PRAISE FOR
KEEPER OF THE LOST CITIES

"A delightful and dangerous adventure with complex characters
and relationships you'll root for till the end of time."
—Lisa McMann, *New York Times* bestselling
author of the Unwanteds series

"*Keeper of the Lost Cities* is a little bit *Alice's Adventures in
Wonderland*, a little bit *Lord of the Rings*, and a little bit *Harry
Potter*. And it's all fun!" —Michael Buckley, *New York Times*
bestselling author of the Sisters Grimm and NERDS series

"A slew of interesting and well-drawn characters, careful
plotting, and just plain good storytelling will have readers
racing through the pages." —*School Library Journal*

ALSO BY SHANNON MESSENGER

Keeper of the Lost Cities

Keeper of the Lost Cities Book Two: Exile

For Older Readers

Let the Sky Fall

Let the Storms Break

KEEPER
LOST CITIES
OF THE

SHANNON MESSENGER

Aladdin
New York   London   Toronto   Sydney   New Delhi

ALADDIN

An imprint of Simon & Schuster Children's Publishing Division
1230 Avenue of the Americas, New York, NY 10020
First Aladdin paperback edition August 2013
Text copyright © 2012 by Shannon Messenger
All rights reserved, including the right of reproduction in whole or in part in any form.
ALADDIN is a trademark of Simon & Schuster, Inc., and related logo is a registered trademark of Simon & Schuster, Inc.
Also available in an Aladdin hardcover edition.
For information about special discounts for bulk purchases, please contact Simon & Schuster Special Sales at 1-866-506-1949 or business@simonandschuster.com.
The Simon & Schuster Speakers Bureau can bring authors to your live event. For more information or to book an event contact the Simon & Schuster Speakers Bureau at 1-866-248-3049 or visit our website at www.simonspeakers.com.
Designed by Karin Paprocki
The text of this book was set set in Scala.
Manufactured in the United States of America 0421 OFF
25 27 29 30 28 26 24
The Library of Congress has cataloged the hardcover edition as follows:
Messenger, Shannon
Keeper of the lost cities/by Shannon Messenger.—1st Aladdin hardcover ed. p. cm.
Summary: At age twelve, Sophie learns that the remarkable abilities that have always caused her to stand out identify her as an elf, and after being brought to Eternalia to hone her skills, discovers that she has secrets buried in her memory for which some would kill.
[1. Ability—Fiction. 2. Psychic ability—Fiction. 3. Memory—Fiction. 4. Identity—Fiction. 5. Foster parents—Fiction. 6. Elves—Fiction. 7.Fantasy—Fiction.] I. Title
PZ7.M5494 Kee 2012 [Fic] 2011042201
ISBN 978-1-4424-4593-2 (hc)
ISBN 978-1-4424-4594-9 (pbk)
ISBN 978-1-4424-4595-6 (eBook)

For Mom and Dad,
who always believed this day would come.
(And because I'm hoping imaginary
grandchildren count!)

PREFACE

BLURRY, FRACTURED MEMORIES SWAM through Sophie's mind, but she couldn't piece them together. She tried opening her eyes and found only darkness. Something rough pressed against her wrists and ankles, refusing to let her move.

A wave of cold rushed through her as the horrifying realization dawned.

She was a hostage.

A cloth across her lips stifled her cry for help, and a sedative's sweet aroma stung her nose when she inhaled, making her head spin.

Were they going to kill her?

Would the Black Swan really destroy their own creation?

What was the point of Project Moonlark, then? What was the point of the Everblaze?

The drug lulled her toward a dreamless oblivion, but she fought back—clinging to the one memory that could shine a tiny spot of light in the thick, inky haze. A pair of beautiful aquamarine eyes.

Fitz's eyes. Her first friend in her new life. Her first friend ever.

Maybe if she hadn't noticed him that day in the museum, none of this would have happened.

No. She knew it'd been too late even then. The white fires were already burning—curving toward her city and filling the sky with sticky, sweet smoke.

The spark before the blaze.

ONE

ISS FOSTER!" MR. SWEENEY'S nasal voice cut through Sophie's blaring music as he yanked her earbuds out by the cords. "Have you decided that you're too smart to pay attention to this information?"

Sophie forced her eyes open. She tried not to wince as the bright fluorescents reflected off the vivid blue walls of the museum, amplifying the throbbing headache she was hiding.

"No, Mr. Sweeney," she mumbled, shrinking under the glares of her now staring classmates.

She pulled her shoulder-length blond hair around her face, wishing she could hide behind it. This was exactly the kind of attention she went out of her way to avoid. Why she wore dull colors and lurked in the back, blocked by the other kids who were at least a foot taller than her. It was the only way to survive as a twelve-year-old high school senior.

"Then perhaps you can explain why you were listening to your iPod instead of following along?" Mr. Sweeney held up her earbuds like they were evidence in a crime. Though to him, they probably were. He'd dragged Sophie's class to the Natural History Museum in Balboa Park, assuming his students would be excited about the all-day field trip. He didn't seem to realize that unless the giant dinosaur replicas came to life and started eating people, no one cared.

Sophie tugged out a loose eyelash—a nervous habit—and stared at her feet. There was no way to make Mr. Sweeney understand why she needed the music to cancel the noise. He couldn't even *hear* the noise.

Chatter from dozens of tourists echoed off the fossil-lined walls and splashed around the cavernous room. But their mental voices were the real problem.

Scattered, disconnected pieces of thoughts broadcast straight into Sophie's brain—like being in a room with hundreds of TVs blaring different shows at the same time. They sliced into her consciousness, leaving sharp pains in their wake.

She was a freak.

It'd been her secret—her burden—since she fell and hit her head when she was five years old. She'd tried blocking the noise. Tried ignoring it. Nothing helped. And she could never tell anyone. They wouldn't understand.

"Since you've decided you're above this lecture, why don't you give it?" Mr. Sweeney asked. He pointed to the enormous orange dinosaur with a duckbill in the center of the room. "Explain to the class how the Lambeosaurus differs from the other dinosaurs we've studied."

Sophie repressed a sigh as her mind flashed to an image of the information card in front of the display. She'd glanced at it when they entered the museum, and her photographic memory recorded every detail. As she recited the facts, Mr. Sweeney's face twisted into a scowl, and she could hear her classmates' thoughts grow increasingly sour. They weren't exactly fans of their resident child prodigy. They called her Curvebuster.

She finished her answer, and Mr. Sweeney grumbled something that sounded like "know-it-all" as he stalked off to the exhibit in the next room over. Sophie didn't follow. The thin walls separating the two rooms didn't block the noise, but they muffled it. She grabbed what little relief she could.

"Nice job, superfreak," Garwin Chang—a boy wearing a T-shirt that said BACK OFF! I'M GONNA FART—sneered as he shoved past her to join their classmates. "Maybe they'll write another article about you. 'Child Prodigy Teaches Class About the Lame-o-saurus.'"

Garwin was still bitter Yale had offered her a full scholarship. His rejection letter had arrived a few weeks before.

Not that Sophie was allowed to go.

Her parents said it was too much attention, too much pressure, and she was too young. End of discussion.

So she'd be attending the much closer, much smaller San Diego City College next year—a fact some annoying reporter found newsworthy enough to post in the local paper the day before—CHILD PRODIGY CHOOSES CITY COLLEGE OVER IVY LEAGUE—complete with her senior photo. Her parents freaked when they found it. "Freaked" wasn't even a strong enough word. More than half their rules were to help Sophie "avoid unnecessary attention." Front-page articles were pretty much their worst nightmare. They'd even called the newspaper to complain.

The editor seemed as unhappy as they were. The story was run in place of an article on the arsonist terrorizing the city— and they were still trying to figure out how the mistake had happened. Bizarre fires with white-hot flames and smoke that smelled like burnt sugar took priority over everything. Especially a story about an unimportant little girl most people went out of their way to ignore.

Or, they used to.

Across the museum, Sophie caught sight of a tall, dark-haired boy reading yesterday's newspaper with the embarrassing black-and-white photo of her on the front. Then he looked up and stared straight at her.

She'd never seen eyes that particular shade of blue before—

teal, like the smooth pieces of sea glass she'd found on the beach—and they were so bright they glittered. Something flickered across his expression when he caught her gaze. Disappointment?

Before she could decide what to make of it, he shrugged off the display he'd been leaning against and closed the distance between them.

The smile he flashed belonged on a movie screen, and Sophie's heart did a weird fluttery thing.

"Is this you?" he asked, pointing to the picture.

Sophie nodded, feeling tongue-tied. He was probably fifteen, and by far the cutest boy she'd ever seen. So why was he talking to her?

"I thought so." He squinted at the picture, then back at her. "I didn't realize your eyes were brown."

"Uh . . . yeah," she said, not sure what to say. "Why?"

He shrugged. "No reason."

Something felt off about the conversation, but she couldn't figure out what it was. And she couldn't place his accent. Kind of British, but different somehow. Crisper? Which bothered her—but she didn't know why.

"Are you in this class?" she asked, wishing she could suck the words back as soon as they left her mouth. Of course he wasn't in her class. She'd never seen him before. She wasn't used to talking to boys—especially cute boys—and it made her brain a little mushy.

His perfect smile returned as he told her, "No." Then he pointed to the hulking greenish figure they were standing in front of. An Albertosaurus, in all its giant, lizardesque glory. "Tell me something. Do you *really* think that's what they looked like? It's a little absurd, isn't it?"

"Not really," Sophie said, trying to see what he saw. It looked like a small T. rex: big mouth, sharp teeth, ridiculously short arms. Seemed fine to her. "Why? What do you think they looked like?"

He laughed. "Never mind. I'll let you get back to your class. It was nice to meet you, Sophie."

He turned to leave just as two classes of kindergartners barreled into the fossil exhibit. The crushing wave of screaming voices was enough to knock Sophie back a step. But their mental voices were a whole other realm of pain.

Kids' thoughts were stinging, high-pitched needles—and so many at once was like an angry porcupine attacking her brain. Sophie closed her eyes as her hands darted to her head, rubbing her temples to ease the stabbings in her skull. Then she remembered she wasn't alone.

She glanced around to see if anyone noticed her reaction and locked eyes with the boy. His hands were at his forehead, and his face wore the same pained expression she imagined she'd had only a few seconds before.

"Did you just . . . hear that?" he asked, his voice hushed.

She felt the blood drain from her face.

He couldn't mean . . .

It had to be the screaming kids. They created plenty of racket on their own. Shrieks and squeals and giggles, plus sixty or so individual voices chattering away.

Voices.

She gasped and took another step back as her brain solved her earlier problem.

She could hear the thoughts of everyone in the room. But she couldn't hear the boy's distinct, accented voice unless he was speaking.

His mind was totally and completely silent.

She didn't know that was possible.

"Who are you?" she whispered.

His eyes widened. "You did—didn't you?" He moved closer, leaning in to whisper. "Are you a Telepath?"

She flinched. The word made her skin itch.

And her reaction gave her away.

"You are! I can't believe it," he whispered.

Sophie backed toward the exit. She wasn't about to reveal her secret to a total stranger.

"It's okay," he said, holding out his hands as he moved closer, like she was some sort of wild animal he was trying to calm. "You don't have to be afraid. I'm one too."

Sophie froze.

"My name's Fitz," he added, stepping closer still.

Fitz? What kind of a name was Fitz?

She studied his face, searching for some sign that this was all part of a joke.

"I'm not joking," he said, like he knew exactly what she was thinking.

Maybe he did.

She wobbled on her feet.

She'd spent the past seven years wishing she could find someone else like her—someone who could do what she could. Now that she'd found him, she felt like the world had tilted sideways.

He grabbed her arms to steady her. "It's okay, Sophie. I'm here to help you. We've been looking for you for twelve years."

Twelve years? And what did he mean by "we"?

Better question: What did he want with her?

The walls closed in and the room started to spin.

Air.

She needed air.

She jerked away and bolted through the door, stumbling as her shaky legs found their rhythm.

She sucked in giant breaths as she ran down the stairs in front of the museum. The smoke from the fires burned her lungs and white bits of ash flew in her face, but she ignored them. She wanted as much space between her and the strange boy as possible.

"Sophie, come back!" Fitz shouted behind her.

She picked up her pace as she raced through the courtyard

at the base of the steps, past the wide fountain and over the grassy knolls to the sidewalk. No one got in her way—everyone was inside because of the poor air quality. But she could still hear his footsteps gaining on her.

"Wait," Fitz called. "You don't have to be afraid."

She ignored him, pouring all her energy into her sprint and fighting the urge to glance over her shoulder to see how far back he was. She made it halfway through a crosswalk before the sound of screeching tires reminded her she hadn't looked both ways.

Her head turned and she locked eyes with a terrified driver struggling to stop his car before it plowed right over her.

She was going to dic.

TWO

THE NEXT SECOND WAS A BLUR.

The car swerved right—missing Sophie by inches—then jumped the curb and sideswiped a streetlight. The heavy steel lantern cracked from its base and plummeted toward Sophie.

No!

It was her only thought as her instincts took over.

Her hand shot into the air, her mind pulling strength from somewhere deep in her gut and pushing it out through her fingertips. She felt the force collide with the falling lantern, gripping on like it was an extension of her arm.

As the dust settled she looked up, and gasped.

The bright blue lantern floated above her, somehow held up by her mind. It didn't even feel heavy, though she was sure it weighed a ton.

"Put it down," a familiar, accented voice warned, bringing her out of her trance.

She shrieked and dropped her arm without thinking. The streetlight hurtled toward them.

"Watch out!" Fitz shouted, yanking her out of the way a split second before the lantern crashed to the ground. The force of the impact knocked them over, and they tumbled to the sidewalk. Fitz's body broke her fall as she landed across his chest.

Time seemed to stop.

She stared into his eyes—eyes that were now stretched as wide as they could go—trying to sort through the flurry of thoughts and questions swirling around in her head to find something coherent.

"How did you do that?" he whispered.

"I have no idea." She sat up, replaying the past few seconds in her mind. Nothing made sense.

"We need to get out of here," Fitz warned, pointing to the driver, who was staring at them like he'd witnessed a miracle.

"He saw," she gasped, feeling her chest tighten with panic.

Fitz pulled her to her feet as he got up. "Come on, let's get out of sight."

She was too overwhelmed to figure out a plan on her own, so she didn't resist when he dragged her down the street.

"Which way?" he asked when they reached the first intersection.

She didn't want to be alone with him, so she pointed north, toward the San Diego Zoo, where there was sure to be a crowd—even during a firestorm.

They took off running, though no one was following, and for the first time in her life, Sophie *missed* hearing thoughts. She had no idea what Fitz wanted—and it changed everything. Her mind ran through terrifying scenarios, most of which involved government agents throwing her into dark vans to run experiments on her. She watched the road, ready to bolt at the first sign of anything suspicious.

They reached the zoo's massive parking lot, and Sophie relaxed when she saw people outside, milling around their cars. Nothing would happen with so many witnesses. She slowed her pace to a walk.

"What do you want?" she asked when she caught her breath.

"I'm here to help you, I promise."

His voice sounded sincere. Didn't make it easier to believe him, though.

"Why were you looking for me?" She tugged out a loose eyelash, more than a little afraid of the answer.

He opened his mouth, then hesitated. "I'm not sure if I'm supposed to tell you."

"How am I supposed to trust you if you won't answer my questions?"

He considered that for a second. "Okay, fine—but I don't know much. My father sent me to find you. We've been looking for a specific girl your age, and I was supposed to observe and report back to him, like always. I wasn't supposed to talk to you." He frowned, like he was disappointed with himself. "I just couldn't figure you out. You don't make sense."

"What does *that* mean?"

"It means you're . . . different from what I expected. Your eyes really threw me off."

"What's wrong with my eyes?" She touched her eyelids, suddenly self-conscious.

"We all have blue eyes. So when I saw them, I figured we had the wrong girl again. But we didn't." He looked at her with something like awe. "You're really one of us."

She stopped and held up her hands. "Whoa. Hang on. What do you mean, 'one of us'?"

He glanced over his shoulder, frowning when he spotted a crowd of fanny-pack-wearing tourists within earshot. He pulled her toward a deserted corner of the parking lot, ducking behind a dark green minivan.

"Okay—there's no easy way to explain this, so I'm just going to say it. We're not human, Sophie."

For a second she was too stunned to speak. Then a hysterical laugh escaped her lips. "Not human," she repeated, shaking her head. "Riiiiiight."

"Where are you going?" he asked as she moved toward the sidewalk.

"You're insane—and I'm insane for trusting you." She kicked the ground as she stomped away.

"I'm telling the truth," he called. "Just think for a minute, Sophie."

The last thing she wanted to do was listen to another word he said, but the plea in his voice made her stop and face him.

"Can humans do this?"

He closed his eyes, and vanished. He was only gone for a second, but it was enough to leave her reeling. She leaned against a car, feeling everything spin around her.

"But I can't do that," she argued, taking deep breaths to clear her head.

"You have no idea what you can do when you set your mind to it. Think of what you did with that pole a few minutes ago."

He seemed so sure—and it almost made sense.

But how could that be?

And if she wasn't human . . . what was she?

THREE

S O ... WHAT?" SOPHIE MANAGED TO SAY when she finally found her voice. "You're saying I'm ... an alien?"

She held her breath.

Fitz erupted into laughter.

Her cheeks grew hot, but she was also relieved. She didn't want to be an alien.

"No," he said when he'd managed to compose himself. "I'm saying you're an elf."

An *elf*.

The word hung in the air between them—a foreign object that didn't belong.

"An elf," she repeated. Visions of little people in tights with pointy ears danced through her brain, and she couldn't help giggling.

"You don't believe me."

"Did you really expect me to?"

"I guess not." He ran his hands through his hair, making it stick out in wavy spikes—kind of like a rock star.

Could someone *that* good looking be crazy?

"I'm telling you the truth, Sophie. I don't know what else to say."

"Okay," she agreed. If he refused to be serious, so would she. "Fine. I'm an elf. Am I supposed to help Frodo destroy the ring and save Middle-earth? Or do I have to make toys in the North Pole?"

He let out a sigh—but a smile hid in the corners of his mouth. "Would it help if I showed you?"

"Oh, sure—this ought to be good."

She folded her arms as he pulled out a slender silver wand with intricate carvings etched into the sides. At the tip, a small, round crystal sparkled in the sunlight.

"Is that your magic wand?" she couldn't resist asking.

He rolled his eyes. "Actually, it's a pathfinder." He spun the crystal and locked it into place with the silver latch at the top. "Now, this can be dangerous. Do you promise you'll do *exactly* what I tell you to do?"

Her smile faded. "That depends. What do I have to do?"

"You need to take my hand and concentrate on holding on.

And by concentrate, I mean you can't think about anything else—no matter what happens. Can you do that?"

"Why?"

"Do you want proof or not?"

She wanted to say no—he couldn't actually prove anything. What was he going to do, whisk her away to some magic elf land?

But she was curious. . . .

And, really, what harm could come from holding someone's hand?

She willed her palms not to sweat as their fingers laced together. Her heart did that stupid fluttery thing again, and her hand tingled everywhere their skin touched.

He glanced over his shoulder, scanning the parking lot again. "Okay, we're alone. We go on three. You ready?"

"What happens on three?"

He shot her a warning look, and she scowled at him. But she bit her tongue and concentrated on holding his hand, ignoring her racing heart. Seriously—when did she become one of those silly girls?

"One," he counted, raising the wand. Sunlight hit a facet in the crystal and a bright beam refracted toward the ground.

"Two." He tightened his grip. Sophie closed her eyes.

"Three."

Fitz pulled her forward, and the warm tingling in her hand shot through her body—like a million feathers swelling underneath her skin, tickling her from the inside out. She fought off a giggle and concentrated on Fitz—but where was he? She knew she was clinging to him, but it felt like her body had melted into goo, and the only thing keeping her from oozing away was a blanket of warmth wrapped around her. Then, faster than the blink of an eye, the warmth faded, and she opened her eyes.

Her mouth fell open as she tried to take it all in. She might have even squeaked.

She stood at the edge of a glassy river lined with impossibly tall trees, fanning out their wide emerald leaves among the puffy white clouds. Across the river, a row of crystal castles glittered in the sunlight in a way that would make Walt Disney want to throw rocks at his "Magic Kingdom." To her right, a golden path led into a sprawling city, where the elaborate domed buildings seemed to be built from brick-size jewels— each structure a different color. Snowcapped mountains surrounded the lush valley, and the crisp, cool air smelled like cinnamon and chocolate and sunshine.

Places this beautiful weren't supposed to exist, much less appear out of thin air.

"You can let go of my hand now."

Sophie jumped. She'd forgotten about Fitz.

Her hand released his, and as the blood tingled in her fingertips, she realized how hard she'd been squeezing. She looked around, unable to make sense of anything she saw. The castle towers twisted like spun sugar, and something seemed oddly familiar about them, but she couldn't figure out what it was. "Where are we?"

"Our capital. We call it Eternalia, but you might have heard it called Shangri-la before."

"Shangri-la," she repeated, shaking her head. "Shangri-la is real?"

"All of the Lost Cities are real—but not how you'd picture them, I'm sure. Human stories rarely get anything right—think of all the ridiculous things you've heard about elves."

She had to laugh at that—and the sharp burst of sound echoed off the trees. It was so quiet there, just the gentle breeze brushing her face and the soft murmur of the river. No traffic, no chatter, no hammering, unspoken thoughts. She could get *very* used to the silence. But it felt strange, too. Like something was missing.

"Where is everyone?" she asked, rising on her tiptoes to get a better view of the city. The streets were a ghost town.

Fitz pointed to a domed building that towered over all the others. The green stones of its walls looked like giant emeralds, but for some reason the building sparkled less than all the others. It looked like a serious place, for serious things. "See the blue banner flying? That means a tribunal is in progress. Everyone's watching the proceedings."

"A tribunal?"

"When the Council—basically our royalty—holds a hearing

to decide if someone's broken a law. They're kind of a big deal when they happen."

"Why?"

He shrugged. "Laws are rarely broken."

Well, *that* was different. Humans broke the law all the time.

She shook her head. Was she really thinking of humans as something *other*?

But how else could she explain where she was?

She tried to wrap her mind around the idea, tried to force it to make sense. "So," she said, cringing over her ridiculous next question. "This is . . . magic?"

Fitz laughed—a full body laugh, like it was the funniest thing he'd ever heard.

She glared at him. It couldn't be *that* funny.

"No," he said when he'd regained control. "Magic is a stupid idea humans came up with to try to explain things they couldn't understand."

"Okay," she said, trying to cling to the remaining strands of her sanity. "Then how can we be here, when five minutes ago we were in San Diego?"

He held the pathfinder up to the sun, casting a ray of light onto his hand. "Light leaping. We hitched a ride on a beam of light that was headed straight here."

"That's impossible."

"Is it?"

"Yeah. You need infinite energy for light travel. Haven't you heard of the theory of relativity?"

She thought she had him stumped with that one, but he just laughed again. "That's the dumbest thing I've ever heard. Who came up with that?"

"Uh, Albert Einstein."

"Huh. Never heard of him. But he was wrong."

He'd never heard of *Albert Einstein*? The theory of relativity was *dumb*?

She wasn't sure how to argue. He seemed so ridiculously confident—it was unnerving.

"Concentrate harder this time," he said as he grabbed her hand again.

She closed her eyes and waited for the warm feather sensation. But this time it was like someone turned on a hair dryer and sent the feathers scattering in a million directions—until another force wrapped around her and pulled everything back together like a giant rubber band. A second later she was shivering from a cold ocean breeze whipping her hair around her face.

Fitz pointed to the massive castle in front of them, which glowed like the stones were carved from moonlight. "How do you think we got here?"

Words failed her. It really had felt like the light passed through her, pulling her along with it. But she couldn't bring herself to say it, because if that was true, every science book she'd read was wrong.

"You look confused," he observed.

"Well, it's like you're saying, 'Hey, Sophie, take everything you've ever learned about anything and throw it away.'"

"Actually, that *is* what I'm saying." He flashed a smug grin. "Humans do the best they can—but their minds can't begin to comprehend the complexities of reality."

"And what, elves' minds are better?"

"Of course. Why do you think you're so far ahead of your class? The slowest elf can still trump a human—even one with no proper education."

Her shoulders sagged as Fitz's words sank in.

If he was right, she was just some stupid girl who knew nothing about anything.

No—not a girl.

An *elf*.

FOUR

THE SCENERY BLURRED—BUT WHETHER it was from tears or panic Sophie couldn't be sure.

Everything she knew was wrong. Her entire life was a lie.

Fitz nudged her arm. "Hey. It's not your fault. You believed what they taught you—I'm sure I'd have done the same thing. But it's time you knew the truth. This is how the world really works. It's not magic. It's just how it is."

The castle bells chimed, and Fitz yanked her behind a large rock as a gateway opened. Two elves with floor-length velvet capes draped over their black tunics emerged, followed by dozens of bizarre creatures marching in military formation down the rocky path. They were at least seven feet tall and wore only black pants, leaving their thick muscles prominently on display. With their flat noses and coarse gray skin, which fell in pleated folds, they looked part alien, part armadillo.

"Goblins," Fitz whispered. "Probably the most dangerous creatures you'll ever meet, which is why it's a good thing they signed the treaty."

"Then why are we hiding?" she whispered, hating her voice for trembling.

"We're dressed like humans. Humans are forbidden in the Lost Cities—especially here, in Lumenaria. Lumenaria is where all the other worlds come together. Gnomes, dwarves, ogres, goblins, trolls."

She was too overwhelmed to even think about the other creatures he was mentioning, so she focused on the better question. "Why are humans forbidden?"

He motioned for her to follow him to a rock farther away, squatting behind it. "They betrayed us. The Ancient Councillors offered them the same treaty they made with all the intelligent creatures, and they agreed. Then they decided *they* wanted to rule the world—like it even works that way—and started planning a war. The Ancients didn't want violence, so they disappeared, forbid any contact with humans, and left them to their own devices. You can see how well that's working out for them."

Sophie opened her mouth to defend her race, but she could see Fitz's point. War, crime, famine—humans had a lot of problems.

Plus, if everything he was saying was true, they weren't *her* race. The realization chilled her much more than the frigid wind licking her cheeks.

"The stories told by the humans who'd known us must've sounded impossible after we disappeared, and eventually they evolved into the crazy myths you've heard. But *this* is the truth, Sophie." Fitz pointed around them. "This is who you are. This is where you belong."

Where you belong.

She'd waited her whole life to hear those three simple words. "I'm really an elf?" she whispered.

"Yes."

Sophie peeked through the rocks at the glowing castle—a place that wasn't supposed to exist but was somehow right in front of her. Everything he was telling her was insane. But she knew it was true—she could feel it. Like a crucial piece of her identity had clicked into place.

"Okay," she decided, her head spinning in a thousand directions. "I believe you."

A loud clang sounded as another gate closed. Fitz stepped out of the shadows and pulled out a different wand—no, pathfinder—sleek and black with a cobalt blue crystal. "Ready to go home?"

Home.

The word jolted her back to reality. Mr. Sweeney would call her mom when she didn't get on the bus. She needed to get home before her mom freaked.

Her heart sank a little.

Reality seemed so bland and boring after everything she'd seen. Still, she took his hand and stole one last look at the incredible view before the blinding light swept it away.

The smoky ash stung her lungs after the crisp, fresh air of Lumenaria. Sophie looked around, surprised she recognized the plain square houses on the narrow, tree-lined street. They were a block away from her house. She decided not to ask how he knew where she lived.

Fitz coughed and glared at the sky. "You'd think humans could handle putting out a few fires before the smoke pollutes the whole planet."

"They're working on it," she said, feeling a strange need to defend her home. "Plus, these aren't normal fires. The arsonist used some sort of chemical when he started them, so they're burning white hot, and the smoke smells sweet."

Usually, wildfires made the city smell like barbecue. This time it was more like melting cotton candy—which was actually kind of nice, if it didn't burn her eyes and rain ash.

"Arsonists." Fitz shook his head. "Why would anyone want to watch the world burn?"

"I don't know," she admitted. She'd asked herself the same question, and she wasn't sure there was an answer.

Fitz pulled the silver pathfinder out of his pocket.

"Are you leaving?" she asked, hoping he didn't notice the way her voice hitched.

"I have to find out what my dad wants to do now—if he even knows. Neither of us thought you were going to be the girl."

The girl. Like she was someone important.

If she could hear his thoughts, she'd know what he meant. But his mind was still a silent mystery. And she still had no idea why.

"He's not going to be happy I took you to our cities," he added, "even though I was careful no one saw us. So *please* don't tell anyone about anything I've shown you today."

"I won't. I promise." She held his gaze so he'd know she meant it.

He released the breath he'd been holding. "Thank you. And make sure you act normal so your family doesn't suspect anything."

She nodded—but she had to ask one question before he left. "Fitz?" She squared her shoulders for courage. "Why can't I hear your thoughts?"

The question knocked him back a step. "I still can't believe you're a Telepath."

"Aren't all elves Telepaths?"

"No. It's a special ability. One of the rarer ones. And you're only twelve, right?"

"I'll be thirteen in six months," she corrected, not liking the way he'd said "only."

"That's *really* young. They said I was the youngest to manifest, and I didn't start reading minds until I was thirteen."

She frowned. "But . . . I've been hearing thoughts since I was five."

"*Five?*" He said it so loud it reverberated off the houses, and they both scanned the street to make sure no one was around.

"You're sure?" he whispered.

"Positive."

Waking up in the hospital after she hit her head wasn't the kind of moment she could forget. She was hooked up to all kinds of crazy machines, with her parents hovering over her, shouting things she could barely separate from the voices filling her mind. All she could do was cry and hold her head and try to explain what was happening to a group of adults who didn't understand—who would never understand. No one could make the noise go away, and the voices had haunted her ever since.

"Is that wrong?" she asked, not liking the worry etched between his brows.

"I have no idea." His eyes narrowed, like he was trying to see inside her head.

"What are you doing?"

"Are you blocking me?" he asked, ignoring her question.

"I don't even know what that is." She stepped away, wishing the extra space could stop him from reading her private thoughts.

"It's a way to keep Telepaths out. Kind of like putting a wall around your mind."

"Is that why I can't hear you?"

"Maybe. Can you tell me what I'm thinking right now?"

"I told you, I don't hear your thoughts the way I do with other people."

"That's because humans have weak minds—but that's not what I meant. If you *listen*, can you hear me?"

"I . . . don't know. I've never tried to read a mind before."

"You just have to trust your instincts. Concentrate. You'll know what to do. Try."

She hated being bossed around—especially since he wasn't answering her questions. Then again, what he wanted her to do might be the only way to find out why he looked so concerned. She just had to figure out what he meant by "listen."

She didn't have to tell her ears to hear—they just did. But listening took action. She had to concentrate. Maybe mind reading worked the same way—like an extra sense.

She focused on his forehead, imagining that she was stretching out her consciousness like a mental shadow, feeling for his thoughts. After a second Fitz's voice swept through her head. It wasn't sharp or loud like human thoughts, more of a soft whisper brushing across her brain.

"You've never felt a mind as quiet as mine?" she blurted.

"You heard me?" He looked pale.

"Was I not supposed to?"

"No one else can."

She needed a few seconds to process that. "And you can't read my mind?"

He shook his head. "Not even when I try my hardest."

A whole new world of worries pressed down on her shoulders. She didn't want to be different from the other elves. "Why?"

"I have no idea. But when you pair it with your eyes, and where you live—" He stopped, like he was afraid he'd said too much, then fumbled with the crystal on his pathfinder. "I need to ask my dad."

"Wait—you can't leave now." Not when she had more questions than answers.

"I have to. I've already been gone too long—and you need to get home."

She knew he was right. She didn't want to get in trouble. But her knees still shook as he held the crystal to the sunlight. He was her only link to the amazing world she'd seen—the only proof that she hadn't imagined the whole thing.

"Will I ever see you again?" she whispered.

"Of course. I'll be back tomorrow."

"How will I find you?"

He flashed a small smile. "Don't worry. I'll find *you*."

FIVE

"*THERE YOU ARE!*" HER MOM SHOUTED. Her panicked thoughts battered their way into Sophie's brain as she entered their cluttered living room and found her mom still on the phone. "Yes, she's home now," she said into the receiver. "Don't worry, I will be having a *very* long talk with her."

Sophie's heart jolted.

Her mom hung up the phone and reeled around. Her wide green eyes glared daggers. "That was Mr. Sweeney calling because he couldn't find you at the museum. What were you thinking, wandering off like that—especially now, with the fires making everyone nervous? Do you have any idea how worried I was? And Mr. Sweeney was about to call the police!"

"I'm—I'm sorry," Sophie stammered, struggling to find a convincing lie. She was a horrible liar. "I . . . got scared."

Her mom's anger faded to concern, and she tugged nervously at her curly brown hair. "Scared of what? Did something happen?"

"I saw this guy," Sophie said, realizing the best lies were based on truth. "He had the article about me. He started asking all these questions and it was freaking me out so I ran away from him. And then I was scared to go back, so I walked to the trolley and took the train home."

"Why didn't you get a teacher or a museum guard—or call the police?"

"I guess I didn't think of that. I just wanted to get away." She tugged out an eyelash.

"Ugh—stop doing that," her mom complained, closing her eyes and shaking her head. She took a deep breath. "Well, I guess the important thing is that you're okay. But if anything like that ever happens again, I want you to run straight to an adult, do you understand?"

Sophie nodded.

"Good." She rubbed the wrinkle between her brows that always appeared when she was stressed. "This is exactly why your father and I were upset about that article. It's not safe to stand out in this world—you never know what some weirdo is going to try to do once they know where they can find you."

No one understood the dangers of standing out better than

Sophie. She'd been teased and tormented and bullied her whole life. "I'm fine, Mom. Okay?"

Her mom seemed to deflate as she let out a heavy sigh. "I know, I just wish . . ."

Her voice trailed off and Sophie closed her eyes, hoping she could close out the rest of the thought.

You could be normal, like your sister.

The words slipped a tiny pin into Sophie's heart. It was the hardest part of being a Telepath—hearing what her parents *really* thought.

She knew her mom didn't mean it. But that didn't make it any less painful to hear.

Her mom wrapped her in a tight hug. "Just be careful, Sophie. I don't know what I'd do if anything happened to you."

"I know, Mom. I'll try."

Her dad came through the front door and her mom let her go.

"Welcome home, honey! I'll have dinner ready in ten," she called to him. "And, Amy!" she added, raising her voice so it would be heard upstairs. "Time to come down!"

Sophie followed her mom into the kitchen, feeling uncase twist in her stomach. Worn linoleum, pastel walls, tacky knickknacks—it all seemed so ordinary after the glittering cities Fitz had shown her. Could she really belong there?

Did she really belong *here*?

Sophie's dad kissed her on the cheek as he set his shabby

briefcase on the kitchen table. "And how's my Soybean?" he asked with a wink.

Sophie scowled. He'd been calling her that since she was a baby—apparently, she'd had a hard time pronouncing her name—and she'd asked him hundreds, no, thousands of times to stop. He refused to listen.

Her mom took the lid off one of the simmering pots, and the smell of garlic and cream filled the room. She handed Sophie the silverware. "It's your turn to set the table."

"Yeah, Soybean. Get crackin'," her sister said as she scooted into the room and plopped into her usual chair.

At nine years old, Amy already had the annoying little sister role mastered.

Amy was Sophie's opposite in every way, from her curly brown hair and green eyes to her lower than average grades and incredible popularity. No one understood how she and Sophie could be sisters—especially Sophie. Even their parents wondered about it in their thoughts.

The silverware slipped through Sophie's fingers.

"What's wrong?" her mom asked.

"Nothing." She sank into her chair.

How could she and Amy be sisters? Amy was definitely human. Her parents were too—she'd heard enough of their thoughts to know they weren't hiding any secret powers. And if she was an elf . . .

The room spun and she lowered her head into her hands.

She tried to concentrate on breathing: Inhale—exhale—and repeat.

"You okay, Soybean?" her dad asked.

For once she didn't care about the nickname. "I feel kind of dizzy—must be from the smoke," she added, trying not to make them suspicious. "Can I go lay down?"

"I think you should eat something first," her mom said, and Sophie knew she couldn't argue. Skipping dinner was definitely not acting normal—especially on fettuccine night. It was her favorite, but the rich sauce did not help her sudden nausea. Neither did the way her family stared at her.

Sophie ignored their mental concern, trying not to tug on her eyelashes as she chewed each bite and forced herself to swallow. Finally, her dad set his fork down—the official end of dinner in the Foster house—and Sophie jumped to her feet.

"Thanks, Mom, that was great. I'm going to do some homework." She left the kitchen and sprinted up the stairs before they could say anything to stop her.

She raced to her room and closed her door, stumbling to her bed. A loud hiss shattered the silence. "Sorry, Marty," she whispered, her heart pounding in her ears.

Her fluffy gray cat glared at her for sitting on his tail. But she reached out her hand and he slunk toward her, settling into her lap. Marty's gentle purring filled the silence and gave her courage to confront the realization she'd made downstairs.

Her family couldn't be *her* family.

She took a deep breath and let the reality settle in.

The strange thing was, in some ways it made sense. It explained why she always felt so out of place around them—the slender blonde among her chubby brunette family.

Still, they were the only family she knew.

And if they weren't her family . . . who was?

Panic closed off her chest and her lungs screamed for air. But another pain throbbed deeper, like something inside had ripped apart.

Her eyes burned with tears, but she blinked them back. It had to be a mistake. How could she not be related to her family? She'd been hearing their thoughts for seven years—how would she not know that? And even if it was somehow possible, not being related to them didn't change anything, did it? Lots of kids were adopted, and they were part of their new family.

Her mom poked her head through the door. "I brought you some E.L. Fudges." She handed Sophie a plate full of her favorite cookies and a glass of milk, then frowned. "You look pale, Sophie. Are you getting sick?" She pressed her palm against Sophie's forehead. "You don't have a fever."

"I'm fine. Just . . . tired." She reached for a cookie but froze when she noticed its tiny elf face. "I need to go to bed."

Her mom left her alone so she could change. She stumbled through her routine and crawled under the blankets, wrapping them as tight as they would go. Marty took his place on her pillow, next to her head.

"Sweet dreams, Soybean," her dad said, kissing her on the forehead. Her parents always tucked her in—another Foster family tradition.

"Night, Dad." She tried to smile, but she could barely breathe.

Her mom kissed Sophie's cheek. "Do you have Ella?"

"Yep." She showed her the blue elephant tucked under her arm. She was probably too old to still have a stuffed animal, but she couldn't sleep without Ella. Tonight she needed her more than ever.

Her mom turned off the light, and the darkness gave Sophie the courage she needed. "Um, can I ask you guys something?"

"Sure," her dad said. "What's up?"

She hugged Ella tighter. "Was I adopted?"

Her mom laughed as her mind flashed to the twelve hours of very painful labor she'd endured. "No, Sophie. Why would you ask that?"

"Could I have been switched at birth?"

"No. Of course not!"

"Are you sure?"

"Yes—I think I would know my own daughter." There wasn't a doubt in her mom's mind. "What's this all about?"

"Nothing. I was just wondering."

Her dad laughed. "Sorry, Soybean, we're your parents—whether you like it or not."

"Okay," she agreed.

But she wasn't so sure anymore.

SIX

THAT NIGHT SOPHIE DREAMED THE Keebler elves were holding her hostage until she perfected all their cookie recipes. Then she told them she liked Oreos better, and they tried to drown her in a giant vat of fudge. She woke in a cold sweat and decided sleep was overrated.

When morning came, she took a quick shower and threw on her best jeans and a shirt she'd never worn—buttery yellow with brown stripes. It was the only item in her closet that wasn't gray, and she'd always been too self-conscious to wear it. But the color brought out the gold flecks in her eyes, and today she would see Fitz again. As much as she hated to admit it, she wanted to look good. She even clipped part of her hair back and toyed with the idea of lip gloss—but that was going too far. Then she snuck downstairs to check outside for him.

She crept into the front yard, blinking to keep the falling ash out of her eyes. The smoke was so thick it stuck to her skin. Seriously, *when* were they going to get the fires contained?

"Looking for someone?" her next-door neighbor asked from his perch in the middle of his lawn. Mr. Forkle could always be found there, rearranging hundreds of garden gnomes into elaborate tableaux.

"No," she said, hating how nosy he was. "I was checking to see if the smoke was any better. I guess it's not." She coughed for added effect.

His beady blue eyes bored into hers, and she could tell from his thoughts that he didn't believe her. "You kids," he grumbled. "Always up to something."

Mr. Forkle loved to start sentences with the words "you kids." He was old and smelled like feet and was always complaining about something. But he was the one who called 911 when she fell and hit her head, so she was obligated to be nice.

He moved a gnome a fraction of an inch to the left. "You should get back inside before the smoke gives you another one of those headaches you're always—"

Loud yapping interrupted him, and a ball of fur with legs streaked up the sidewalk, barking its tiny head off. A blond guy in spandex jogging shorts chased after it.

"Would you mind grabbing her?" he called to Sophie as the dog raced across her lawn.

"I'll try." The dog was quick, but Sophie managed to step on the leash with a clumsy lunge. She kneeled, stroking the wild-eyed, panting creature to calm her down.

"Thank you so much," the guy said as he ran up the path. As soon as he drew close, the dog growled and strained against the leash, barking like mad.

"She's my sister's dog," he shouted over the noise. "She hates me. Not my sister—the dog," he added. He held out his hand, displaying several half-moon bite wounds, fresh and still bleeding. One was so deep it would definitely leave a scar.

Sophie picked up the trembling dog and hugged her. Why was the dog so afraid?

"I don't suppose you'd be willing to carry her back to my sister's house. It's just a few blocks away, and she seems to like you better than me." He winked one of his piercing blue eyes.

"She most certainly will not," Mr. Forkle yelled before she could open her mouth to answer. "Sophie, go inside. And you"—he pointed to the jogger—"get out of here right now or I'm calling the police."

The guy's eyes narrowed. "I wasn't asking you—"

"I don't care," Mr. Forkle interrupted. "Get. Away. From. Her. Now."

The barking grew louder as the guy moved toward Sophie.

She could barely think through the chaos, but there was something in his expression that made her wonder if he was planning to grab her and drag her away. And that's when it hit her.

She couldn't hear his thoughts. Even with the barking—she should've heard *something*.

Would Fitz have sent someone else in his place?

But if he had, why wouldn't the jogger say that? Why try to trick her?

Before she could react, Mr. Forkle stepped between them, stopping the jogger in his tracks. Mr. Forkle might be on the old side, but he was a large man, and when he straightened up to his full height, he made quite an intimidating figure.

They stared each other down for a few seconds. Then the jogger shook his head and backed off.

"Sophie, let the dog go," Mr. Forkle ordered. She did as he said and the dog raced away. The jogger glowered at them both before he took off after it.

Sophie released the breath she'd been holding.

"You're okay," Mr. Forkle promised. "If I see him again, I'll call the police."

She nodded, trying to find her voice. "Uh, thanks."

Mr. Forkle snorted, shaking his head and grumbling something that started with "you kids" as he returned to his lawn gnomes. "Better get inside."

"Right," she agreed, moving up the path on shaky legs.

As soon as the front door closed, she leaned against it, trying to make sense of the scattered questions racing through her brain.

Why would that guy try to grab her? Could he be another elf? Fitz had some serious explaining to do—whenever he decided to make his next appearance.

There was still no sign of Fitz when she got to school, and now she wasn't sure what to do. He might be waiting for her to be alone before he appeared, but after the dog incident, she wanted a few eyewitnesses around. Unless Fitz had sent the jogger to get her. . . .

It was all so frustrating and confusing.

She headed for class when the bell rang, lurking a few steps behind the other students.

A hand grabbed her arm and pulled her into the shadows between buildings. Sophie stopped her scream just in time when she recognized Fitz.

"Where have you been?" she demanded—a little too loudly. Several heads turned their way. "Do you have any idea what I've been going through?"

"Missed me bad, huh?" he whispered, flashing a cocky smile.

She felt the blood rush to her face and looked away to hide her blush. "More like you left me alone with a ton of unanswered questions and no way to find you, and then this guy shows up and tries to grab me and—"

"Whoa—wait. What guy?"

"I don't know," she said. "Some creepy blond guy tried to trick me into wandering off with him, and when I wouldn't, it looked like he was going to snatch me but I wasn't sure because I couldn't hear his thoughts and I think he might be another elf."

"Okay, slow down." Fitz swept his hair back. "No one else knows you're here. Only my dad, and he sent me to get you."

"Then why couldn't I hear his thoughts?"

"I don't know," he admitted. "Are you sure you couldn't?"

She replayed the scene, trying to remember. There had been a lot of barking and growling. Her heart pounding in her ears. She couldn't even remember hearing Mr. Forkle's thoughts—now that she thought about it—and she could always hear his.

"Maybe not," she said quietly.

"My guess is he was human, and maybe his mind is just quieter than the others. But we'll check with my dad. We'd better move though." He pointed to a teacher who was eyeing them like she suspected impending mischief. "We can't leap with people around."

"Leap?" she squeaked as he pulled her behind the English building. "I can't ditch class, Fitz. They'll call my parents—and after yesterday I think my mom might strangle me."

"This is important, Sophie. You have to come with me."

"Why?"

"Just trust me."

She locked her knees so he couldn't pull her any farther. She couldn't keep disappearing all the time. Elf or not, she had a life *here*, with classes she could fail and parents who could ground her. "How am I supposed to trust you when you won't even tell me anything?"

"You can trust me because I'm here to help you."

That wasn't good enough. If he wouldn't tell her what was going on, she knew how to find out.

It was strange to willingly use her telepathy, after so many years trying to block it. But it was the only way to find out what he was hiding. So she closed her eyes and reached for his thoughts the way she had the day before. The breeze brushed through her mind, whispering scattered pieces of information—nothing she needed, though. But when she pushed a little further, she found what he was hiding.

"A test?" she shrieked. "What am I being tested for?"

"You read my mind?" He dragged her deeper into the shadows, shaking his head. Hard. "You can't do that, Sophie. You can't listen to someone's thoughts any time you want to know something. There are rules."

"You've tried to read my mind without my permission."

"That's different. I'm on assignment."

"What's that supposed to mean?"

Fitz ran his hands through his hair, which he seemed to do when he was frustrated. "It doesn't matter. What matters is you could get in big trouble for invading someone's mind like that. It's a *serious* offense."

The way he said "serious" made everything inside her scrunch and twist together.

"Really?" she asked quietly.

"Yeah. So don't do it again."

She started to nod, but a small movement at a nearby oak caught her attention and she froze, her heart hammering so hard it drowned out everything else. It was only for a second—but she could've sworn she saw the jogger's face.

"He's here," she whispered. "The guy who tried to grab me."

"Where?" Fitz scanned the campus.

She gestured toward the tree, but there was no one around. No thoughts nearby either.

Did she imagine it?

Fitz pulled the silver pathfinder from his pocket and adjusted the crystal. "I don't see anyone—but let's get out of here. We shouldn't keep everyone waiting, anyway."

"Who's everyone?"

"My parents, and a committee of our Councillors. It's part of the test you heard me thinking about when you broke into my head." He shot her a sidelong glance, and she felt her cheeks heat up.

"Sorry," she mumbled.

She'd never thought of telepathy as "breaking in" before, but she could see his point. His thoughts hadn't automatically filled her mind the way they did with humans. She'd shoved her way in and took them. She'd be furious if someone did that to her.

She wouldn't make that mistake again.

It wasn't like she'd ever enjoyed being a Telepath anyway. Reading minds always caused way more problems than it solved.

Fitz took her hand and led her into the sunlight. "Ready?" he asked as he held up the pathfinder.

She nodded, hoping he couldn't feel the way her arm was shaking. "Can you tell me what the test determines?"

He grinned as his eyes locked with hers. "Your future."

SEVEN

SOPHIE HAD TO SHIELD HER FACE AS she surveyed her new surroundings. The enormous metal gate in front of them glowed as bright as sunlight, nearly blinding her.

"Welcome to Everglen," Fitz said, leading her toward the doors. "What do you think?"

"It's very bright."

He laughed. "Yeah. The gate absorbs all the light, so no one can leap directly inside. My dad works for the Council, so he likes his privacy at home."

"I guess." After her stressful morning it was nice to know she would be safe, but she couldn't help wondering what they were trying to keep out. She doubted King Kong could get past the massive doors.

A faint click sounded, and the gate swung inward. A striking figure stood in a small, grassy clearing surrounded by the same enormous trees she'd seen growing along the river in the capital. A floor-length, midnight blue cape was fastened across his shoulders with a clasp that looked like a pair of yellow, diamond-encrusted wings. He was tall and lean, with the same vibrant teal eyes and dark wavy hair—it was impossible to miss the family resemblance.

"Sophie, this is my father, Alden," Fitz introduced.

She wasn't sure if she should bow or curtsy or shake hands. How should she greet an elf? She managed a shy wave.

"It's a pleasure to meet you, Sophie," Alden said with an accent more prominent than Fitz's. "I see Fitz wasn't kidding about the brown eyes. Most unusual."

She could feel her cheeks flush. "Oh. Uh. Yeah."

Alden smiled. "There's nothing to be embarrassed about. I think the color is quite pretty. Don't you, Fitz?"

She couldn't look at Fitz as he agreed. Her face felt like it might actually be on fire.

"Did you tell anyone else where Sophie was?" Fitz asked.

"Only the Council. Why?"

"Sophie said someone tried to take her this morning."

Alden's eyes widened. "Are you okay?" he asked, scanning Sophie like he was checking for injury.

"Yeah. He never got close enough to grab me. He just looked like he wanted to."

"Humans," Alden muttered.

"Actually, Sophie thought he might be an elf," Fitz told him.

Father and son shared a look. Then Alden shook his head. "Kidnapping is a human crime. I've never heard of an elf even considering such a thing—much less trying it. What made you think it was one of us?"

"I might've been wrong," she said, feeling silly and paranoid. "I just can't remember hearing his thoughts—which has only happened around Fitz. And now you."

"Yes, Fitz told me about your telepathy." He reached out to touch her forehead. "Do you mind?"

"Um." She didn't want to be rude, but she couldn't help taking a step back.

"I mean you no harm, I assure you. I'd love to see your memories of the kidnapper, if that's okay?"

She was surprised he'd asked her permission. Fitz really was right about the rules for Telepaths. Didn't mean she liked the idea of having her memories searched though.

She glanced at Fitz and he nodded, trying to reassure her, but it was the kindness in Alden's eyes that made her agree.

Alden placed two fingers gently against her temples and closed his eyes. She tried to hold still—and avoid thinking about how good Fitz looked in his dark jacket—but as the seconds ticked by, she could feel her knees start to shake.

"Well," Alden said as he pulled his hands away. "You are indeed a fascinating girl."

"Couldn't hear her either, could you?" Fitz asked him, sounding triumphant.

"No." Alden took both of her hands. "Well, I'll look into what happened this morning, but I'm sure there's no reason to worry. You're here now, and it's perfectly safe in our world—"

He frowned and his head jerked toward Fitz. "I specifically told you not to let her leap again without a nexus."

"Sorry, I forgot. Sophie thought she saw the guy who tried to grab her, so we had to get out of there quick. But we're fine. I had us covered."

"That's not the point." Alden held out his hand, and Fitz dug a small black cuff out of his coat pocket and handed it to him. Alden clamped the bracelet around Sophie's right wrist, twisting until it fit snug. "Is that comfortable?"

She nodded, staring at her new accessory. The wide band had a single teal jewel set into the front, a smooth gray rectangle on the back, and intricate symbols etched all around. She blinked when she realized they were letters. Letters that spelled out gibberish. Which seemed like an odd way to decorate a bracelet. But what *wasn't* odd about this world?

Alden twisted the band again and it clicked with finality. "There. All set."

"Um. What is it?"

"A safety precaution. Your body has to break into tiny particles to be carried by the light, and the nexus holds those particles together until your concentration is strong enough to do it for you. Fitz never should have let you leap without one—even with the stressful circumstances."

"But Fitz doesn't have one." Sophie pointed to his bare wrist.

"I got mine off early. My concentration is strong enough for three people—which is why we're fine. Sophie's not even a little bit faded, and you know it."

"Only fools overestimate their skills, Son. You've never had to watch someone fade away. Perhaps if you had, you would be more cautious."

Fitz's eyes dropped to the ground.

"What does it mean to fade away?" Sophie asked quietly.

A second passed before Alden answered, and he looked like he was watching a memory. "It's when you lose too much of yourself in a leap. Your body isn't able to fully reform, and eventually the light pulls the rest of you away and you're lost forever."

Sophie felt goose bumps dimple her skin.

Alden cleared his throat. "It's only happened a few times, and we'd prefer to keep it that way." He shot a reproving look at Fitz.

Fitz shrugged. "Fine. The next time you send me on a secret mission to collect a long-lost elf, I'll be sure to put the nexus on *before* I leap her here."

Alden's lips looked like they wanted to smile as he motioned for Sophie and Fitz to follow him down the path. "We shouldn't keep our guests waiting."

Sophie wiped her palms on her jeans and took a deep breath before she followed him down the narrow path lined with trees blooming blue and red and pink and purple—every color of the rainbow. The air was so thick with the perfume of their flowers it was almost dizzying, a nice change from the smoky air back home. "How exactly does this test decide my future?"

"They're testing you to see if you qualify for Foxfire." Fitz paused, like that was supposed to mean something.

"Isn't that glowing fungus?" she asked.

Alden cracked up.

Fitz looked a little insulted. "It's our most prestigious academy."

"You named your most prestigious academy after fungus?"

"It represents a bright glow in a darkened world."

"But . . . the light comes from fungus."

Fitz rolled his eyes. "Will you stop saying 'fungus'? Only those with the strongest talent qualify for Foxfire, and if you don't get in, you might as well kiss your future goodbye."

Alden placed his hand on her shoulder. "You'll have to excuse my son. He's very proud to attend Foxfire—and it's definitely an accomplishment. But don't let him worry you. The earliest levels are more of a testing ground, to see who develops abilities that qualify them to continue with their studies."

The idea of going to an elvin academy made her head spin. Would she have to sneak away every day? She didn't see how that could work, but she doubted her parents would knowingly let her light leap to a secret elvin school, either.

If they really were her parents . . .

Cold chills mixed with sudden nausea as last night's troubling revelation rushed back, but she shoved the sickening thought to a dark corner of her mind.

One problem at a time.

"Is it going to be hard to get into Foxfire?" she asked.

"Councillor Bronte will be difficult to impress," Alden admitted. "He feels your upbringing and lack of proper education should disqualify you. Plus, he doesn't like surprises. The Council had no idea you existed until today, and he's more than a little miffed about it. But you only need two out of three votes. Just do the best you can."

The Council didn't know about her? Then why did Fitz say they'd been looking for her for twelve years?

Before she could ask, they arrived at another clearing, and all coherent thoughts vanished.

Dozens of squat, earth-toned creatures with huge gray eyes tended a garden that belonged in a fairy tale. Lush plants grew up and down and sideways and slantways. One of the females shuffled by in a dress woven from grass, carrying a basket filled with twinkling purple fruit.

"What?" It was the only word Sophie could come up with.

"I'm guessing this isn't quite how you pictured gnomes, is it?" Alden asked.

"Um, no." These definitely weren't little old men in pointy hats, like Mr. Forkle's lawn statues. "So . . . you have gnomes for servants?"

Alden stopped to stare at her. "We would never have servants. The gnomes *choose* to live with us because it's safer in our world. And they help in our gardens because they enjoy it. We're privileged to have them. You'll get your first taste of gnomish produce during lunch, and you're in for quite a treat."

She watched a gnome dig slimy yellow tubers that looked like giant slugs out of the ground. She hoped none of those was on the menu.

She peeled her eyes away from the strange scene as Alden led her out of the garden to a meadow with a house in the center, one so large, so elegant, she couldn't believe anyone could call it "home." Part castle, part manor, it was made almost entirely of intricately cut crystal, and among the numerous turrets and gables rose a tower that resembled a lighthouse.

They passed through two massive doors made of braided silver, and entered a round foyer, which sparkled like a prism in the sunlight.

"This way," Alden said, taking her hand and bringing her down the widest hallway, lined with fountains that spouted streams of colored water over their heads. The hall dead-ended at a pair of doors encrusted with a jeweled mosaic—two diamond unicorns racing across a field of amethyst flowers. Sophie couldn't help wondering just how rich Fitz's family had to be to live in a place like this. Though everything she'd seen in the elvin world spoke of wealth. It felt very intimidating.

Alden squeezed her hand. "You have nothing to be afraid of."

She tried to make herself believe him as Fitz pulled the doors open and led them into a formal dining room. Sheer silk curtains covered the glass walls, drawing the eye up to an enormous chandelier—a waterfall of long, shimmering crystals—that hung over a round table set with domed platters and fancy goblets. Three figures in jewel-encrusted circlets rose from the plush, thronelike chairs surrounding the table.

A second too late Sophie realized she should have curtsied—not that she knew how.

She stared at the silver capes fastened at the base of their necks with clasps that looked like glowing, golden keys and felt horribly underdressed. Everyone wore jewels and lush fabrics except her and Fitz—and he was in "disguise."

"Councillors, this is Sophie Foster," Alden introduced with a quick bow. "Sophie, this is Kenric, Oralie, and Bronte."

Kenric was built like a football player, with wild red hair and a big, toothy grin. Oralie looked like a fairy princess—rosy cheeks and long golden ringlets. And then there was Bronte.

As Sophie met his cold gaze, she could see what Alden

meant about Bronte being hard to impress. He was the smallest of the three, with cropped brown hair and sharp features. He wasn't bad looking, but there was something strange about his appearance she couldn't put her finger on.

She gasped when she realized what it was.

"What?" Bronte demanded.

Five pairs of blue eyes focused on her and she stared at the floor as she mumbled, "Sorry. I was surprised by your ears."

"My ears?" Bronte repeated, confused.

Fitz's whole body shook with laughter. Sophie squirmed as one by one the others joined him. Bronte did not look at all pleased to be left out of the joke.

"I think she's surprised that your ears are . . . *pointy*," Alden finally answered. "Our ears change shape as we age. Eventually it'll happen to all of us."

"I'm going to get *pointy ears*?" Her hands darted to her head, like they might have already transformed.

"Not for a few thousand years," Alden promised. "By then I doubt you'll mind."

Sophie sank into a chair, barely noticing that Fitz sat next to her. Her brain was on autorepeat: *Thousand years, thousand years, thousand years.* "How long do elves live?" she asked. Everyone looked young and vibrant—even Bronte.

"We don't know," Kenric said, scooting his chair a touch closer to Oralie's than he really needed to. "No one's died of old age yet."

Sophie rubbed her forehead. It actually hurt her brain trying to understand this. "So, you're saying elves are . . . immortal?"

"No." A trace of sorrow hid in Alden's voice. "We can die. But our bodies stop aging when we reach adulthood. We don't get wrinkles or gray hair. Only our ears age." He smiled at Bronte, who glowered back. "Bronte belongs to a group we call the Ancients, which is why his ears are so distinct. Please, help yourselves," he added, pointing to the domed platters in front of each guest.

Sophie uncovered hers and fought to hide her grimace. Black strips and purple mushy glop didn't exactly scream *Eat me*. She forced herself to take a bite, stunned when the purple goop tasted like the juiciest cheeseburger ever. "What is this stuff?"

"That's mashed carnissa root. The black strips are umber leaves," Alden explained.

Sophie took a bite of umber leaf. "Tastes like chicken."

"You eat animals?" Fitz asked in a tone that would have made more sense if she'd said she ate toxic waste.

Sophie nodded, squirming when Fitz grimaced. "I take it elves are vegetarians."

Everyone nodded.

She took another bite to hide her horror. It wasn't that she liked eating animals, but she couldn't imagine living off only vegetables. Of course, if the vegetables tasted like cheeseburgers, maybe it wouldn't be so bad.

"So, Sophie." Bronte sneered her name like it bothered him to say it. "Alden tells me you're a Telepath."

She swallowed her mouthful, and it sank into her stomach with a thud. It felt wrong discussing her secret so openly.

"Yes. She's been reading minds since she was five. Isn't that right, Sophie?" Alden asked when she didn't respond.

She nodded.

Kenric's and Oralie's jaws dropped.

"That's the most absurd thing I've ever heard," Bronte argued.

"It's *unusual*," Alden corrected.

Bronte rolled his eyes as he turned to Sophie. "Let's see how good you are, then. Tell me what I'm thinking."

Sophie's mouth went dry as everyone fell silent. Waiting for her.

She glanced at Fitz, remembering his warnings about the rules of telepathy.

"He gave you permission," Fitz told her.

She nodded, taking a deep breath to stay calm.

Apparently, the test had begun.

EIGHT

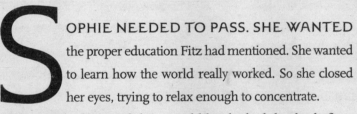

SOPHIE NEEDED TO PASS. SHE WANTED
the proper education Fitz had mentioned. She wanted
to learn how the world really worked. So she closed
her eyes, trying to relax enough to concentrate.

She reached out with her mind like she had the day before.
Bronte's mind felt different from Fitz's—deeper somehow,
like she was stretching her mental shadow much further. And
when she finally felt his thoughts, they were more like an icy
gust than a gentle breeze.

"You're thinking that you're the only one at this table with
any common sense," she announced. "And you're tired of
watching Kenric stare at Oralie."

Bronte's jaw fell open and Kenric's face turned as red as

his hair. Oralie looked down at her plate, her cheeks flushing pink.

"I take it that's right?" Alden asked, hiding his smile behind his hand.

Bronte nodded, looking angry, chagrined, and incredulous all at the same time. "How can that be? An Ancient mind is almost impenetrable."

"The key word in that sentence is 'almost,'" Alden reminded him. "Don't feel bad—she's also breached Fitz's blocking."

Guilt tugged at Sophie's conscience as she watched Fitz flush red. Especially when Bronte grinned and said, "Sounds like Alden's golden boy isn't as infallible as everyone thinks."

"It's more likely that Sophie is exceptionally special," Alden corrected. "Fitz also saw her lift more than ten times her weight with telekinesis yesterday."

"You're kidding!" Kenric gasped, recovering from his embarrassment. "At her age? Now *that* I have to see."

Sophie shrank in her chair. "But . . . I don't know how I did it. It just sort of happened."

"Just relax, Sophie. Why not try something small?" Alden pointed to the crystal goblet in front of her.

That didn't sound *too* hard—and maybe it was like her telepathy. Another sense she had to learn how to use.

She replayed the accident, remembering the way she'd found the strength deep inside, and pushed it out through her fingers. Could she do that again?

She raised her arm and imagined lifting the goblet with an invisible hand. Nothing happened for a second, and her palms started to sweat. Then something pulled in her stomach, and the glass floated off the table.

Sophie stared at the goblet in wonder. "I did it."

"That's it?" Bronte scoffed, unimpressed.

He needed more? Seriously?

"Give her a second. She's still getting used to her ability." Alden put his hand on her shoulder. "Take a deep breath—relax—then see what else you can do. And remember, your mind has no limitations—unlike your physical body."

Alden's calm confidence gave her the courage to try harder. She tried to think about the clue he was giving her. No limitations. What did that mean?

Maybe she could lift more than one thing at once. She blew out a breath, pretending she had five more imaginary hands to extend. The tug in her gut felt sharper, but it was worth it when the other five goblets rose like crystal flying saucers.

Kenric applauded. "Excellent control."

Her cheeks grew warm with the praise. "Thanks."

Bronte snorted. "It's a couple of glasses. I thought she was supposed to be able to lift ten times her body weight."

Sophie bit her lip. She wasn't sure how much more she could handle, but she was determined to impress Bronte.

She must be stronger than she realized—how else could she have stopped the lantern? She took another deep breath and shoved every ounce of the force she could feel in her core toward the empty chair next to Bronte.

A collective gasp rang in the air as three chairs floated off the ground, including the one Bronte sat on.

"Incredible," Alden breathed.

Sophie didn't have time to celebrate. Her stomach cramped from the strain and her hold broke. She screamed as the goblets shattered against the table and the chairs crashed to the floor, knocking Bronte flat on his back with a thunderous collision.

For a second no one said anything; they just stared in openmouthed shock. But when Bronte hollered for someone to help him up, everyone burst into a fit of laughter.

Except Sophie. She'd *dropped* one of the Councillors. She was pretty sure she'd sealed her future with that mistake.

Kenric clapped her on the back, pulling her out of her worries. "I've never seen such natural talent. You're even a natural at our language. Your accent is perfect. Almost as perfect as these guys'." He pointed to Alden and Fitz.

"I'm sorry, what?" she asked, assuming she'd heard him wrong.

Fitz laughed. "You've been speaking the Enlightened Language since we leaped here—just like you did yesterday."

She was speaking a different language—with an accent?

"Our language is instinctive," Alden explained. "We speak from birth—I'm sure people thought you were an interesting baby. Though to humans our language sounds like babbling."

Her parents were always teasing her about what a noisy baby she was. She gripped the table. "Is there a word that sounds like 'soybean' in English?"

"Soybean?" Alden asked.

"I used to say it as a baby. My parents thought I was trying to say my name and mispronouncing it. They even turned it into a nickname—a really annoying one." She blushed when Fitz chuckled beside her.

Kenric shrugged. "I can't think of what that would be."

Fitz and Oralie nodded. But Alden looked pale.

"What is it?" Bronte asked him, still dusting off his cape from his fall.

Alden waved the words away. "Probably nothing."

"I'll decide if it's nothing," Bronte insisted.

Alden sighed. "It's . . . possible she was saying *suldreen*—but it's a stretch."

Bronte's mouth tightened into a hard line.

"What does *suldreen* mean?" Sophie asked.

Alden hesitated before he answered. "It's the proper name for a moonlark, a rare species of bird."

"And that's bad because . . . ?" She hated the way everyone was looking at her—like she was a puzzle they couldn't solve. Adults were always looking at her that way, but usually she could hear their thoughts and know why they were so bothered. She missed that now.

"It's not bad. It's just interesting," Alden said quietly.

Bronte snorted. "Troubling is what it is."

"Why would it be troubling?" Sophie asked.

"It would be an uncomfortable coincidence. But most likely you *were* trying to say your name. You were hearing it all the time so it's natural that you would try to repeat it." Alden said it like he was trying to convince himself as much as her.

"Well, I think I've heard quite enough to make my decision," Bronte barked, shoving all thoughts of moonlarks out of her mind. "I vote against—and you will not convince me otherwise."

Sophie wasn't surprised, but she couldn't fight off her panic. Had she failed?

Kenric shook his head. "You're being absurd, Bronte. I vote in favor—and you won't convince *me* otherwise."

She held her breath as all eyes turned to Oralie for the final vote. Oralie hadn't said a word the entire time, so Sophie had no idea where she stood.

"Give me your hand, Sophie," Oralie said in a voice as fragile and lovely as her face.

"Oralie's an Empath," Fitz explained. "She can feel your emotions."

Sophie's arm shook as she extended her hand. Oralie grasped it with a delicate touch.

"I feel a lot of fear and confusion," Oralie whispered. "But I've never felt such sincerity. And there's something else. . . .

I'm not sure I can describe it." She opened her huge, azure eyes and stared at Sophie. "You have my vote."

Alden clapped his hands together with a huge grin. "That settles it then."

"For now," Bronte corrected. "This will be revisited. I'll make sure of it."

Alden's smile faded. "When?"

"We should wait till the end of the year. Give Sophie some time to adjust," Kenric announced.

"Excellent," Alden agreed.

"Fools," Bronte grumbled. "I invoke my right as Senior Councillor to demand a probe."

Alden rose with a nod. "I'd planned as much. I've arranged to bring her to Quinlin as soon as we're done here."

Sophie knew she should probably celebrate, but she was too busy trying to decipher the word "probe." That didn't sound fun.

"What's a probe?" she asked Fitz as Alden led everyone else out of the room.

Fitz leaned back in his chair. "Just a different way to read your mind. It's no big deal. Happens all the time when you're in telepathy training—which it looks like you'll be. I can't believe you passed. It looked iffy there for a minute."

"I know." She sighed. "Why did Bronte demand a probe?"

"Because he's a pain. Well, that and I think he's worried that my dad couldn't read your mind."

"Worried?"

"I guess maybe 'bothered' is a better word. My dad's *really* good. And so am I." He flashed a cocky smile. "So if we can't read your mind, it's kind of like, who can?"

"Okay," she said, trying to make sense of what he was saying. "But why does he care if no one can read my mind?"

"Probably because of your upbringing."

She took a deep breath, reluctant to say the next words. "You mean the fact that my family is human. And I'm not."

A second passed before he nodded.

Emptiness exploded inside her. So it wasn't a mistake. She really wasn't related to her family—and Fitz knew. He wouldn't look at her, and she could tell he was uncomfortable.

She choked down the pain, saving it for later, when she'd be able to deal with it in private. She cleared her throat, trying to sound normal. "Why would that concern him?"

"Because it's never happened before."

The warm, bright room felt suddenly colder. "Never?"

"No."

It was a tiny word, but the implications it carried were huge. Why was she living with humans?

Before she could ask, Alden swept back into the room. "Sophie, why don't you come with me, and we'll get you something else to wear. You'd better change too, Fitz."

Sophie hesitated. She should probably make them take her home. Her parents had to know by now that she'd ditched school.

Then again, she was already in trouble—might as well stall the punishment as long as possible. Plus, she wasn't ready to go home yet. She needed more answers.

"Where are we going?" she asked as she followed Alden out of the room.

Alden smiled. "How would you like to see Atlantis?"

NINE

*T*HIS IS ATLANTIS?" SOPHIE COULDN'T quite hide her disappointment.

They were in the middle of nowhere, on a patch of dark rocks surrounded by white-capped waves. The only signs of life were a few seagulls, and all they did was screech and poop. It was hardly the lost continent she'd expected.

"This is how we get to Atlantis," Alden corrected as he stepped across a tide pool toward a triangular rock. "Atlantis is underneath us, where light doesn't reach. We can't leap there."

It was hard not to slip on the slick rocks as she followed Fitz, especially in the red shoes Alden insisted she wear to match the long gown. She'd begged to wear pants, but apparently it was a sign of status for a girl to wear a gown, especially in Atlantis, which Alden explained was a *noble city*, which meant members of the nobility had offices there. The empire waist and beaded neckline of her dress made her feel like she was wearing a costume.

It was even stranger seeing Fitz in elvin clothes: a long blue tunic with elaborate embroidery around the edges and slender pockets sewn into the sleeves—the exact same size as his pathfinder. Black pants with pockets at the ankles—so he didn't have to sit on the stuff he carried, he'd explained—and black boots completed the look. No sign of tights or pointy shoes—thankfully—but he looked more like an elf now, which made everything more real.

A rock moved under her foot and she fell into Fitz's arms. "Sorry," she whispered, knowing her face was as red as her dress.

Fitz shrugged. "I'm used to it. My sister, Biana, is clumsy too."

She wasn't sure she liked that comparison. "So, Atlantis really sank?" she asked, changing the subject as she followed him to a ledge high above the water.

"The Ancients engineered the catastrophe," Alden answered. He opened a secret compartment in the side of the strange rock, revealing hundreds of tiny glass bottles, grabbed one, and joined them on the ledge. "How else would humans think we disappeared?"

Sophie glanced at the label on the bottle. ONE WHIRLPOOL. OPEN WITH CARE.

"Step back." Alden uncorked the top and flung the bottle into the ocean. A huge blast of wind whipped against their faces, and the roar of churning water filled the air.

"Ladies first," Alden shouted, pointing to the edge.

"I'm sorry—*what?*"

"Maybe you should go first, Dad," Fitz suggested.

Alden nodded, gave a quick wave, and jumped. Sophie screamed.

Fitz laughed beside her. "Your turn." He dragged her toward the edge.

"Please tell me you're joking," she begged as she tried—and failed—to pull away.

"It looks worse than it is," he promised.

She gulped, staring at the maelstrom swirling beneath her. Cold, salty water sprayed her face. "You seriously expect me to jump?"

"I can push you if you'd prefer."

"Don't even think about it!"

"Better jump then. I'll give you to the count of five." He stepped toward her. "One."

"Okay, okay." She wanted to keep what little dignity she had left.

She took a slow, deep breath, closed her eyes, and stepped off the edge, screaming the whole way down. It took her a second to realize she wasn't drowning, and another after that to stop flailing around like an idiot. She opened her eyes and gasped.

The whirlpool formed a tunnel of air, dipping and weaving through the dark water like the craziest waterslide ever. She was actually starting to enjoy the ride when she launched out of the vortex onto an enormous sponge. It felt like being licked from head to toe by a pack of kittens—minus the kitten breath—and then the sponge sprang back, leaving her standing on a giant cushion.

Her hands froze as she smoothed her dress. "I'm not wet."

"The sponge absorbs the water when you land. Incoming!" Alden yanked her out of the way as Fitz rocketed onto the sponge, right where she'd been standing.

She jumped off the sponge to the slightly squishy ground. It felt like packed wet sand.

"Now, *this* is Atlantis." Alden gestured to the gleaming metropolis ahead of them.

Sophie's eyes felt like they had to stretch to take it all in. The city was wrapped in a dome of air, which faded into the ocean beyond. Twisted crystal towers soared into the skyline, bathing the silver city in the soft blue glow radiating from their pointed spires. The buildings lined an intricate network of canals, interconnected by arched bridges. It reminded her of pictures she'd seen of Venice, but everything was sleek and modern and clean. Despite being at the bottom of the ocean, the air was crisp and fresh. The only clue that they were underwater was a muted hum in the background, like the sound she'd heard when she put a seashell to her ear.

"You guys build with crystal a lot," Sophie observed as she followed Alden into the city.

Alden smiled. "Crystal stores the energy we use to power everything, and it's cut to let precisely the right amount of light in. Of course, we had to make some changes when we moved Atlantis underwater. We plated the buildings with silver so they'd reflect the firelight we created in the spires and help illuminate the city."

"Why did you sink Atlantis, and not the other cities?"

"We built Atlantis for humans. That's why you know the real name of the city. A long time ago humans walked these very streets."

Sophie looked around. Elves wandered the shops looking young and elegant. The men wore heavy velvet capes, like they belonged at a Renaissance fair, and some of the women's gowns shifted color as they moved. Signs advertised two-for-one specials on bottled lightning or fast approval on Spyball applications. A child strolled past with some sort of hybrid chicken-lizard on a leash. No wonder humans invented crazy myths after the elves disappeared.

They reached the main canal, and Alden hailed one of the carriages floating along the water—a silver, almond-shaped boat with two rows of high-backed benches. A driver in an elbow-length green cape steered from the front bench, drawing the reins of some sort of brown creature skimming the surface of the waves.

Sophie shrieked as the eight-foot-long scorpion with deadly pincers reared against the reins. Its tail curled up, looking ready to sting. "What is that thing?"

"An eurypterid," Alden explained. "A sea scorpion."

"You're not afraid, are you?" Fitz asked.

She moved farther away.

"What is it with girls?" Fitz leaned down and stroked the shiny brown shell along the eurypterid's back. Sophie waited for the pincers to slice him in half, but the creature held still, emitting a low hissing sound, like it enjoyed being petted. "See? Harmless."

Fitz jumped into the carriage.

Alden followed, holding the door open for her. "Quinlin's waiting, Sophie. It's time to find out what's in that impenetrable mind of yours."

TEN

EVERY FIBER OF SOPHIE'S BEING wanted to run far, far away from the mutant insect of doom, especially since it would take her to get *probed*. But she gritted her teeth and ran into the carriage, pressing her back against the bench to be as far as possible from the hideous sea scorpion.

"Where to?" the driver asked Alden with a laugh.

"Quinlin Sonden's office, please."

The driver shook the reins, and the giant scorpion thrashed its tail against the water, pulling them along.

"So who is this Quinlin guy anyway?" Sophie asked.

Alden smiled. "He's the best probe I know. If anyone can slip into your brain, it's him."

Something about the words "slip in" gave her the heebie-jeebies. She tried to think about something else to stay calm. "Why does he work down here?" Atlantis wasn't a bad place, but she imagined the commute would get annoying after a while.

"Atlantis is our most secure city. Anyone and anything that needs added protection is here. Including your file."

"I have a file?"

"A highly classified one."

"What's in it?"

"You'll see soon enough."

She opened her mouth to ask another question, but Alden shook his head and pointed to the driver. She'd have to wait till they were alone.

The carriage entered some sort of business district. The streets were packed with elves, all in long black capes, and the silver buildings stood taller than the others, with round windows tracing down the sides and glowing signs bearing their names. TREASURY. REGISTRY. INTERSPECIESIAL SERVICES. But half the signs were unreadable.

"What's with the random strings of letters?" she asked, pointing to a building with gibberish for a sign.

Alden tried to follow her gaze. "The runes?"

"Is that what these are?" She held out her wrist, running her fingers along the nonsense writing on the nexus.

Alden nodded. "That's our ancient alphabet."

"You can't read it?" Fitz sounded more surprised than she

would have liked. Being the clueless one was getting old—fast.

Alden stroked his chin. "But you can tell they're letters?"

"Yeah, but it's just a big jumble. Is that going to be a problem for school?" She held her breath. What would the other kids think if she couldn't even *read*?

"Nah, it's rarely used," Fitz said, and she could breathe again. "Only when they want to be fancy or something."

She hesitated, hating that she had to ask her next question again. "Is it wrong that I can't read them?"

"Reading should be instinctive," Alden admitted. "But maybe your human education affected you somehow. We've never had anyone with your upbringing, so it's hard to say."

There was that word again. "Upbringing." This giant gap between her and everyone else.

How was she ever supposed to fit in if she was the only kid who went home to her human parents every night? But what other option did she have? No way her parents would let her move here. They wouldn't even let her move across the country to go to college.

"How—" she started to ask, but Alden cut her off.

"No reason to worry, Sophie. I'm sure we'll figure it out with further testing."

That wasn't what she was going to ask, but the idea of more weird elf tests made her forget her other problems. She hoped she'd get through the next one without dropping a member of the Council.

They turned down a narrow, quiet canal lined with purple trees with thick, broad leaves like kelp. The water dead-ended at a single silver building, a square tower with no windows or ornamentation, other than a small sign with precise white letters that read: QUINLIN SONDEN: CHIEF MENTALIST. All signs of life had vanished, and the small black door was closed tight. But the sea scorpion slowed to a stop, and Alden took a small green cube from his pocket. The driver swiped it across the cuff above his elbow and handed it back to Alden after it made a tiny *ping*.

Sophie's legs wobbled as she followed Alden toward the door. Despite Fitz's earlier assurances, she couldn't help wondering if the probe would hurt. Or worse—what humiliating memories Quinlin would find.

Alden bypassed the receptionist in the dim foyer and headed to the only office in back. The small square room smelled damp, and half the space was filled with a massive stone desk. A tall, dark-skinned elf with chin-length black hair jumped from his seat and gave an elegant bow.

"Please, there's no need for ceremony, my friend," Alden said with a wink.

"Of course." Quinlin's gaze settled on Sophie. "Brown eyes?"

"Definitely unique," Alden agreed.

"That's an understatement." He stared at Sophie long enough to make her squirm. "You really found her—after all these years?"

And they still hadn't explained why they'd been looking for her.

"You tell me," Alden told Quinlin. "Do you have her file?"

"Right here." Quinlin held up a small silver square before handing it to Sophie.

"You lick it," Fitz explained. "They need your DNA."

She tried not to think about how unsanitary that was as she gave the square the tiniest lick. The metal grew warm, and Sophie nearly dropped it when a hologram flashed out of the center: two strands of DNA—rotating in the air with an unearthly glow. The word MATCH flashed across them in bright green.

It took Sophie a second to realize she'd stopped breathing.

She was a *match*. She really did belong.

"So this is why Prentice sacrificed everything," Quinlin breathed, staring at the glowing double helixes as though seeing a long-lost child.

Prentice? Was that a name?

And what did he sacrifice?

Alden answered before she could ask. "He definitely had his reasons. You'll see when you try the probe."

Sophie jumped as Alden squeezed her shoulders. He probably meant to reassure her, but it didn't help as Quinlin reached toward her.

"It's no big deal, Sophie," Fitz promised.

"I'll be done in less than a minute," Quinlin added.

She swallowed her fears and nodded.

Two cold, slender fingers pressed against her temples, and Quinlin closed his eyes. Sophie counted the seconds as they ticked by. Two hundred seventy-eight passed before he pulled away—so much for less than a minute.

Quinlin's mouth hung open.

"That's what I thought," Alden murmured, almost to himself. He turned and began pacing.

"You can't hear anything either?" Sophie asked. Part of her was relieved—she hated the idea of having her private thoughts invaded. But she didn't like the look on Quinlin's face, like all the wind had been knocked out of him.

"What does that mean?" Quinlin asked quietly.

"It means she'll be the greatest Keeper we've ever known, once she's older," Alden said through a sigh.

Quinlin snorted. "If she isn't already."

Alden froze midstep. When he turned to face her, he looked pale.

"What's a Keeper?" Sophie asked.

A second passed before Alden answered. "Some information is too important to record. So we'll share it with a Keeper, a *highly* trained Telepath, and leave them in charge of protecting the secret."

"Then why would I already be one?"

"Quinlin was joking about that." Alden's smile didn't reach his eyes, which made it harder to believe.

Then again, the only secret she was currently keeping was

where she'd hidden her sister's karaoke game, so she didn't have to listen to Amy sing off-key all the time. How could she be a Keeper?

"Perhaps we should talk upstairs." Alden gestured to the foyer, where the receptionist was leaning toward them, making notes. Clearly eavesdropping.

Quinlin led them to the far end of the small office. He licked a silver strip on the wall, and a narrow door slid open, revealing a winding stairway. They climbed to an empty oval room with live footage of brush fires projected across the walls.

A cold chill settled into Sophie's core when she recognized the city.

"Why are you watching the San Diego wildfires?" She pointed to the aerial view of Southern California. White fire lines formed an almost perfect half circle around San Diego.

"You know the area?" Quinlin asked.

"Yeah, I live there."

Quinlin's gasp made her ears ring.

Thin lines etched into Alden's forehead as he stared at the images. "Why didn't you tell me there were fires?" he asked Fitz.

"I didn't know they were important."

"I didn't ask you to tell me what was important. I asked you to tell me *everything*." Alden turned to Quinlin. "Why were you watching the fires?"

"They're burning white hot—against the wind. Like they were set by someone who knew what they were doing. Plus . . . doesn't it look like the sign?"

Sophie had no idea what "the sign" was, but she didn't like the way the lines on Alden's forehead deepened. Little valleys of worry.

"I'm guessing this is how you found the article you sent me," Alden murmured. "I'd wondered why you were looking there. We ruled that area out years ago."

"Article?" Quinlin asked.

"The one about the child prodigy in San Diego. Led me right to Sophie."

Reflections of the glowing flames made Quinlin look even more haunted as he shifted his weight. "I didn't send you any articles. Did it have a note from me?"

Alden frowned. "No. But you were the only one who knew what I was up to."

"Not the only one," Quinlin said quietly.

"What's going on?" Sophie asked. She didn't care about interrupting—or the warning Fitz was trying to communicate with his waving hands. "What sign? What's wrong with the fires? Should I warn my family to get out of there?"

Not being allowed to read minds was turning out to be more frustrating than she'd ever imagined. The answers she needed were right there—within her reach. But what would happen if they caught her taking them?

She didn't want to find out.

"There's no reason to worry, Sophie," Alden promised. "I know this all seems very strange to you, but I assure you we have everything under control."

The calm tone to his voice made her cheeks feel hot. Maybe she was overreacting. "Sorry. It's just been a weird day. Between the guy trying to grab me this morning and—"

"What?" Quinlin interrupted, glancing between Sophie and Alden. "Was he . . . ?"

"An elf?" Alden finished. "I doubt it."

"How can you be sure?" Quinlin asked.

Alden turned to Sophie. "Why didn't he take you?"

She shuddered, remembering the desperate look in the kidnapper's eyes before Mr. Forkle stepped in. "My neighbor threatened to call the police."

"See?" Alden told Quinlin. "They never would have backed down so easily."

"They?" Sophie didn't like the idea the word implied—a nameless, faceless entity out to get her.

Alden smiled. "I meant an elf—any elf. You've seen how quickly we can light leap. If one of us were really there to get you, no human threatening to call the authorities would stop them. They would've just grabbed you and leaped away."

She shivered at the thought. "But what about the fires? Why are they white?"

"The arsonist probably used a chemical accelerant.

Humans do so love their chemicals. I'll look into it," Alden promised. "I follow suspicious leads all the time, and they never amount to anything. Humans are always doing crazy, dangerous things. If they're not lighting something on fire, they're spilling oil in the ocean or blowing something up. Every time they do, I investigate to make sure things don't get out of hand—but that doesn't leave this room. The Council's official position is to leave humans to their own devices. That's another reason Quinlin works down here: The Council rarely takes the time to visit and find out what we're up to."

"Bronte has his babysitter sitting outside my office all day, taking notes though," Quinlin grumbled. "He could've at least picked someone who's a decent receptionist."

Alden rolled his eyes. Then his smile returned. "At least she's equally bad at spying. You should've seen Bronte's face when he learned about Sophie. I thought steam might come out of his ears."

Quinlin laughed. "Keeping that secret for twelve years has to be a record."

"Why didn't the Council know you were looking for me?" Sophie had to ask. *Why all the secrecy?*

"Bronte had specifically ordered us to ignore the evidence we found of your existence," Alden explained. "He thought the DNA we'd discovered was a hoax and that my search was a waste of time. That's why he was so hard on you today. He

doesn't like being wrong. And he really doesn't like knowing that I've been working behind his back. So can I trust
you to keep this quiet?" Alden waited for Sophie and Fitz to
nod.

Sophie couldn't help feeling like she was missing something, so she wasn't quite ready to agree. "Do you promise
you'll keep me updated on the fires?"

Alden sighed. "I will, if there's anything important. Agreed?"

Sophie nodded, trying to make sense of the pieces she'd
learned. Why would her DNA be a hoax? How did they even
have her DNA?

Alden turned to Quinlin. "Send me everything you have on
the fires. I need to get Sophie back home."

"The information will be waiting for you," Quinlin promised with a slight bow.

"Thank you. Good to see you, my friend."

Alden's pace felt rushed as he led Fitz and Sophie downstairs, bypassing the receptionist without so much as a nod.
He hailed another sea scorpion carriage, but this time Sophie
was too distracted to care about the evil-looking creature as it
pulled them through the canals.

Random facts floated through her mind. Prentice. DNA
matches. Keepers. White-hot fires wrapping around the city
where she lived. A "sign," Quinlin had said. A sign of what?

And why couldn't anyone read her mind?

She was no closer to the answer when the carriage slowed

to a stop. They'd reached a small blue lagoon so far outside the city that the silver spires were nothing more than a tiny glint in the distance. Shimmery white dunes surrounded the small lake, and on the west shore stood a strange black statue—a narrow round base, which rose at least two stories high, topped with a wide hollow circle. An iridescent film shimmered across the center of the loop, making the whole apparatus resemble a giant bubble wand.

"Hold on tight," Alden said as he moved between Sophie and Fitz and took their hands.

Before Sophie could ask why, Alden's feet lifted off the ground, his strong arms pulling her—and Fitz—along with him as he floated out of the carriage. She clung to his hand with every bit of strength she had, shrieking as the ground grew farther and farther away.

She blushed when Fitz chuckled. She needed to be better about keeping her cool.

But now elves could levitate?

What *couldn't* they do?

"Do I want to know what we're doing?" she asked as Alden steered them toward the statue.

"You'll see," Fitz told her.

They passed through the center of the loop and the iridescent film stretched, forming a giant bubble around them.

Sophie couldn't resist touching the bubble's side, which was warm and wet like the inside of her cheek. But a low rumble coming from beneath them demanded her attention.

She glanced down just in time to see a giant geyser shoot up from the lagoon, and it launched their bubble out of Atlantis.

ELEVEN

ON'T ELVES EVER DO ANYTHING the normal way?" Sophie asked as she watched the waves crash far below. Their bubble bobbed on the breeze, high in the clouds.

"Where's the fun in that?" Alden's smile lifted the worry she'd been carrying since they left Quinlin's office. If he could relax, maybe things weren't as scary as they seemed. Plus, it was hard to feel anything other than pure joy as she floated above the world in a giant bubble.

Especially when Fitz took her hand again. "Ready to go home?" he asked, holding his pathfinder in the sunlight.

She barely had time to agree. The bubble popped, and

she could only get half her scream out before the warm rush whisked them away.

Sophie squinted in the glaring light. "I thought you meant *my* home," she said as she stared once again at the enormous gates of Everglen.

She was actually relieved. They still hadn't explained what she was supposed to tell her family about all of this. In fact, there were quite a few things they hadn't explained. Her brain felt ready to burst with all the unanswered questions. "So what am I supposed to—"

Her question was cut short by a flash of light that made everyone shield their faces. When Sophie opened her eyes, a tall elf in a simple black tunic strode toward them. His olive skin stood in sharp contrast to his pale blond hair, and while his face held youth, something ancient shone in his dark blue eyes.

"You've got some nerve summoning me," he shouted, stepping right into Alden's personal space. He was a couple inches shorter than Alden, but he didn't seem the least bit intimidated by the height difference. "I'd sooner be exiled than train anyone in your family."

From the corner of her eye, Sophie saw Fitz's hands clench into fists. Alden barely blinked. He took a small step backward, and smiled.

"Yes, Tiergan—I'm well aware of your opinion of me. I can

assure you, I wouldn't have summoned you if I wasn't convinced that it would be what Prentice would want."

Tiergan's fierce expression crumbled. He backed away, crossing his arms against his chest. "Since when are you the expert on anything Prentice wanted?"

"Who's Prentice?" Sophie had to ask.

Tiergan spun toward her and his eyes did a quick inventory, widening when they locked with hers.

"Yes," Alden said when Tiergan gasped. "Whatever you're thinking, yes, Tiergan, I'd like you to meet Sophie Foster. Foxfire's newest prodigy, who happens to need a telepathy Mentor."

Tiergan swallowed several times before he spoke. "She's the one, isn't she? The one Prentice was hiding?"

"Yes," Alden agreed. "She's been living with humans for the past twelve years."

"Okay, seriously," Sophie interrupted. The way Tiergan was staring at her—like he'd just watched someone kill his favorite puppy—was officially weirding her out. "Who is Prentice, and what does he have to do with me?"

"I'm sorry, that's classified information, Sophie," Alden said quietly.

"But it's about *me*." She glanced at Fitz for help, but he shrugged, like it was out of his hands.

"If it becomes important for you to know, I will tell you," Alden promised. "For now, all anyone needs to know is that you are the most incredible Telepath I've ever seen, and you need a Mentor. Which is why I summoned you," he added, turning to Tiergan. "Sophie has already broken through Fitz's and Bronte's blocking without training. She needs the best Mentor we can provide. I know you're retired, but I thought—given the circumstances—you might be persuaded to return to Foxfire."

Anger and resentment danced across Tiergan's features, so the last thing Sophie expected was for him to nod.

"You'll do it?" Alden asked, his voice a mixture of surprise and relief.

"Yes. But only for this year. That will be more than enough to hone her abilities. Then you leave me alone and never ask for my assistance again."

"That's more than reasonable," Alden agreed.

"Wait," Sophie interrupted. "Do I get any say in this?"

"What do you mean?" Alden asked.

She needed a deep breath before she could answer. "I'm not sure I want to get better at telepathy." She'd always hated reading minds, and that was before she had to worry about serious rules and restrictions on it. And Tiergan didn't seem like he even wanted to train her. Maybe it was better to just pretend she wasn't a Telepath at all.

"Are you crazy?" Fitz asked. "Do you have any idea what an opportunity this is—"

Tiergan raised a hand, silencing him. He took a step closer

to Sophie, waiting for her to meet his eyes. "Being a Telepath around humans is quite a burden. I'll bet you've had terrible headaches and heard all kinds of things you didn't want to hear. Right?"

She nodded, stunned by his sudden change in mood. He sounded almost . . . kind.

He frowned and looked away, mumbling something she mostly didn't understand. But she thought she caught the word "irresponsible."

"It doesn't have to be that way," he said after a second. "With proper training you'll learn to manage your ability. But you do have a choice. There should *always* be a choice." He said the last part louder, like it was for Alden's benefit. "If you don't want telepathy training, you don't have to have it."

Sophie could feel the weight of everyone's stares. She knew what Alden and Fitz wanted her to say. And it would be nice to control her ability. "I guess I can give it a try."

"You guess," Fitz snorted, so low he probably thought she couldn't hear it.

Tiergan glared at him, and Fitz looked away, his cheeks flushing pink.

Alden cleared his throat. "Well, that settles that, then. I'll notify Dame Alina that you'll be returning to Foxfire. But the name of your prodigy will be kept classified. The Council doesn't want anyone knowing Sophie's a Telepath until she's older."

"Why do I have to hide it?" she asked. His words touched a bruise. She thought she was done hiding her abilities.

"You won't have to hide it forever," Alden said gently. "Just for a little while, to give everyone time to adjust to you. In the meantime, the session will be listed as remedial studies on your schedule."

Adjust. Like she was a problem they'd have to get used to. And why didn't they call it *Elf Lessons for Dummies*, while they were at it?

"I know this is all very confusing, Sophie, but I will do my best to explain everything when we get inside, okay?" Alden asked.

She nodded. What choice did she have?

"Good." He turned to Tiergan, who had backed a few feet away from everyone. "I'm assuming you don't want to come in."

"Finally, a correct assumption." Tiergan's voice was cold, but it warmed when he looked at Sophie. "I'll see you Tuesday." Then he raised a pathfinder to the light and vanished in a brilliant flash.

Alden laughed. "Well, that went better than expected." He licked a panel on the enormous gates, taking Sophie's hand as they swung inward. "Come on, Sophie. Let's see if I can't answer some of those questions I'm sure are floating around in your head."

He led her through Everglen's sprawling grounds, explaining how her new school schedule would have two sessions a day plus lunch and study hall. She'd be a "prodigy"—their word for student—and she would carry eight subjects, most of which were taught one-on-one by a Mentor, who were members of the nobility. Sophie's nerves tingled at the idea of one-on-one sessions with royalty. Talk about pressure to succeed.

Not to mention how behind she would be. The school year was already in session, and she was starting as a Level Two, the proper grade level for her age. So she'd be starting over, relearning everything she'd ever been taught, and already behind. It was a long way to fall from being the top of her class her whole life.

Self-doubt weighed heavier on her shoulders with each step, but she fought against it. She belonged here. She needed to believe that. Her fragmented life was finally coming together.

Well . . . almost.

"What am I supposed to tell my family?" she asked Alden. "They're not going to let me disappear every day with no explanation."

Alden bit his lip as he opened the doors to Everglen and stepped aside to let her and Fitz pass. "About that, Sophie. You and I need to have a talk."

The sorrow in his eyes made her feel like she'd swallowed something slimy. Clearly, it wasn't going to be a pleasant conversation.

"My office is this way," Alden said, leading her through

another shimmering hall. "We can talk there. There is much to dis—"

The sound of arguing cut him off, and when they entered a wide sitting room filled with overstuffed armchairs and elegant statues, they found a dark-haired girl about Sophie's age, who appeared to be shouting at herself.

A woman wearing an elegant purple gown appeared out of thin air next to the girl and said, "You're home."

Sophie squealed. Fitz snickered. So much for keeping her cool.

"Sophie, this is my wife, Della." Alden's cheeks were pinched—like he was trying not to laugh. "And my daughter, Biana," he added, gesturing to the girl. "My dear, I don't believe our guest is used to being around Vanishers."

"I'm so sorry," Della said, smiling at Sophie. She had a musical voice with just a hint of Alden and Fitz's accent. "Are you okay?"

"Yes," Sophie mumbled, trying not to stare. Della's beauty was like a force, pulling every eye to her as she tossed her long, chocolate brown hair and pursed her heart-shaped lips. And Biana had all of her parents' best features, combined in the best possible way. It was hard not to feel like a gangly troll, especially when Biana frowned and asked, "Is that my dress?"

"Yes." Alden interceded. "Sophie needed to borrow it to go on a few errands."

"I can go change," Sophie offered.

"No, that's fine," Biana said, looking away. "You can keep it. It's kind of frumpy."

"Oh . . . thanks."

"Quinlin sent the files you requested," Della told Alden. "I put them in your office." Her smile faded. "And the Council denied our request. But they did approve Grady and Edaline."

Alden ran a hand through his hair—the same way Fitz did when he was frustrated. "In that case, I'd better make a call." He turned to Sophie. "Then we'll have a long talk, okay?"

She nodded, a little torn when he set off down the hall. She had a feeling she knew what he was going to say—and she wasn't ready to hear it. But she wasn't sure what to say to Della or Biana. She could feel them staring at her.

"The Council sent these for you," Della said with a radiant smile. She held out two small parcels wrapped in thick white paper as she walked toward Sophie, blinking in and out with every step, like a strobe light.

"She doesn't realize she does it," Fitz explained when Sophie's eyes widened. "Vanishers let light pass through their bodies, so they can turn invisible, even when they move."

Della unwrapped the packages. "Hold up that pretty blond hair, will you?"

Sophie did as she asked, and Della clasped a thick silver cord around her neck. It fit like a choker, with a single pendant—an etched silver loop with a small clear crystal set in the center. Her registry pendant, Della explained. Everyone had to wear one, so they could be easily found. It was kind of pretty. But mostly it was one more elf-y thing she'd have to explain to her family.

Della handed Sophie a tiny green cube. "Anytime you need to pay for anything, just give them that. Your birth fund's been activated."

It took a minute for the words "birth fund" to register. "I have money?"

Della nodded. "The standard five million."

"*Dollars?*"

"Lusters," Fitz corrected, laughing. "One luster is probably worth a million dollars."

"What's a dollar?" Biana interrupted.

"Human money."

She crinkled her perfect little nose. "Ew."

Sophie ignored the insult. How could the elves afford to give away so much money?

"We do things differently around here," Della explained. "Money is something we have, not something we need. No one ever has to go without."

Sophie couldn't believe it. "But . . . why does anyone work, then—if they already have money?"

"What else would we do with our time?"

"I don't know. Something fun?"

"Work *is* fun," Della corrected. "Remember—we're not limited to seventy or eighty years. Once you get used to that idea, I think you'll find our way makes much more sense."

"Maybe," she agreed, still trying to wrap her head around it.

"All set?" Alden asked, coming back into the room.

Della nodded. "Were you able to change their minds?"

Alden shook his head, and Della's face fell. In fact, everyone looked . . . sad—except Biana, who looked relieved.

"What's going on?" Sophie asked, trying to ignore the panic rising in her chest.

Alden let out a long, slow sigh. "Come on, Sophie. Let's go have that talk."

TWELVE

ONE WALL IN ALDEN'S OFFICE WAS a large, curved window overlooking a silvery lake. A floor-to-ceiling aquarium wrapped the rest of the room. Sophie waited in an enormous wingback chair facing Alden, who sat behind a black desk piled with books and scrolls. Anxiety tightened her chest as the walls of water seemed to close in.

Sophie sucked in a breath to remind herself she wasn't drowning, and pointed to the stacks of human newspapers piled next to her chair. Articles were circled in red and then crossed out. "Keeping up with the news?"

"Looking for you." He removed another newspaper from a drawer and handed her the article with her picture circled.

"You don't know who sent this to you?" she asked.

"I have a few theories. No reason to worry."

"You keep saying that." A hint of irritation crept into her tone.

"Because it's true."

She sighed. "Well, if you figure it out, maybe you can find out how the reporter knew about me. My parents were super upset about it."

Her heart stuttered as Alden's face fell.

"I think I know what you're going to say," she said as he opened his mouth to speak. She needed to say it first. That would be the only way to survive it. "You're going to tell me I'm not related to my family." She felt a pull in her chest as the words floated away, like they were taking part of her with them.

"Yes, I was planning to discuss that." A shadow passed over his features. "But what we really need to talk about is why you can't live with them anymore."

The words swam inside her head, refusing to make sense.

Alden moved to her side, leaning against the chair as he took her hand. "I'm so sorry, Sophie. We've never faced anything like this, and there's no perfect solution. You can't hide your abilities forever—especially as they get stronger. Sooner or later someone will suspect that you're something *other*, and we can't allow that to happen, for your safety—and ours. Now that the Council knows you exist, they've ordered that you move here. Effective immediately."

She felt the blood drain from her face as his words sank in. "Oh."

The too-simple word couldn't communicate what she felt, but she couldn't come up with anything better. Part of her refused to believe him—refused to accept the impossible things he was saying. The same part wanted to kick and scream and cry until he took her home to her family.

But a tiny voice of reason wouldn't let her.

Deep, *deep* down—beneath the fear and hurt and pain—she knew he was right.

She'd lived every day since she was five in constant fear of discovery. She wasn't sure how much longer she could keep it up. The headaches from her telepathy were almost unbearable—and if they were going to get stronger . . .

Not to mention the loneliness. She'd never felt right with her family. She'd never had any friends. She didn't belong in the human world, and she was tired of pretending she did.

But knowing he was right didn't make it hurt any less. Didn't make it any less terrifying.

"Will I get to visit my family?" she asked, grasping for something to calm the fear threatening to overwhelm her.

Alden didn't look at her as he shook his head. "I'm sorry. I'm afraid that would be impossible. We call the areas where humans live the "Forbidden Cities" for a reason. Access is severely restricted. Plus they're going to think you're dead."

She was on her feet without deciding to stand up. "You're going to kill me off?"

"As far as your family and the rest of the humans are concerned . . . yes."

For a moment she was too stunned to speak—her mind filled with creepy images of gravestones reading HERE LIES SOPHIE FOSTER. But one image was even worse.

She closed her eyes, desperate to block out the horrifying mental picture, but it only became more vivid: her parents, hovering over her grave with tearstained faces.

"You can't do that to my parents," she whispered, blinking back tears of her own.

"We have to. If you disappeared, they would never stop trying to find you. It would draw too much attention to everything."

"But don't you know what this will do to them?"

"I wish there were another way."

She refused to accept that. Elves could travel on a beam of light and read emotions and probe minds. There had to be a way her family wouldn't suffer.

A sickening idea struck her. "Could you make them forget me? Make it like I never existed?"

Alden bit his lip. "It's more complicated, but it can be done. But would that really be better? They'd be relocated. They'd lose their jobs, their house, all their friends—"

"That's better than thinking their daughter is dead."

Her words seemed to hit him, and he turned away, staring

deep into the aquarium. "What about you?" he said after a stretch of silence. "These are people you love, Sophie. If we erase you, they won't miss you, they won't even know you exist. Wouldn't that be too painful?"

A single tear slipped down her cheek. "Yes. But only for me. For them . . ." She squared her shoulders and set her jaw. "It's the best thing for them."

Seconds passed before Alden turned to her, obvious pain in his eyes. "If that's what you want, we'll do it that way."

"Thank you," she whispered, hardly believing what she was saying. It felt like her brain was shutting down, too overwhelmed to function.

Had she really agreed to have her whole life erased?

She sank back into the massive armchair. Tears streaked down her cheeks and she scrubbed them away. "Will I get to say goodbye?"

Alden shook his head. "The Council specifically forbade me to take you back."

The room spun and a small sob slipped out. It never occurred to her when she left for school that it would be the last time she'd see her family—ever. It was too much. "Please. I need to say goodbye."

Alden studied her face for a long minute before he nodded. "I can't take you without risking a tribunal, but I can give you twenty minutes before I alert the Council to the change of plans and let Fitz take you. You'll have to change clothes before you go, and get out of there before anyone sees you or it would be very bad for him. Can you do that?"

She nodded, wiping away more tears. "Thank you."

Alden rushed to the door and called Fitz. Sophie couldn't focus as Alden explained what was happening. She was too busy trying to figure out what she would say to her parents.

How was she going to tell her family goodbye?

THIRTEEN

WHERE HAVE YOU BEEN?" HER dad shouted as Sophie set foot through the door. His round face—usually so soft—was bent and twisted into hard lines. Her mom rubbed her temples. "We almost called the police."

Sophie's eyes burned with unshed tears. Her parents, her house, her whole life for the past twelve years—this was the last time she would see any of it. It was far, far too much for her brain to process, so she did the only thing she could do. She raced across the room, threw her arms around them, and hugged as hard as she could.

"Did something happen, Sophie?" her dad asked after a

minute. "Your school called and said you left early." His mind flashed to unspoken horrors.

Sophie cringed away from his thoughts. "Nothing bad happened. It's just been a strange day." She buried her face into her mom's side. "I love you guys."

"We love you too," her mom whispered, totally confused.

"What's going on, Soybean?" her dad asked.

Sophie trembled at the nickname—proof that she really didn't belong with her family.

"She's just trying to get out of trouble," Amy said, bouncing into the room. She loved watching Sophie get busted.

"Amy, how many times have I told you not to cavesdrop?" her mom asked.

Amy shrugged. "How long is she grounded for?"

"Three months," her dad answered.

Amy shot Sophie a triumphant look.

"It doesn't matter," Sophie said, still hugging her parents. "I'm sorry for worrying you guys. I won't do it again, I promise." For once she would be able to keep her word.

"Well, maybe two months," her mom decided, rubbing Sophie's back.

Amy pouted and Sophie couldn't help smiling at her pettiness.

She was stunned to realize at that moment that she was going to miss Amy. Her bratty, obnoxious, pain-in-the-butt little sister. Sure, they fought all the time, but fighting with her was . . . fun. Why had she never realized that before?

She ran over and wrapped Amy up in a hug.

Her parents gasped.

"Ugh, what are you doing?" Amy asked, squirming in Sophie's tight embrace.

Sophie ignored her struggles. "I know we don't always get along, Amy, but you're my sister, and I love you."

Amy jerked away. "Why are you being weird?"

"I'm not being weird. I just wanted to tell you I love you. I love all of you." She turned to her parents, who were watching the strange scene play out between their daughters with their mouths open. "I couldn't have asked for a better family."

"What happened to you?" Amy asked.

"Nothing." She turned away to blink back tears. "I'm going to my room now."

Her dad cleared his throat, coming to his senses. "You're not off the hook yet, Soybean. We still need to talk about what happened today."

"We will," she agreed, desperate to get out of there. Fitz was keeping watch outside, and she had to hurry. "Later."

She raced to her room and packed in a daze. She didn't take much. Everything felt like it belonged to someone else—to another life.

When she was done, she allowed herself one minute to rememorize every detail of her old room: the pale blue walls, the dusty stacks of books piled on every available surface, the blue and yellow quilt her mother made for her when she was a baby. Her room looked empty now. Maybe that was because she felt empty.

Then she took a deep breath, turned off the light, and closed the door.

She tripped over Marty's furry body in the hall. "Sorry, boy," she whispered, crouching next to him. She rubbed his soft fur, trying not to cry. He'd been her only friend—but she couldn't take him with her. Her family would need him.

"Amy will take care of you," she promised as she stood up.

His pink mouth opened, releasing one tiny, pathetic meow "I'll miss you too."

Fitz had given her a disk of sleeping gas to release if she couldn't sneak out. She'd hoped she wouldn't have to use it— the idea of drugging her family made her physically ill—but they were waiting at the base of the stairs.

"Where do you think you're going?" her dad demanded, glaring at the backpack slung over her shoulder.

Amy giggled. "Aren't you in enough trouble already?"

"Sophie Elizabeth Foster, you tell us what's going on right now!" her mom yelled.

Sophie stared at them, clutching the sleeping gas, too afraid to use it. "I'm sorry," she managed to say. "I have to leave."

Her dad moved between her and the door. "You're not going anywhere."

"It's not up to me."

"Sit down," he demanded, pointing to the living room couch.

Clearly, they weren't going to let her go, and time was all but up. "Fine. I promise I'll explain everything if you just sit down and listen to me."

She cringed at the lie, hating herself for saying it. But it worked. They moved to the couch and waited for her to start talking.

She fingered the disk, ordering her hands to spin the top the way Fitz had shown her. But she couldn't—she couldn't let the last words she said to them be a lie.

"Please, please know that I love you. I can't thank you enough for everything you've done for me. I have to go now, but I will never forget you."

Tears blurred their faces as she held her breath and twisted the disk between her hands. Air rushed past her fingers as the gas released, and she dropped it and backed away.

Somehow she managed to count to thirty to let the gas clear before she breathed. Then she crumpled to the floor, burying her face in her hands.

"It's okay, Sophie. It's going to be okay."

It took her a second to recognize that the voice belonged to Fitz. He crouched on the floor, holding her against his shoulder. Some part of her brain knew she should be embarrassed about smearing tears and drool and snot all over his jacket, but she couldn't make herself care.

"I drugged my family," she whispered.

"You did the right thing."

"It doesn't feel like the right thing."

He squeezed her tighter as another round of sobs overcame her. "Look, Sophie, I feel like a jerk for saying this, but we have to get out of here. The Washers could be here any second, and they can't find us here."

"Washers?"

"Telepaths trained to erase memories. I'm sure the Council has sent them by now."

She forced her arms to let go of him and wiped her tearstained face on her shirt. "Just give me a second."

"I'll go get your bags. Are they upstairs?"

She pointed to her worn purple backpack. "This is all I'm taking."

"That's all?"

"What am I supposed to take? What am I going to need it for?"

"It's now or never, Sophie. Don't leave anything behind that you might regret later."

"No, there's nothing—" She stopped as she realized there was. Something she'd decided to leave because she was too embarrassed to take it with her. Something she suddenly couldn't bear to leave without.

"Ella," she whispered. Saying the name made her feel a tiny bit better. "I haven't slept without her since I was five. I thought I should leave her behind, but—" She couldn't finish.

"Where is she?"

"Upstairs, on my bed. She's the bright blue elephant wearing a Hawaiian shirt." She blushed, but he didn't laugh. Somehow he seemed to understand.

"I'll be right back," he promised.

She closed her eyes so she wouldn't have to see her family's limp bodies, and counted the seconds until Fitz returned. When he handed her the worn blue elephant, she was surprised at how much better she felt. Now she had something to hold on to. One thing she loved was coming with her.

"I'm ready to go," she said with sudden determination.

Fitz helped her to her feet and led her to the door. A big part of her wanted to look back one last time, but she kept her eyes forward. Then, clutching Ella with one arm and Fitz with the other, she took the two hardest steps she'd ever taken—out of the past, and into the future.

FOURTEEN

ALDEN AND DELLA WAITED OUTSIDE, pacing in the glow from Everglen's enormous gates. As soon as the doors swung open, Della wrapped Sophie in a tight hug, stroking her hair and whispering that everything would be okay. Sophie waited for the tears to come, but she'd cried herself out.

"No one saw us," Fitz assured Alden, handing over the black pathfinder.

"Thank you, Fitz. My dear, you might want to let her breathe," he told Della.

Della released her from the stranglehold, and Sophie took a shaky breath.

"Are you okay?" Alden asked, deep shadows haunting his face.

"No," she admitted.

He nodded. "It gets easier from here."

"I hope so." She hugged Ella. "What happens now?"

"Della and I are going to personally oversee your family's relocation. Fitz can help you get settled in here while we're gone."

"Here? I'll be living here?" Hope flared. Living with Alden and Della would be amazing.

Della wrung her hands. "Oh, Sophie, we would love that—we even offered. But the Council wanted you placed with other guardians."

Guardians? The title sounded cold and formal.

"I selected them personally," Alden assured her. "They're good friends of ours. You're going to like them."

"Okay," she agreed without much enthusiasm. It was hard to be excited about living with strangers, but she was too worn out to think about it.

"We'll talk more tomorrow," Alden said. "Right now we have to get going. Fitz, Elwin's waiting to see Sophie."

Fitz nodded.

Della gave Sophie one more hug before she moved to Alden's side. He held the blue-crystaled pathfinder to the light.

"Where are you moving my family to?" Sophie had to ask.

Alden sighed. "I'm sorry, Sophie. I can't tell you that."

It took her a second to understand why. "You're afraid I'll try to see them."

"The temptation might be hard to resist."

A shiver raked through her as the reality settled into her bones. She would never see her family again. She was an orphan.

"Why don't you take Sophie inside, Fitz?" Alden suggested quietly. "Elwin's waiting for her in the conservatory."

Fitz tried to léad her away, but Sophie turned back to face Alden. "My family always wanted a house with a big backyard, so they could get a dog."

"That can be arranged," Alden promised.

"We'll take good care of them," Della added. "They'll have money, security, everything they could ever want, well, except . . ."

She didn't finish the thought.

Any doubt Sophie might have had about choosing to be erased disappeared in that moment. Knowing she'd saved her family from feeling the throbbing ache she was suffering made it worth it. Her last gift to them, to thank them for everything they'd done for her. They didn't ask to raise an elf as their daughter—and it certainly hadn't been easy.

Which made her wonder . . . why them?

How had two average humans ended up raising an elf—without knowing it?

More important, why?

She met Alden's eyes, her lips already forming the question, but stopped at the last second. She wasn't ready to hear about the family who'd abandoned her. Whatever their story was, she doubted it was a good one, and she'd had pretty much all the bad news she could take for one night. So she let Fitz lead her, deciding not to watch as Alden and Della disappeared to wipe away all trace of her existence.

"Who's Elwin?" Sophie asked as Fitz led her down another long, glittering hallway.

"He's a physician. He's going to do a quick physical on you."

She froze as needles and other medical horrors flashed through her head.

"What's wrong?"

"I *hate* doctors." She knew she should put on a brave face in front of Fitz, but she couldn't. She still had regular nightmares about her brief hospital stays.

"You'll be fine, I promise." He grabbed her hand and pulled her forward, laughing as she struggled to resist. He didn't seem to notice the way her whole body trembled.

"What are you doing?" Biana asked from behind them.

"Nothing," Fitz told her, dragging Sophie a few steps in the right direction.

"Where were you? I asked Dad, but he wouldn't tell me."

"That's because it's none of your business," Fitz said.

"Will you tell me later?"

"Drop it, okay? I'm a little busy right now."

"I can see that," Biana grumbled, glaring at their hands.

Sophie tried to jerk free, not sure if she liked what Biana was implying.

Fitz tightened his grip. "Don't even think about it. I'm taking you to Elwin, and you're going to see it's no big deal."

She lost the will to resist under Biana's glare, so she let him pull her to an arched, golden door at the end of the hall.

Fitz stood behind her, blocking any possible escape. "I'll take your stuff to your room. Why don't you hang on to Ella?" he whispered. "Maybe she'll help."

"Thanks," she mumbled.

She handed over her backpack but made no move to open the door.

Fitz leaned toward her. "I tell you what. If anything bad happens in there, I'll let you punch me in the stomach as hard as you can. Sound fair?"

She nodded.

She caught Biana glaring at them again as Fitz pulled the door open and nudged her inside, but she was far too terrified to care.

The glass walls of the conservatory bathed everything in soft moonlight, and enormous plants grew in glowing pots around the room. Some of the gigantic flowers looked like they could eat her, but Sophie barely noticed them. She kept her eyes glued to the man—the elf—leaning over her low, cushioned cot, ready to bolt the second he pulled out a syringe.

"This goes a lot faster if you hold still," Elwin said as he adjusted her pillow.

She nodded and tried not to fidget, but between his wild dark hair and huge, iridescent spectacles, he reminded her way too much of a mad scientist.

He lifted her right arm.

"What are you doing?"

He snapped his fingers and a ball of green light formed around her elbow. "See? Painless."

She stared at the glowing orb. "How did you do that?"

"I'm a Flasher. I can manipulate light the way I want it—though I'm not as skilled as Orem Vacker. You'll see his crazy light show on the next total eclipse. It's one of our biggest celebrations."

It was strange to think that the elves had their own traditions, but it also made sense. The elves lived in their own world, and she needed to learn more about it—and quick—so she didn't look like an idiot all the time.

"Whoa, that is some serious damage. It's not permanent," he added when she tensed. "And it's not your fault. Toxic food, toxic water, toxic air. What chance do your poor innocent cells have?"

"You can see my cells?"

"Of course. Did you think I was wearing these glasses because they make me look dashing?"

She smiled. "What do they do?"

"Anything, depending on what color of light I use."

He snapped again, flashing blue and purple and red orbs

of light around her body and squinting through the lenses. Then he took the glasses off, and Sophie was relieved to see he wasn't as stunningly perfect looking as the other elves she'd met. His eyes were more of a gray than a blue, and his mouth was a little too small for his broad jaw. But when he smiled, his whole face lit up.

"You can sit up now," he told her, holding a small silver square in front of her eyes when she did. He frowned.

"What? Just tell me. I can take it."

He laughed. "You're so dramatic. I was expecting your eye color to be from the toxins. But your eyes are perfect. They're just . . . brown."

"They always have been. Even when I was a baby. Do you know why?" The last question came out as a whisper.

"No idea. I'm sure there's a reason, but I'd have to do some research. It'll be a great case study for the books once I figure it out."

"What? No—you can't!" How was she ever supposed to fit in if they were running case studies on her?

"All right, all right. Relax. I won't."

Sophie released the breath she'd been holding. "Thanks."

"No problem." Elwin laughed. He rifled through the satchel slung across his shoulder and removed tiny vials of colored liquids. "Now, try not to let this worry you, but your body needs a *major* detox. We'll start with these."

Sophie braced for the bitter burn of medicine, but the bottles were filled with sweet syrups, like nectar from unknown fruits. They made her tingly and warm inside.

"Good girl," Elwin said as he cleared the empty vials away. He placed a large, clear bottle in front of her. "All of us drink one of these every day, but I want you to drink two for a while, to make up for lost time."

"'Youth in a Bottle,'" she read from the label. "Like the fountain of youth?"

"I suppose that is where those legends come from," he agreed. "It has a few enzymes that are essential for our health."

The water was cold and slightly sweet, and somehow more refreshing than what she'd tasted before. She downed the contents in one gulp and handed the empty bottle back to him. He gave her another, and she drank it just as fast.

"I don't have a few of the medicines you need, but I'll give Alden a list. I want you to come see me in a couple weeks for a follow-up."

Her face twisted into a scowl before she could stop it.

Elwin laughed. "It won't be so bad—just a quick checkup. I work at Foxfire, so you can stop by anytime."

Mention of her new school made her tug out a couple of loose eyelashes.

"What are you doing?"

"Sorry. Nervous habit."

"You tear out your eyelashes?"

"It doesn't hurt."

"Still."

"You sound like my mom." The warmth of the medicines faded as the reality of everything that had happened rushed back. "Well, I thought she was my mom."

He sat next to her on the cot. "Alden told me about that. Do you want to talk about it?"

"Not really." She stared at Ella, hugging her tighter.

He whistled. "You're a pretty brave kid, you know that?"

She shrugged. "Sometimes you have to be brave."

"True," he agreed, laughing.

"What?"

"That just sounds funny coming from someone hugging a stuffed elephant."

Her cheeks heated up. "I know it's lame but—"

"I'm teasing. Personally, I can't sleep without Stinky the Stegosaurus—there's no shame in that." He laughed. "Anyway, you should get some sleep. You've had a big day. I'll see you in a few weeks."

"So, you gonna punch me?" Fitz asked as he showed her to her room.

"I guess not," she mumbled, feeling horrified about the big production she'd made. He must think she was the biggest wimp *ever*.

Fitz grinned. "What's with the 'doctor phobia' thing? You

were more afraid of Elwin than you were of jumping into the whirlpool."

"I guess you've never had anyone stick a needle in your arm or strap you to a bunch of machines."

"You're right about that." He shuddered and she felt a little better. And least he understood her fear now. "Why did they do that to you?"

"The shots were because I had an allergic reaction a couple years ago." She rubbed her arm, remembering the bruise the needles gave her. "The machines were because I hit my head when I was five."

"How'd you do that?"

"I guess I passed out and cracked my head on the concrete— I don't remember. All I know is I woke up in the hospital and my parents were freaking out, saying my neighbor had called nine-one-one and that I'd been unconscious for hours."

"That happened when you were five?"

She nodded.

"Was that before or after your telepathy started?"

"The same time. I started reading minds in the hospital. I always thought something happened to my brain when I fell, but I guess it was my elf genes kicking in."

He didn't respond.

"What?"

"It's just . . . telepathy doesn't *kick in* at that age. Something would have to trigger it."

"Trigger it how?"

"I have no idea. Not many things trigger a special ability—and none of them exist in the Forbidden Cities. My dad will have to look into it."

She repressed a sigh. Alden had a *lot* to look into, thanks to her.

Fitz stopped in front of a bedroom fit for a princess—huge canopied bed, crystal chandeliers, and glass walls overlooking the lake. "This is you. If you need anything, my room's just down the hall."

Her heart did that weird fluttery thing when their eyes met, and she had to look away to speak clearly. "Thanks for your help today. I don't think I could've gotten through all this without you."

He cleared his throat. "I don't deserve your thanks."

"Why?"

He kicked the ground. "Because—I knew what was going to happen and I didn't tell you when I made you come with me. I never realized it would be hard for you to move here—not until I found you there on the floor. I feel like I ruined your life."

"Fitz." She paused to find the right way to explain the crazy emotions spinning through her. "Today was hard. But you were right about what you said yesterday. This is where I belong."

Fitz straightened up, like a weight was lifted off his shoulders. "Really?"

"Really. Don't worry about me. I'm going to be okay."

She willed the words to be true, chanting them like a mantra as she shut herself in her room and changed into her pajamas.

Still, alone in the dark, with no one to tuck her in and no Marty on her pillow, she couldn't keep up the brave face any longer. She curled into a ball and cried for everything she'd lost. But when she fell asleep, she dreamed of a life filled with friends and fun and finally belonging.

FIFTEEN

S HE'S ALIVE!" FITZ TEASED WHEN SOPHIE wandered into the living room the next day. He sat in an overstuffed armchair reading a book called *Twenty-Five Ways to Catch the Wind.* "You do realize you slept through breakfast and lunch, right?"

"I did?" Sophie looked around, trying to find a clock, but everything was covered in weird clothes—like a costume shop threw up on the furniture. "Sorry. I guess I was tired."

"You had a rough day yesterday. Plus, your body needs rest while it detoxes," Della said, materializing in the center of the room.

Sophie clutched her chest. She couldn't understand how anyone could get used to the ghostly way Vanishers appeared.

Della frowned as she met Sophie's eyes. "How are you doing?"

Sophie shrugged. She didn't know how to answer.

"Well, you look great. Not that you weren't pretty before, but I think that detox made a difference. You should see how shiny your hair is, and your eyes are so . . . striking. You're going to be quite the heartbreaker when you grow up."

"Who is?" Biana strode into the room in a fitted dress with intricate gold embroidery that shimmered with every step. She looked way more glamorous than any twelve-year-old had the right to look.

"Sophie," Della said, smiling at Sophie. "Doesn't she look pretty today?"

There might've been things that were less embarrassing than that moment, but Sophie couldn't think of any. Especially when Biana shrugged, and asked, "Isn't that the same dress you wore yesterday?"

"All my other clothes were—" she started to explain, but Della held up her hand.

"I'm sorry. I should've sent something up for you. I've been shopping all morning." She waved her arms at the explosion of clothes. "Behold. Your new wardrobe."

"That's all for me?" Was she going to be wearing five outfits a day?

Della winked. "I got you everything you'll need, plus a few extras. The only thing I didn't get was a new nexus. I figured you'd want to pick your own. Unless you want to keep Fitz's old, beat-up one."

Sophie stared at the cuff on her wrist. "This was yours?" she asked Fitz.

He nodded.

She liked that—more than she wanted to admit. She fingered the sparkly stone, which was exactly the same color as his eyes. "Do you want it back?"

"I don't need it anymore. It's yours if you want it."

She was very aware of everyone watching her, so she tried hard to sound casual as she said, "Might as well keep this one then, so it doesn't go to waste."

"If that's what you want," Della agreed with a smile. "I should be done packing all of this in a few minutes, and then I'll get you some lunch."

"Packing?" Her heart sank as Alden entered the room holding her backpack and Ella. "Are you kicking me out?"

She tried to make it a joke, but a touch of hurt leaked into her words.

Della rushed to take her hands. "Of course not. We thought you'd want to get settled into your new home. If you want to wait a few days, we'll unpack your stuff right now."

Sophie swallowed to steady her voice. "No, it's fine. In fact, I don't really want lunch. I'm not hungry." Her stomach was so knotted with nerves there wasn't room for food.

Della smiled sadly. "You're going to like Grady and Edaline."

Her palms dampened at the strange names. "What are they like?"

"They're great," Alden promised. "They run an animal preserve at Havenfield, so they always have all kinds of exciting things going on."

"Do they have any kids?"

Della glanced at Alden.

He looked away. "Grady and Edaline lost their only daughter about fifteen years ago. Her name was Jolie. She was twenty when she died. It was a . . . terrible accident."

Della covered her mouth with her hand.

Alden shook his head. "I'm not sure if they'll mention it, so you might want to wait to see if they bring it up. That way you'll know they're ready to talk about it. And please don't let that make you more nervous to meet them. I won't deny that their loss has affected them, but they're still two of the most wonderful people I know. You're going to like them." He offered her his hand. "Come on. Let's go meet your new guardians."

"What kind of animal preserve *is* this?" Sophie asked as a booming roar shook the ground. Fenced-in pastures spread as far as she could see, filled with creatures that looked like mutant, scrambled versions of animals. Ella—in her bright blue glory—suddenly looked normal.

"Havenfield is one of the rehabilitation centers for our Sanctuary," Alden explained. "The animals are brought here first for training, before we release them into their protected home—and they're not easy to catch. We're still trying to trap Nessie. She's quite the escape artist."

"These things live around humans?"

"Where do you think the legends come from? Which is why it's not safe for them. We've even had to collect endangered species—gorillas, lions, mammoths—"

"Mammoths are extinct," she interrupted.

"Tell that to the thriving herd we have at the Sanctuary."

"You have a herd of woolly mammoths?" Somehow that was harder to believe than goblins or ogres.

"We have colonies of everything. Mammoths, saber-toothed tigers, dinosaurs." He laughed when her jaw fell slack. "Every species exists for a reason, and to allow one to die off would rob the planet of the unique beauty and qualities it provides. So we make sure they all continue to thrive. Grady and Edaline train the animals to be vegetarians by feeding them gnomish produce; that way they won't hunt one another once they're moved to the Sanctuary."

Another roar interrupted their conversation. Whatever it was sounded like it wasn't happy about its new diet plan.

The path they followed split, part of it winding down steep cliffs to a rocky beach lined with dark caves. Still, that path looked much less scary than the wide, flower-lined one they took to meet her new guardians.

The path led to a wide meadow, where gnomes were using

thick ropes to lasso what looked like a giant lizard covered in neon green feathers. The beast thrashed in protest.

"Oh, stop being such a drama queen," a husky male voice commanded from somewhere among the ropes and feathers.

ROAR!

"Okay. Here goes nothing," he called.

The gnomes tugged on the ropes, pulling the beast's neck low enough for a blond elf to heave himself up—no easy feat considering the beast was twice the size of an elephant.

SNAARRLL!

"I'm trying to help, you silly girl," he yelled as the beast bucked and thrashed.

Sophie cringed, hoping she wasn't about to watch her new guardian become lizard food.

"Need a hand, Grady?" Alden called.

"Nah. Almost got it." He lunged and grabbed something black tangled in the feathers. It twisted and writhed, but Grady yanked it off, nearly losing his balance in the process. The fluffy lizard stopped struggling as Grady tossed the black thing to one of the gnomes and slid down the beast's back. "Sorry about that," he called to Alden, once he was back on the ground.

"No problem, my friend. Verdi giving you trouble again?"

"That's why she's our permanent resident."

"Would you like to meet a tyrannosaurus, Sophie?" Alden offered.

Her eyes stretched wide at the name. So the dinosaurs

really weren't extinct. The idea was so impossibly cool. And they looked nothing like what humans thought. Now she knew what Fitz meant with his smug comments at the museum.

"Is it safe?" she asked as she followed Alden forward. She wasn't sure if she was more nervous about the deadly dinosaur or about meeting Grady.

"It is now that he got that jaculus off her neck. It's a winged serpent that feeds off blood."

She clung to Ella for support and moved to Alden's other side, away from the gnome struggling to contain the bloodsucking snake.

"Easy there, Verdi," Alden said as the giant beast whipped her head toward him and Sophie.

Verdi was more intimidating up close, with huge yellow eyes, sharp claws, and a pointed snout. Sophie tried not to tremble as Verdi bent down in front of her, lowering her giant head to Sophie's height. Rows of sharp fangs glinted with dinosaur slobber in the sunlight.

"Are you surprised by what dinosaurs really look like?" Alden asked, motioning for her to come closer.

"I wasn't expecting the neon feathers," she admitted, her legs refusing to take another step forward.

Grady laughed beside her, and she whipped around to get a better glimpse of her new, dinosaur-riding guardian. With his chiseled features and feather-covered tunic, she couldn't decide if he reminded her more of James Bond or Robin

Hood—which felt wrong. He was so unlike her chubby, balding dad she wasn't sure how to relate.

His handsome face stretched into a smile. "You must be Sophie."

She shook the feathery hand he offered and squeezed Ella tighter. He didn't *look* scary—but her knees banged together anyway.

"Want to pet Verdi?" Grady asked.

She really didn't want to get closer to those deadly looking teeth, but she didn't want Grady to think she was a wimp either. So she took a deep breath and stepped close enough to rub the T. rex's cheek with a light touch. Verdi stayed docile, watching Sophie with her unblinking yellow eye. Sophie lost herself in the stare.

"She's still in pain," she said, not entirely sure how she knew.

"Is she?" Grady separated the feathers on Verdi's neck. "The wound is pretty deep. Maybe I should treat it."

Sophie stepped back, and plugged her nose as Grady spread stinky brown slime over the wound. It smelled like death and rot and tuna fish—*not* a good combination.

"Kelpie dung," Alden explained. "Takes the sting out of most bites."

She hoped she wouldn't have to touch any dung while living there.

Grady closed the stinky jar and wiped his hands on a cloth

the gnome handed him. "I think you were right, Sophie. She seems more relaxed now. You must be good with animals."

"I can be—with normal animals at least." She stole another look at the gigantic feathery lizard. Verdi was still watching her, and maybe she was crazy, but she could swear she was trying to thank her.

"Well, come on, Edaline's probably waiting." Grady's voice sounded wary, and his steps were almost as reluctant as Sophie's as he led them to a house overlooking the ocean. It was small compared to Alden and Della's palatial estate but a mansion by human standards. The house was taller than it was wide, with golden columns breaking up the etched glass walls, and a glittering cupola rose from the center of the roof.

There was no fancy entryway like Everglen's, just a huge room with clear walls overlooking the ocean and scattered furniture breaking up the space. A wide central stairway curved to the upper floors, and a chandelier of intricately braided crystals cascaded from the domed ceiling. It was simple but elegant, and very, very clean. So clean It didn't look lived in.

Edaline swept into the room in a pale blue dress made of wispy fabric that floated around her as she moved. She had soft pink cheeks, wide turquoise eyes, and amber hair that fell past her shoulders in soft curls. Aside from Della, she was the most beautiful woman Sophie had seen—except for the purple shadows under her eyes. Sophie's human mom had similar dark circles sometimes, but only when she was stressed.

She wondered what Edaline was stressed about. She hoped it wasn't the idea of having her live with them.

Edaline frowned when she saw Grady. "You're covered in dinosaur fluff! I'm sorry, I told him to be presentable," she told Alden.

Alden laughed. "I've yet to see someone ride a T. rex without picking up a few feathers."

"You've never seen Edaline in action," Grady corrected with a smile.

Sophie tried to imagine someone so delicate playing rodeo cowboy with a dinosaur. Nope, she couldn't picture it.

"I'm going to wash up," Grady said, dashing up the staircase.

Edaline nodded. Then she took a deep breath and turned to Sophie. "Welcome to our home." Her shaky voice sounded more nervous than Sophie felt, which actually made Sophie feel better. At least Edaline thought this process was scary too.

"Thank you for having me." She didn't know what else to say.

Edaline smiled, but sadness lingered in her eyes. "I hope you can stay for tea," she told Alden. "There's mallowmelt."

Alden's face lit up. "If you insist."

Mallowmelt turned out to be a gooey cake that tasted like fresh-baked chocolate chip cookies soaked in ice cream and covered in frosting and butterscotch. It melted on her tongue and was, hands down, the best thing Sophie had ever tasted.

She giggled as Alden helped himself to three pieces. Grady joined them a few minutes later—his hair still dripping from a hasty shower—and helped himself to *four* slices.

Tea was served in a nook in the kitchen, and even though Sophie could see orange, feathery dinosaurs grazing outside in one of the pastures, it reminded her a little of home. Maybe it was the pastel linens on the table, or the intricate flowers painted on the china—but for the first time all day she didn't feel the empty, homesick ache she'd woken up with.

"Would you like some lushberry juice?" Edaline offered Sophie.

"Um, sure."

Edaline snapped her fingers. There was a tiny *pop* and a flash of light, and a bright green bottle appeared on the table.

Sophie scooted back like the bottle was possessed.

Grady laughed. "Guess you've never seen a Conjurer in action before."

"How?" she asked when her mouth was able to form words again.

Edaline smiled for real this time, and it lit up her whole face. "If I know where something is, I can bring it here with my mind. It's kind of like teleporting, but with objects."

That was pretty much the coolest ability ever. "What can you do?" Sophie asked Grady.

His smile faded. "Nothing nearly as fun, trust me."

She waited for him to elaborate, but he looked away.

Alden rose. "I, unfortunately, must get going." He dug a scraggly paper out of his pocket and handed it to Edaline. "Elwin wants her to take these medicines for the next few weeks. You should be able to find them at Slurps and Burps."

All the color faded from Edaline's face. "I guess I'll take her tomorrow. Is there anything else she needs?"

"Della took care of the rest. You know how she is when it comes to shopping."

"I do. I made the mistake of letting her help me shop for a gift for . . . a friend's daughter one time. Four hours later I had a whole new wardrobe and still no gift."

Grady took Edaline's hand and she turned away, staring out the window.

Sophie's heart ached for them. She knew their pain—she'd lost an entire family. Maybe that was why Alden put them together. They all knew what it was like to grieve. But she didn't feel like talking about it, so she kept quiet.

Alden fished a thin crystal square out of his pocket and handed it to Sophie. "This is an Imparter. It'll allow you to communicate with anyone in our world. So if you need anything, or simply want to talk, say my name to the screen and you'll reach me. Okay?"

"Okay." She strangled Ella as her heart pounded in her ears. It wasn't that she didn't like Grady and Edaline—but it would be weird to be alone with them. What would they talk about?

Alden leaned closer, so he could whisper. "It's going to be

okay, Sophie. If you need anything—anytime—I'm here. Use the Imparter."

She nodded.

"Good." He waved to Grady and Edaline, gave Sophie one more reassuring smile as he held up his pathfinder, and vanished in a flash of light.

The silence he left behind was deafening.

Grady snapped out of it first. He jumped to his feet and nudged Sophie. "Let's show you your new room."

"This is really all mine?" Her bedroom took up the entire third floor.

Star-shaped crystals dangled from the ceiling on glittery cords, and blue and purple flowers weaved through the carpet, filling the room with their sweet scent. A giant canopy bed occupied the center of the room, and a huge closet and dressing area took up an entire wall. Bookshelves full of thick, brightly colored volumes filled the other walls. She even had her own bathroom, complete with a waterfall shower and a bathtub the size of a swimming pool.

"I hope it's okay," Edaline said, biting her lip.

Was she kidding?

"It's awesome," Sophie said, feeling more excited about her new home already. She dropped her backpack off, but decided to keep Ella with her. It helped having something to hold.

Half of the second floor was Grady and Edaline's bedroom, and the other half was a long hall with three closed doors. Two were their personal offices. One they didn't explain, but Sophie assumed it was Jolie's room. They didn't forbid her from going to that part of the house, but they didn't give her a tour either, and with the way their voices strained as they spoke about it, she decided it would be best to stay away.

After an awkward but delicious dinner of soupy green stuff that tasted like pizza, Grady and Edaline left Sophie alone to unpack—which turned out to be a good thing.

Unpacking made everything real.

She *lived* here now, in this strange, slightly too perfect world where everything she knew was wrong and all she had to show for the past twelve years of her life was a backpack stuffed with wrinkled clothes she'd never wear, an iPod she couldn't charge, and a scrapbook full of memories that had been erased from everyone except her.

At least she knew her family wasn't missing her the way she missed them. Their new life—wherever it was—would be better without her. Alden and Della would've made sure of it.

Tears welled in her eyes as she put the last remnants of her human life away. Then she curled up on her bed with Ella and let herself have one last good cry.

When her eyes finally dried, she promised herself she wouldn't look back anymore.

Grady and Edaline weren't like her parents, and Havenfield wasn't like her old house—but maybe that was better. Maybe it was easier if they were different. And maybe, with time, it would really feel like home.

SIXTEEN

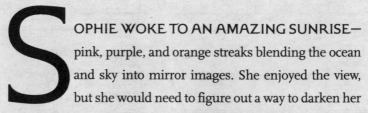

OPHIE WOKE TO AN AMAZING SUNRISE— pink, purple, and orange streaks blending the ocean and sky into mirror images. She enjoyed the view, but she would need to figure out a way to darken her glass walls. Sunrise was too early to be awake every day.

Grady and Edaline were in the kitchen finishing up breakfast when she came downstairs. Sophie hovered in the doorway, not sure if she should interrupt.

"Either you're an early riser," Grady said as he moved the scrolls he was reading to make room for her, "or you didn't close the shades."

She sank into a chair next to him. "How do I do that?"

"Just clap your hands twice."

"How about some breakfast?" Edaline asked. Her voice sounded tired, and the shadows around her eyes were so dark they looked like bruises. At Sophie's nod she conjured up a bowl of orange glop and a spoon. Each bite tasted like warm, buttery banana bread, and Sophie was tempted to ask for seconds, but she didn't want to impose.

She didn't know how to talk to them, so she stared at Grady's scrolls. The sloppy handwriting was impossible to read upside down, but she did notice a symbol in the corner: a hooked bird's neck, with the beak pointing down. The image tickled her mind, like she should know what it meant, but she couldn't find the memory it belonged to.

Grady caught her looking and rolled them up. "Boring stuff from a long time ago." He said it with a smile, but it was obvious he didn't want her seeing the scrolls, which only made her more curious. Especially when she spotted a line of runes running along the bottom, and this time they made sense.

"'Project Moonlark,'" she blurted, before she could think it through.

"You can read that?" Grady asked.

Sophie nodded, scooting back a little when she saw the look in his eyes. Anger, confusion—and fear. "Usually I can't, but this time I could. What's Project Moonlark?" she whispered.

Grady's mouth tightened. "Nothing you need to know about."

But Alden had said the word she used to babble as a baby

might mean "moonlark." That couldn't be a coincidence. She tugged out an eyelash.

Grady ran a hand across his face and took a deep breath. "I'm sorry. I didn't mean to scare you. It's just, these are extremely classified documents, and those are cipher runes. No one is supposed to be able to read them unless they've been taught the key."

She swallowed, trying to get enough moisture on her tongue to make it work. "Why can I read it, then?"

"I have no idea." He shared a look with Edaline. "Maybe the way humans taught you to read, or write, made your mind see things a little different."

That was the same excuse Alden had given for why she couldn't read normal runes. It wasn't particularly believable, but she couldn't think of anything better. She was pretty sure she'd remember being taught to read cipher runes.

"If you're ready to go, we should get those medicines Elwin prescribed," Edaline interrupted, standing. Each word was drawn out, like the whole sentence was one long sigh, which didn't exactly make Sophie eager to go. But she couldn't really say no, so she rose, fidgeting with the ruffles on the purple dress she was wearing. It was the simplest dress Della bought her, but she still felt ridiculous. Did the elves have something against jeans?

Grady nodded. "Say hi to Kesler for me."

Edaline groaned. "This is going to be interesting."

Sophie glanced at Grady, hoping he wasn't mad about the scrolls. He gave her a small smile. Then Edaline took her hand, and they glittered away.

They leaped to an island called Mysterium. Small, identical buildings lined the narrow streets like they'd been cut from a mold. Street vendors filled the air with the scent of spices and sweets, and conversation buzzed around the crowded sidewalks. Sophie's and Edaline's gowns stood out among the simple tunics and pants of the other elves.

"Hey, how come they don't have to dress up?" Sophie complained.

"Mysterium is a working-class city."

"Oh. But wait—doesn't everyone get the same amount of money in their birth fund?"

Edaline nodded. "Money has nothing to do with social rank. Our world is 'talent based.' Those with simpler abilities work simpler jobs—and they dress correspondingly."

"Seems kind of unfair," Sophie mumbled. "You can't control how much talent you're born with. Why should you live a lesser life?"

"Their lives aren't lesser. They have houses just as fine as Alden's or ours. But when they come to work, they come to a different type of city. A city designed for *their* kind of work." Edaline's grip tightened on Sophie's hand as several people waved at her.

"You okay?" Sophie asked.

"Yes, I'm just not used to being around so many people." She kept her head down as she led Sophie through the busy village, avoiding the other elves they ran in to. Everyone seemed to recognize Edaline, though, and whispers followed them wherever they went.

"Look, it's Edaline Ruewen—can you believe it?"

"I thought she never left the house."

"She doesn't."

Edaline pretended not to notice, and they didn't slow their pace until they reached the only building that was different: a store painted twenty different colors, with curved walls and a crooked roof—like it belonged in a nursery rhyme.

SLURPS AND BURPS: YOUR MERRY APOTHECARY.

The door belched as they entered.

The store was a maze of shelves filled with colored bottles of liquids and pills. Edaline went straight to the back, to a laboratory complete with beakers bubbling over burners with rainbow-colored flames. A slender man in a long white lab coat hovered over the experiments with a skinny boy at his side—probably his son, since they both had the same tousled strawberry blond hair and periwinkle eyes.

"I'll be with you in two minutes," he promised as he added a blob of orange slime to one of the test tubes. "Get ready to add the amarallitine, Dex."

The boy used a long pair of tongs to pick up a glowing yellow vial and hold it over the experiment from a safe distance. "Ready?"

"Not yet." He slipped on a pair of thick black glasses. "Okay. Now!"

He jumped back as the boy poured in the contents of the vial. The beaker sparked and released an enormous plume of smoke, filling the room with the smell of dirty feet. Sophie fought off a gag and hoped the concoction wasn't on Elwin's list.

The man pounded the boy's back and removed his glasses. "First one we haven't exploded all day. Edaline!" he exclaimed, finally looking up. "Is that really you?"

"Hello, Kesler."

"'Hello, Kesler,'" he repeated, with a convincing impersonation of her soft voice. "That's all you have to say? Get over here and give me a hug!"

Edaline moved across the room like sludge, but he wrapped her in a big bear hug anyway. "You look good, Eda—but what are you doing here? You *never* come to town."

"I know." She handed him the crumpled scrap of paper. "Elwin said I need to get these for Sophie."

Kesler scanned the sheet for half a second before his head snapped up. "Sophie?" His eyes found where Sophie was standing and his jaw fell slack. "Did I . . . miss something?"

"Yes." Edaline took a deep breath. "Sophie lives with us now."

Kesler's eyes darted between Sophie and Edaline, like he

couldn't decide who was more fascinating. "Since when?"

"Since yesterday—it's a long story." She gestured for Sophie to join them. "Sophie, this is my brother-in-law, Kesler, and my nephew Dex."

"Hi," Sophie mumbled, too nervous to make eye contact, especially since these were Edaline's *family*. She could practically feel their stares.

"Sophie will be starting at Foxfire on Monday," Edaline explained.

"Cool," Dex exclaimed. "What level will you be?"

"Level Two."

"Me too! Do you know your schedule al—whoa!" He leaned close to her face and pointed to her eyes. "How'd you do that? I turn mine red sometimes—totally freaks everyone out—but I've never seen brown before. I like it."

She could feel her cheeks blush. "Actually, I just have brown eyes."

"Really? Excellent. Do you see them, Dad?"

"I do." Kesler studied her like she was one of his experiments. "Where exactly are you from, Sophie?"

"I . . . uh . . ." She wasn't sure if she was allowed to tell the truth.

"Sophie's been living in the Forbidden Cities until a few days ago," Edaline answered for her.

Sophie cringed as Kesler asked, *"What?"* at the same time Dex shouted, "That's the coolest thing I've ever heard! Was it awesome? I bet it was awesome. Hey, are you human? Is that why you have brown eyes?"

"I'm not human. I was just raised by them." The words came out, but they felt wrong on her tongue.

"Dex, I think you're making Sophie uncomfortable," Edaline said, before he could ask another question.

"Am I? Sorry. I didn't mean to."

Sophie shrugged. "It's okay. I know I'm strange."

Dex smiled, flashing deep dimples. "I like strange. Hey, do you—"

The door burped again.

"You!" A tall woman in a dark green cape stalked through the store, pushing past Sophie and Edaline. A beanpole of a girl in a hooded pink cloak dragged behind.

"What's wrong now, Vika?" Kesler asked with obvious annoyance.

"Ask your son. This has his handiwork written all over it." She whipped the hood down from the girl's head, revealing a shiny bald scalp underneath

Edaline, Sophie, and Kesler gasped at the same time. Dex, meanwhile, seemed to be trying very hard not to smile. "Hey, Stina. Did you change something? 'Cause you look different today. Wait, don't tell me. . . ."

"Mom!" Stina growled.

Kesler's cheeks twitched, like he was battling a laugh. "We don't sell any balding solutions here, Vika."

"Just because you don't sell them doesn't mean you don't make them," she insisted.

Kesler glanced at Dex.

"You know how to make them too," Dex reminded him.

"I know it was you, you stupid *sasquatch*!" Stina screamed.

Dex rolled his eyes and pointed to a spot behind her ear. "Did you know you have a dent in your skull right there?"

Sophie bit back a laugh as Stina lunged for him in a flurry of bony appendages.

"That's enough!" Kesler shouted, pulling them apart. "Control your daughter, Vika."

"Why should I? It's not like you control your children."

Kesler looked like he wanted to throttle her, but instead he gritted his teeth and said, "We have Hairoids in stock. Take some on the house, and she'll have her hair back in a week."

"A week?" Stina wailed. "I can't go to school looking like . . . like . . ."

"Like an ogre?" Dex suggested with a wicked grin.

Stina screamed.

"If my daughter misses any days of school because of *your* son, I will make sure he is held responsible," Vika yelled.

"You can't prove anything," Dex grumbled.

"I won't need to. They'd expect nothing less from a bad match!"

Kesler's friendly features twisted with obvious rage, and he needed several deep breaths before he spoke. Sophie didn't know what a "bad match" was, but it must be a heavy insult.

"Okay, here's what we're going to do," Kesler practically spat. "You two are going to get out of my sight, and when I finish helping these customers, I'll see if I can make the Hairoids more potent. If I can't, wear a hat."

Vika stared him down, but he didn't flinch. "I guess we have no choice. It's not like anyone else would waste their lives making ridiculous medicines in a useless shop."

"If it's so useless, why does *everyone* buy from me?" Kesler countered.

Vika couldn't seem to find a retort. So she threw the hood back over Stina's head and dragged her toward the door.

"I'll get you for this," Stina promised Dex.

"Oooh, I'm really scared."

Stina's bitter eyes focused on Sophie. "What are you looking at?"

Sophie looked away. "Nothing."

The door burped again, then slammed.

Kesler pounded his fist against the table, making everyone jump. "Do I want to know what that was all about, Dex?"

"Probably not."

Kesler sighed. "You need to be more careful, Dex. You know how some people feel about our family—especially Vika and Timkin Heks."

"Well," Edaline said quietly, "this store hardly helps the situation. Perhaps if you made it more traditional—"

"Absolutely not," Kesler interrupted. "Nothing brings me more joy than watching all the stuffy nobles squirm in here."

"Just like nothing makes me happier than a shiny bald Stina," Dex added, grinning.

Kesler couldn't help laughing. "Well, Dex, since you made the mess, you get to tweak the Hairoids. I need to help Edaline with Elwin's list."

Dex scowled and stalked off to collect the supplies from the back. He returned a few seconds later with an armful of vials and spread them on the worktable with a sneaky smile. "This will make her hair grow faster," he whispered to Sophie. "But it'll also give her a beard."

Sophie giggled, and made a mental note never to get on Dex's bad side. "What did that girl do to you?"

"She's just evil," he said as he ground black leaves with a mortar and pestle. "Trust me."

Edaline disappeared to her room when they returned to Havenfield, and Grady tried to teach Sophie how to light leap alone. She'd never been so horrible at anything in her life.

The first twenty times she tried, she couldn't feel the warm feathers—no matter how many times Grady told her to concentrate on the tingle in her cells. After that she couldn't hold on long enough to do anything except break out in a full body sweat from the heat.

On attempt fifty-seven she finally made a solo leap to the

other side of the property. She completed the next five in a row and felt ready to collapse, so she wanted to cry with relief when Grady announced she'd practiced enough. But when he checked her nexus, he frowned.

He pointed to the gray rectangle, which displayed only a sliver of blue. "That means your concentration is at ten percent. Everyone your age is at least at thirty percent by now."

Yeah, and they'd been light leaping their whole lives—but she chose not to point that out. She didn't want Grady to think she was difficult. "I'm trying as hard as I can."

"I know," Grady said, worrying the edge of his tunic with his hands. "But I don't think you have any idea what you're up against. Alden told me Bronte doesn't want you at Foxfire, which means he'll be watching you like a hawk. He'll check with your Mentors. He'll monitor your tests. And at the first sign of weakness, he'll step in and try to have you expelled. I wouldn't be surprised if he pushes for you to be transferred to Exillium—and let's just say it's somewhere you don't want to go."

She nodded, swallowing a mouthful of bile. If she hadn't been freaked out about starting Foxfire before, *she was now*.

How was she supposed to pass when she was so far behind?

Grady forced a smile. "I know you're struggling to adjust and have a ton to learn, but you're going to have to push yourself as hard as you can. And I promise I'll help you every way I can. Edaline will too."

A flash of light pulled her out of her mounting panic attack, and two people appeared a few feet up the path. She recognized Dex from Slurps and Burps, and the woman he was with resembled Edaline, except her hair was messy and her yellow gown was wrinkled and plain.

"Had to come see for yourself, Juline?" Grady asked.

"I'm allowed to visit my sister, aren't I?" she asked, her eyes riveted to Sophie.

Grady laughed. "Where's the rest of the family?"

"Home with Kesler. I didn't want to overwhelm you."

"And maybe you wanted time to gossip without interruption?" Grady teased. "Sophie, why don't you show Dex your room? I have a feeling the girls have a lot of talking to do."

Sophie had no idea what to do with Dex. She'd never had a friend before—much less a boy—much less an elf. Dex seemed pretty comfortable, though. He wandered her room, touching everything that caught his interest. He thought her human clothes were hilarious, and was even more excited when he found the scrapbook she'd hidden on the bookshelf.

"Hey, is that you?" he asked, pointing to the photo mounted to the cover.

Sophie's eyes stung as she glanced at the picture. Her dad and sister waved at the camera while she hid in the background building a sand castle. "Yeah. That was last summer."

"Is that your dad?"

"Yeah. Well—um—that's the guy who raised me," she corrected, blinking away the tears that had formed. It was going to be hard to get used to saying that. But she had to. She wasn't his daughter. He didn't even know she existed anymore.

Dex frowned. "What happened to them?"

"I'm not allowed to know." She couldn't keep the sadness out of her voice. As much as she didn't want it to matter, it was hard not knowing where they were or how they were doing.

"Sorry." He shuffled his feet. "Do you want to talk about it?"

"Not really." She wasn't sure she was ready to look through the scrapbook, but Dex already had it open and was flipping through the pages. She hoped there weren't any naked baby pictures in there.

"Why did you take your picture with a guy in a giant mouse suit? Actually—better question: Why would anyone wear a giant mouse suit?"

"We're at Disneyland."

His head snapped up. "I have my own land?"

"What?"

"My last name is Dizznee."

She laughed. "I'm pretty sure it's a coincidence."

He squinted at the picture. "Are you wearing fairy wings?"

"Okay, I think we've had enough fun with the photos." She pulled the scrapbook away from him before he found anything else to make fun of.

"Sorry. I just can't get over it. I mean, I've never seen a human, in real life. And you *lived* with them." He shook his head. "How come you live with Grady and Edaline? Are you related to them?"

Her jaw tightened. "I'm not related to anyone."

"You're alive. You must have parents."

She shook her head. "My real parents didn't want me to know who they are, so as far as I'm concerned, they don't exist."

Dex didn't seem to know what to say to that. Honestly, she didn't either.

"Hey, this is one of those music things," he said, picking up her iPod.

"Yeah. How did you know?"

"My mom's into human movies. She doesn't have many, but one of them had one of these things in it, and I've always wanted to see one. We don't have anything like them."

"Really? Why not?"

"Elves aren't really musical—not like dwarves. They have some awesome music." He slid his fingers across the screen. "It's dead."

"No outlets here. No way to charge it."

Dex flipped it over. "I don't know much about human technology, but I bet I could make it solar powered."

"Really?"

"Well, I can give it a try." He slipped it into his pocket and went over to her desk, rifling through all her Foxfire stuff. He scanned her schedule. "Sir Conley's pretty cool, I hear. But good luck with Lady Galvin. She has the highest fail rate of any Mentor—ever. I'm pretty sure she failed her last prodigy a few weeks ago."

Sophie's heart slammed so hard she was surprised it didn't punch through her chest. Were they *trying* to make her fail? She wouldn't put it past Bronte to rig her schedule.

But . . . this was school. She'd always been great at school.

She took a deep, calming breath.

"Hey, I could help you find your way around tomorrow," Dex offered.

Relief flooded through her. She wouldn't have to do this alone. Except . . .

"You wouldn't mind being seen with the weird new girl with the weird brown eyes and the weird human past?"

"Are you kidding? I can't wait to tell everyone you were my friend first."

She smiled. "We're friends?"

"Yeah. I mean—if you want to be."

"Of course!"

Dex's smile widened, flashing his deep dimples. "Cool. I'll see you tomorrow morning."

SEVENTEEN

SOPHIE WAS STILL TRYING TO FIGURE out which of the strange gadgets from Della were school supplies when the chimes rang. Dex had arranged to meet her at Havenfield so she wouldn't have to arrive at Foxfire alone.

She laughed as she let him inside. "And I thought my uniform was bad."

She couldn't believe she had to be seen in a blue pleated skirt with black leggings and shirt-vest-cape combo. Dex's was worse, though. The blue lace-up jerkin over a black long-sleeved shirt and blue slacks with pockets at the ankles wasn't so bad. But the waist-length cape made him look like a really lame superhero—Captain Blueberry to the rescue!

"What's with the capes?" she asked.

"I know, they're stupid, right? But they're a sign of status, so we have to wear them."

"Capes?"

"Yeah, haven't you noticed that only the nobility have them? Foxfire is the only *noble* school—meaning you have to go there in order to be in the nobility—so we wear half capes to demonstrate that. At least next year we get rid of the wimpy halcyon." He pulled on the blue, jeweled bird that clasped the cape against his neck. "We'll be mastodons."

He laughed when he caught her confused expression. "Each grade level has a mascot. Level Two is a halcyon, these dumb birds that can sense when a storm is coming. But Level Three is a mastodon, so at the opening ceremonies on the first day of school we get to dress in these cool elephant costumes. Be glad you missed wearing the halcyon costume. We looked like idiots."

Dressing like an elephant didn't sound nearly as appealing as Dex seemed to think, but she'd worry about that next year. Assuming she was allowed to stay at Foxfire.

One problem at a time, she reminded herself.

"Hey, you're wearing the Ruewen crest," Dex said, pointing to the triangle patch sewn where her cape hung over her heart: a scarlet eagle soaring with a white rose in its talons. His patch was square and looked like a bunch of chemistry equipment twisted into a tree. "We wear our family's crest on our uniform.

If Grady and Edaline are letting you wear theirs, they must be serious. Are they adopting you?"

"I don't know." She'd never thought about adoption—she was still getting used to the idea of being an orphan.

What if they didn't adopt her?

Everything in her life was so temporary. Her enrollment at Foxfire. Her home. It felt like any second it could all be ripped away.

"Where are they, anyway?" Dex asked, looking around.

"A gnome ran in during breakfast and yelled something about a manticore stinging a stegosaurus, and they both ran off."

"And people say my parents are weird."

"It's pretty crazy here. But they seem nice enough."

"Grady and Edaline? Oh yeah, they're great. They keep to themselves a lot because of what happened to Jolie. I never knew them before it happened, but my mom said they used to throw these huge parties everyone looked forward to all year. Now they never leave the house. So weird."

Sophie shrugged. "A lot of people are never the same after someone they love dies."

"Really?"

"Yeah." She started to ask why he seemed surprised, but then she remembered what Alden had explained about the elvin life span. Death was probably a rare thing in this world. Which must make it even harder for the few elves who'd had to cope with it.

"My mom thinks it'll be good for them having you around," Dex told her. "Maybe they'll get over it."

She wasn't sure they would ever *get over it*, but his words calmed her panic. If she was good for them, maybe they'd want to keep her. She did understand what they were feeling—maybe better than most other elves.

"Hey, wait a minute," she said, frowning. "How do you know about adoption? I'm guessing you don't get a lot of orphans around here."

"We don't," Dex agreed. "We had a big drama a few years back—some kid named Wylie whose dad was exiled had his mom die too. Something broke her concentration while she was leaping and she faded away, I guess. I don't know much, just that Sir Tiergan adopted him and retired from Foxfire."

"Sir Tiergan—the telepathy Mentor?"

"Yeah. Wait—how do you know about him?"

"Uh, Alden mentioned him," she mumbled, trying to recover. She'd forgotten to pretend she had no connection to Tiergan.

"Oh yeah, he *hates* Alden. Blames him for the dad being exiled or something. But I might be remembering wrong. Wylie's a few years older than me, so I've never met him or anything. You ready to go?"

She slipped her satchel over her head. "Yep. How do we get there?"

He led her up to the cupola and pointed to hundreds of

crystals hanging in a round chandelier. "The Leapmaster 500. You're lucky. My parents aren't nobility, so they're only authorized to have the 250—it's missing tons of cool places. *Foxfire!*" he shouted.

The crystals rotated until one lowered, casting a beam of light toward the ground.

"You ready?" he asked.

She wasn't. But she forced a smile across her lips, took a deep breath, and let the warm feathers whisk through her and pull her away to her first day at Foxfire.

"That's a school?" Sophie asked, trying to make sense of the bizarre structure spread before them.

A five-story glass pyramid towered over everything from its place in the center of a wide stone courtyard. The main building wrapped around the pyramid in a sharply angled U and was made entirely of stained glass. Six towers—each a different color—separated the wings, and a seventh tower—another Leapmaster—stood in the center, taller than the others.

To the left sat a domed amphitheater and two smaller buildings, all built from the same glowing stones as the castle Fitz had shown her in Lumenaria. To the right, two giant towers, one gold and one silver, twisted around one another. Combined with extensive fields of purple grass, the place seemed more like a small city than a school, and Sophie tried not to imagine how hopelessly lost she would be.

Dex led her into the bottom floor of the glass pyramid, which was packed with prodigies in uniforms the same colors as the building's six towers. All hope of finding Fitz faded when she saw the chaos, and Sophie ducked behind Dex, hoping no one would notice her.

"What are we doing here?" she leaned in and whispered.

"Every morning starts with orientation. It's no big deal. Dame Alina—our principal—just reads off any announcements while they take attendance."

"How can they take attendance with this many people?"

He pulled his registry pendant out from under his collar. "They track us with these."

Thousands of bells chimed an intricate peal, and everyone faced the far wall, which now showed a close-up of Dame Alina, a stunning beauty with porcelain skin and fragile features.

She smoothed her caramel-colored hair and pursed her lips. "Good morning, prodigies. First and foremost, whoever put reekrod in my desk over the weekend *will*— It's not funny!" she snapped as everyone cracked up. Her eyes narrowed. "Mark my words—whoever it was *will* be punished to the fullest extent of my abilities."

She let the threat dangle before she continued. "Last week we had fourteen prodigies detect special abilities—a new record." She clapped and everyone joined her. "And—last but not least—where is she? . . . Ah, there!"

A spotlight focused on Sophie.

"Everyone, please welcome Sophie Foster—a Level Two prodigy, starting her first day at Foxfire."

Every eye turned to look at Sophie. Her name hissed around the room like a viper's nest. "Sssssssophie."

Dame Alina cleared her throat. "Is that how we welcome someone?"

A second of silence passed before everyone clapped. Sophie looked around for a hole she could crawl into.

"That's better," Dame Alina said. "That concludes today's announcements. Have a wonderful day!"

Everyone applauded as Dame Alina flashed a brilliant smile and blinked off the screen. Then all eyes returned to Sophie. The whispering started again.

"Get me out of here," she begged Dex.

He laughed and led her out the nearest exit.

"I can't believe that just happened."

"It's not a big deal."

"She had to force them to clap, Dex." She buried her face in her hands.

"Everyone was just surprised. We've never had a prodigy start in the middle of the year."

She groaned. Why did she have to be the exception to *everything*?

"Just relax. You'll be fine. Come on."

He led her into the main building, which was divided into

six different wings by the towers, one wing for each lower grade level. The walls of the Level Two wing were the same blue as her uniform, and the banners bore a halcyon in midflight.

Dex switched halls so many times Sophie lost count, and she was beyond confused when they entered an enormous quad with glittering crystal trees scattered throughout the room. A statue of a halcyon filled the center, sparkling like it was carved from sapphire instead of stone. Prodigies chatted as they put books and supplies into the narrow doorways lining the walls, but everyone fell silent when they noticed Sophie.

"Okay, this is the atrium," Dex explained, ignoring the spectacle they were creating. He checked her schedule and led her toward the far wall, to a door marked with a rune she couldn't read. "This is your locker. See that silver strip?" He pointed to a shiny mirrored rectangle just underneath the symbol. "Lick it. The lock uses your DNA."

"That's gross."

"It tastes good."

She doubted that, but she could feel everyone watching her so she licked the silver rectangle. "Mallowmelt?"

"The faculty picks the flavors. They change every day—but watch out for Elwin's picks. Last week it was pepper. Made everyone sneeze like crazy."

Dex's locker was two doors down, and a loud *croak* sounded as he opened the door. Dex yelped and slammed it closed, but the whole room filled with the stench of rotten eggs mixed with morning breath and a dash of dirty diaper.

"She put a muskog in my locker!" he screamed.

A high, wheezy snicker erupted behind them.

They whirled around to face a girl towering over them like a giant stick insect. The girl's head was covered with a mass of frizzy brown curls, so it took Sophie a minute to recognize her as the bald girl from Slurps and Burps. Two girls stood next to her cackling like evil hags.

"How did you get in my locker?" Dex demanded, stalking up to Stina's towering body. His head barely cleared her shoulders.

"You left it open, idiot. I guess remembering to close doors is too hard for the son of a bad match to remember."

Dex ground his teeth. Then his eyes lit up, and he pointed to a row of scraggly hairs along her jaw. "Nice beard you're grow-ing there. Hope you know how to shave."

Stina felt her chin and shrieked. She grabbed Dex by the shirt. "You little—"

"That's quite enough, Miss Heks!" a slender woman in a deep blue gown and cape ordered as she stepped through the wall and pulled them apart. "What's going on here? And what on earth is that smell?"

"She put a muskog in my locker!" Dex told her.

"He put balding serum in my lushberry juice on Friday!" Stina retorted.

The woman shook her head, her long raven hair swishing

behind her. "Such behavior—and in front of our new prodigy." Her eyes darted to Sophie. "I'm sorry you had to see this, my dear."

"You just walked through a wall," was all Sophie could think to say.

"Phasers do that sometimes." She turned back to Dex and Stina. "You two should be ashamed of yourselves. Apologize."

Dex scowled. Stina glared. But they both mumbled, "Sorry."

"You two obviously need time to bond, so you can spend all week together in lunch detention."

"But, Lady Alexine—"

"I don't want to hear it. Dex, get that muskog out of here before it stinks up the whole place. And, Stina? You seem to have some strange hairs on your chin. You might want to have Elwin check them."

Dex cracked up and Stina turned beet red. She covered her beard with her hand and stalked off, followed by her minions. Lady Alexine swept across the atrium, disappearing through the far wall.

"See what I mean?" Dex asked as he kicked his locker. "She's evil."

Sophie nodded. "What exactly is a muskog?"

"It's kinda like a frog, but it burps stinky gas when it's scared. So you should probably get away from here—unless you want to smell like muskog fumes all day."

He didn't have to tell her twice. She was already the weird

new girl. She didn't need to be the stinky, weird new girl.

"Hey, you're the prodigy Dame Alina told us about, right? The new one?" a small boy asked, catching up with her as she set off through the halls. He was a couple of inches shorter than her, with messy brown hair and a very round face.

"Sophie," she corrected.

"I'm Jensi—whoa—you have really weird eyes—cool— anyway—so—everyone wants to talk to you—but they're all afraid—so I decided to show them how it's done."

"Um . . . thanks," she said, struggling to keep up with his rapid-fire speech. He talked like he'd had buckets of sugar for breakfast.

"See, I told you she'd be nice," he shouted, making several kids around them turn bright red. Sophie's cheeks were probably redder.

"I've never heard of you before—and I know pretty much everyone—so where have you been all this time?" Jensi asked.

She'd been hoping no one would ask that question. Alden had instructed her to be honest. "I was living with humans," she whispered.

"Humans!"

Everyone fell silent. Sophie managed a nod.

"Well—that's weird—but cool—you'll be 'Human Girl'— it'll be awesome!"

She cringed. "How about just 'Sophie'?"

"If that's what you want."

"Thanks." They hit a fork in the hallway, and she took the right path on a whim.

Jensi followed her. "Where are we going?"

"Elementalism." She didn't miss the fact that he used the word *we*.

He laughed. "Boy, are you going the wrong way. Come on. I'll take you there."

Part of her wanted to run from the humiliating boy who was drawing way too much attention to her. But she did need help, so she swallowed her pride.

They backtracked, making so many twists and turns Sophie had to admit she never would've found it without him. Finally, they entered a narrow hall that smelled like a storm, right before the first drops of rain fell.

Jensi pointed to a warped wooden door. "Your session's in there—oh—and be careful—I'd hate you to get zapped on your first day!"

"Okay—wait!" she added as his words sank in. "What do you mean, 'zapped'?"

Jensi was already gone. She stared at the door, wondering if he was kidding. This was a school. They wouldn't allow anything dangerous around the prodigies, would they?

She took a deep breath to calm her nerves, squared her shoulders, and pushed the door open. A loud thunderclap shook the floor, and a bolt of lightning shot out of the ceiling, knocking her off her feet.

EIGHTEEN

HOW WAS YOUR FIRST SESSION?" Dex asked as he handed her a tray and made room for her in the lunch line.

"Oh, fine—except I was almost electrocuted." She tried to keep the quiver out of her voice. Sir Conley stopped the lightning from hitting her, catching it in a tiny fluted vial at the last possible second. But the hairs on her arms still stood on end. Especially since she'd also botched the class assignment, and she caught Sir Conley making notes about it. Would he be sending them to Bronte?

"That's elementalism for you," Dex said. "Wait till they make you collect your first tornado. They're *not* easy to catch."

Of course they weren't. *Because they were tornadoes!* "Why do we have to learn to bottle that stuff, anyway?"

"Mastering all the elements is one of the steps toward entering the nobility."

"Why?"

"No idea. Neither of my parents are in the nobility, so I don't know much about it."

Right. His parents were a "bad match"—whatever that meant. "Hey, what are you doing here? I thought you had detention?"

"I still have to eat," he grumbled, filling his tray with brightly colored foods.

The lunch line wound through a series of stalls, like a food court at the mall. None of the food was recognizable, so Sophie grabbed whatever Dex took.

"Sorry I got detention on your first day. Are you going to be okay without me?"

"Sure." She'd eaten lunch alone her whole life—what was one more day?

Except there were no empty tables inside the cafeteria, which took up the whole second floor of the glass pyramid. Sophie scanned the faces hoping to find Fitz, but all she saw were strangers, most of whom looked away, like they were tying to discourage her from joining them.

She was on the verge of panic when a pair of teal eyes caught her attention. Unfortunately, they were set into Biana's perfect face.

Biana held her gaze and shook her head—barely perceptible—but the message came through loud and clear: *Don't even think about sitting here.*

Sophie ignored the sting of the insult, focusing on the bigger problem. Biana was sitting next to Fitz. Where was she supposed to go now?

Jensi rushed to her side. "Hey, my friends and I have a table—it's only guys—and most of them are pretty lame—but you can totally sit with us."

She might've hugged him if her hands hadn't been full. "Thanks, Jensi."

If Jensi's friends were human, they would've been skinny, with acne and braces. Since they were elves, they were fairly good looking—or they could've been if they hadn't slicked their hair into greasy ponytails. They stared at her like they'd never seen a girl up close before. One of them even drooled.

"Sorry," Jensi mumbled, setting his tray down with a bang. "C'mon, guys. I said be cool!"

"Sorry, dude," they all said in unison, and went right on staring at Sophie.

Jensi sighed. "So, how was the E?"

"'E'?"

"Elementalism," one of the greasy ponytails explained. "Dude, you don't know that's what we call it?"

"Of course she doesn't. She's been living with humans," Jensi explained before she could say anything. He grinned like he'd just done her a huge favor. But she had to fight the urge to crawl under the table. Especially when all his friends leaned back in their chairs and said, "Dude."

She barely held back her sigh. "Elementalism was good. I wasn't zapped."

"Well, duh," the drooly one volunteered. "Your clothes would be all singed and stuff if you were."

Jensi rolled his eyes. "Anyway—what do you have next?"

"The Universe." The name alone sounded daunting.

"Don't you mean the U?" the drooly one asked with an exaggerated wink. The other guys giggled.

Jensi shot them all death looks. "That's not what we call it. Stop messing with her."

"Sorry, dude," they mumbled.

"Enough with the 'dude'—you guys are killing it!"

"Sorry, dude."

Jensi looked ready to explode. Sophie covered her laugh with a cough.

"Thanks for taking care of her, guys, but I'll take it from here," a girl's voice interrupted.

All the greasy ponytails stared and drooled again as a pixie-like girl grabbed Sophie's tray and motioned for her to follow.

"What are you doing?" Sophie hissed.

"Rescuing you," she whispered, tossing her blond hair.

Not sure what else to do, Sophie murmured a quick goodbye and caught up with the girl.

"You can pay me back later," she said without turning her head. She was extremely petite, and her uniform looked like it spent the night balled up on the floor, but she still looked pretty. Maybe it was the way she'd twisted some of her hair into tiny braids, or her huge, ice blue eyes.

"Sitting with those guys is social suicide," she explained.

"Jensi's not so bad," Sophie argued. Sure he was a little over-eager, but he'd come to her rescue twice already.

"Yeah, he's fine, but those other guys . . ." She shuddered. "My name's Marella. Not Mare. Not Ella. No nicknames." She led Sophie to her table and set the tray down next to hers. "Most of the people here aren't worth my time. But I figured anyone who got Stina to hate her in less than a day is my kind of girl. Take a seat."

For some reason Sophie obeyed. "Stina hates me?"

"Oh yeah. But you're better off. She's evil."

"So I keep hearing." She wasn't sure it was a good idea to have enemies though. Would Bronte use that against her if he found out?

"Anyway, I saw you over there with the drooly boys and felt sorry for you, so I thought I'd try making a friend." The way she said it was almost like Sophie should feel honored. "You gonna eat or what?"

"Oh. Right." Sophie took a small bite of a green puffy ball and felt her lips pucker. It tasted like sour licorice soaked in lemon juice. "Do you usually sit by yourself?" she asked when she could move her face again.

"Sometimes I let boys sit with me, but I'm not a fan of girls. Girls are annoying." She shot Sophie a warning look, like she was ordering her not to be obnoxious. "Like, check out Princess Prettypants over there." She pointed to Biana and rolled her eyes. "I'd rather hang out with a bunch of goblins."

Sophie grinned. She couldn't understand how such a grumpy brat could be related to Alden and Della—or Fitz.

"Her brother's cute, though," Marella said, her voice turning dreamy. "What I wouldn't give . . ."

It took all of Sophie's willpower not to agree. She took another bite of the green ball.

Marella smiled when she cringed. "Too sour?"

"Way. I guess that's what I get for copying Dex." She took a sip of lushberry juice to wash away the taste.

"Dex . . . strawberry blond curly hair and dimples, right? He's cute. His family's a little"—she looped her finger around her ear—"but that's not really his fault."

"His parents seemed okay when I met them," Sophie said, defending her friend.

"The Dizznees are nice, but they're odd. I mean, they have triplets!"

"And having triplets is . . . bad?"

"Yeah. I mean, I don't know how it is in the Forbidden Cities, but here we have our kids one at a time. So to have three at once is *weird*. My mom says it's because his parents were a bad match."

Sophie tensed at the insult. "What exactly is a 'bad match'?"

"A couple that was ruled genetically incompatible. Usually means their kids will be inferior—and if you'd met the triplets, you'd believe me. No way those kids will be normal." She shrugged. "Even his aunt and uncle are superstrange."

"Grady and Edaline?"

She nodded. "They used to be celebrities—like, more famous than the Vackers."

"Who?"

Marella shot her another warning look. "Fitz and Biana. Their dad's superimportant—their whole family is. But Grady was even more important, 'cause he has such a rare special ability. Then their daughter died and they freaked out and cut themselves off from everyone."

Sophie wasn't sure she liked Marella's tone. There wasn't even a hint of sympathy. "You guys really don't understand how hard death is, do you?"

"And you do?"

She nodded. "My grandma died when I was eight, and my mom cried for weeks."

She'd had to hear every one of her mom's heartbroken thoughts, and there was nothing she could say to make her less sad—or to bring her grandma back. It was the most helpless she could remember feeling.

"Weird," was all Marella had to say to that. "Anyway, Dex

seems okay. I know some people think he'll end up in Exillium, but I doubt it."

Ice ran through Sophie's veins at the name. "What's Exillium?"

"The school where they send the hopeless cases. It's pretty much a guarantee you'll end up scooping mammoth poop at the Sanctuary when you grow up—and that's if you're lucky."

Sophie couldn't hide her shudder. She had to do well in her sessions. There was no way she was going to that awful place. She'd do whatever it took.

Her afternoon session was the Universe, and it was as daunting as she'd feared. Every star. Every planet. Every possible astronomical object—she'd be learning them all.

But Sir Astin—a pale blond elf with a soft, whispery voice—said she was a natural. Apparently, he'd never taught a prodigy with a photographic memory strong enough to remember the complex star maps he projected across the walls of the dark planetarium. Sophie had no idea why it was so effortless for her, but she wasn't complaining. At least she had one session she excelled at. She hoped Sir Astin sent Bronte a note about *that*.

Every day ended with an hour of study hall on the first floor of the pyramid with the rest of the school. Dex waved her over to a seat he'd saved for her. "You survived," he said as she plopped down next to him.

"So far." She smiled as she dug out her Universe homework.

"There you are," Fitz said, approaching their table. His green Level Four uniform somehow looked better on him than on anyone else—even the cape looked good, especially with the green dragon clasp. "Why didn't you sit with us at lunch?"

She chose not to tell him about Biana's hateful glare. "Jensi invited me to sit with him, and I didn't want to hurt his feelings."

"Ah. Well, maybe tomorrow then. Oh, and"—he handed her a folded slip of paper—"my dad asked me to give you this."

Inside the note were two short sentences in precise letters:

The San Diego fires have been extinguished.
No reason to worry.

Sophie smiled. Her family didn't live there anymore, but it was still a relief that the fires were out. Everything was back to normal.

Dex cleared his throat.

"Oh, sorry. Do you guys know each other?" she asked, stuffing the note in her satchel.

Dex said, "Yes," at the same time Fitz said, "No." *Awkward.*

"Well," she said, trying to fill the silence. "This is Dex."

"Nice to meet you."

"Right," Dex snorted.

"What?"

"Nothing, apparently."

Fitz frowned. Dex glared. Sophie watched them, trying to make sense of the animosity.

"I should get started on my homework," Fitz said after a second. He smiled and her heart did that stupid fluttery thing again. "I just wanted to check on you. I'll see you tomorrow?"

"Sure."

"Oh, and uh, nice to meet you, Deck," he added with a hasty nod as he walked away.

"It's Dex," he growled.

"What is up with you?" she whispered.

"Me? 'Nice to meet you, *Deck*,'" he repeated in an uncanny impersonation of Fitz's precise accent.

She fought off her smile. "I'm sure that was an innocent mistake."

"Please. I see him all the time—not that his royal highness bothers remembering. But he remembers *you*. Why is that, by the way—and why did he give you a note from his dad?"

"I stayed with his family my first night here, and Alden promised to get back to me about something. It's about my old life. I'm not supposed to talk about it."

"Figures."

"What?"

"Nothing. I just hate that family. Everyone thinks they're so cool and talented. But they're totally overrated. '*Deck*,'" he muttered.

"Maybe Fitz just heard me wrong."

"Yeah, right. Listen to you defending him. You're just like

all the other girls, you know that? I saw what you did when he smiled at you. You lit up."

"I did not!"

"Yes, you did. You were beaming."

Beaming? Did Fitz see that too? "I wasn't beaming," she argued.

Dex rolled his eyes. *"Girls."*

NINETEEN

THE WHOLE SCHOOL HAD PHYSICAL education together every Tuesday and Thursday morning—the only session that wasn't one-on-one. Sophie was so nervous she couldn't even think about breakfast. She'd always been a disaster at anything physical. Her goal was to hide in the back and hope her Mentor didn't notice her.

The locker rooms were outside, sandwiched between a huge field of purple grass and the amphitheater that looked like a domed Colosseum. As soon as she set foot through the door, hundreds of girls stopped talking to stare at her.

Sophie kept her head down and rushed to what she assumed was her PE locker. Instead, the door led to a personal changing area, complete with shower and vanity. Her uniform hung from a hook near the door: blue tunic, black leggings, black sneakers—finally something without a cape. She changed fast, swept her hair into a loose ponytail, and emerged into the main room just as Stina and her minions stalked by like they owned the place.

Stina laughed when she spotted her. "I give the new girl six months before they ship her off to Exillium," she said, loudly enough for everyone to hear.

The word "Exillium" felt like a slap. Sophie couldn't think of a reply.

Marella's voice cut across the room. "That's about how long your dad lasted, wasn't it?" She stalked over and got in Stina's face. "Actually, I doubt he even made it that far."

"You want to compare parents, Redek?" Stina hissed.

Marella was so tiny Stina looked like she could squish her—but she didn't flinch. "My family may not be nobility, but at least we're not trying to fool anyone—unlike *some* people in this room."

"Take that back," Stina demanded.

"I will when it stops being true." Marella dragged Sophie outside and into the amphitheater as Stina shouted idle threats.

All the prodigies were grouped by level, and Marella led her to the crowd of Level Twos.

"I'm sorry you had to get in the middle of that," Sophie mumbled.

"I didn't *have* to. I wanted to. She tromps around here like she's so special 'cause her mom's an Empath for the nobility. Meanwhile, her dad never manifested and she only has a fifty-fifty chance of manifesting herself. I can't wait to watch you put her in her place."

"Wait—I'm going to put her in her place? Me?"

"Of course you. You're the new girl with the mysterious past who probably has all these weird powers. I mean, just look at your eyes."

Sophie shuffled her feet. Marella's remark hit a little close to things she was required to keep secret. "I'm not special, Marella. Trust me."

"Whatever. My point is, none of us has been able to take Stina down, not even Princess Prettypants Biana. You're the new variable—something no one expected—so you get to end Stina's reign of terror. Everyone's waiting for it."

"What do you mean 'everyone'?" She was stunned to notice several prodigies watching her. They didn't really think she'd change anything, did they?

"Are you ready for this?" Dex interrupted, jumping up and down—and getting some impressive height. He grabbed Sophie's shoulders, like he wanted to jolt enthusiasm into her.

Before she could answer, twelve Mentors strode into the room in dark gray capes. Each of the six grade levels had two Mentors to supervise, one for the boys and one for the girls. Lady Alexine, the Mentor who gave Dex and Stina detention the day before, and Sir Caton, who had the muscles of a Titan god, informed the Level Twos that they'd be working on channeling.

"It's about focusing your concentration," Dex explained. "Mind over matter. Don't worry. It's supereasy."

It wasn't.

Sophie was supposed to channel the strength of her mind to different parts of her body: jumping to super heights, running at super speeds, crushing things with super strength. But no matter how hard she tried, or how much Lady Alexine helped her, she couldn't do anything better than she normally did, which was horribly unimpressive. She could imagine the kind of report Bronte would get.

After several failed attempts she noticed a few prodigies watching her. Then a few more, and a few more after that, until all the Level Twos were watching—and a few Level Threes. She didn't have to read their minds to know what they were thinking.

If she'd had any doubt, it was settled in the locker room. Stina bumped her into the wall and said, "I take it back. She won't last six weeks."

This time, no one came to her defense.

Too embarrassed to face the cafeteria after PE—she'd lost her appetite anyway—Sophie used her lunch break to find her next session.

Telepathy training required a special room in the Level

Four wing. Her bright blue uniform shone like a spotlight was trained on it in the emerald green halls, so she was glad she found the room before the end of lunch.

"Sorry, am I too early, Sir Tiergan?" she asked as he startled to his feet.

He tugged at the edge of his faded black cape. "Of course not. But please just call me Tiergan. I am *not* a member of the nobility—Mentor or no."

"Um . . . okay," she agreed, not sure what to say to that. She scanned the round green room. Other than two silver chairs that looked like they belonged on a spaceship, the place was bare and unremarkable.

She waited for Tiergan to tell her what to do, but he just stood there, studying her superintently, like he was searching for something. "Uh, should I sit?" she finally asked.

He shook his head, snapping out of his daze. "Actually, I prefer to probe thoughts standing up. I think better on my feet."

She tensed as he moved toward her, the coarse fabric of his cape scraping across the floor. Fitz had told her probing would be part of telepathy training, but the whole concept still freaked her out.

Their eyes met as he reached for her forehead, and he must've noticed the fear in them because he hesitated. "I know this process is unsettling, Sophie, given your background. But a crucial step to telepathy training is to establish a connection between Mentor and prodigy."

She nodded, forcing herself to hold still as he placed a hand on each of her temples and closed his eyes. The bells chimed the end of lunch. She counted eighty-seven more seconds before his eyes popped open and a wrinkle puckered his brow.

"I take it you couldn't hear anything either," she mumbled.

"If you weren't so obviously alive, I would assume I was probing a dead mind."

Well, *there* was a cheerful thought. She scraped together the courage to ask her next question. "Does that mean there's something wrong with me?"

He frowned, like his mind had wandered somewhere else again. "I have no doubt you are exactly the way you were intended to be."

She'd heard people use that expression before, and it was usually reassuring. But the way he said it made the hairs on her arms stick up. Especially when she noticed the way his hands had started shaking.

"Can you tell me what I'm thinking right now?" he asked quietly.

She stretched out her consciousness, feeling for his thoughts. "You're wondering how to train me if you can't probe my mind."

All color drained from his face and he turned away, steadying himself against one of the chairs. "In that case, I suggest you have a seat. We need to have a very long talk about ethics."

* * *

Grady was outside when Sophie leaped home to Havenfield, holding a thick cord that floated into the sky and appeared to be attached to nothing. She squinted at the clouds and then at Grady. "Um, what are you doing?"

"Giving the meganeura some exercise."

She didn't want to annoy him, so she decided not to ask what it was.

Grady fidgeted and glanced at her out of the corner of his eye as she stood there in silence. "How was your second day?" he eventually asked.

"Fine."

"Just fine?" He cocked his head and gave her a look like he could see right through her. "Wanna talk about it?"

He seemed so much like her human dad at that moment, it felt like her heart dropped into her stomach. "Well—"

Loud buzzing cut her off.

"Step back!" Grady locked his legs as something big and green with iridescent wings circled above, then dived straight down. Sophie screamed and jumped out of the way seconds before a vulture size insect landed where she'd been standing.

"Don't tell me you're afraid of dragonflies," Grady said as he patted the freaky-looking bug on the back.

"I don't mind them when they're *normal* size." Blown up to gargantuan proportions was a whole other story. The eyes were pretty much the creepiest things she'd ever seen—like disco balls on the sides of its head.

"This is the normal size for a meganeura. Well, this one's a baby. He'll probably get twice this size when he's full grown."

Sophie shuddered. Grady cracked up and motioned for her to follow him as he steered the monster insect into its enclosure. "So, what were you going to say?"

"Nothing really. I'm awful at phys. ed. and telepathy was . . . intense."

"I'm guessing Tiergan gave you the ethics lecture."

She nodded.

Being a Telepath had *serious* restrictions. She wasn't supposed to block her thoughts, especially from the elvin authorities, which was a problem considering she didn't know how she was doing it, much less how to turn it off. She also wasn't supposed to read minds unless someone gave her permission—just like Fitz had told her. Not unless it was an emergency, or she was on an assignment from the Council.

And that was the weirdest part: Telepaths were in high demand. Once she'd proven trustworthy, she'd receive assignments from the Council. But Tiergan warned her that her impenetrable mind would make it hard for anyone to trust her—she could hide something too easily. Which made her wonder about Quinlin's "joke" about her being a Keeper. The Council didn't think she was hiding something, did they?

"Wait," she said as Grady's words clicked. "Are you a Telepath?"

"No. Why would you think that?"

"How else would you know about the ethics lecture?"

"Everyone gets lectured on ethics when it comes to their talent. Manifesting a special ability comes with great responsibility. Not everyone gets one, you know."

She did know. She'd already learned that having a special ability was a *big* deal. In fact, while she was in her telepathy sessions, Dex—and all the other prodigies who hadn't manifested—was taking ability detecting, hoping to discover his talent. If a prodigy hadn't manifested by Level Four, they might be expelled—and even if they stayed at Foxfire, they couldn't take the elite levels, which meant they'd never be nobility. Most ended up working class.

But once again it didn't escape her notice that Grady avoided telling her what his special ability was. It couldn't be something bad.

Could it?

TWENTY

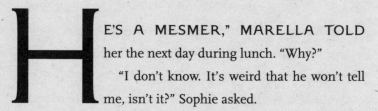E'S A MESMER," MARELLA TOLD her the next day during lunch. "Why?"

"I don't know. It's weird that he won't tell me, isn't it?" Sophie asked.

"It's Grady and Edaline—everything about them is weird. I still can't believe you're living with them. Are they adopting you?"

"I . . . don't know. What exactly is a Mesmer?" she asked, changing the subject to something that didn't make her nauseated.

"Wow, you really don't know anything, do you?"

"Never mind."

"I'm just teasing—sheesh. A Mesmer can put you in a trance and make you do anything they want while you're in it. It's rare. Not as rare as inflicting, but close."

She *really* didn't want to have to ask another stupid question, but curiosity won out. "And inflicting is . . . ?"

"When someone makes you feel things. Makes you laugh, makes you cry, causes you incredible pain—whatever they want. It's extremely rare. I only know of one, and he's on the Council. But there might be another. Your history Mentor would know."

Sophie cringed at the word "history." She'd had her first session with Lady Dara that morning, and it was . . . strange.

Impossible pictures flashed across the walls during the entire lecture: elves using telekinesis to help the humans build the pyramids, a tidal wave swallowing Atlantis, an army of hairy, brown dwarves hollowing out the Himalayas to build the Sanctuary. But the strangest part was Lady Dara. She kept losing her train of thought every time her eyes met Sophie's. Then she'd mumble something about "history in the making" and return to the lecture. It had totally creeped Sophie out.

"Hey, did you hear?" Marella interrupted. "Sir Tiergan's back."

"Who's he?" she asked, relieved she'd remembered to lie.

"Only like the most famous telepathy Mentor ever. He retired when his friend Prentice ended up in exile—it was like a protest or something."

"Prentice?" She tried not to sound too interested, but she'd been dying to know more about him since Alden had told her the information was classified.

"Yeah. He was this supertalented Telepath, but he got exiled like twelve years ago."

"How do you get exiled?"

"You have to break a fundamental law. The Council holds a tribunal, and if you're found guilty, they lock you away deep underground for the rest of eternity." Marella shrugged. "I don't know what he did, but I think it had to do with him being a Keeper. It had to be pretty bad for the Council to ruin his life. Especially since it ruined his family's life too. His wife died in a fluke leaping accident not long after, and his son, Wylie, was adopted by Tiergan."

Sophie's lunch churned in her stomach as Quinlin's words flashed through her mind.

So this is why Prentice sacrificed everything.

Quinlin had also implied she was a Keeper. So if Prentice was a Keeper, could that mean they were . . . related?

Could he be her father?

The pieces fit. Abandoning a child was illegal for humans—she doubted it was any less of a crime here. And if Prentice was a talented Telepath, maybe he was a Washer. Maybe he could alter the minds of two human parents and make them believe the child was theirs.

But why? He didn't get rid of Wylie—so why dump her? Was there something *that* wrong with her?

Unless it had something to do with her eye color. Or the way her brain worked . . .

"Do you know Wylie?" Sophie asked quietly. She doubted she'd be brave enough to meet someone who could be her brother, but she was still curious.

Marella shook her head. "He's in the elite levels, so he's secluded from the rest of us, in the elite towers. We're not allowed to go over there and interrupt their studies."

Sophie couldn't decide if she was disappointed or relieved. Most likely he didn't know anything. No one else seemed to. Except Alden—and he wasn't telling. She'd have to figure it out on her own.

She sorted through the scrambled bits of information in her head. Searching for the clue that would finally put the pieces together.

"You okay?" Marella asked, reminding her that she wasn't alone.

"Yeah. Sorry." She tried to sound casual when she asked her next question. "Have you ever heard of something called Project Moonlark?"

Marella frowned. "Is that a Sanctuary effort to rescue moonlarks?"

"I have no idea. I heard it somewhere and didn't know what it was. I thought you might know." She'd tried to find out more, but Grady never brought the scrolls out again—and she was too afraid to search the house. What if they caught her and kicked her out?

"Nope, never heard of it. But I doubt it's anything interesting. I know everything cool that goes on around here." Marella opened a can of strawberry flavored air and took a deep breath of the pink flumes that spritzed around her. She licked her lips. "Want some?"

Sophie shook her head, deciding to shove the disturbing questions to the dark corner of her mind, where she'd pushed everything else that was too painful to think about. She had enough to deal with already.

"Worried about your next session?" Marella asked.

Sophie nodded. Dex's warning about Lady Galvin failing prodigies had her terrified. It didn't help when Marella smirked and said, "Yeah, good luck with that."

"That bad?"

"Uh, yeah. Lady Galvin only Mentors for the title. Being good at alchemy isn't the same as having a special ability, so unless she wanted to run some crazy apothecary like the Dizznees, it was Mentor or nothing. She hates it—and she takes it out on her prodigies. But who knows? Maybe you'll become her new star pupil."

The words would have been encouraging—if Marella hadn't burst into a hysterical fit of giggles right after. She was still cracking up when the bells chimed their intricate melody.

Maybe Sophie imagined it, but the tone sounded ominous.

The wide, round alchemy room smelled like burning hair, and the walls were lined with curved shelves. Half were filled with tiny pots of ingredients, and the other half were filled with what

Sophie thought were trophies, but up close she realized they were just random gilded items. Hats. Books. Pieces of fruit. A pair of curved, pointy-toed shoes that looked suspiciously like the ones she'd grown up believing elves wore. It was like King Midas had come through and turned everything he touched to gold.

The center of the room held two empty lab tables—one gleaming silver, the other sleek and black—and the strangest experiment Sophie had ever seen. Lady Galvin wasn't there, so she dropped her stuff on a table and took a closer look at the giant bubble hovering over a ring of fire on the floor. Milky liquid filled the bubble, dancing up and down to the rhythm of the flames.

"Step back!" Lady Galvin shouted, rushing over in a rustle of fabric. She yanked Sophie away. "Do you have any idea what that is?" She looked Sophie up and down and rolled her eyes. "No, I suppose you don't."

Lady Galvin was slender and wore her red-brown hair in an updo so tight and full of twists it gave Sophie a headache just looking at it. Her cape was hunter green, made of silky fabric decorated with emeralds sewn in elaborate patterns. It swished with the slightest movement.

"It's *alkahest*," she announced. "The universal solvent. It can only be stored in a bubble of itself because it dissolves everything else. Wood. Steel. Flesh."

Sophie backed another step away. "Is that what we're making today?"

Lady Galvin sighed the way Sophie's dad used to while doing his taxes. "It's the second hardest substance for an alchemist to make. Don't you know anything about alchemy?"

"I guess not," she admitted. And it probably wouldn't be wise to ask what the hardest substance to make was—even though she was curious.

"All I ask for is a decent prodigy—and what do I get?" Lady Galvin stalked across the room to one of the shelves. "I should be teaching masters to turn living matter into gold, not little girls who don't know the difference between a tincture and a poultice. Dame Alina probably thinks this is funny, forcing me to teach basic serums. Well, I won't have it."

She removed a yellowed card from a small box, grabbed an empty flask, a few jars of ingredients, and a long twisted silver spoon from the shelves and returned to Sophie. "This serum is the first step to turn glass into iron. I'll have you transmuting metals if I have to walk you through it. Step. By. Step."

Sophie glanced at the recipe. The chemical formula didn't look too hard. The ingredients weren't familiar, but the jars were labeled, and there were only two simple instructions.

Lady Galvin fiddled with her cape and rolled her eyes as Sophie checked and rechecked each amount to be sure she wasn't making any mistakes. When she felt confident that she had it right, she poured everything into the flask. Then she plunged the spoon in and whipped the liquid the same way she'd learned to whip cream.

"Don't!" Lady Galvin shouted, rushing forward to stop her—a second too late.

The liquid fizzed and rumbled.

Sophie jumped out of the way just as sticky gray jelly exploded all over Lady Galvin's exquisite cape.

Sophie watched in horror while the sludge dissolved the luxurious fabric. "I'm so sorry." She reached for the damaged cape to see if there was anything she could do to salvage it, but Lady Galvin grabbed her hand to stop her. That's when she noticed the red welt on the back of Sophie's wrist, where some of the slime caught her.

She sighed. "Better head to the Healing Center."

"Yes, ma'am." Sophie was hardly eager to see another doctor, but Lady Galvin looked ready to murder someone. She rushed to retrieve her satchel. "Should I come back here afterward?"

"No!"

Sophie slunk toward the door. "Okay. See you next week?"

Lady Galvin's face darkened, and she turned away muttering under her breath about incompetence.

Sophie stumbled through the halls, the panic making it hard to think straight. Would Lady Galvin flunk her? Should she use the Imparter to call Alden and see if he could help?

"You must be lost."

The boy's deep voice brought her out of her trance. He wore a green Level Four uniform, and was sprawled across a bench, watching her with curious, ice blue eyes.

She blinked, noticing the hallways were stark white now. "How did you know?"

He smirked. "It's the middle of session. Either you're lost, or you're ditching—and clearly you're not ditching."

"Why couldn't I be ditching?" she asked, not exactly sure why she was arguing.

"Are you?"

"No," she admitted.

His lips twisted into a crooked grin. "You're the new girl, aren't you?"

She sighed and nodded.

"I'm Keefe."

"Sophie—but I'm sure you already know that."

He laughed. "You may be the biggest news to hit the academy since the Great Gulon Incident three years ago—which, by the way, I had nothing to do with." He flashed a slightly wicked smile. "But that's not a bad thing. Personally, I've always enjoyed being the center of attention."

She didn't doubt that. From his disheveled blond hair to the way he'd rolled up his sleeves and left his shirt untucked, she could tell—he was cool. Probably popular, too. So why was he talking to her? She almost asked him but stopped herself at the last second.

"Where are you supposed to be?" she asked instead.

"The Universe. I ditch whenever I can. Lady Belva has the

worst crush on me. I mean, I can't really blame her"—he gestured to himself—"but still, it's awkward, you know?"

She was 90 percent certain he was joking, but he was also *very* good looking. She was sure at least half the girls in school had a crush on him.

"And now I get to meet the mysterious new girl," he added. "So I'd say ditching paid off pretty well."

She felt herself blush, and hoped he didn't notice. "I'm hardly mysterious."

"I don't know. You won't tell me why you're not in session. Don't think I haven't noticed."

She stared at her feet. "That's because it's too embarrassing."

"I love embarrassing!" He laughed when she stayed silent. "Will you at least tell me where you're supposed to be?"

She sighed. "Alchemy with Lady Galvin."

"Ugh, she's the worst. I had her as a Level Three—and she hated me, probably because I turned the lab table to silver. But she said she wanted me to impress her." He winked. "Still, I wouldn't mention that we're friends if I were you."

Friends?

Since when did cool, cute boys want to be her friend? Not that she was complaining. . . .

"So, what, did Lady Galvin kick you out or something?" he asked.

"Kind of."

"Now this I have to hear."

"You're going to laugh at me."

"Probably," he agreed.

He clearly wasn't going to let it go, so she kept her eyes glued to the floor. "I accidentally exploded the serum I was making."

Right on cue, he burst into laughter. "Did you do any damage?"

"Only to her cape—"

"Whoa, whoa, whoa. Do you have any idea how epic that is? That cape is her pride and joy! Did she send you to Dame Alina's office?"

"No, she sent me to the Healing Center. A little of it got on my hand." She glared at the ugly red welt.

He studied her for a second, then shook his head. "Wow, most girls would be crying about a wound like that—most guys too. Even I'd be playing it up for sympathy and stuff."

"It must look worse than it is."

"Still, don't you think you should get it treated?"

"I guess."

He laughed again. "You just turned whiter than these walls. What's wrong?"

"Nothing." There was no way she was telling him about her doctor phobia—she'd never hear the end of it.

"Come on, then. I'm taking you to the Healing Center so you don't get lost again." He hooked his arm through hers and dragged her away before she could resist.

The Healing Center consisted of three rooms: a treatment area with four empty beds, a huge laboratory where strange alchemy experiments were brewing, and the physician's personal office, where a familiar face sat at an enormous desk covered in paperwork.

"Sophie?" Elwin asked. "I figured I'd have to drag you back here to check up on you."

"I know," she said, very aware of the way Keefe had cocked his head toward her. "I have a tiny burn I need you to treat—no big deal."

"Well, let me check it out." As he got up, a slinky gray creature hissed and scurried across the floor. "Don't mind Bullhorn," Elwin said as Sophie backed against the door. "He's harmless."

Bullhorn looked like a demented ferret with beady purple eyes. "What is he?"

"A banshee. Adorable, isn't he?"

"Uh, sure." Bullhorn snapped at her ankles. Keefe laughed.

"What brings you here today, Keefe?" Elwin asked.

"Just helping a fellow prodigy, sir."

Elwin grinned. "I notice you've had to miss your session to do it."

"I know. Such a shame." He sighed dramatically. "But Sophie needed help, so what could I do?"

"What, indeed? And I suppose you'll be wanting a pass to excuse you."

"What a good idea."

"You always have been one to seize an opportunity." Elwin handed Keefe a slip of paper. "Session won't be over for another half hour, so I'd walk slow if I were you."

"Oh, I can't leave yet—not until I know Sophie will be okay."

"Mmm-hmm. So, where's the burn?" he asked Sophie.

She wanted to be brave in front of Keefe, but her arm still shook when Elwin put his funny glasses on and flashed a blue orb of light around her hand.

Elwin frowned. "This looks like an acid burn. How did you manage that?"

"Um . . . slight accident in my alchemy session."

Keefe mimed a huge explosion, complete with sound effects. "Destroyed Galvin's cape."

Elwin dropped her hand, cracking up. "Wish I could have seen *that*! Sorry," he added when he caught her scowl. "Have a seat so I can treat it."

He had Sophie sit on one of the beds and grabbed a small jar from one of the shelves. She tried to stay calm as he rubbed purple salve on the burn, but Keefe saw her flinch.

"Out of curiosity," Elwin asked. "How did you explode the serum?"

"I'm not sure. I measured everything twice, and added it in the order I was supposed to, but when I whipped it, it exploded."

"Whipped it?" Keefe interrupted.

"Yeah. At first I thought it said 'whap,' but I figured I read it wrong so I whipped it."

Elwin and Keefe both burst into hysterical laughter.

"*WHAP* means 'wash hands and present,'" Keefe managed to explain between laughs.

Oh.

She was officially an idiot. Why didn't she ask for clarification?

Elwin cleared his throat. "It's an honest mistake. Could've happened to anyone."

It didn't. It happened to *her*. She knew she wasn't going to live this down anytime soon.

"This is going to be *epic!*" Keefe said, confirming her fear. "I can't *wait* for tomorrow!"

She sighed. At least that made one of them.

TWENTY-ONE

A HIGHLY EMBELLISHED VERSION OF the Great Cape Destruction spread through the school faster than the white fires in her old city, and Sophie knew Keefe had everything to do with it. Even her Mentors had heard about it.

Sir Conley joked that they'd have to work their way up to bottling fire in elementalism, so she wouldn't burn down the school. Lady Anwen told her in multispeciesial studies that she hadn't laughed so hard in 324 years. And Sir Faxon had to cancel his metaphysics lecture because he snorted lushberry juice all over his clothes.

Once again Sophie could feel everyone watching her as she wandered the halls—except this time they wanted to know her.

Kids invited her to sit with them during lunch. They introduced themselves during orientation, between classes. They complimented her eyes. Dex told her the next week they were getting requests for brown-eye drops at Slurps and Burps. He was in the process of trying to create them.

Sophie couldn't believe it. Overnight she'd somehow become . . . popular.

Grady was relieved when she told him. The more she belonged at Foxfire, the harder it would be for Bronte to get her expelled.

But she refused to take anything for granted. She still sat with Marella during lunch. Dex joined them when his detention was over, and Jensi slipped in a few days later—but he'd reached out to her on her first day, so he was allowed.

Plus, her sessions were incredibly challenging. Lady Galvin didn't fail her, but she made her work on the opposite side of the room, which turned out to be a wise decision. Fires and explosions were a regular occurrence. The problem was, Sophie didn't just have to learn, she had to *unlearn* a lifetime of human knowledge, where things like alkahest didn't exist. All the laws she'd learned in chemistry were wrong, and tripped her up.

She had the same problem with some of her other sessions. Levitating was supposed to be impossible. So was catching wind in jars and bottling rainbows. She constantly had to remind herself not to trust her instincts, because they were all wrong, and even when she tried her hardest, she still messed things up.

Which was why her telepathy sessions became the highlight of her week. Every skill came effortlessly, and she was amazed at the things she could do with her mind. Tiergan taught her how to shield her brain from unwanted human thoughts—in case she was ever around humans again—and how to transmit her thoughts into someone else's mind. She even learned how to project mental images onto special paper—like a psychic photograph.

For the first time in her life, she didn't mind being a Telepath. It was actually pretty cool—and no one could deny her talent. Even Bronte wouldn't be able to.

Too bad she had to keep it secret. It would've been fun to shut Stina up whenever she teased Sophie about needing *remedial studies*. Stina still hadn't manifested a special ability, so it would kill her to know Sophie was a Telepath—being trained by the greatest telepathy Mentor ever. But she'd have to be patient. Stina would learn the truth eventually.

Plus, she had other problems. Biana avoided her like the plague, and Sophie had a strong suspicion she was keeping Fitz away from her. Two months had passed since she'd moved to Havenfield, and except for a couple waves across the hall, she hadn't seen or talked to him. She missed him—more than she wanted to admit.

The next week Sophie finally saw Biana waiting for the

Leapmaster without her snotty friend Maruca—another member of the I-Hate-Sophie-Foster Club—and decided to try reaching out.

Biana spotted her and cut in line, leaping home before Sophie could reach her.

The sigh Sophie let out sounded more like a growl.

"What's wrong?" Dex asked, catching up with her.

"Biana. I don't know what her problem is, but I'm really getting sick of it."

"She's just jealous. She's used to being the prettiest girl in school." As soon as the words left his mouth, he turned bright red.

Sophie knew her face had to be redder than his.

Neither of them seemed to know what to say after that, so she waved goodbye and leaped back to Havenfield without another word.

She came home to total bedlam. Grady and Edaline were struggling to subdue a very angry woolly mammoth, and the gnomes were chasing a small pack of rabbits with antlers.

"You're just in time," Grady called to her as he ducked under a swinging trunk. He pointed to a lump of trembling purple fur. "Can you get the verminion in a pen?"

"Uh . . . sure."

"Thanks." Grady boosted Edaline onto the mammoth's back. The huge, hairy elephant trumpeted in protest—an earthshaking squeal that left Sophie's ears ringing.

Sophie crept toward the purple mound of fur, hoping the verminion was as timid as it looked. A twig snapped under her foot.

Hiiiissssssssssss!

The creature uncurled, revealing a giant rodent face with glassy black eyes, pointy fangs, and bulging cheeks. She'd always thought hamsters were pretty cute, but this rottweiler-size beast was Hamsterzilla, and it looked ready to trample her like a Japanese city.

"Nice hamster—verminion—thing," she cooed, taking a step away.

SNAARRRLLL!

Hamsterzilla was not impressed.

"You have to make it chase you to the pen, Sophie," Edaline shouted as she tried to steer her mammoth by its furry ears.

"How do I do that?"

Grady dashed after Edaline. "Get it mad."

"But—what if it catches me?"

"It won't," Edaline promised.

"Better run really fast, just in case," Grady added.

Sophie knew this would probably end up in the top fifty stupidest things she'd done, but she picked up a huge clod of mud and nailed the verminion in the gut.

GROOOWWWWLLLL!

She took the hint and bolted for the nearest pen, only to realize Grady's plan had a fatal flaw. The verminion blocked the only exit, and he seemed to know it. She could've sworn his beady eyes were laughing at her.

"A little help here?" she called as the mutant hamster closed in.

"On it!" The gnomes took over helping Edaline, and Grady raced across the yard, jumped the verminion, and pinned it. Purple fur flew as the beast thrashed to escape.

Grady grunted. "Okay, Sophie. I want you to put one hand on each of his cheeks and press as hard as you can."

After a few tries—and a lot of snarling—she managed to get her hands in position and squeeze. The verminion's jaw unlocked and an assortment of dead furry things spewed all over the ground.

"Ew," she whined.

"I know," Grady agreed. "There's a pile of bags and some gloves in the shed so you can clean it up."

She stared at the mound of flesh and fur.

"We can trade jobs," Grady offered. The verminion growled again.

Sophie sighed as she trudged to the shed, slipped on the oversize gloves, and made her way back to the pile. "I am so taking a shower after this."

She threw dead squirrels and rats and things she couldn't begin to identify into the heavy burlap sack. One moved in her hand and she squealed, jumping back.

"What?"

"That thing isn't dead!"

"You'd better take it to Edaline, then, see if there's anything she can do."

Sophie stared at the quivering ball of gray fur, afraid to touch it again.

"My arms are getting pretty tired here, Sophie."

SNARL! the verminion added.

She steeled her nerves and threw the rest of the dead things into the sack. Then she picked up the live creature, trying not to shriek as he trembled in her hands.

He was the size of her palm, with enormous green eyes, furry ears, and batlike wings. His tiny chest heaved as he struggled to breathe.

Sophie raced across the pastures toward the shed. "Edaline! I need your help."

Edaline rushed to her side, wiping mammoth wool off her tunic.

Sophie held out the suffering creature. "Do you think you can save him?"

Edaline's gentle fingers probed through the fur. "He has some deep scratches, and his leg looks broken—but we can try."

Sophie followed Edaline into one of the stone outbuildings. Beyond the shelves of carefully organized supplies was a space set up like a veterinarian's office. Edaline laid the creature flat on its back on a sterile table, spreading out his limbs and wings. She smeared a yellow salve over the wounds, then set the leg and conjured up an eyedropper and a bottle of Youth. She dripped a single drop of liquid onto his furry lips. Sophie squeezed Edaline's arm as a tiny purple tongue popped out and licked the drop of water.

Edaline stared where Sophie's hand touched her. Her eyes turned glassy.

Sophie pulled away. "Sorry."

"No, it's . . ." She cleared her throat. "Can you keep an eye on him while I help Grady finish up?"

"Sure." She waited for Edaline to leave, then placed another drop on the creature's lips. "Don't die, little guy," she whispered, watching his tongue pull the water into his mouth. Twelve drops later and his breathing was steady. He curled into a tiny ball.

"That's a good boy," Sophie cooed, stroking the fur along his back. He rewarded her with a squeaky rumbling in his chest. She smiled, remembering Marty's crackly purr.

"How's the patient?" Grady asked from the doorway. He stood next to Edaline, both of them watching Sophie with small smiles.

"I think he's doing better. He drank a bunch of water and now he's sleeping."

Edaline nodded. "That's a good sign. Do you want to wash up and have some dinner?"

"Can I bring him with me? I don't want to leave him alone."

Grady grabbed a small cage from one of the shelves and filled it with dinosaur fluff from a nearby barrel before handing it to her. "Good job, Sophie. You saved his life."

She brought the cage inside and—after an incredibly hot, soapy shower—met Grady and Edaline downstairs for dinner. She kept the cage with her at the table to keep an eye on the creature. He'd rolled onto his back with his mouth open and his tongue hanging out. If it weren't for the chain-saw-esque snores vibrating the cage, she might have worried he was dead.

"What is he?" she asked with a mouthful of brattail, a tuber that tasted like sausage.

"An imp," Grady grumbled. "They're trouble. When I was a kid, one got inside my tree house. I've never seen such a disaster."

"You want to keep him, don't you?" Edaline guessed.

Sophie shrugged. "Maybe."

Edaline smiled.

"You aren't seriously thinking about this, Eda? Have you been around an imp before?"

"Please tell me you're not afraid of a six-inch ball of fur," Edaline teased.

"You should've seen my tree house. Plus, they bite—did you know that? And their bite is venomous. It won't kill you, but it stings—a lot."

Sophie looked at the tiny snoring body and tried to see the vicious monster Grady was describing. All she found was a cute little lump of fur, whose life she had saved.

"Grady, we tame dinosaurs and yetis. We can handle an imp," Edaline argued.

Grady laughed. "I can see I'm outnumbered here. But don't say I didn't warn you."

Sophie and Edaline shared a smile. Then Edaline helped her bring the cage to her room. Sophie chose a table by the window so the little guy would have sunlight during the day, and crouched down to check on him. He was still conked out, snoring like a wood chipper.

"What do you want to name him?" Edaline asked.

Sophie blushed. "I know it's silly, but I kind of like Iggy."

"Iggy the imp. I like it." She placed a hand on Sophie's shoulder, and Sophie straightened. "Sorry, do you mind?"

"No . . . it's nice," Sophie whispered. It was the first time Edaline had touched her.

Edaline held her breath as she used her other hand to brush a strand of hair off Sophie's cheek.

Sophie closed her eyes and leaned into Edaline's hand. Her heart seemed to swell inside her chest, filling an empty space she'd almost forgotten was there. Her human parents had been generous with hugs and touches, and she hadn't realized how much she'd missed those gestures. She held still, afraid to do anything to ruin the moment.

Edaline swept her hand across Sophie's forehead again and let out a sigh. "You should get to bed." Her fingers brushed down Sophie's cheek as she pulled away.

Sophie blinked and nodded. "I'll get ready."

"Good." Edaline smiled, and her eyes glistened with tears. "I hope you sleep okay," she added, with a dubious glance at the noisy cage.

"Me too." Sophie's cheek still tingled where Edaline's fingers had left tiny trails of warmth. "Edaline?" she asked, as Edaline turned to leave.

Edaline's eyes met hers.

"Thank you."

It took Edaline a second to answer. "You're welcome. Good night, Sophie."

"Good night."

When Sophie climbed into bed a few minutes later, it finally felt like home.

TWENTY-TWO

S HARING A ROOM WITH IGGY WAS KIND of like having a congested warthog for a roommate, but Sophie didn't mind. She was warm and snuggly with the feeling of home, and even a sleepless night couldn't spoil it.

Grady and Edaline promised to check on Iggy during the day to make sure he was okay, and Sophie left for Foxfire not even caring that it was a Thursday, and she had another humiliating PE session ahead of her.

"Who's ready for the Ultimate Splotching Championship?" Sir Caton asked as the Mentors strode into the amphitheater carrying huge sacks of tiny, brightly colored balls.

Everyone cheered.

"What's the Ultimate Splotching Championship?" Sophie asked Dex.

"Telekinesis," he grumbled. "I suck at telekinesis."

She tried to look sympathetic, but secretly she was celebrating. Finally—something she knew how to do! Well, sort of—but that was better than nothing. "How does this work?" she asked as everyone partnered up. Naturally, she teamed with Dex.

"We push the splotcher at each other with our minds," he explained, "and whoever gets splattered loses. The winners play each other until there's only one left, and that person wins."

"Everyone, on your marks," Sir Caton ordered, as Lady Alexine handed Dex a bright pink splotcher. "Get set!"

Dex tossed the splotcher toward Sophie. "Catch."

It very nearly splattered the floor, but at the last second she managed to catch it with her mind.

"Sorry, I forgot you're worse at this stuff than me," Dex said smugly. "At least I'll win one match this time."

She rolled her eyes. He shouldn't count her out yet.

She took a deep breath, focusing on the power she knew was deep within her core. She could almost feel it swirling around, like a warm buzzing in her stomach.

"Splotch!"

Sophie pushed the warmth out through her fingers and sent it toward the splotcher.

Splat!

A stunned Dex stared at Sophie with bright pink slime running down his chin. She'd nailed him right on his smug little grin.

"Sorry," she said, not quite able to hide the smile in the corners of her mouth.

"It's okay," he said through a sigh. "I guess I deserved it."

"Well done, Sophie!" Sir Caton interrupted, sounding more surprised than she would've liked. "Go ahead and move up to the winners. Dex can join those colorful prodigies over there." He pointed to a group forming on their left.

Dex scowled.

"So what's the prize for this contest, anyway?" Sophie asked before Dex wandered away.

"Usually a pardon from one punishment—but don't get your hopes up. Fitz always wins—not that Wonderboy ever does anything to need a pardon." He mimed gagging. "Anyway, I hope you win a few more rounds."

"Thanks."

Marella made it to the winners. So did Biana and Maruca. Even Jensi. Unfortunately, so did Stina.

"Even a muskog could beat Dex," Stina sneered. "Let's see how you do against a *real* opponent." She tossed a bright blue splotcher at Sophie's head.

Sophie caught it with her mind, floating it in the space between them. She ignored the knots in her stomach. She wasn't backing down.

"I'm going to enjoy this," Stina sneered. "I'll aim for your eyes—finally turn them blue."

Sophie gritted her teeth. She didn't care how she did it, but Stina was going down.

"Get set!" Sir Caton called. "Splotch!"

Sophie threw her hands out, pulling a bigger burst of strength from her gut as she shoved the splotcher.

Splat!

"Ow!" Stina screamed, rubbing her slimy blue cheek.

"Sorry," Sophie said, her eyes wide. Had she pushed too hard?

"No reason to apologize," Lady Alexine corrected. "Well done, Sophie. I haven't seen such raw telekinetic power in a long time."

Sophie flushed. That was the first compliment Lady Alexine had ever given her.

"But she hurt me!" Stina argued. "That disqualifies her, doesn't it?"

"I didn't mean—" Sophie started to explain but Lady Alexine held up her hands.

"You didn't do anything wrong. If you're hurt, Miss Heks, go to the Healing Center. Either way, Sophie won fair and square."

Marella caught her eye and pumped her arms in victory. Sophie's face felt hotter. Especially when she noticed the other prodigies cheering for her. Did they think she'd actually taken Stina down?

"As for you, Miss Foster," Lady Alexine added, "I think it might be a good idea to put you with the Level Threes so your opponents can match your mental strength."

Since when did she have the mental strength to face off against older kids with a lot more training and experience? She'd been ahead around humans, of course, but here she felt so far behind it wasn't even funny. Was she starting to catch up?

It seemed like she was. She took out the Level Threes in duel after duel, and before she knew what was happening, there were only nine other prodigies left.

"A Level Two making it to the top ten," Keefe said behind her. He flashed a crooked smile. "And you said you weren't mysterious."

She stared at her feet to hide her blush. "Must be beginner's luck."

Keefe snorted. "Or maybe you've got all kinds of talents we don't know about."

He couldn't know about her telepathy, could he?

"Look who went pale again. Interesting . . . ," he murmured.

She opened her mouth to make some excuse, but he cut her off.

"I have a feeling you'll be the one to take down the mighty Fitz."

Sophie froze. She wasn't surprised that Fitz was still in the competition—especially after Dex's earlier grumblings—but it hadn't occurred to her that she might have to battle him. Her palms slicked with sweat, but she shook the idea away. What were the odds she would be able to beat a bunch of older, much more experienced prodigies?

Evidently, the odds were good.

Soon enough she was in the final four: her, Fitz, and two Level Sixes named Trella and Dempsey. Everyone seemed as surprised as she was—even the Mentors.

Sir Caton paired Fitz against Trella, and Sophie toyed with the idea of not even trying in her match with Dempsey—so she wouldn't have to face Fitz. Then she caught the hopeful look on Stina's face and found a new determination to win.

"Splotch!"

Dempsey was fast on the draw and the splotcher was halfway to her face before she stopped it. She locked her jaw and threw out her hands, pushing with every bit of strength she could muster. Her stomach cramped and the splotcher splattered so hard it knocked Dempsey back a step.

"That hurt!" He rubbed his cheek, smearing the orange goo.

She rushed toward him. "Sorry, are you okay?"

He flinched, not looking happy to have the girl who'd just bested him trying to help him. Sophie stepped back.

"Winner," Lady Alexine announced, and Sophie spun around. Fitz waved to the cheering crowd before he turned and met her eyes. Her heart fluttered.

"It appears we've reached our final battle," Sir Caton announced. "I think it's safe to say that this is the most unusual match we've had in Foxfire history. Are the competitors ready?"

Fitz stepped toward Sophie with a smug smile. "I am."

"Uh, me too." Her voice shook, betraying her nerves.

"Go, Fitz!" Biana shouted. Her voice hid an edge that made Sophie wonder if Biana wanted her to lose more than she wanted her brother to win. She wouldn't be surprised.

"Kick his butt, Sophie!" Keefe cheered. "It's about time someone took Fitz down."

"Some best friend you are," Fitz shouted. But he said it with a smile.

"Any preference on splotcher color?" Sir Caton asked.

"Pink! Pink! Pink! Make Fitz look pretty in pink!" Everyone joined Keefe's chant.

Sophie glanced at Fitz, trying to read his expression.

He grinned. "Ladies' choice."

"Pink," she decided, to make Keefe happy. And it *would* be kind of funny to splat him with pink—not that she expected to win. Dex said Fitz *always* won.

"Pink it is." Sir Caton tossed the splotcher, and Sophie and Fitz made it float in the space between them.

"On your marks!"

Sophie's hands clenched into fists. If she was going to beat Fitz, she was going to have to give it everything she had—and then some.

Adrenaline surged through her veins. The murmur of the audience faded, and she became aware of another buzzing in the back of her mind, like a back-up pool of energy she'd never noticed before. It felt stronger than the other energy. Could she draw from there instead?

"Get set. . . . Splotch!"

Sophie threw her hands out, pushing toward the splotcher with her mind. Her brain seemed to stretch, like someone snapping a rubber band, and her ears rang, but she didn't break her concentration.

The splotches exploded as her force met Fitz's and Sophie felt the energy rebound. The next thing she knew, she was flying backward across the room. She caught the surprised look in Fitz's eyes as the same phenomenon happened to him.

For a long second she was weightless, then her back collided with the wall and the wind was knocked out of her. An almost simultaneous crash told her Fitz had met the same fate.

Pain shot through her whole body and she collapsed. The last thing she saw was Fitz crumpled on the floor. Then everything went black.

TWENTY-THREE

WELCOME BACK," ELWIN SAID, placing a cool compress across her forehead. "You know, for a girl who hates doctors, you sure can't seem to stay away from the Healing Center."

She pulled herself into a sitting position, wincing as pain whipped through every muscle.

"Easy there. You've been out nearly ten minutes." Elwin flashed an orb of yellow light around her and put on his glasses.

"Ten minutes? What happened?"

"No idea. I've never heard of anyone getting seriously injured while splotching. Leave it to you." He chuckled.

Her memories flooded back. Splotching. Flying backward through the room. Fitz's crumpled body. "Where's Fitz? Is he okay?"

"He's fine." Elwin pointed to her left, where Fitz lay in a bed with his eyes closed.

"He's unconscious!"

"He'll come around any minute." Elwin placed a cold compress across Fitz's forehead and his vivid eyes sprang open.

"WhermIwhahapped?" he mumbled, closing his eyes.

Elwin chuckled. "Must've been *some* splotching match."

"Will he be okay?"

"Of course. If he weren't, Bullhorn would be freaking out right now—or worse: laying next to him." He pointed to the slinky gray creature curled up in the corner. "Banshees can sense when someone's in mortal danger. Fitz hit his head a little harder than you, so he needs another minute for the medicine to set in."

"This is all my fault," Sophie groaned. She wasn't sure if that was true, but it seemed like the most likely option.

"What did you do during the match?" Elwin asked.

"I don't know."

Fitz stirred, and he looked more lucid when he opened his eyes.

"How are you feeling?" Elwin asked him.

"I've been better, but I'll live." Fitz winced as he sat up.

"Are you okay?" he asked Sophie, rubbing the back of his head.

She nodded, feeling shy. She hadn't really talked to him since the first day of school.

Elwin handed them each a blue vial. "This will ease the pain. You'll still be stiff tomorrow, but I can't help that."

The glands behind her tongue zinged as Sophie swallowed the sour medicine, but the ache in her back vanished.

"Do either of you remember what happened?" Elwin asked as he collected the empty bottles.

"Not really," Fitz admitted. "I remember pushing toward the splotcher, but then it was like it rebounded or something."

"Rebounded?"

"Yeah. I felt my force hit hers and bounce back at me."

"That's what I felt too," Sophie agreed.

Elwin's eyes widened. Then he shook his head. "Nah. Couldn't be."

"Couldn't be what?" Sophie asked, with a horrible feeling he was going to tell her it really *was* her fault.

"That sounds like what happens when someone does a brain push—using mental energy for telekinesis instead of core energy. But a brain push is a highly specialized skill only the Ancients can pull off."

Sophie's heart hammered in her ears. She had pulled energy from her mind in the match—was that a brain push? "Doesn't telekinesis always use mental energy?"

"It uses mental *control*," Elwin explained. "Your concentration controls how you use the energy—where you send it, how much you send. But the actual energy and strength comes from your core. Don't you feel the pull in your gut when you draw on it?"

She did. "But why would a brain push send us flying across the room?"

"Mental energy doesn't mix with core energy, so they'd rebound."

That matched what she'd felt. But how could that be? "Is it something you could do by accident?"

"No way. It's a less draining way to move things, but it takes years and years to train your mind to store energy like that. Then it takes a lifetime of practice to use that mental power. It must just be that you and Fitz were evenly matched. Which is still weird—don't get me wrong. You're awfully young to have that kind of strength. But I wouldn't worry about it too much, Sophie. Fitz, on the other hand, might want to worry about being beat by a Level Two."

Elwin laughed and Sophie's face caught fire. She was too afraid to look at Fitz to see if the teasing bothered him. Plus, she couldn't help wondering if Elwin was wrong, if she'd done a brain push. But . . . what she'd done had been almost effortless. If it was a brain push, wouldn't she have had to try a lot harder?

"You two are cleared to return to session," Elwin announced, interrupting her thoughts. "But I want you sitting on the sidelines. And take it easy for the rest of the day."

"Thanks, Elwin." Fitz stood on shaky legs, leaning on the bed for a second.

Sophie jumped up, wobbling as the blood rushed to her head.

"Take it easy," Elwin repeated as they made their way to the door. "Oh, and, Sophie?" He grinned when she met his eyes. "I'm sure I'll see you soon."

Fitz stayed quiet as they walked back to the auditorium.

Sophie bit her lip. Was he mad at her? She'd just worked up the courage to ask him when they reached the amphitheater, and a round of applause drowned out the question.

"Yes, yes, welcome back, Fitz and Sophie. Glad to see you're feeling better," Sir Caton said, looking a teensy bit annoyed by the interruption. He tried to call everyone back to order, but Dex, Marella, Biana, and Keefe broke rank and rushed over to them.

Biana got there first and threw her arms around Fitz, hugging him so tight he winced. It would have been a touching moment if Keefe hadn't copied her and grabbed Fitz, pretending to cry. Fitz shoved them both away, blushing.

"Beat by a Level Two," Keefe said, elbowing Fitz in the ribs.

"It was a tie," Sophie protested.

Keefe snorted. "Please. You totally kicked his butt."

"Totally," Dex agreed. "He hit the wall *way* harder than you did. That was the greatest present you could have ever given me, by the way," he whispered.

Sophie shook her head. He was hopeless.

"Even the Mentors declared you the winner," Keefe added, wrapping an arm around her shoulders. "If you don't think you'll need your pardon, I'll be happy to take it off your hands—"

"Keefe! Dex! Marella! Biana! Need I remind you that you are not excused from this lesson?" Sir Caton yelled.

"Think about it," Keefe said, then ran to rejoin the class.

Fitz sat next to Sophie on the sidelines, watching everyone practice telekinesis with the remaining splotchers. She tried not to worry, but she couldn't help glancing at him from the corner of her eye, wondering why he still hadn't said anything to her.

"Why aren't you and Biana friends?" he asked after a minute. "It seems like you guys would get along. You have a lot in common."

She wasn't sure she wanted to have things in common with someone who acted like such a brat. "I don't think she has time for another friend. She's always busy with Maruca."

He frowned.

Before she could think of anything else to say, Lady Alexine delivered her prize, a small golden square with an intricate *P* etched on the top.

"Any Level Two who holds her own against Fitz is the clear winner," she explained. "Congratulations, Sophie."

"Thank you." She peeked at Fitz to see if he looked bothered. He grinned. "I couldn't agree more." But his smile faded after Lady Alexine left. "You really don't know what happened during the match?"

"I . . . don't know. I do remember pushing some energy from my mind," she whispered, afraid to look at him. "But that couldn't have been a brain push, could it?"

Fitz had no idea how much she needed him to tell her that it couldn't. Instead he said, "I'll have to ask my dad."

She tried to smile, but she couldn't help feeling like she'd somehow done something wrong. The worry in Fitz's eyes seemed to confirm her fears.

So later that afternoon she worked up the courage to ask Grady about brain pushes while she helped him give Verdi a bath.

"Why?" he wanted to know.

Sophie focused on lathering Verdi's feathers as she told him what had happened in PE. Grady and Edaline knew about her telepathy and her silent mind, but she hated reminding them how different she really was. Who'd want to adopt a freak as their daughter?

She'd tugged out three loose eyelashes before he finally spoke.

"That does sound like a brain push." His voice was a whisper. "When you were around humans, did someone train you how to use your abilities?"

"No one knew about my abilities—not even my parents. Why?"

Verdi stirred, getting annoyed with her distracted bathers. Grady waited until the soggy dinosaur had settled before he answered. "The way you use your mind, Sophie—someone *had* to teach you. It's not possible that you just instinctively know these skills."

"But . . . no one taught me anything. I'd remember that."

"Would you?"

How could she not? "Besides, how would a human even know *how* to teach me to use my abilities? It's not like they can do what we can."

Grady stared in the distance. "No, you're right. Only an elf could teach you."

"And the first elf I met was Fitz," she added, reminding him as much as herself. She didn't like the worry lines that creased his forehead.

She couldn't have met an elf without knowing it, could she?

No. She'd never met anyone else with a silent mind. Except for that jogger that day. But she'd barely talked to him for five minutes. He couldn't have done something to her, could he?

Wouldn't she have felt something?

And why would he do that?

Plus, Fitz said they'd been looking for her for twelve years. Even the Council didn't know where she was. There was no way she could've met any other elves.

But if humans didn't teach her, and elves didn't teach her . . . who did?

She searched her memories for the rest of the night, but when she went to bed she was no closer to the solution. So many things about her past raised more questions than they did answers—it was enough to drive her crazy.

She had to let this go. She had enough to worry about with her adoption and Bronte and gaining the Council's permission to stay at Foxfire. Once she had her future settled, she could search her past. Until then, she'd try to put it out of her mind.

TWENTY-FOUR

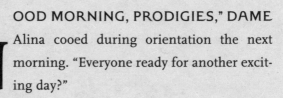OOD MORNING, PRODIGIES," DAME
Alina cooed during orientation the next
morning. "Everyone ready for another exciting day?"

"Hey, check it out," Dex whispered to Sophie. He pointed
to the meter on his plain blue nexus. "I finally passed the
halfway point."

"Really?" She tried to be excited for him, but she hadn't even
reached the one-third point.

"Yep. Not much further till I can have my own Pathfinder.
Maybe I'll even get my nexus off younger than Fitz—man,
that'd be awesome! I'd love to see Wonderboy's face if a
Dizznee broke his precious record."

She was about to defend Fitz when Dame Alina caught her attention.

"We are now four weeks away from midterms. For those of you worried you won't be able to score the required seventy-five percent to pass, I recommend seeing Lady Nissa in the Tutoring Center."

"Maybe you should sign up for alchemy tutoring," Marella whispered. "Not sure you'll pass without it."

Marella's tone was teasing, but her words hit a nerve. Sophie was barely scraping by in alchemy, and that was with Lady Galvin shouting instructions across the room. She couldn't imagine how hard it would be on her own. And she had Bronte to consider. He was probably waiting for her to fail her midterms.

Everything in her shrank at the idea of needing a tutor. She wasn't used to struggling with her grades. It felt so humiliating.

Not as humiliating as getting expelled. . . .

"That's it for today. Everyone work hard," Dame Alina finished, tossing her hair before her projection disappeared.

"Ugh, what is that?" Sophie gagged and glared at the silver strip on her locker.

Dex looked a little green. "I think it's reekrod. Elwin must've picked the flavor today."

"Remind me to yell at him the next time I see him."

"Planning another visit to the Healing Center?" Marella asked. "Going to make it a daily habit?"

"Very funny."

Marella gave her locker the tiniest lick and shrugged. "He's done worse."

"Yeah, well, I'm taking all my books with me now," Sophie said.

"Oooh—smart thinking," Dex agreed, reaching for the rest of his books. He grabbed a small silver box and tore it open. "Here. Take a Prattle to get rid of the taste."

For once Dex had good taste in candy. It was sweet and chewy—like caramel mixed with peanut butter and filled with cream.

"Which pin did you get?" Marella asked as he pulled out a small velvet pouch, like a Cracker Jack prize.

Dex removed a tiny silver horse with a glittering black mane.

Marella gasped. "A Prattles' unicorn? Please tell me you want to trade."

"Maybe." His eyes darted to Sophie. "Unless you want it?"

"I don't have any to trade."

Marella's eyes stretched as wide as they would go. "You don't have any Prattles' pins?"

Sophie stared at her feet, hating how out of touch she still was.

"I think Sophie should have it." Dex placed the pin in her hand before she could argue.

Marella snorted. "Of course you do."

"What? She needs to start her collection."

"Whatever you say."

Dex blushed and Sophie pretended not to notice. She examined the little horse, amazed by the detail. The back had a tiny digital screen that read: #122 OF 185. "What's the number mean?"

"There's one pin for every creature alive on the planet—that we know of. Right now there are only one hundred and eighty-five unicorns—so that pin is super-rare." Obvious bitterness leaked into Marella's voice.

"Hey, Sophie?" a vaguely familiar voice asked behind her. "Can I talk to you?"

Sophie spun around and froze when she saw Biana. "Uh, sure," she said as her brain struggled to compute this unexpected development.

Biana glanced at Dex and Marella. "Can we go somewhere more private?"

Sophie hesitated half a second, then shrugged to her friends and followed Biana toward a deserted corner of the atrium. "Um, what's up?"

"I was wondering if you wanted to come over after school today."

Sophie waited for the punch line, but Biana seemed serious. "Why?"

Biana looked at her hands, twisting her fingers together. "I don't know. I thought it might be nice if we could . . . try to be friends." The last words came out barely louder than a whisper.

"Friends?" The word sounded like a foreign language coming from Biana. Her eyes narrowed. "Did Fitz put you up to this?"

"No! Why would Fitz care if—" She took a deep breath. "He didn't put me up to this."

"But . . . I thought you didn't like me."

"I never said that."

"You didn't have to. It was pretty obvious."

"Well, I'm sorry you felt that way. I guess I'm not good at meeting new people."

Talk about the understatement of the century. Sophie had half a mind to tell her that she didn't need her too-little-too-late olive branch. But . . . she was Fitz's sister. It would be easier if they could get along. "Fine."

"Really?"

"Sure. I guess it's worth a try."

They both stood there, not quite meeting each other's eyes.

"So . . . what time should I come over?" Sophie eventually asked.

"Um, why don't you go home and change and come over after that? You know how to get there, right?"

"Yeah. I have been there before."

A bit of the old glare flared in Biana's face, but it was quickly replaced with an uncomfortable smile. "Well, good. I guess I'll see you then."

Sophie watched Biana walk away, replaying the conversation in her mind, trying to make sense of it.

"Are you going to tell us what that was all about?" Dex asked, already at her side. He and Marella must've made a beeline the second Biana's back was turned.

"She invited me to come over after school today."

"What?" they asked simultaneously.

"She said she wanted to be friends."

"Why?" they both asked.

Sophie shrugged. "She didn't say."

"Please tell me you told her to go sniff a gulon," Dex begged.

Sophie looked down, unable to meet his eyes.

"Aw, come on!"

"I didn't know what else to say."

"You could have told her she's a stuck-up snob and you don't want to be her friend," Marella offered.

"Look, I know you guys aren't going to like this, but my life would be a lot easier if Biana and I got along. If it doesn't work out, then I wasted one afternoon of my life. So what?"

"How do you know this isn't a trap?" Marella asked. "Invite you over, then humiliate you. You could be walking into an ambush."

"That's not what this is."

"What? You think she isn't capable?" Dex sneered.

"No, but she would never do it at her house. Not with Fitz there."

"Right. I forgot. You and *Wonderboy* are friends."

Sophie blew out a breath. "Aren't you guys the teeniest bit curious what she's up to?"

She had them there.

"I want details later," Marella agreed.

"And you'd better not leave anything out," Dex added.

TWENTY-FIVE

HEY," BIANA SAID AS SHE OPENED the gates of Everglen to let Sophie in. "You made it."

"Yeah." Sophie managed a half smile. Despite her earlier enthusiasm, she was having second thoughts.

The gate clanged closed. Somewhere in the distance a cricket chirped.

Sophie pulled on the sleeves of her pale yellow tunic, glad Biana was also dressed casual—though Biana's turquoise tunic had pink beaded flowers embroidered around the edges and a pink satin sash. "So, what are we going to do?"

Biana stared at the ground as she shrugged.

Okay. . . .

"Is your family around?"

Biana's eyes narrowed. "I knew you'd ask that."

"What?"

"I know you like my brother."

"What?"

"Please. It's pretty obvious."

"He's my friend." Sure, she liked him. But she didn't *like him*, like him. "This was a bad idea."

Biana grabbed her arm to stop her from walking away. "Wait. I'm sorry. It's just . . . girls always use me to get to my brother. I guess I sort of expect it."

Sophie could imagine how annoying that might get—but still. "That's not what I'm doing—and *you* invited *me* over, remember?"

"I know." Biana stared at her hands, wringing her fingers so tight it looked painful. "Can we maybe start over?"

Sophie bit her lip. "I guess we can try."

Biana exhaled, seeming relieved. "Good." Her eyes lit up. "I know. We can give each other makeovers. I have all the serums to change our hair color, and we can try on some of my mom's gowns."

Wrestling the verminion would've sounded more fun, but Sophie couldn't think of a polite way to say that. Fortunately, she didn't have to.

"Makeovers?" Keefe scoffed behind them. "You girls sure

know how to have fun. Maybe you can braid each other's hair and giggle about boys while you're at it."

Sophie spun around to face him, and she felt her heart flutter when she noticed Fitz standing next to him.

Keefe grinned. "Actually, maybe that last part is a good idea. You could get the dirt on Foster, find out which guys make her heart go pitter-patter."

"Um, that would be none," Sophie insisted, hoping her face wasn't as red as it felt.

"Eh, that's what they all say. But deep down girls *always* have one guy they can't take their eyes off—isn't that right, Fitz?"

"Why are we talking about this?" Fitz complained.

Keefe shrugged. "Just sayin'."

"What are you guys doing here?" Biana asked, shooting Fitz a pointed look.

"We came to see if you guys want to play base quest," Keefe answered for him.

"What's base quest?" Sophie asked, grateful for the subject change.

"Only the most awesome game ever. I call Foster for my team," Keefe announced.

Jealousy flared in Biana's eyes as Keefe wrapped an arm around Sophie's shoulders. Sophie shrugged away from him. "How about we play boys against girls?"

Fitz explained the rules. One team guarded its base while

the other team launched a raid. If the questers made it to the base without getting tagged, they won.

"Light leaping isn't allowed, but special abilities *can* be used," Fitz added, looking right at Sophie, like he was saying it for her benefit.

"That's not fair. Sophie and I don't have . . ." Biana's voice trailed off when Fitz shot her a warning look. "Fine. But you guys have to quest first."

Sophie chose to be sentry at the vivid red tree they'd picked as their base. She didn't like being the last defense—especially considering how fast Fitz and Keefe could run—but she didn't know the grounds, so it made more sense to let Biana try to hunt them down. Plus, if abilities were allowed, she knew how to keep tabs on the boys.

Tiergan had taught her how to track where thoughts came from. Most Telepaths could only isolate a general area, but Sophie could nail down the exact spot. She'd never tried it on moving targets, but it was worth a shot. So as soon as Biana ran off, she opened her mind and *listened*.

Fitz's thoughts were softer than ever—he must be trying to block her—but Keefe's were loud and clear. He was thinking about the lake, so she listened in that direction and instantly *felt* their presence. She couldn't think of a better way to explain it—even Tiergan didn't understand. Her mind somehow touched them through the air, telling her exactly where they were.

She needed a tremendous amount of concentration to stay connected as they snuck through the meadow, but she didn't lose them, even when they dashed into the forest to slip by Biana. Her head ached, but she held on, following them through the trees. When their thoughts focused on the base, her heart thundered. They were closing in.

She took off, not sure if she was seeing with her eyes or theirs as she plowed through the trees. She didn't know where she was, or how long she ran, or if she felt anything—until her hands connected with skin and her vision cleared.

Fitz and Keefe stared at her with wide eyes. She gripped their arms.

"How did you do that?" Keefe demanded. "You ran straight to us, like you knew where we were."

"I"—she racked her brain for a credible excuse—"heard you."

"Heard us how?" Keefe cocked his head, glancing at her hand on his arm, then back at her. "Hiding something, Foster?"

"She probably heard you crashing through the bushes like a sasquatch," Fitz said, coming to her rescue. "I think the whole world did."

"No, I don't think that's what it is."

"You're just mad because you lost," Biana teased, catching up with them. "I can't believe Sophie tagged you both on her own—she can be my base quest partner anytime." She grinned, and Sophie couldn't help smiling back.

She was actually having fun—with Biana, of all people. Who would've guessed?

"Do my eyes deceive me, or is that Sophie Foster?" Alden asked behind them.

"We've missed you around here," Della added, rushing over and wrapping Sophie up in her arms.

Sophie sank into the hug, swallowing the emotions rising in her chest. She hadn't seen Alden or Della since she moved to Havenfield, and she hadn't realized how much she missed them. She took a deep breath to clear her head and her nose tingled. "Whoa, you smell like smoke. Is there a fire?"

Della glanced at Alden as she pulled out of the hug, backing a few steps away.

Alden cleared his throat. "Just something we're looking into. No reason to worry."

Sophie repressed a sigh. "No reason to worry" seemed to be Alden's favorite words.

Then again, he'd never found anything suspicious about the San Diego fires—or if he had, it hadn't been important enough to hit the gossip circles. Sophie was sure Marella would've heard otherwise.

"So, what are you guys up to?" Della asked.

"Getting stomped in base quest," Keefe grumbled. "You should've seen it—Sophie tagged us out like she knew where we were."

Alden glanced at Fitz—who gave the slightest nod—before

he grinned at Keefe. "Sounds like someone's not happy about losing."

"I'd just like to know how she did it, but she insists on being all mysterious." Keefe narrowed his eyes at Sophie. "She still hasn't explained how she slammed Fitz into the wall yesterday."

Sophie flushed, and when she met Alden's eyes she could see clear concern. "Fitz said he was going to talk to you about that," she said quietly. "Any theories?"

"None that makes any sense," Alden admitted.

A second of silence passed. Then Della came to the rescue. "Besides, we girls never reveal our secrets. How else can we keep you boys on your toes? So, who's staying for dinner?" She glanced at Sophie.

"Sorry. I told Edaline I'd be home. Maybe next time." She flushed when she realized she'd invited herself over.

But Biana smiled. "Sounds good."

"Do you need to use the Leapmaster?" Alden asked.

"No, Grady and Edaline gave me a home crystal." She held up a long silver chain that hung to her waist. The crystal pendant only had a single facet, the path to Havenfield. They'd given it to her that morning, apologizing for not giving her one sooner.

She really felt like family.

"Don't stay away too long this time," Alden told her. "We've missed you around here."

"I've missed you guys too. I'll see you soon."

On Monday Biana, Keefe, and Fitz sat with Sophie at lunch.

Jensi and Marella kept giggling and staring at their visitors—Marella especially. Dex spent the entire lunch sulking at his tray.

"Hey, Dex," Sophie said, trying to draw him out of his funk. "Can you come over after school today?"

He glared at Fitz before his eyes met hers. "You don't have other plans?"

She ignored his snipe. "I was hoping you'd tutor me in alchemy. I'm going to need help before midterms, and you're the best alchemist I know."

Dex straightened up at the compliment. "Sure, if you really need me."

Keefe wagged a finger at her. "Aw, don't go getting good at alchemy, Foster. Who else can we count on to destroy Lady Galvin's capes?"

"Don't worry, I don't think Sophie can ever get *good* at alchemy," Marella told him. "Do you have any idea how many things she's exploded?"

"There've been other explosions?" He flashed Sophie a wicked grin. "This I have to hear."

Sophie sighed as Marella filled everyone in on her almost weekly explosions. Now she had a reason besides Bronte to get better at alchemy. If sitting with Keefe was going to be a regular thing, she would never hear the end of the jokes.

Keefe got detention a week later, so she was off the hook for the teasing. But it was a lucky break, because even with Dex's expert instructions, she couldn't get the hang of alchemy. She almost caught her room on fire twice before Dex moved their practice experiments to the caves that lined the beach at the base of Havenfield's cliffs. Rock couldn't burn and the ocean was nearby if they needed it. And they needed it. A lot. She even caught Dex's tunic on fire.

Maybe it was because the rules of alchemy defied every rule of chemistry she'd ever learned, or maybe it was because the ingredients were so foreign, but two weeks away from exams she was panicking. Her only chance of passing would be if she knew what would be on the test so she could practice until she got it right. Too bad Lady Galvin refused to give a study guide. Sophie was fairly certain she was hoping she'd fail so she'd be rid of her.

Of course, Sophie could always read her mind.

The thought was so terrible she was ashamed for even thinking it.

But . . .

No one would ever know.

And she'd still have to complete the assignment for the test without any help. Narrowing down what to study wasn't so wrong, was it? Plus, if she didn't pass, Bronte would have what he needed to get her expelled, maybe even shipped off to—

She refused to finish the terrifying thought. The fear made up her mind.

At her next alchemy session she dropped her books. She kept her back to Lady Galvin as she bent to retrieve them, and—before she could wimp out—she closed her eyes and concentrated on her thoughts.

It was easier than she had planned. Lady Galvin had the exam on her mind, so Sophie didn't have to probe deeper into her memories. She was deciding between making Sophie turn a rose to iron or making her turn brass to copper—the hardest basic transmutations. Sophie tucked both ideas away, then closed her mind and picked up her books like nothing had happened.

She'd expected to feel triumphant. Now she had a fighting chance. Plus, she was right. Lady Galvin was giving her the hardest challenges to try to fail her, and she'd thwarted her plan. So why did she feel like she'd eaten a huge bowl of slime?

Distracted and uncomfortable, she spilled the gashrooms and made the whole room reek of rotten fungus.

Study hall was worse. Everyone pored over their notes while Sophie sat frozen, afraid to open her books. By the time she got home she was on the verge of tears. She couldn't touch her dinner, couldn't bear the concerned looks on Grady's and Edaline's faces. She didn't deserve sympathy. She didn't deserve anything. She hid in her room the rest of the night.

Sleep was a lost cause.

Alone in the darkness, with a snoring imp shattering the silence, and Ella in her arms, she forced herself to admit the truth.

She'd broken the rules for Telepaths.

Even worse: She'd cheated.

Just thinking the word made her skin crawl. From now on, anything she accomplished at Foxfire would be because she cheated on her alchemy exam. Could she really live with that?

No.

But what could she do?

How could she study without focusing on those things? And, if she didn't study them, she'd be sure to fail. It wasn't like she could tell Lady Galvin what happened. She wasn't allowed to tell anyone about her telepathy. She *had* to cheat now—no way around it.

Unless . . .

Her heart sank as another option occurred to her. It was far from ideal, but it was her only way out—and better than living with guilt for the rest of her life.

Fear weighed her down as she crept out of bed and dug out the Imparter Alden had given her. But she had to do this now, before she changed her mind.

She cleared her throat, took a deep breath, and forced her lips to say three words she was dreading. "Show me Alden."

TWENTY-SIX

DAME ALINA'S OFFICE WAS A TRI-angular room with glass walls and a high, pointed ceiling at the apex of the pyramid at Foxfire. Morning sunlight streamed through the clear windows, but every other pane was a mirror, tilted at just the right angle to show Dame Alina's reflection as she sat behind her mirrored desk, examining her hair from all sides.

Sophie kept her eyes on her hands as she confessed her crime. She didn't want to see the disappointment on Alden's or Tiergan's face, or Dame Alina's reflections glaring at her from every direction. This was so much harder than telling Grady and Edaline before she left for school. They'd just nodded, forgave her, and hoped she didn't get in too much trouble.

"What do you think, Dame Alina?" Alden asked when Sophie finished. His voice was neutral. Not angry, but not gentle either.

Dame Alina pursed her lips. "She violated the ethical regulations of telepathy."

"She did indeed," Tiergan murmured. "And I'm sure some here feel she should be exiled for that." He glared at Alden.

Sophie froze. Would the Council *exile* her? And here she'd thought all she was facing was expulsion.

Alden sighed. "No one is suggesting anything of the sort."

Sophie released the breath she'd been holding.

"Right," Tiergan grumbled, "because it would be absurd to exile an innocent girl. But a man with a family to care for—"

"I will not have this argument again, Tiergan. It was the Council's ruling. I had no choice but to obey."

"There's *always* a choice," Tiergan insisted quietly.

Sophie knew they were talking about Prentice, and she knew she should be curious. But ever since she realized he was the one who'd abandoned her, she didn't want to be interested in what had happened to him. It hurt too much to think about.

"Now, now, boys," Dame Alina said, rising from her chair with an elegant flourish. She smoothed her hair in her dozens of reflections. "Can't we play nice?"

No one said anything.

Dame Alina sighed. Then she turned to Alden, flashing a wide smile. "What do you think the punishment should be?"

Tiergan snorted. "Yes, let's leave it up to him. Why bother asking her *telepathy* Mentor how she should be punished for violating the rules of *telepathy*?"

"He's the one reporting on her to the Council," Dame Alina argued.

Sophie had to stifle her gasp. Alden was reporting on her too? How closely was the Council watching her?

"Yes, everyone knows he's good at that," Tiergan growled.

Alden sighed but said nothing.

"Don't forget your place, *Sir* Tiergan," Dame Alina said icily. "As long as you are a Mentor you will respect my authority. And I'd like to know what Alden advises."

"Of course you do," he said under his breath. "Everyone knows how you favor him."

"Excuse me?" Dame Alina hissed.

Alden closed his eyes, shaking his head. But Tiergan straightened his shoulders, like he wasn't backing down. "It's hardly a secret that you tried to stop his wedding to Della."

"Really?" Sophie blurted, unable to stop herself.

Dame Alina flushed bright red, and her mouth flapped a few times, like she wanted to speak but couldn't get her tongue to work.

Alden ran his hands through his hair. "All of that is neither here nor there."

"Isn't it?" Tiergan asked. "This whole process is pointless.

Sophie won a pardon from the splotching match. Can't she hand that over and consider it punishment served?"

"And allow her to believe that cheating is tolerated?" Dame Alina huffed, still struggling to recover her dignity. "Certainly not."

"But she didn't actually cheat," Tiergan pointed out.

"And the fact that we're here at all tells us she regrets it. She didn't have to confess," Alden added.

Tiergan stared at him for a second, like he couldn't believe they were on the same side.

"She should still have to serve detention, at minimum," Dame Alina insisted.

"That's ridiculous," Tiergan argued.

"Can I say something?" Sophie asked, stunned by her sudden courage. Her mouth went dry as they all turned to stare at her. "I'll serve the detention."

Seeing how she'd disappointed everyone made her ill. She didn't deserve to get off easy. And the smile hiding in the corners of Alden's mouth told her she'd made the right decision.

Dame Alina nodded. "Good. Then I'm assigning you detention until the end of midterms, and you are not to tell anyone the reason you're being punished, is that clear?"

"What will you tell Lady Galvin?" Sophie asked.

"I'll explain the situation to her. No reason to worry." The warmth in Alden's voice melted the sickening guilt in her stomach. It wasn't a perfect solution, but at least she'd be able to sleep at night again. Well . . . once she stopped worrying about her midterms. And Bronte.

One problem at a time.

It was becoming a theme in her life.

"Where are you going?" Dex asked when Sophie turned to head away from the cafeteria. So much for her plan of slipping away unnoticed.

She stared at her feet. "I can't sit with you guys today. I have detention."

"Detention?" they all repeated, loud enough to turn a few heads.

"How long do you have it for?" Dex asked.

"Till the end of midterms," she mumbled.

"The end of midterms!"

Jensi whistled. "Dude. What'd you do?"

"I don't want to talk about it." She gave a small smile and bolted before they could ask more questions.

The detention hall was in the glass pyramid, one floor beneath Dame Alina's office. The ceiling was low and the windows blocked more light than they let in, giving the room a gloomy atmosphere. Sophie tried to sneak in without being seen by the twenty or so other kids, but Sir Conley recognized her from their elementalism sessions.

"Welcome, Miss Foster," he announced, and every head turned her way. He brushed a hand across his long dark hair and waved toward the rows of uncomfortable desks. "Take a seat and settle in. I have *quite* a treat for everyone today."

She ignored the stares as she sank into the first empty chair. She caught Keefe's eye from a desk in the corner. He grinned and gave her a thumbs-up.

"Ready for more siren song?" Sir Conley asked.

Everyone groaned.

"You have no appreciation for art or nature," he grumbled, clapping his hands. An earsplittingly shrill whine—part whale song, part nails on a chalkboard, with just the right amount of screaming toddler—reverberated through the room. "Uncover those ears—I am broadening your horizons, and you will listen to every note!"

Everyone glared at him as they lowered their hands.

"What are you in for?" Keefe asked with a crooked smile. Somehow he'd slipped into the empty desk behind her.

"None of your business," she whispered.

He laughed. "You keep claiming you're not mysterious, but who are you kidding?"

She sighed. "What are you doing here?"

"Remember the reekrod someone put in Dame Alina's office a few months ago?"

"That was you?"

"Of course. Took her long enough to trace it back to me." He laughed, not even a little repentant. "Will you at least tell me how long I'll get to enjoy your company here?"

She bit her lip. "Till the end of midterms."

"Sounds like Miss Foster did something *very* bad. In the future you should leave the mischief making to me."

Sophie cringed as a shrill whine rang through the air. "Is it always this loud?"

"Oh, no. That's just Sir Conley. Tomorrow it's Lady Belva."

"What's her brand of torture?"

"You'll see."

Ballroom dancing—that was Lady Belva's idea of punishment. Given the choice, Sophie would have taken the screeching sirens any day.

The desks were shoved aside so the dances could be done in a line, like at old Edwardian balls. Keefe tried to grab her as his partner, but Lady Belva claimed him for herself and paired Sophie with Valin, one of Jensi's greasy, ponytailed friends. His palms were cold and sticky and a blob of drool settled in the corner of his mouth and never went away. Keefe snickered every time it was her turn to promenade through the other dancers on Valin's sweaty arm. She'd never been so happy to hear the bells chime the end of lunch.

"I hope you know Valin is in love with you now," Keefe teased when he caught up with her in the hall.

"And you would know that because . . . ?"

"Please. You could see the stars in his eyes all the way across the room. They shined brighter than that blob of spit on his lips."

She couldn't help laughing. "You're terrible."

"I know." He grinned wickedly. "But I'm serious. I bumped his arm on my way out the door, and he was crushing hard. The Sophie Foster Fan Club has a slobbery new member."

She opened her mouth to argue when she caught what he'd said. "Wait—are you an Empath?"

He winked, reaching for her hand. "Want me to tell you what you're feeling?"

She jerked away. "Thanks, I'll pass."

"Too bad I can read what you're feeling even without physical contact." His voice shifted up a few octaves as he fanned the air. "I hope Keefe's right about Valin liking me. Guys who drool are *so* cute."

"Will you keep your voice down?" she hissed, glancing around to make sure no one was within earshot.

Keefe laughed. He fanned the air again. "Hmm. Now I can tell you're embarrassed. And a tiny bit irritated."

"You're wrong. I'm *just* irritated."

"Nah. You're flattered." He scooted away before she could shove him.

They walked in silence for a minute before Sophie's eyes dropped to her feet. "Could you really feel that I was irritated or were you guessing?"

"You look worried—you wouldn't have something to hide, would you? A secret crush, maybe?"

"Never mind. Forget I asked."

He cracked up. "It's almost *too* easy to annoy you, you know that?"

She sighed.

"Oh, all right. If you must know, yes, your emotions are a little stronger than others. I can't really understand what they are, but I can feel them—and no, I don't know why, in case you're going to ask. Scored me major points with my empathy Mentor when I told him, though."

She wasn't quite sure what to say to that, so they walked in silence until the hallway forked and she went left at the same time Keefe turned right.

"See you tomorrow in detention," he said with a smirk. "It's Lady Galvin. Hope you're good at ironing. It probably wouldn't be good to burn more holes in her capes."

He was gone before she could ask him if he was joking.

Keefe wasn't joking. Lady Galvin brought an enormous stack of capes for the detained prodigies to iron and hang as their punishment. Sophie wasn't allowed anywhere near them, forced instead to sit alone in the corner while Keefe winked at her and Valin stared and drooled. She wasn't sure which was worse.

She spent most of the time glaring at the level on her nexus, which still hadn't increased, despite practicing leaps with Grady. He kept telling her to give her brain time to get used to it—she was learning an entirely different way of making her mind work—but it was still annoying.

She flipped the nexus over so she couldn't see the meter anymore, and her eyes found the sparkly aquamarine stone. Her mind wandered automatically to Fitz.

Someone cleared his throat.

Sophie locked eyes with Keefe. She turned away when he raised one eyebrow. It was a coincidence, she told herself. There was no way he could feel what she was feeling from all the way across the room. No Empaths were *that* powerful.

Still, she kept her mind on mundane things until the bells chimed.

"Oh, Miss Foster," Lady Galvin called when she was halfway out the door. "How's your studying going?"

Her mouth went dry. "Good."

"Glad to hear it. You're going to need it."

She nodded and turned to leave.

"You might want to brush up on iron purification," she added quietly.

Sophie spun back around. "Iron purification?"

"In case you've been wondering what to study. Your exam will be in that vein. Even you should be able to handle that."

Lady Galvin waved her away and Sophie left the room in a daze.

Did she really tell her what would be on the test?

Did she really pick iron purification—the easiest transmutation in alchemy?

"How was detention?" Dex asked when she found him at the lockers.

"Good," she said, still struggling to wrap her mind around what happened. Actually, it was better than good, but he was looking at her like she was a freak, so she didn't elaborate as she traded books. "Hey, Dex?"

"Yeah?"

"Do you think you can help me practice iron purification this weekend?"

TWENTY-SEVEN

EVERYONE EXCITED FOR MIDTERMS?" Dame Alina's projection chirped.

Sophie locked her legs to keep her knees from banging together as Dame Alina continued in her annoyingly cheerful voice.

"Your thinking caps are in your lockers, and remember, anyone found without one for the rest of the day will be disqualified for cheating—is that clear?" She waited until everyone nodded. "Good. Have fun with midterms."

The chorus of groans echoed through the air as Dame Alina flashed away and everyone left for exams. Sophie froze, too terrified to move.

Dex pulled her toward the atrium. "Will you relax? We've been practicing nonstop for a week. You're ready."

She nodded, afraid that if she spoke, her voice would tremble.

Her hands shook as she slipped on the thinking cap from her locker. The white cloth wrapped around her head and hung in a point. She glared at her reflection. "I look like a Smurf."

The thick fabric consisted of an amalgam of metals, made to dull telepathic abilities and preserve the integrity of the exams. But the second she concentrated she could feel Dex's voice rushing through her mind like a blast of air, so it clearly didn't work on her. She wasn't surprised.

"Well . . . here goes nothing." She forced a smile before stumbling down the hall on shaky legs.

She wrote an extensive essay on the human betrayal for elvin history, named more than a hundred stars in the Universe, and won the mind-over-matter debate with Sir Faxon in metaphysics. Tiergan was so amazed that the thinking cap had no effect on her, he gave her an automatic 100 percent.

But her harder exams were after lunch, and alchemy was up first. Thinking about it made her stomach twist in ways that couldn't be natural.

Lady Alexine allowed last-minute studying in detention, so Sophie spent the time mentally repeating Dex's purification tips.

"Will you chill?" Keefe whispered. He waved at the air, like he was trying to fan her negative vibes away. "You're starting to stress me out."

"Aren't you nervous?"

"Nah, I'm awesome at tests. Photographic memory."

Sophie's eyes widened. "You too?"

"You have a photographic memory? Then what are you freaking out about?"

"Because it doesn't help as much as you think."

"Sure it does. How else do you think I got a year ahead? It sure wasn't my work ethic."

"You're a year ahead?" She'd never realized he was younger than Fitz.

"Yep. It's my big claim to fame. I skipped Level One. Kinda like you."

"I didn't skip it. I missed it."

"Same thing."

It wasn't, but she didn't have time to argue. The bells chimed the end of lunch.

For a second she wasn't sure if she'd be able to get up.

Keefe pulled her to her feet. "That means it's time to go, in case you didn't realize. Seriously, Foster, you have to relax. You're going to make yourself sick."

"I feel sick," she admitted, wobbling.

He jerked away. "Thanks for the warning. No need to share *that* feeling. Look, I'm not good at the serious, supportive thing—but trust me, you're going to be fine."

"How do you know?"

He grinned. "I have a feeling you can do pretty much anything you put your mind to. So stop doubting yourself and go prove me right. You know, so I can brag about it."

She couldn't help smiling. "Thanks." She took a deep, calming breath, squared her shoulders, and ordered her legs to walk. Mercifully, they obeyed.

Lady Galvin was still setting up when she entered the room. Sophie's heart stalled when she saw the deep magenta berries and the rusty iron key. Lady Galvin may be giving Sophie the easiest discipline, but she certainly hadn't chosen an easy project.

"Does the cap even work on you?" Lady Galvin asked, her eyes boring into Sophie's.

Sophie shook her head, not quite brave enough to speak the words.

"Will you be picking the secrets out of my brain, then?"

She shook her head again.

"Why should I believe you?"

She cleared her throat and forced her mouth to work. "I want to pass on my own."

Lady Galvin stared at her for a second before she blinked. "You must purify the iron key using only ruckleberries. You have fifty-five minutes. I suggest you get started."

Ruckleberries were nasty, stinky little berries that brought impurities to the surface of a metal. They also made your skin wrinkle like an elderly human's if any of the juice got on you—and you'd smell like feet all day—so most alchemists used other methods to purify metal. But it was the assignment. Sophie had no choice but to dive in and do her best.

Her palms were so sweaty it was hard to hold the knife as she pierced the first berry and dribbled the juice on the key. She tried to work slow and careful, but a few drops still ended up on her pinky, making it look crinkled and haggard, and the glacial pace made her run out of time. Only three quarters of the key had turned the gleaming black color she was going for, but she hoped it was enough. Lady Galvin's face was unreadable when she turned it in, and she glared at Sophie's wrinkled pinky. Points would clearly be deducted.

Sophie finished out the day with a decent essay on ogres for multispeciesial studies and a mediocre performance on her last two exams. Her channeling went well in phys. ed.—until Lady Alexine ran back and forth through the walls and broke her concentration. And she managed to bottle three different clouds in elementalism, but it took four tries to bottle a whirlwind and the bottle had a crack from the pressure. Sir Conley didn't look impressed when she handed it in.

Completely exhausted, she trudged back to the atrium to meet Dex.

"Well, *that* was brutal," he whined, slamming his locker closed. "How'd it go for you?"

She slumped against the wall. "I did the best I could."

"I guess you can't ask for more than that." He tried to smooth his wild hat hair. "You staying home tonight?"

"No. Grady and Edaline are taking me shopping."

"Whoa. That'll be the first time they've gone out in public together since . . . you know."

She did know. Grady and Edaline hadn't left the house together since Jolie died. Sophie told them they didn't have to, but Grady insisted. Foxfire tradition held that at the end of midterms all the prodigies hung their thinking caps upside down from hooks on their lockers. The next day everyone filled each other's hats with presents and opened them while their parents met with their Mentors to find out their grades. Sophie's legs felt weak just thinking about it.

She loved the idea of presents and hanging out with her friends, but having Grady and Edaline know if she failed before she did sent chills down her spine. Why couldn't elves send out report cards like human schools?

"Are you going shopping tonight?" she asked Dex.

"Nope. My parents think it's too much hassle to take all four of us, and they can never find babysitters for the triplets." Bitterness edged into his voice. "But don't worry"—he nudged her arm—"I already made your present."

"You made my present?" At first she was touched, but then she thought about it. "Wait, it's not some solution that's going to turn my hair green, is it?"

Dex flashed a slightly evil grin. "I guess you'll have to wait and see."

Grady and Edaline took Sophie to Atlantis. She hadn't been there since the day Alden and Fitz brought her—the day her human life ended—and she still hadn't figured out how to feel about any of that. She'd been with the elves a little more than three months now, and she'd come a long way. But she still had a long way to go.

Passing her midterms was the biggest obstacle.

She glared at her wrinkled pinky. How many points would she lose for the mistake? And how many more for not finishing?

Grady squeezed her shoulder when he caught her tugging out an eyelash. "Try to stop stressing, Sophie. We're here to have fun, not worry about grades."

She was tempted to point out that Grady and Edaline looked more stressed than she did. Their shoulders were rigid, their jaws set, and Edaline had deep shadows under her eyes. But they were making a huge sacrifice for her. The least she could do was enjoy herself.

It took seven stores to find suitable gifts for all of her friends, and with each store Grady and Edaline looked more strained. The worst was the jewelry store. The woman who ran the shop remembered them. Apparently, they used to come in all the time to buy new charms for a charm bracelet—which had obviously belonged to Jolie.

Sophie took Edaline's hand.

Edaline jumped. Then her eyes welled with tears and she squeezed Sophie's hand and didn't let go. Grady took Sophie's other hand, and they walked that way for the rest of the night.

When they got home, Grady stopped her on her way to her room.

"I'm glad you came to live with us, Sophie. It's . . ." His mouth formed a word, then changed to a different one. "It's nice."

"I'm glad I live here too," she whispered.

He cleared his throat. "Big day tomorrow. Better get some sleep."

"Good night, Grady."

Even though she was terrified about her exam grades, she fell asleep believing that everything was going to be okay.

TWENTY-EIGHT

FOXFIRE WAS ALMOST UNRECOGNIZable. Silver streamers wrapped every tree, every shrub, every tower—like the school had been toilet-papered with tinsel. Confetti and flowers covered the floor, and giant bubbles filled with prizes floated through the halls. Prodigies ignored their parents as they dashed around popping as many as they could.

Grady and Edaline were overwhelmed by the crowd, so they went straight to where they'd meet for their first Mentor appointment and left Sophie to celebrate on her own. She made her way to the Level Four wing, deciding to drop off Fitz's and Keefe's presents before meeting up with her friends.

A tiny part of her had been hoping she'd find Fitz at his

locker, but all she found was a long line of Level Four girls, all of whom glared at her as she added her small, teal-wrapped package to his nearly full hat. The glaring turned even uglier when she added a bright green box to Keefe's collection.

Girls.

She kept her head down as she slunk away, hurrying back toward her own wing. Which was how she ended up plowing straight into Sir Tiergan.

"Sorry," she exclaimed as he struggled to regain his balance. He'd been moving fast, and they'd crashed pretty hard. She rubbed her forehead where it had slammed into his elbow.

"Sophie!" He glanced around, thin lines stretched across his brow. "What are you doing here?"

"I just came to drop off some gifts. Why? Is everything okay?"

He smiled, but it looked forced. "Of course. I just didn't expect to run into you here. Especially so literally." His smile turned real with his joke.

"Well, well, who do we have here?"

Sophie's heart sank as she turned around, expecting to find Keefe with lots of prying questions and one of his trademark smirks. And he was there. But his grin was gone, and it wasn't he who'd spoken.

A tall, slender man in a sapphire-encrusted navy-blue cape stood next to him, studying Sophie intently. The family resemblance was striking, though Keefe's disheveled hairstyle and untucked shirt sharply contrasted his dad's slicked blond hair and pristine tunic.

"This must be the girl who was raised by humans," he said, much louder than Sophie would've liked. "How curious to find her in the Level Four wing, talking to Foxfire's most *infamous* Mentor."

"Infamous?" Sophie couldn't help asking. She glanced at Keefe, but he was staring at the ground. It was strange to see him so . . . deflated. Like he'd wilted in his father's presence.

Keefe's father grinned, an oily sort of smile that dripped with insincerity. "Few Mentors have resigned, then returned years later—out of the blue—to train a mystery prodigy." He winked with the last two words, like he knew exactly who the prodigy was.

Sophie felt her cheeks flame and searched for some sort of lie. But Tiergan beat her to it.

"Interesting theory, Cassius—"

"*Lord* Cassius," he corrected.

Tiergan's jaw tightened. "*Lord* Cassius. But do you really think I could be tempted back by a little girl? Especially one performing so unremarkably in her sessions?"

She knew he didn't mean it. That Tiergan was only trying to keep her telepathy hidden. But the words still stung. A lot.

"Come on, Dad," Keefe said, looking at Sophie, not his father. His eyes radiated the apologies he couldn't say. "I'm sure Fos—er—Sophie has somewhere she needs to be."

Cassius glared at his son. "Yes, of course. And I need to meet with your Mentors. See how disappointing your scores will be this time."

Keefe rolled his eyes as his father turned to Sophie with another fake smile. "Fascinating to meet you. I look very forward to seeing what you can do."

Sophie nodded and took off down the hall without saying goodbye. She felt bad leaving Keefe and Tiergan that way, but she had to get away from that man. It wasn't because he was intimidating—though he was definitely that. She felt sorry for Keefe, having to go home to a cold, critical father every day.

But what she really didn't like was the way Cassius had looked at her, like he was trying to see through her. And the last thing he'd said: *I look forward to seeing what you can do.* Almost like he knew something she didn't. Totally gave her the creeps.

It was a relief to reach the safety of the Level Two wing, which was packed with prodigies running around, popping the prize-filled bubbles. She poked a bubble floating by her locker and a box of Prattles dropped into her hands.

"Good catch," Dex said, running up beside her. He jumped for a bubble but didn't quite reach it. Before he could try again, Stina shoved by, raised a bony arm, and popped it.

She waved the bottle of lushberry juice in Dex's face. "Must get frustrating being shorter than the average dwarf."

Sophie snorted. "This coming from someone who looks like

a giant lollipop. If your head gets any bigger, you'll topple over."

Dex cracked up.

"Awfully brave words coming from a girl who's going to flunk out of here today," Stina growled.

Sophie opened her mouth but couldn't find a snappy comeback. Stina could be right, and Sophie was trying very hard not to think about that. Especially after Tiergan's comment.

Stina giggled. "Enjoy your last day at Foxfire, loser." She bumped Sophie into the wall and stalked away.

"Don't let her get to you—and if Lady Galvin fails you, I'll organize a protest." Dex pointed to her thinking cap, which was overflowing with presents. "Look at how many people care about you here." He frowned at his own, half-empty cap.

Sophie nudged his arm, pulled a package from her satchel— the Disneyland watch she'd been wearing when she moved to the Lost Cities. She figured he'd get a kick out of that—and dropped it in.

He grinned, flashing his dimples. "I slipped your present in before you got here." His eyes dropped to his feet. "I hope you like it."

"I'll love it. Just let me drop off Biana's gift and we'll go to the cafeteria."

"Ugh—why did you buy Biana a present?"

"She's my friend."

"Yeah, and like a month ago you guys hated each other."

"That was a misunderstanding."

"Yeah, well . . . I don't trust her. I don't think you should either. Why would she reach out to you for—"

Sophie shushed him as Biana entered the atrium, followed by Maruca. They looked like they were talking, but when Sophie got closer she realized they were arguing.

Biana bit her lip. "Oh, hey, Sophie."

Maruca glared at Biana.

Sophie cleared her throat. "Sorry. I just wanted to drop this off." She handed Biana a pink box—the charm bracelet she'd bought her—and turned to leave.

"Wait." Biana pulled out a slim purple parcel and handed it to Sophie. "You're coming over for dinner tonight, right?"

"Of course. I can't wait! Well . . . I'll see you later," Sophie said, wondering why Maruca was glaring at her. Then again, so was Dex. "What?" she asked as soon as they were out of earshot.

"You're going over there for dinner?" He said something else too, but the chiming bells drowned him out.

Sophie froze.

The bells signaled the start of parent-Mentor conferences. Which meant Grady and Edaline were finding out right now if she was going to stay at Foxfire.

Dex dragged her to the celebration feast in the cafeteria, but Sophie couldn't relax—even surrounded by friends.

The bells chimed every twenty minutes. Four had already

passed, which meant in twenty minutes Grady and Edaline would know if she'd failed alchemy. Her palms were so damp she struggled to unwrap her presents.

"What do we have here?" Keefe asked, snatching a red box from her thinking cap. He was definitely back to his old self without his father around. He glanced at the card and cracked up. "'Dear Sophie. I really enjoyed our dance, and I hope we can do it again sometime. *Love*, Valin.'"

Her face burned as everyone at the table laughed—even Fitz.

"Who's Valin?" Dex asked.

"Vice president of the Sophie Foster Fan Club. Don't worry, I'm president, so I'll take care of her." He winked as he tossed the present back to her. "Go on. Open it."

There didn't seem to be a way to avoid it, so she tore off the paper, wishing she could disappear when she unwrapped a bracelet of little heart charms.

Keefe cracked up again. "Aw, Foster has a boyfriend."

"She does not!" Dex snapped. "You don't, right?"

She shook her head so hard her brain rattled.

"I'm just teasing—sheesh." Keefe nudged Dex's arm, then grinned at Sophie. "Interesting."

"What?" Dex asked.

"Which one's your gift, Dex?" Sophie interrupted. She didn't have to be a mind reader to know what Keefe was going to tease Dex about.

Dex glared at Keefe as he grabbed a small package wrapped

in plain white paper and handed it to Sophie. "Sorry, we didn't have any ribbon."

"Please, I still can't believe you made me something." She tore through the paper and gasped. "My iPod." She tapped the screen and the gadget sprang to life.

"Yeah." He pointed to a green rectangle about the size of his fingernail set into the back. "It's solar powered now, and it has a speaker in case you don't want to use those ear thingies."

She stared at Dex for a minute, so amazed she wanted to hug him. She knew Keefe would have a field day, though, so she fought the urge. "This is amazing, Dex. How did you do it?"

He shrugged, pink coloring his cheeks.

"Well, thank you. Best. Gift. Ever."

"I dunno," Keefe interrupted. "You haven't opened mine yet."

She bit her lip, a little afraid of what Keefe might give her. "Which one's yours?"

"Your hat was overflowing, so it's waiting in your locker."

"How did you get in my locker?"

"I have my methods."

She shook her head in disbelief as Marella shoved a box wrapped with crooked green paper into her hands. "Open mine next."

Marella gave her a variety pack of flavored air, plus she got a ton of candy from prodigies she barely knew. Biana gave her a set of edible lip glosses, and Jensi gave her a speckled spider snapper—a plant that fed off spiders. Clearly, he didn't know how to shop for girls.

The only real disappointment was Fitz's gift. He gave her a riddler—a pen that only writes the words of a riddle until someone writes the correct answer. It was kind of cool, except he also gave one to everyone else. She'd spent forever trying to find him something personal, settling on a miniature Albertosaurus covered in deep violet feathers. She knew it was silly, but it reminded her of the day they met, and in the card she thanked him for showing her what dinosaurs really looked like.

Fitz giving her a fancy pen—especially the same fancy pen he gave everyone else—made it seem like he hadn't thought about her at all. But maybe he hadn't. He'd hardly looked at her gift when he opened it, too distracted by the tunic Keefe gave him, which had I KNOW WHAT YOU'RE THINKING—AND YOU SHOULD BE ASHAMED OF YOURSELF embroidered across the front. She tried not to let that bother her.

The doors burst open and parents streamed in. Sophie couldn't breathe as she scanned the faces, desperate to find Grady and Edaline.

Dex squeezed her shoulder and told her it would be okay no matter what, but she barely heard him. She'd found Grady and Edaline, and their faces were unreadable as they searched the room, not seeing her as she shoved toward them. She was halfway there before she locked eyes with Grady. A huge grin lit up his face.

"You passed," he shouted over the crowd.

A hysterical laugh erupted from her lips as she ran the rest of the way and threw her arms around them. When her brain caught up, she wondered if she'd crossed a line, but their arms wrapped around her, and when they let her go their eyes were misty.

"I really passed?" she asked, needing to hear it again. "Even alchemy?"

"You got a seventy-nine on your purification. Still room for improvement, but within passing range."

She squealed, hugging them again.

Grady grinned. "I'm sensing you're happy about this."

She laughed so hard tears streamed down her face, but she didn't care. She passed! She could stay at Foxfire. Sure, she still had to face Bronte and the Council in five months about permanent enrollment, but right now she was going to celebrate.

She raced back to the table and threw her arms around Dex. "I couldn't have done this without you." His face was tomato red when she let go, and she couldn't help giggling.

Everyone congratulated her—except Keefe, who leaned in and whispered, "Told you so," when his dad wasn't looking. All her friends had passed their exams. In fact, it looked like most of the school had. A few parents had to comfort sobbing prodigies, but everyone else was tossing confetti and partying. Unfortunately, that included Stina.

Her face twisted into a sneer when she noticed Sophie celebrating. Then she rolled her eyes and stomped away. Sophie giggled.

She wanted to stay for the party, but she could tell Grady and Edaline were a little overwhelmed. She ran back to the atrium to pick up Keefe's gift, so she would be ready to go home. Inside her locker she found a giant box of mood candy, a small black cube, and a note:

For the Mysterious Miss F—
If you don't relax, this candy will always taste bitter—so snap out of it! And try to stay out of detention! —K

The candy tasted like sugarplums, and inside the black cube she found a round silver pendant with a cobalt blue crystal in the center.

The candy turned sour.

Since when did Keefe give her jewelry?

He didn't *like* her

She wouldn't finish the thought. There was no way a guy like Keefe would ever, could ever—why was she thinking about this? Marella's boy-craziness must be rubbing off on her.

It was just a necklace. He probably gave them to all the girls.

She didn't know what to do with it, so she shoved the

pendant to the back of her locker, and was glad she didn't see Keefe before she left. She needed to figure out how to thank him for such a strange present.

Thankfully, Keefe didn't bring it up at dinner that night. He was more interested in teasing her about Valin, or teasing Fitz about all the girls who gave him crush cuffs—wristbands embroidered with their names, hoping he'd wear them and show the whole school he liked them. Sophie couldn't decide which was more annoying.

Halfway through the feast of epic proportions, a dark-haired guy rushed into the room and sank into an empty chair. He was a Vanisher, blinking in and out of sight with every step.

"Sorry I'm late, Mom," he said as Della brought him a platter of food. "I got held up at Customs."

Mom? Fitz and Biana had an older brother? How did she not know that?

Same wavy hair, same square jaw—but he had Della's pale eyes. He was also ridiculously good looking, but he clearly worked hard to look good. Every hair was gelled to perfection, he was built like he went to the gym twice a day, and his ornate cape was immaculate. Not as over the top as Lady Galvin's, but headed that direction.

"You must be the famous Sophie Foster," he said, smiling at her. "I'm Alvar."

She ignored Keefe as he snickered at the word *famous*. "I didn't realize there was another brother."

"I see my family talks about me a lot."

"No—I'm sorry. I—"

"It's fine. That's what I get for moving out. Out of sight, out of mind." He winked at Della. "I guess I need to stop by for dinner more often."

"We know you're busy," Della told him, rumpling his hair as she brought him a glass of fizzleberry wine.

"Yeah, busy juggling two girlfriends," Keefe interrupted.

Alvar grinned. "Three."

"Three?" Della's voice was as horrified as her expression. "Alvar, that's awful."

"Are you kidding? It's awesome!" Keefe corrected. "You're my hero."

Alvar beamed and Della glared at both of them.

"How are things with the ogres?" Alden asked Alvar, changing the subject.

"Drama. They're not happy about the smoke—like it's our fault the humans can't put out their piddly little fires. I can't believe they haven't learned to make Quicksnuff yet."

"What fires?" Sophie asked, not missing the way Alden tensed at her question.

"Just some wildfires," Alden answered after a second.

"Yes," Alvar added, swallowing his wine in one gulp. "And they're certainly not worth sending Emissaries to investigate." He shot Alden a pointed look.

Sophie's breath caught. Alden had told her he was only sent to investigate *suspicious* things. "Are they burning white hot again?"

"Yeah. How did you know?" Alvar asked, frowning.

"Never mind," Alden interrupted. "And why have you been keeping an eye on me?" he asked Alvar.

"I tend to do that when I hear my father's off chasing imaginary enemies. Please tell me you don't buy the conspiracy theories."

"Certainly not without proof." Alden's voice was hard. "But you would be a fool to believe it's not a possibility."

"You really believe the Black Swan exists?"

"Yes. I've seen their handiwork myself."

Sophie watched them stare each other down, wishing she were allowed to read their minds. Something about the "Black Swan" felt familiar. . . .

Alvar shook his head. "Well, I don't buy it."

"That's what that symbol was!" Sophie said as her memories pieced together.

"Symbol?" Alden asked.

Sophie flushed as she realized she had everyone's undivided attention. "Just something I saw on some scrolls Grady had. There was a black, curved swan's neck at the bottom."

Alvar snorted. "Ah, yes—*the sign of the swan*. What a bunch of nonsense."

Alden said something, but Sophie's racing heart drowned out his words.

The *sign.*

The curve of the swan's neck matched the pattern of the fires that wrapped around San Diego. Quinlin had even called it "the sign."

Which meant the fires had something to do with the Black Swan—whatever that was.

"What's Project Moonlark?" she asked quietly.

Alden dropped his fork. "How do you know that term?"

"It was on those scrolls. Grady was surprised I could read it. He said the words were written in cipher runes."

The silence felt so heavy it pressed on her shoulders, but she held Alden's gaze, waiting for his answer.

"That's classified," he finally replied.

Sophie sighed. She was getting tired of important things being *classified.*

"It's also a hoax," Alvar added. "But what's this about a cipher? And why would Grady have scrolls about the Black Swan?"

Sophie was wondering the same thing herself.

"Grady used to look into certain things, back when he was active in the nobility," Alden explained.

"So why does he still have them?" Alvar pressed.

And why was he reading them so recently? Sophie wondered.

"Enough, Alvar. This conversation is over. And everything

that's just been said is classified—is that understood?" Alden waited for everyone at the table to nod. Then his eyes met Sophie's. "I know you find this all very interesting, Sophie, but you need to understand—any unauthorized investigation into these subjects will land you in deep trouble with the Council. So no more questions, okay?"

Sophie nodded, her head buzzing with fear and frustration. She couldn't shake the feeling that all of this had something to do with her—maybe even with how her brain could do such weird things. But she had too much to lose, too many things the Council could take away if she upset them. So she took a deep breath and focused on her plate.

Keefe nudged her. "Earth to Foster—Della asked you what you're doing over the break."

"Sorry." She shook her head, trying to snap back to the present. "I'm not sure yet."

"I hope you'll spend some time over here." Alden glanced at Biana.

Biana nodded. "Anytime she wants to come over."

"Then I'll be here as much as I can," Sophie said, glad for the excuse. She may not be allowed to look into whatever was going on. And she may not be allowed to read Alden's mind. But maybe she could find something out, just by being around.

It was the best plan she had.

TWENTY-NINE

EX REFUSED TO HAVE ANYTHING to do with Fitz and Biana, so Sophie had to alternate spending time with him at Havenfield and hanging out at Everglen. Alden and Della were gone a lot, and they usually came home smelling of smoke. They never talked about it, and Sophie was too afraid to ask questions after Alden's warning—but she wasn't giving up.

If she couldn't get any new information, maybe she could make sense of the pieces she already had. She tried to fit the clues together.

Project Moonlark had to have something to do with the Black Swan—whatever that was. And they had to be behind the fires. But . . . why set fires—especially around humans? What would that accomplish?

The fires consumed her thoughts so much they crept into her dreams. Vivid nightmares of her human family, trapped in their old house, surrounded by fire. She knew it wasn't real, but she still woke up shivering every night. It got so bad she slept with Iggy on her pillow so she wouldn't be alone.

Pretty soon she was counting down the days until school resumed. School was safe. She'd passed her exams. Once school started she would have nothing to worry about.

"Congratulations to everyone who passed their midterms," Dame Alina said during their first orientation. "I hope you enjoyed your six-week vacation, because it's time to get serious. Anyone who got lower than eighty-five percent on their midterms needs to step it up or you will not pass your finals."

Sophie sighed. Aside from the seventy-nine in alchemy, she'd received an eighty-one in elementalism, and an eighty-three in physical education.

"Your Mentors also tell me there are one hundred nine Level Threes who haven't manifested abilities, and more than double that of Level Twos—which is unacceptable. Be prepared to be pushed *much* harder in ability detecting from now on."

Groans chorused through the room.

The next week everyone looked sweaty and wilted as they trudged into study hall after ability detecting. Even Marella's poufy hair had thrown in the towel and drooped against her head.

"What did they do to you guys?" Sophie asked.

"Stuck us in an oven and roasted us for two hours trying to figure out if we were Frosters," Dex grumbled.

"Which none of us were, because frosting is a stupid talent almost no one has," Marella added. She slumped into a chair. "What did you do in remedial studies?"

"Same old boring stuff."

Actually, she'd had a blast. Tiergan had her test her transmitting distance, and it was off the charts. Fitz almost had a heart attack when she transmitted into his mind from all the way across the school. She couldn't blame him for his surprise— even Tiergan didn't know that was possible—but she'd never forget the way his mind actually jerked when she reached it. She hoped he hadn't peed his pants.

She fought off her smile, feeling guilty that everyone else suffered while she had fun. "What are Frosters?"

Dex rested his cheek against the table. "Cryokinetics. They freeze things by manipulating the ice particles in the air. It's totally useless. I don't know why they even test us for it."

"They have to test us for everything," Jensi reminded him.

"That's not true. They don't test us for pyrokinesis," Dex argued.

"Yeah, because that's a forbidden talent," Marella said.

"There are forbidden talents?" Sophie asked.

"Only one," Dex told her. "Mesmers and Inflictors are closely monitored, but Pyrokinetics are forbidden."

"Why?"

"Too dangerous."

"How could it be more dangerous than someone who can inflict pain?"

"Because fire's too unpredictable. No one can truly control it."

"Plus, people died," Marella added.

"Who?" Dex asked.

Marella shrugged. "I don't know. I heard five people died, and that's why it's forbidden now."

"But how can they forbid something like that?" Sophie asked. "Isn't that kind of like forbidding someone to breathe?"

"Nah. Some talents happen on their own as you get older, like telepathy and empathy. Others you would never know you have if something didn't trigger them."

Sophie shook her head. "That still seems wrong. It's like they're not allowed to be who they are."

"Oh, relax. There's only been like twelve—ever—so it's not exactly a huge problem."

"I guess." She wasn't really listening anymore, because she'd remembered what Alvar had said about the fires.

Conspiracy theory.

Could a Pyrokinetic be part of that?

It was an interesting idea—and left her head spinning for

the rest of study hall—but she needed more information. She swung by the library to see if they had any books on the subject. Surely Alden wouldn't mind her doing a little innocent research at school, right?

The Level Two library didn't have any books on Pyrokinetics. Neither did Level Three's. The Level Six librarian finally told her most books on the subject were banned, but she took Sophie's name and promised to check the archives and send anything she found to Sophie's locker. In the meantime, Sophie wondered if Grady and Edaline had any books in the libraries at Havenfield.

The main library downstairs was a bust, but Grady and Edaline had to have personal libraries in their offices on the second floor. Seemed like the perfect place to hide banned books. Only problem: Even after living there for a little more than five months, Sophie wasn't sure she was allowed in that section of the house, and she didn't know how they'd react if they caught her—especially after Alden's warning.

But she couldn't let it go. So she waited until Grady and Edaline were busy outside with a pair of dire wolves and snuck upstairs for a quick peek, promising herself she'd be careful not to leave any trace she'd been there.

The first door she tried was Grady's office. Rolled scrolls were stuffed in bins, a mountain of paperwork littered the desk, and books were shoved haphazardly on the shelves. No pictures, no knickknacks—nothing personal to make the place feel warm. But there were empty spaces where they might have been.

The bookshelves were filled with law and history books. They probably talked about Pyrokinetics in there somewhere, but Sophie didn't have time to scan through them all. The scrolls tempted her, but they were rolled up too tight to read, and she was afraid he'd be able to tell if she unrolled them. She wasn't brave enough to flip through the papers on his desk either, in case they were in a special order. She hoped Edaline's office would be more helpful.

She'd assumed the door across the hall was Edaline's, so she almost gasped when she stepped into a dim bedroom. Lacy curtains blocked most of the sunlight, crystal chandeliers were dulled with dust, and there were scattered remnants left behind from childhood: stuffed unicorns, Prattles' pins strung on lanyards, dolls, books. On the desk was a framed photo of a beautiful girl.

Jolie.

Her blond hair hung in soft curls to her waist, and she had Edaline's turquoise eyes and Grady's striking bone structure. She wore a white Level Six uniform in the photo, so she was probably sixteen when it was taken. Next to it was another picture: Grady, Edaline, and Jolie, when she was close to Sophie's age, standing in a breathtaking garden. It was the old them— happy, wearing the capes of the nobility—before their lives were struck by tragedy. Sophie could have spent the whole day drinking in the glimpse of who they used to be, but she knew this was the worst place they could find her. She peeled her eyes away and left.

The last room had obviously been Edaline's office, but it had turned into the place where leftover junk went to die. Stacks of locked trunks littered the floor, covered with piles of folded linens, unopened presents, and random objects she couldn't identify. A huge bin of unopened letters blocked most of the doorway, so Sophie couldn't get inside—which was fine. The bookshelves were full of thick, dusty volumes, and anything she disturbed would be too obvious.

She'd have to figure out another way to find books on Pyrokinetics. Maybe Biana would let her look through the library at Everglen—but she'd have to come up with a good excuse, in case Alden found them in there. She was on murky ground, but she was close to something—she could feel it. Her mind wouldn't let her drop it until she figured out what it was.

THIRTY

SOPHIE GAGGED AS SHE LICKED OPEN her locker. "Elwin's choice again?" she whined to Dex. In the three weeks since midterm they'd already suffered through burned hair and sweaty feet flavors. Elwin was on a roll.

Dex plugged his nose as he licked his panel, but he still winced. "Ugh, that's exactly how I imagine a fart would taste."

Sophie giggled and grabbed a small scroll waiting on her top shelf—a special assignment from the Universe Mentors. Each list had six stars that fit some sort of pattern, and each prodigy was supposed to bottle a sample of the starlight from each, figure out what the pattern was, and choose a seventh star that fit with the others. She and Dex had plans to work together that night.

Dex took her to Moonglade: a wide, round meadow filled with thousands of fireflies flickering in the darkness.

"Everyone else goes to Siren Rock," Dex explained as he set up the stellarscope, which looked like a bent, upside-down spyglass. "But it's so crowded there it's hard to find a space to work. Plus, the view's better here." He pointed to the sky, where billions of stars sparkled through the inky black, then handed her a thick wad of star maps. "Finding stars takes forever, so let's tag team it. First star on my list is Amaranthis."

Sophie stared at the sky, following trails she'd already memorized. "It's right there—fourth star to the left of Lambentine."

Dex's jaw dropped. "How did you do that?"

"Photographic memory. Remember?"

"I know. But . . . the stars?"

She nodded smugly.

"Wow—well, awesome." He stuffed the maps into his bag, and attached a small glass bottle to a spout at the wider end of the stellarscope. "Want to go first?"

She took the scope from him and held it up to her eyes. "How does this work?"

"It's easy. You find the star and use the knobs to isolate it." He came up behind her and used one arm to level the scope. His other arm wrapped around her and his hand slid her fingers down to a cluster of dials. "Sorry, um, is this okay?" he asked as she stiffened.

"Sure."

But it was strange having him so close. She could feel her cheeks warm and was glad it was too dark for him to see her blush.

Dex cleared his throat. "Did you find Amaranthis?"

"Yep."

"Good. Then turn the knobs until you see the star change color, and flip the lever by your thumb. The stellarscope will do the rest."

She did as he said, and a bright purple flash filled the bottle. The glass clinked as the scope sealed the light in.

It only took them a few minutes to fill bottles with scarlet light from Rubini, yellow light from Ororo, pale blue light from Azulejo, deep orange light from Cobretola, and dark blue light from Indigeen.

Dex stared at the six twinkling bottles, scratching his head. "I don't see a pattern."

"It's the colors of the spectrum." She rearranged the bottles in the right order. "Red, orange, yellow, blue, indigo, and violet. What's missing?"

"Green! Can you find Zelenie?"

She pointed to an isolated star to the left. "There."

He bottled the deep green glow. "This'll be the first time I get it right. I usually just pick a random star and try to bluff."

Sophie laughed and dug her list from her pocket. Her stars were much harder to find, and she had to really push her memory, but eventually she had bottles of silver, gold, black, white, copper, and green light.

"Any idea what the pattern is?" Dex asked

"I'm not sure." Something felt familiar, a shadow of an idea, not formed enough to make sense. She poured through her memories, scrounging for the clue she was missing. The pieces clicked. "Elementine."

"What's the pattern?"

"I don't know, but I know Elementine is right." She grabbed the stellarscope.

"Are you sure? I've never heard of it before."

"I think I would know better than you. Besides, why would I make that up?"

"Good point."

She followed strange trails through the stars as the minutes ticked by. "I know it's there."

She focused on a dark space and fiddled with the dials.

"I don't see anything," Dex told her.

"I think it's just *really* far away."

More turning and adjusting. Still nothing. Dex was getting fidgety when she finally said, "There!" and flipped the latch.

The stellarscope hummed, then turned white hot. Sophie yelped, dropping the scope.

"What happened?"

"Ow, ow, ow!" She waved her hands, trying to cool the burning, but the pain made her eyes water.

"Let me see." Dex took a jar of moonlight from his bag and

grabbed her wrists, shining the light on them. "Whoa. Are you okay?"

She wanted to be brave, but her eyes teared when she saw the purple welts on her palms.

"What should I do?" Dex asked, sounding frantic.

She tried to think through the pain. She could go home, but she wasn't sure how Grady and Edaline could help. What she really needed was a doctor.

Her face fell as she realized what she had to do. "Can you get my Imparter from my satchel?" She'd been carrying it with her ever since the cheating disaster.

Dex dug through her bag until he found the silver square. "Who are we calling?"

She sighed. "Elwin."

THIRTY-ONE

NOW YOU'RE CALLING ME AT HOME and dragging me out of bed? Maybe it was better when you were afraid of me," Elwin teased. His smile faded when she showed him the blackish-purple blisters on her hands. "How did you do that?"

"I was just trying to bottle the light from Elementine."

"Elementine?" He pulled a small pot from his satchel and spread a thick green salve over the burns. "Never heard of it."

"I told you it wasn't real," Dex said.

"But I found it," she insisted as Elwin sprinkled purple powder on top of the salve. "The scope got really hot when I flipped the latch, and it burned me."

Elwin wrapped her hands with thick blue cloth. "I've never

heard of *that* happening. It's always an adventure with you, Sophie—I'll give you that."

The annoying part was she couldn't argue. Why did weird things keep happening to her?

"Is that helping the pain?" Elwin asked.

"Yes. Thanks."

"Good." He poured a bottle of Youth over the cloth, soaking it through. "Did you bottle the light?"

"I don't know." In all the chaos she hadn't bothered to look.

"I'll check it." Dex ran over to the scope, which was still where Sophie had dropped it. "There's something in it, but it's weird."

"Don't touch it," Elwin ordered. "Last thing I need is another patient."

Sophie hung her head. "I'm sorry I woke you."

"Don't worry about it. Gives me a good story to tell tomorrow."

She sighed. Marella and Keefe were going to have a field day with this.

Elwin unwrapped her hands. The blisters were gone, but the skin was red and raw. He stroked his chin. "That should've worked better."

"It doesn't hurt anymore."

"That's because the salve numbs you. I'm going to have to make a stronger balm. Wait right here."

She nodded miserably. Where would she go?

Elwin glittered away, and Dex plopped beside her.

"You don't have to wait with me."

"Like I would leave you in the middle of nowhere at night, injured. What kind of friend do you think I am?"

"But you must be cold."

"Nope. I can regulate my body temperature. See?" He touched her cheek, and she was surprised at how warm his skin was. "Want me to teach you how to do it tomorrow?"

"I can't. I'm going to Fitz and Biana's."

"Ugh. Another day at the palace. Be sure to wear your crown."

"Are you ever going to stop that?"

"Doesn't look like it."

"They're my friends. I wish you could be a little nicer about it."

"Hey, I hold a lot back."

She laughed. "Somehow I doubt that."

He ripped a handful of grass and tossed it away. "You just like seeing Wonderboy. Please don't tell me you have some stupid crush on him."

"Of course not." She could feel her cheeks blush and was glad once again for the darkness.

Dex ripped more grass by the roots. "Then what is it? Why do you like him?"

"He's the one who found me." As soon as the words left her mouth, she realized her slip.

Dex stiffened. "That's a story you haven't told me."

"I know." She tried not to talk about her past—it brought up too many questions she didn't have the answers to.

"There's a lot you don't tell me, isn't there? Like your session in the Level Four wing. It's not remedial studies, is it?" He waited for her to deny it.

She didn't.

"What do you really do there?"

"I can't tell you."

"Does Wonderboy know?"

She sighed. "Yes."

He was quiet for a long time, mutilating more innocent blades of grass. "Well, that stinks."

"I didn't tell him—if that's what you're thinking. He's just . . . involved . . . so he gets to know certain things."

They sat in silence, destroying the grass and waiting for the other to speak. Dex finally sighed. "I'm sorry. I'm being a jerk."

"I'm sorry too. I hate keeping secrets from you. You're my best friend."

His head snapped up. "I'm your best friend?"

She shrugged, looking away. "If you want to be."

"Are you kidding? Of course!"

She smiled. "Do you think you could do me a favor, then?"

"Sure. Anything."

"Could you try to keep the Fitz bashing to a minimum?"

"Ugh. Anything but that."

"Please, Dex?"

He glowered at the ground. "Fine. But I'm only doing it for you—I still won't like him."

She smiled at his stubbornness. "Thank you. That means a lot."

Light flashed in front of them and Elwin reappeared, clutching a pot of ointment. "Okay, let's see those hands again."

Sophie crinkled her nose as he spread the golden sludge across the burns. "Ew, Elwin. What's in that stuff?"

"Trust me, you don't want to know. It needs to sit for a minute, so let's see this starlight you bottled." He knelt next to the stellarscope and his brows furrowed.

"What is it?" Dex asked.

"I don't know." He tapped the bottle quickly with one fingertip. "It's cold. What star did you say this came from?"

"Elementine."

"Doesn't sound familiar. Well, don't do anything with this until you show Sir Astin. And be careful." He gently removed the bottle from the scope and handed it to Dex. Then he wrapped the bottle in one of his rags and tucked it in Sophie's bag. He checked Sophie's hands again, and this time the burns were totally gone.

"Thanks, Elwin," she mumbled.

"That's what I'm here for. You guys okay now?"

"Yep. We're going home."

"Good. Come by my office tomorrow, Sophie. I want to make sure I didn't miss anything."

She sighed. He should set up a permanent spot for her.

"All right, my work is done here. Get home safe. Oh, and, Sophie? Better wash your hands, like, twenty times."

Sophie didn't feel like getting into the whole long story, so when Grady and Edaline asked how her night went, she just shrugged and said, "Good." Then she took the longest, hottest, soapiest shower of her life. She planned to tell them in the morning, but one of the griffins escaped, so she figured she'd tell them about it when she got home. Maybe by then her Mentors would have explained what went wrong.

She got to school early to stop by Elwin's office discreetly. He was pleased with the healing but made her drink sour medicine just to be safe.

She'd planned to ask Sir Conley about the strange starlight during elementalism, but he had her bottling flames, and she almost caught her cape on fire—twice. He gave her a thick, boring-looking book on firecatching to read before finals. Stupid cape.

The worry caught up with her in the cafeteria. It seemed she was the only one who had any problems with the starlight assignment, which did not bode well for her grade. It didn't help that as soon as she set out her bottles, Sir Astin frowned. "Where's your seventh star?"

She bit her lip. She'd been hoping he wouldn't count. "Something weird happened. The stellarscope burned me when I bottled it."

His eyes widened, but he shook his head. "No—that's absurd. It couldn't be. . . ."

"Do you want to see the bottle? I think there's something wrong with it, but you tell me."

She dug the bundle out of her satchel. The icy chill stung her fingers even through the thick fabric, and it was heavier than the other bottles, almost like there was something solid inside. The glow was blinding when she unwrapped it.

Sir Astin was always pale, but he looked downright ghostly as he jumped back and screamed, "Don't move!"

She froze. "Should I wrap it back up?"

"I said don't move! I need to think." He started pacing, mumbling incoherently.

"Okay, will you please tell me what this is? You're freaking me out."

He laughed darkly. "Have you ever heard of Quintessence?"

"The fifth element? I thought that was just a myth."

"I'm sure what you've heard is a myth. But the element is real. Quintessence is light in its truest, most powerful form. Under the right conditions, that little bottle could blow up this whole building—or worse."

She gulped. What was worse than blowing up a building? "What do we do?"

"I have no idea!" He wrung his hands. "How did this happen?"

"I don't know. I was just trying to fit the pattern."

"The pattern was metals! The stars on the list have metallic-toned light. You should have bottled something bronze or brass. Not *this*!" He gestured wildly at the bottle.

Her cheeks flamed. Now that he mentioned it, the pattern did seem pretty obvious. "I'm sorry. For some reason I thought I needed to find Elementine."

He froze. "Where did you learn that name?"

"I don't know. Probably from one of those star maps I memorized."

"No, Sophie. I never taught you that name. No one teaches that name." His voice was hushed—barely audible.

That explained why Dex and Elwin had never heard of it. "But I had to learn it here," she insisted. "How else would I know it?"

"I have no idea. Elementine is one of the five unmapped stars. Only the Councillors know their exact locations—and *no one* is allowed to bottle their light." He swallowed loudly. "You've broken a *very* serious law, Sophie. This will merit a tribunal to decide how you should be punished."

THIRTY-TWO

THE HEARING WAS IN ETERNALIA, IN Tribunal Hall. A blue banner flew from the dome, just like it had the first time Fitz took Sophie there. But this time it was for her.

Sophie sat next to Alden on a raised platform facing the twelve empty thrones of the Councillors. Behind her sat Grady and Edaline, Dex, Sir Astin, Dame Alina, and Elwin— everyone remotely involved with the Quintessence incident. The rest of the enormous room was empty. The proceedings had been closed to the public, a rare procedure for a tribunal. But Alden explained that anything involving Quintessence had to be kept top secret.

Each throne had a name carved across the top. Oralie's

had velvet cushions and a heart-shaped back covered in pink tourmaline. Kenric's was sturdy and simple, made of polished wood encrusted with large pieces of amber. Bronte's was plain silver dotted with onyx. The rest were names she'd never heard: Clarette, Velia, Terik, Liora, Emery, Ramira, Darek, Noland, Zarina. Their names alone were intimidating. She tugged out an eyelash and flicked it away.

A mere two hours had passed since the moment Sophie showed Sir Astin the glowing bottle, but it felt like everything had changed. Foxfire was evacuated—a first in its three-thousand-year history. A special task force moved the Quintessence to an undisclosed location. Now she sat in the capital city—on trial for violating a major law. Bronte was probably salivating over the chance to convict her.

Sophie sat up straighter as a dozen goblins marched into the room and stationed themselves in front of the thrones. She remembered them from Lumenaria, but she'd forgotten how huge they were.

"Bodyguards for the Councillors," Alden explained.

Her eyes focused on the strange swordlike weapons slung through their belts, and she couldn't help wondering what the Councillors needed protection from. Alden was always saying how safe their world was.

A loud fanfare blasted through the room, and everyone rose as the Councillors appeared in front of their thrones. Dripping in jewels, draped in gleaming silver capes, and crowned with circlets, they made human royalty look like amateurs. Sophie's lunch churned in her stomach.

"Please be seated," announced a Councillor with shoulder-length black hair and eyes that matched the sapphires in his crown. His throne said Emery across the top. "Thank you for coming on such short notice. We shall begin with you, Miss Foster."

She stood and gave the world's most ungraceful curtsy. Oralie moved to Sophie's side, placing one hand on her shoulder and holding her hand with the other.

"Answer my questions honestly and there will be no problems," Emery warned.

Sophie nodded, the fear so consuming she wondered if she would be sick. She kept her eyes away from Bronte, knowing if she caught his cold gaze, she might lose it.

"Where did you learn of the existence and location of Elementine?"

"I don't know." Her voice trembled.

Emery glanced at Oralie. She nodded.

"What made you look for it?"

"My Universe homework."

Sir Astin coughed behind her, like he was unhappy with her answer.

"What was it about your homework that made you think of it?" Emery asked.

"Honestly? It just sounded right."

Oralie nodded again and Sophie finally understood. Oralie was reading her emotions—a living, breathing lie detector.

"Have you any idea what to use Quintessence for?" Emery asked. "Consider your answer carefully, Miss Foster—this is crucial."

She racked her brain. There was something there—an idea so fuzzy she couldn't make sense of it. "I don't know."

"Oralie?" Emery asked when Oralie frowned.

"She's confused," she said in her fragile voice. "But not lying."

Emery nodded and closed his eyes, placing his hands against his temples.

The silence stretched endlessly, and Sophie wondered if she'd said something wrong. Finally, Emery opened his eyes. "Thank you, Miss Foster. You may be seated."

Her legs felt like Jell-O, but somehow she hobbled back to her seat beside Alden.

"Sir Astin," Emery said, and Sir Astin jumped out of his chair. Oralie returned to her throne. A Telepath could monitor Sir Astin's thoughts for honesty. His mind wasn't impenetrable, like Sophie's. "What stars was she assigned?"

"They were, uh . . ." Sir Astin cleared his throat and fidgeted. "I believe they were . . ."

Emery's sigh echoed off the walls. "Do you remember, Miss Foster?"

She leaped to her feet and gave another awkward curtsy.

"Yes. It was Argento, Auriferria, Pennisi, Merkariron, Styggis, and Achromian."

Emery closed his eyes. "Can you repeat those one more time, slower?"

She did, noticing that Kenric was plotting the stars on a map. He sucked in a breath.

"Who created this list?" Emery demanded, glancing at Kenric.

"I'm not certain," Sir Astin admitted, cowering. "All the Universe Mentors submit them, and it wasn't one of the lists I made."

"That's convenient," Bronte scoffed, and Sophie's gaze followed his voice, against her better judgment. She shivered. He looked even more frightening seated at his jeweled throne.

Emery held up his hand and Bronte fell silent. "Who assigned her that list?" The velvet folds of his voice hardened, but his face remained expressionless.

"The lists are assigned at random," Sir Astin stammered. "It was pure chance."

Emery closed his eyes, rubbing his temples. "Are you aware of any connection between those stars and Elementine?"

Sir Astin shook his head. "I know nothing about Elementine except its name."

"Thank you." Emery motioned for everyone to sit. The room fell silent again.

"What's going on?" Sophie whispered to Alden.

"Emery mediates their discussion telepathically. He'll only speak once they've reached a consensus, so that the Council always presents a united front."

She supposed that made sense, but she felt sorry for Emery. He looked like he would need some strong aspirin after this.

"Enough!" Emery ordered, holding his hands out like stop signs after what felt like an eternity. "We have reached a decision. It's not unanimous"—he glared at Bronte—"but in this situation it does not need to be. Please rise, Miss Foster."

She leaned on Alden for support.

"What you did was very dangerous—and violates one of our most fundamental laws. But we do not believe your actions were intentional, and because of that, you will not be held accountable. You will return to Foxfire tomorrow, and no mention will be made of this tribunal."

Sophie released the breath she'd been holding. Alden squeezed her hand.

She was safe. It was over.

"No one will know the details of this incident, or of Miss Foster's involvement," Emery continued, addressing the others in the room. "The official story will be that a suspicious substance was found, removed, and destroyed. No further details will be given. Is that understood?"

Everyone murmured agreement.

"Good. And, Lord Alden?"

Alden held Emery's gaze and nodded.

"Thank you for your assistance with this matter." Emery motioned for everyone to rise. "That concludes the tribunal."

"I'm so sorry," Sophie said for the millionth time to Grady, Edaline, and Dex as they met her and Alden outside Tribunal Hall. She wished she'd never have to set foot in the terrifying building again. But she knew she'd be back at the end of the year. Her knees shook at the thought.

Dex grinned. "Are you kidding? This has been the coolest day *ever*! I finally got to see Eternalia. Foxfire was evacuated! I missed the Great Gulon Incident three years ago, but I bet it had nothing on this."

"What was the Great Gulon Incident?" she asked.

Alden cleared his throat. "Perhaps we can discuss this another time? There's still a few things Sophie and I need to do."

Grady and Alden exchanged a quick look, and Grady nodded. "We'll take Dex home. Where should I tell his family he's been all afternoon?"

The adults got their stories straight, and Dex leaned toward Sophie, a huge smile dimpling his cheeks. "Will Fitz get to know what *really* happened today?"

"I doubt it."

"Excellent. I finally know something Wonderboy doesn't."

She couldn't help laughing.

"Come on, Dex, time to go," Grady interrupted. He looked at Sophie and smiled. "See you at home, kiddo."

Everyone flashed away, leaving Sophie alone with Alden.

"Come on, Sophie. Let's take a walk."

THIRTY-THREE

ALDEN LED HER ALONG THE BANKS of the river that cut a winding path through the heart of Eternalia. "Do you know what these trees are called?" he asked, pointing to the mammoth trunks all around them. Burnt sienna bark braided up to the hunter green leaves, which fanned out like paintbrushes.

"No," Sophie admitted. She'd seen them around—there were even a few at Havenfield—but she never thought to ask what they were.

"Their full name is *Purfoliage palmae*, but everyone calls them the Pures, because their leaves filter the air, keeping out any pollution or impurities. Every house and city has at least one to keep the air clean, and with so many growing here, Eternalia has the freshest, crispest air in the world." He frowned at the sky, where a tinge of gray fuzzed through the blue. "Well, it does when there isn't a fire nearby—but that's not important. Do you wonder why I ask?"

She nodded.

"I was thinking how strange it is that you don't know the name of one of our most common trees—and yet you knew the name and location of a star only a handful of us have ever heard of, and only the Councillors know how to find."

She stared at her feet. "I don't know why. Honestly."

"I know, Sophie. No one thinks what happened is your fault. But we are concerned about what else might be stored away in that mind of yours."

Her head snapped up. "You think there's other stuff?"

"It's possible. You knew how to read the cipher runes on those scrolls, didn't you?"

Her blood ran cold. Was *that* what Quinlin meant about her being a Keeper, all those months ago? "But . . . how would it get there?"

"We don't know." The hesitation in his voice said otherwise, and it made her desperate to shove into his thoughts. But she was in enough trouble already. And maybe she didn't want to know. . . .

"Is that what Emery said to you at the end?" She remembered Alden's quick nod. "He told you something telepathically, didn't he?"

"You are observant, aren't you?" He sighed. "He was giving me another instruction for you."

Her stomach lurched. "Is it bad?"

"Of course not. Come with me."

He took her hand and leaped them to the edge of Eternalia, where a row of identical crystal castles glowed pink and orange in the sunset.

"Where are we?" Sophie asked as he led her toward the farthest one.

"These are the Councillors' offices. You have an appointment with Councillor Terik."

Her legs went weak from nerves, and she missed a step on the way to the door. Alden steadied her before she fell.

The door opened before Alden knocked, and an elf with wavy brown hair and an emerald-encrusted circlet examined Sophie with curious, cobalt blue eyes. She dropped a shaky curtsy as Alden bowed.

"Do you want me to stay?" Alden asked.

Terik waved him away. "It works better one-on-one—you know that."

"Then I'll be back in ten minutes." He squeezed Sophie's shoulder. "Just relax, Sophie. No reason to worry."

She nodded, her mouth too dry to speak.

Terik led her inside, to an oval sitting room off the main

entryway. He motioned for her to take a seat in one of the plush armchairs, and sat across from her. "Did Alden explain why you're here?"

She shook her head, unable to find her voice.

He laughed, a soft, pleasing sound, which rang off the crystal walls and lifted the heavy atmosphere of the room. "There's no need to be afraid. What's about to happen is quite an honor. Parents beg me to do this for their children and I refuse. Causes too many problems." He sighed. "It's quite a burden being the only Descryer."

He seemed to be waiting for a response, so she nodded again.

"You have no idea what that means, do you?"

She hesitated a second before shaking her head.

"How delightfully refreshing. It means I can sense potential. So you can see why parents are always clamoring for me to meet their children. I used to agree, but then I noticed how often it backfired. Potential is nothing if it's never lived up to, now is it?"

She cleared her throat, realizing she hadn't said a word since she'd arrived. "No."

"She speaks! I was beginning to wonder if you'd forgotten how." He smiled. "I know you're nervous, Sophie, but I promise, you have no reason to be. The Council decided that—given today's unusual circumstances—it might be a good idea for me to see what I sense about you. It's painless, I promise. All I have to do is hold your hands and concentrate. Do you think you can handle that?" He extended his hands to her.

She hesitated half a second before placing her hands in his. A tiny part of her feared what he would find, but she also understood that this wasn't optional. She took a deep breath as he closed his eyes, counting the seconds to stay calm.

Five hundred thirteen seconds passed before he opened his eyes again.

"Fascinating," he whispered, staring into space.

Another 327 seconds passed before he released her hands and stood up. "Incredible."

"Am I allowed to know what you sensed?" she asked quietly.

"I would tell you if I knew what to say. I felt something—something strong. But I couldn't tell what it was."

She already knew the answer, but she had to ask. "Has that ever happened before?"

"No. It's definitely a first." He moved toward the door, opening it before Alden could knock.

Alden glanced between Terik and Sophie. "How did it go?"

"Interesting," Terik murmured, his mind far away.

When he said no more, Alden turned to Sophie. "Are you ready to go home?"

She nodded. Terik didn't say goodbye, and he was still standing there, lost in his own thoughts, as the light swept them away.

Alden handed her a parcel wrapped in green paper when they reached Havenfield. "The Council also insisted you keep one of these."

She unwrapped the thick teal book, running her fingers across the silver bird etched into the cover. It had long legs like a crane, sweeping tail feathers like a peacock, and a curved neck like a swan. "It's beautiful."

"It's a memory log." He opened the book to the smooth white pages inside. "Has Tiergan taught you how to project?"

She nodded.

"Good. The Council wants you to keep track of your memories—to see if we find any that aren't yours."

"How do I do that?" They couldn't expect her to record every memory she'd ever had. That would be impossible.

"Just record anything that seems important. And record all the dreams you remember."

She bit her lip. "Even the nightmares?"

"Have you been having nightmares?"

"Sometimes." Since school started she'd stopped having them every night, but at least once a week she still woke up in a cold sweat. "Sometimes I dream that my family is trapped in a burning house, trying to get out." She shivered as the terrifying images flashed through her mind.

Alden was quiet for a second before he said softly, "Your family is safe, Sophie. You have no reason to worry about them."

She met his eyes. "You won't tell me what's going on with the fires?"

He took a step back, like he needed distance between her and her question.

"Do the fires have something to do with me?" She held her breath as he seemed to debate about his answer.

"I . . . don't know," he whispered. "Which is why this memory log is so important. I'll be checking it regularly to see if there's anything useful. Make sure you record those nightmares."

She nodded.

"There's a good girl." He pulled her in for a one-armed hug, then froze. "You haven't told Grady and Edaline about those dreams, have you?"

"No. Why?"

"Jolie died in a fire. Didn't they tell you?"

She shook her head. "They never talk about her. I don't think they know that I know."

Sadness crept across his face in thin lines. "It's hard for them. You can't imagine how hard. Death is such a common thing for humans. For us . . ." He stared into the distance. "Her fiancé's house caught fire. He tried to save her, but there wasn't time. He barely made it out alive, and even then . . ." He didn't finish, but something in his eyes told her it did not end well.

Sophie tried not to imagine the horror he was describing. Burning to death—the thought alone made her shudder. "I won't mention the dreams, I promise."

"Thank you." He smiled sadly, and left her.

She went straight to her room and closed the door.

Projecting her nightmares into the memory log was easy. Seeing them so vividly was awful. Her whole body shook as she stared at her terrified family surrounded by smoke and flames. She slammed the log shut, hiding it behind her bookshelf so no one could find it.

Desperate to replace those horrifying images, she grabbed her old scrapbook and sank onto her bed. She hadn't touched it since the day Dex looked through it.

She never made it past the cover.

Edaline found her later, still staring at the closed album. "Everything okay?"

Sophie jumped, pressing the scrapbook into her chest. "I'm fine." Her voice sounded sharper than she meant it to be.

Edaline frowned. "Dinner's waiting downstairs."

The thought of food turned her stomach. "I'm not really hungry. But thanks."

"Oh . . . okay." Edaline sat next to her on the bed. "Did something happen with Alden? You can tell me." She reached out to stroke Sophie's arm, but Sophie flinched—afraid Edaline might touch the scrapbook.

Edaline retracted her hand, looking anywhere but Sophie.

"Sorry, I didn't—" Sophie started.

Edaline waved away the apology, forcing a smile on her lips as she stood. "Don't worry about it. You want to be alone. I'll send some dinner up later, in case you get hungry."

Sophie watched her leave, hating herself for hurting Edaline's feelings. But she'd have to set it right later. Right now she had bigger problems.

She took a deep breath and forced herself to look at the photo mounted to the cover of the scrapbook again, to make sure her eyes weren't playing tricks on her.

Bile rose in her throat.

There she was, eleven years old, building a sand castle on the beach. But it wasn't an imaginary castle, like she'd thought it was at the time.

She recognized that castle.

She'd been inside it this afternoon.

The twisted turrets. The sweeping arches. It was an exact replica of the crystal castles in Eternalia.

So how could she build a model of it a year before she knew it existed?

THIRTY-FOUR

THE COUNCIL WAS RIGHT. INFORMATION had been planted in her brain.

The idea was too huge, she couldn't make it fit inside her head.

Her hands shook as she ripped the photo off the scrapbook. She was violating everything Alden told her—everything the Council *ordered*—but if anyone found out, her life would never be the same again. She couldn't face that.

She slipped the photo into the middle of a thick book and shoved the book among a dozen other thick books on the highest shelf. It should be safe there. For now.

All she wanted was to curl into a ball and never get up again, but she didn't have time. Someone stuck stuff in her brain and she needed to find those memories—before they got her in trouble again.

What had made her think of Elementine?

She pulled out her star maps and plotted the stars on her list on one page—like she'd seen Kenric do at the tribunal. The six stars formed two lines, pointing straight to Elementine.

The room swam around her.

It couldn't be an accident. That list must've been made specifically for her. Which meant someone *wanted* her to find Elementine.

But who? And why?

And what would they want next?

She stayed up all night projecting anything she could think of into her memory log, but when the sun rose she was no closer to the answer. All she knew for sure was that she had to keep it secret. If the Council found out, they'd never let her stay at Foxfire—Bronte would make sure of it. They might even decide she was dangerous, and she didn't want to think about what they'd do then.

Especially since she couldn't be sure she *wasn't* dangerous. She'd almost blown up the school—or worse. What if that had been the plan when someone gave her that list?

Nowhere seemed safe enough to hide the memory log, so she stuffed it in the bottom of her satchel to keep with her at all times. None of her friends noticed how stressed she was. They were used to her difficulties in PE, and during lunch they were too distracted by all the pressure they were getting to manifest special abilities. It wasn't until telepathy that she wished she'd stayed home sick.

"Did you sleep at all last night?" Tiergan asked as she slumped into her chair.

"No." There was no point lying. She'd seen her reflection. Her dark circles rivaled Edaline's.

"I expected as much." He cleared his throat. "Alden told me what happened yesterday."

She should have guessed that. Which meant he knew about her special assignment. She gripped her satchel, like holding it tighter would protect the secrets inside.

"Have you started the memory log?" he asked, confirming her fear.

She hesitated for a second before she nodded.

"I assume you don't want to show me."

Silence stretched between them until Tiergan removed a black pathfinder from his pocket. "Concentrate," he commanded, and a wave of blue light swept them away.

Noise hammered into her brain as the scenery glittered back into substance.

"Remember to shield," Tiergan shouted as she covered her ears, trying to squeeze out the pain.

She closed her eyes and pushed against the noise with her mind. The chaos quieted and she started breathing again. Tiergan led her to a bench and she sank down, exhausted.

He plopped beside her. "Welcome to Los Angeles. Actually, I believe they call this place Hollywood."

She'd been away from humans for almost six months—long enough to forget the traffic, pollution, and trash. It turned her stomach. "Um, aren't we a little conspicuous?" She pulled on her stupid cape.

"Here?" Across the street Spider-Man and Batman posed for pictures outside Mann's Chinese Theatre.

"No, I guess not." If anything, they blended right in. "What are we doing here?"

"Breaking the law." He held up the pathfinder, casting blue beams of light on the ground. "Only blue crystals take you to the Forbidden Cities, and only certain members of the nobility are allowed to have them. Mine was issued back when I worked for the Council, and I 'forgot' to give it back when I resigned. So this trip is our little secret, okay?"

She nodded.

"I come here sometimes. I'm not supposed to, but it helps to see them in real life." He pointed to the humans wandering the streets, oblivious to the elves sitting among them. "We've cut ourselves off—vanished into the light. Makes it easy to forget how similar we are. Or could be—if they weren't so stubborn."

He paused, like he was waiting for her to speak. But she didn't know what to say.

"Do you miss your human life?" he asked.

She thought about the headaches, the fear of discovery, how out of place she always felt, and opened her mouth to say, "No." But, "Sometimes I miss my family," slipped out instead.

His expression softened. "That's good, Sophie. You, of all people, should never forget where you came from. If you ever need reminding, let me know and I'll bring you here."

She nodded.

"Do you wonder why you were hidden with humans?"

Her mind darted unwillingly to Prentice. "My real parents must've wanted to get rid of me," she whispered.

He closed his eyes, and pain seeped into his features. "Trust me, Sophie—no one 'got rid of' you. Don't you know how special you are?"

"Yeah, special enough to have secret information stored in my brain without my permission," she mumbled. Which was probably why Prentice got rid of her. Who'd want a freak for a daughter?

Or maybe he was the one who planted the information. Her hands clenched into fists.

"That's not the only reason you're special, believe me." Tiergan cleared the strain out of his voice. "Have you remembered anything else since the tribunal?"

She watched an ant crawl across the dirty pavement.

"I understand if you aren't ready to talk about it. But don't be afraid to explore your memories. They might be the only way to understand who you really are."

"What if I'm someone bad?" she whispered, putting words to the fear that had consumed her since yesterday.

"I can assure you you're not," he promised.

She shook her head, refusing to believe him. "What do you know about Prentice?"

Tiergan shifted in his seat.

"I know that's classified information, but I think I deserve to know who he was." She took an extra breath for courage. "He was my father, wasn't he?"

Tiergan sucked in a breath. "Of course not. Why would you think that?"

"He was a Keeper, and he was exiled because of me. It's not hard to put the pieces together."

"Sophie, look at me," Tiergan said, waiting until she did. "Prentice was exiled because he was hiding your existence— not because he was responsible for it."

"What do you mean?"

He hesitated, and she could tell he was warring with himself, deciding how much to say.

"Please," she whispered. "No one will tell me *anything* about my past."

He sighed and looked away. When he spoke, his words were hurried, like he was forcing them out before he could change his mind. "Prentice was a Keeper for a group called the Black Swan, and the information he was hiding was *you*. Where to find you. I'd warned Prentice there would be consequences for helping the Black Swan, but he didn't listen. And when he was captured, he sacrificed his sanity to keep you hidden. Now he lives in exile, his mind a shattered, useless mess."

"That's why you're so upset with Alden?"

He nodded. "Alden was the one who found him. I pleaded for mercy on Prentice's behalf, but the Council demanded to know what Prentice hid in his mind, so Alden oversaw something called a memory break. It's a type of probe that shatters someone's sanity in order to access their hidden memories."

Sophie shivered. She couldn't picture Alden carrying out that kind of order—unless he knew he was right. But why wouldn't Prentice just tell them where she was? "What exactly is the Black Swan?"

"Something our society doesn't know what to do with." He wrung the edge of his cape between his hands. "The name is a metaphor. For thousands of years humans were convinced there was no such thing as a black swan. So when a black swan was found, it became a symbol of something that shouldn't exist but does. A small group of insurgents in our society adopted the name. A brewing rebellion—a black swan—in a society where rebellion isn't supposed to exist."

"How do you know so much about them?" she had to ask.

"You're not the only one with secrets you'd rather not share."

Sophie swallowed, realizing how little she knew about her favorite Mentor. He couldn't be involved in anything . . . wrong, could he?

No. Tiergan was one of the kindest people she knew. He could never be bad.

Bad.

"So, the Black Swan are the bad guys, right?" she whispered, staring at her hands. "And if they have something to do with me . . ." She couldn't bear to follow the thought to its end.

Tiergan took her hands and waited for her to meet his eyes. "Whatever the Black Swan is, it has nothing to do with who you are. When I look at you, I only see good. You came forward when you cheated—you even chose to serve your detention when you didn't have to. Whatever's in your mind is just information. And whatever secrets lie in your past do not change who you are now. I have no doubt you'll make the right decisions, whenever the time comes to make them."

His words felt more healing than the balm Elwin used to cool her burns. Her voice was thick when she spoke. "Thank you, Tiergan. I'll try to remember that."

She wasn't sure what to do with the other things he told her. The bits and pieces belonged to a puzzle she didn't know if she wanted to solve. For now she tucked them away, clinging to the hope that Tiergan was right—that she was good. As long as that was true, she could survive pretty much anything else.

Despite Tiergan's encouragement, Sophie didn't feel ready for anyone to know about her revelations. Especially Bronte.

She kept the memory log with her at all times and only took

it out to work on when she was alone. Grady and Edaline were used to her practicing alchemy in the caves, so they didn't question her disappearing after school every day with Iggy. And Dex was so busy with the added ability-detecting exercises, he didn't notice they weren't hanging out as much. The only one who seemed concerned was Biana.

She cornered Sophie in the hallway. "Are you mad at me?"

"What? No. Why?"

"You haven't come over in at least three weeks. It was before the school was evacuated."

Had it really been that long? "Sorry. I've been superbusy."

"Do you want to come over this weekend?"

"I don't think I can." She needed to avoid Alden, so he wouldn't ask to see her memory log.

"What about next weekend?"

"Uh . . . sure." Biana seemed so insistent, and she could always cancel.

Biana straightened, like a weight had been lifted off her shoulders. "Cool. I'll tell my parents so they know to be home."

"Oh. Good." She was sure her smile looked more like a grimace.

Deep down she knew she was overreacting. Other than Elementine and the photo of the sand castle, she hadn't found anything significant. She'd poured through her scrapbook for anything elf-ish and recorded every dream, but there was nothing worth hiding. Maybe Elementine was a one-time thing. She wasn't going to stop searching, but maybe she didn't need to stress so much about the memory log.

So she didn't cancel her plans with Biana. She went to Everglen. And it felt like coming home.

They played base quest, and this time she was on Fitz's team. His eyes held a tiny bit of envy when Sophie showed him the way she tracked thoughts to an exact location. She tried to teach him, but his mind couldn't master it, so she did the tracking and transmitted the location to him so he could tag Keefe and Biana out. She was so familiar with the *feel* of Fitz's mind after all the times she'd transmitted to him across the campus during her telepathy sessions, she barely had to concentrate to find him.

After losing three rounds in a row, Keefe refused to play unless Sophie was on his team. She agreed to the switch, and then transmitted their hiding spots to Fitz so they'd lose and keep the suspicion off of her. Keefe looked ready to explode when Fitz tagged him out the second time, and he spent the rest of the night grumbling about conspiracies. Sophie laughed until her sides hurt. She couldn't believe she'd let fear keep her away from this much fun for over a month.

Especially since Alden never asked to see her memory log. He and Della hugged her, told her to visit more often, and disappeared for the rest of the day on official business. For once she didn't want to know where they went.

She was done asking questions. Done investigating conspiracies—not that she'd made any headway. She didn't want to accidentally trigger any more memories. Ignorance was safer.

Whatever was going on was the Council's problem, not hers. She wouldn't let fear control her again.

She made it one whole month without unnecessary stress or worry, and then Dame Alina said the two most terrifying words ever: "final exams."

One month until finals. And even if she passed the tests, she still had to face another tribunal, where the Council—Bronte—would permanently decide her future at Foxfire. She felt like throwing up every time she thought about it.

Alchemy was still her worst subject, but she also struggled with elementalism and PE—all the subjects where she had to do things, not just learn. She still hadn't figured out how to turn off the part of her brain that screamed levitating was impossible, that lightning couldn't be jarred, that the law of conservation of mass was a legitimate scientific principle—and it always messed her up.

Dex had been nagging her for months to try an elixir he invented called Nogginease, which contained limbium, a rare mineral that could supposedly clear her mind. She'd resisted, since she couldn't use it during the exams, but maybe it was like learning to ride a bike. She needed training wheels to start.

Dex looked downright giddy when she asked for a bottle—probably because her lack of skill caused him to lose when they were on the same team in PE. He brought her a week's supply the next morning.

She swallowed the unnaturally cold syrup in one gulp, wincing as the chill ran down her throat. "I don't feel different."

Dex laughed. "Give it a chance. Your body needs time to absorb it."

"I should probably change into my uniform then."

A few steps toward the locker room her mind fuzzed. She leaned against the wall for support. "I don't think it's working right."

She couldn't describe what was happening, but she was pretty sure it wasn't a good thing.

Dex rushed to her side. "You don't look so great."

"I don't feel so great." She closed her eyes—the blurry vision was nauseating—and tore at her clothes. It was far, *far* too hot to wear a cape.

"Here, let me," Dex said, unfastening the clasp on her cape. "What's wrong?"

"I don't know." She tugged at her vest. "My skin's on fire."

"Whoa, what are those?" Dex pointed to the huge red bumps popping up on her arms.

"Oh no," she gasped, collapsing. "Allergy . . ."

Dex caught her before she hit the ground. "Allergy? What's an allergy?"

She wanted to explain, but her chest felt like something was crushing it and she couldn't get enough air. The world spun harder and her vision dimmed.

"Hang on. I'll take you to Elwin." Dex threw her over his shoulder, and then they were moving. He was strong, but they were the same height, and she weighed almost as much as he did, so their progress was slow. Maybe too slow. Fear settled into every muscle, making her tremble.

Then someone else grabbed her, cradling her in their arms. She heard some sort of discussion—an argument maybe— and then she was moving much faster. She was too far gone to make sense of it. There was a tugging in her stomach and a burning in her throat, and then she was out cold.

THIRTY-FIVE

DON'T TRY TO SPEAK YET, SOPHIE," a familiar voice whispered as her eyes fluttered open.

She couldn't, even if she wanted to. Her throat chafed like sandpaper and her tongue felt like a foreign object. Her blurry eyes focused on the wild-haired head hovering over her.

"Nod if you can understand me," Elwin instructed.

She nodded, surprised by how much energy the simple movement took.

"That's the first good news today." He smiled, but it didn't erase the worry in his eyes as he held a small bottle against her lips. "I need you to swallow something for me."

Some of it dribbled across her chin, but she managed to get most of it down.

"That's a good girl." He wiped her face with a soft cloth and placed a cold compress against her forehead. "Just rest for now, okay?"

She nodded again, exhausted from the effort.

The warm liquid soothed her dry throat and sent cool, tingling sensations rushing through her body. After a few minutes she could swallow normally again. "What happened?"

"I'm not exactly sure. Dex said you told him it was an allergy. He thinks it might be the limbium in a solution he gave you, because you'd never had it before."

Her fuzzy memories focused. "Where is Dex?"

"I made him and Fitz wait outside till I had things under control. Things got a little too messy for spectators."

Fitz?

She vaguely remembered stronger arms carrying her to safety. Had that been Fitz? She was about to ask when she caught what Elwin said. "Messy?"

"Don't worry, I cleaned up all the vomit. But you need to change your shirt."

She bolted upright. "I threw up?"

"Everywhere. Never seen anything like it. It's always an adventure with you, isn't it? But don't worry, I don't mind— and neither did Fitz. It was only his PE uniform."

She threw up on Fitz?

"Oh no," she wailed, wondering if it was possible to die of embarrassment.

"What's the matter? Are you in pain?"

"No," she moaned, trying to crawl under the blankets and disappear. She could smell the mess on her uniform now and she couldn't decide which was worse, knowing it was on her or knowing it was on Fitz, too. "Why? Why did this have to happen?"

"I don't know much about allergies. Never seen one before—and I can't say I'd like to see another. Bullhorn screamed his head off when you came in. Scared the wits out of me."

She cringed. "It was that close?"

He bit his lip. "Bullhorn's never done that before."

They both shivered.

"How did you know what to do?" she whispered.

"I didn't. I just took my best guess and hoped it would work. When Bullhorn left you alone, I knew I was on the right track."

"Well . . . thank you." The words felt trite, considering he'd saved her life. But what else could she say?

"Just don't ever do that to me again! I'm going to make up a bottle of what I gave you, and I want you to keep it with you in case you ever have another reaction—and stay away from limbium."

"I'll try."

He gave her one of his huge tunics and left her alone to change. Her soiled uniform went into an airtight bag to block the smell.

"You up for company?" Elwin asked when she finished. "Fitz and Dex won't leave until they see that you're okay."

She sank lower in her bed and nodded, wondering how to apologize to someone for vomiting on them.

"You guys can come in," Elwin called.

Dex rushed to her side, followed closely by Fitz.

Dex's eyes were red and swollen. "I'm so sorry, Sophie. I had no idea you'd react like that. I'd never—"

"It's okay, Dex," she interrupted. "It wasn't your fault. And I'm fine now. See?" She held up her arm, showing him the blotch-free skin.

Dex let out a deep breath. "You're really okay?"

"Yeah. Just humiliated." She scraped together the courage to look at Fitz. He wore a fitted white undershirt, his PE tunic noticeably absent. "I'm so sorry, Fitz. I can't believe I—"

He held up his hands and smiled his dazzling smile. "Don't worry about it. It wasn't nearly as bad as the time Alvar's pet raptor peed all over me. Now *that* was disgusting."

She wanted to believe him, but she was fairly sure she'd always be the girl who threw up on him. It was hard to resist the urge to crawl under a rock and disappear for a decade or two. "Still. I'm sorry."

"You don't need to be. I'm just glad you're okay and I was there to help."

Dex reeled on Fitz. "I didn't need your help."

"Please, you never would have made it in time."

"I would too!" He looked to Sophie to back him up.

"I . . . don't remember." She wanted to spare Dex's feelings, but deep down she knew Fitz was right. Which was a scary thought.

Dex scowled.

"Has that ever happened to you before?" Fitz asked.

"Only once—when I was nine."

"Had you had any limbium when it happened?" Elwin asked.

"I'd never heard of it before Dex told me about it. Humans don't have stuff like that."

"Then what caused it last time?"

"The doctors ran a ton of tests, but they never figured it out. So they just injected me with a bunch of medicines and steroids and told me to be more careful." She shivered at the memory of the needles.

Elwin stroked his chin. "I honestly can't do much better. The best I can say is to stay away from limbium and wear this all the time." He handed her a tiny black bottle hanging from a cord. "If anything like that ever happens again, drink that immediately and find me."

"I will." She tied the cord around her neck. "Can I go to PE now?"

"Are you crazy?" Elwin asked. "I'm taking you home to rest—don't even think about arguing."

She could tell he wouldn't budge, so she slid out of bed,

wobbling as the blood rushed to her head. Fitz caught and steadied her.

She blushed in his arms. "Thanks."

"You shouldn't be on your feet yet," Elwin scolded, grabbing her arm and wrapping it across his wide shoulders to support her. "You guys should get to session. Well, Fitz might want to hit the showers first."

Dex snickered and Sophie hung her head. "I'm so sorry," she whispered.

Fitz smiled. "Forget it, okay?"

"I will if you will."

"Deal." Then Elwin stepped into the light and the warmth pulled them away.

"Elwin?" Grady called, dropping everything when he saw them. He raced over with Edaline hot on his heels. "What's going on?"

"I brought Sophie home to rest. She had a bit of a crisis."

"Crisis?" Edaline sounded panicked as she ushered everyone inside, and Elwin led Sophie to the couch. "What happened?"

Sophie hid her face as Elwin gave them the full story, but she peeked through her fingers when Grady and Edaline gasped over Bullhorn screaming.

They both looked deathly pale.

"Did Bullhorn lay down beside her?" Grady asked. His voice sounded hollow. Banshees only did that when someone was on their final breaths.

"Yes," Elwin admitted quietly. "At first he was just scream-ing, but then he got quiet and curled up against her chest—nearly gave me a heart attack."

"So . . . she almost died," Edaline whispered. Her eyes darted to Sophie, and widened. "You almost died!"

Sophie couldn't quite hide her shiver.

Grady cleared his throat and squeezed Edaline's hand. "She's okay now, right?"

"She should be. She's tough. How else could she survive so many disasters?"

Grady and Edaline didn't smile.

"She looks so pale," Edaline whispered. She reached for Sophie but retracted her hand before actually touching her.

"She just needs to rest. She'll be back to normal tomorrow."

"I'm already back to normal," Sophie said, hating how wor-ried Grady and Edaline looked.

"But what if this happens again?" Edaline asked.

"It won't," Sophie promised.

"Is that true?" Grady asked Elwin.

"I'll have to do some research. In the meantime, I gave her an emergency solution to keep with her. Let's hope she won't need it, and that it works if she does."

They both nodded blankly.

Elwin squeezed Edaline's arm. "She's fine now. Once she rests and has something to eat she'll be back to her old self."

"I am back to my old self," Sophie insisted.

Edaline nodded, but she didn't look convinced.

"Well," Grady said, turning to Elwin. "We should let you get back to work. Thank you for all you did to save her."

"Just doing my job. Besides, Sophie's my best patient." He gave Sophie a small smile. "Just make your next crisis less dramatic, okay?"

"Maybe this is my last catastrophe," she mumbled.

Elwin laughed. "You? Never."

Grady's lips tightened and Edaline looked at the floor. Clearly, they agreed with Elwin. Except they didn't seem to think it was funny.

Grady helped her up the stairs and Edaline brought her a bowl of brothy soup in bed, but their minds seemed to be elsewhere. When Sophie finished eating, Edaline clapped twice and the shades plunged the room into darkness. The shadowy light made them both look worn and haggard.

"Are you okay?" Sophie asked.

"We're worried about you," Edaline whispered, her eyes on the floor.

Sophie opened her mouth, searching for a way to convince them that she really was okay, but her soft bed and the comforting darkness turned it into a yawn.

"Get some sleep," Grady said as he tucked her in for the first time since she'd moved in.

Maybe it was the way he wrapped the blankets extra snug.

Or maybe it was Edaline handing her Ella. Or maybe it was almost dying. Whatever it was, she snuggled into her pillow feeling so much like family she couldn't help whispering, "I love you guys," into the silence.

But her exhausted body fell asleep before she heard their answer.

THIRTY-SIX

A HIGH-PITCHED SCREECH—LIKE TIRES squealing across pavement mixed with hundreds of shrieking girls—jolted Sophie out of her dreams. She threw on work clothes and rushed outside to see if Grady and Edaline needed her help.

It was still dark, but once her eyes adjusted Sophie could see an eagle-size golden pterodactyl trying to escape the leash Grady held. It somersaulted in the sky, dragging Grady like dead weight, while Edaline and the gnomes tried to calm the nearby animals.

Screeeeeeeeeeeeeeeeech!

Sophie covered her ears. "How can I help?" she shouted to Grady.

"You shouldn't be up. Go back to bed, Sophie. We don't need any help." Grady wrapped the leash around his legs for extra stability and then yanked the cord, trying to rein the creature in. The beast fought back, using speed and momentum to pull Grady over as it gained headway.

Screeeeeeeeeeeeeeeeeeech!

Kinda looked like he needed help. . . .

Sophie stared at the pterodactyl, trying to figure out what to do. Two enormous golden eyes locked with hers, and as she held its gaze an image filled her mind.

Fire.

Sophie wasn't sure how, but she knew what to do. She raced for the shed, grabbed the alchemy torch Edaline used when she made solutions for the animals, and raced back outside. A pile of dried umber leaves sat in the middle of the pasture, waiting to be dispersed to the animals for breakfast. Sophie ran straight for it and lit the mound before she could change her mind.

"What are you doing?" Edaline screamed as Sophie jumped back from the enormous blue flames that smelled uncannily like fried chicken. "Someone get some quicksnuff."

"Just wait a second," Sophie said, pointing to the pterodactyl, which had quieted down. "I know what I'm doing." She *really* hoped that was true.

The creature circled once, then dived nose first into the blaze. Sophie couldn't help shrieking as the fire engulfed its golden body, but the pterodactyl flapped its wings in the flames like a bird in a birdbath. Sophie had to back away to avoid the flying sparks.

"What on earth were you thinking?" Edaline demanded, jerking Sophie farther away from the fire. "What would possess you to do that?"

"It was cold." Sophie pointed to the pterodactyl, still playing in the flames.

"Cold?" Grady asked, joining them. He was covered in bits of grass and mud.

"Yeah," Sophie told him. "She needed fire."

Grady stared at Sophie, then at the creature. "I think you're right. I bet this is a flareadon. They have fire-resistant fur—and they have to be around flames or they'll freeze to death. It's why they're so rare. But how did you know that?"

"I'm not sure, but I think . . ." She tried to replay the moment. It wasn't a triggered memory—she'd been worried about that at first. It was more like . . .

"I think I read its mind. Is that possible?"

Grady ran his hand across his face. "I don't know. I've never heard of anyone reading an animal's mind before."

"Who cares?" Edaline interrupted, her voice an octave higher than normal. "You could've been burned! You could've been killed! And you're supposed to be in bed, resting from your last brush with death!"

Sophie backed a step away from the wild-eyed Edaline. "I was just trying to help."

"We don't need your help, Sophie. We need you inside—where it's safe. Now go!" She pointed to the house.

Sophie glanced at Grady, hoping he'd defend her—she did solve the problem, after all. But Grady was too busy holding a trembling Edaline. That's when it hit her.

Fire.

Death.

Jolie.

"I'm—I'm sorry," Sophie stammered, not sure what to say. "I didn't mean to worry you."

"It's fine," Grady said, as much to Edaline as to Sophie. He turned to Sophie. "Go back inside and rest. We'll talk in the morning." He sounded calm and quiet. But something in his expression warned her not to push.

"Okay," she mumbled, dropping her eyes. "I guess I'll see you when I wake up."

Neither of them said anything as she walked back to the house. No good night. Certainly no hugs. And when she turned back to wave, they'd already turned away.

Things weren't much better at breakfast the next morning. Grady and Edaline's smiles looked forced, and neither had much to say.

"So where did the flareadon come from?" Sophie asked, trying to fill the silence.

"She flew into our pasture, screeching her head off, and we

scrambled to calm her down," Grady answered. "That's when you found us. It's strange. Flareadons live near volcanoes—that's why it didn't occur to me to use fire. Gildie strayed a long way from home."

"Gildie?"

"We were up late with her, calming her down, and it felt silly calling her 'flareadon.' So when we figured out it was a female, Edaline named her Gildie."

"It's a good name."

Edaline gave a forced smile, and looked away.

"You really think you read her mind?" Grady asked.

"How would I have known about the fire? I think I might go practice with Gildie for a few minutes before school."

"Absolutely not," Edaline snapped, instantly on her feet. "You're staying home to rest. And you're not to go anywhere near those animals. Is that understood?"

"But I'm fine now. And I always help you guys outside."

"Well, that was a mistake on our part—one I'm correcting now. I don't want you outside in the pastures anymore."

Grady wouldn't meet her eyes. "Is this about last night?" Sophie whispered.

"It's about a lot of things. We haven't been looking out for your safety, and I'm trying to correct that." Edaline sighed. "Why don't you go study? Finals are less than a month away."

Unfortunately, Edaline was right.

Sophie spent the rest of the weekend trying to wade

through the horrible firecatching book Sir Conley had assigned her to read the day of the Quintessence debacle. She had a feeling firecatching would be on the final exam. But it was so dry, she kept taking breaks to experiment with Iggy.

Most of the time she couldn't decipher what he was thinking, but she suspected it was because Iggy didn't think before he acted. Like when he wrestled with one of her socks and rolled off the bed, or shredded her homework for no apparent reason. But other times she did wonder if she could feel his thoughts. It was more of a vague emotion than a concrete thought—which actually made sense. Human thoughts felt different from elvin thoughts. Maybe each creature's mind was different. She'd have to ask Tiergan to know for sure.

"If *anyone* else told me that, I would question their sanity." Tiergan chuckled. "But with you, I'm learning anything is possible."

Sophie blushed. "You've really never heard of anyone reading animals' minds?"

"No. I've also never heard of anyone transmitting across impossible distances, or having an impenetrable mind, or tracking exact locations, so I can't say I'm surprised. In fact, I wonder . . . Do you think you could transmit to an animal? Or track them?"

"I guess I could try."

His face lit up. "Yes—you must. And if you can, I think that would qualify as passing your final exam."

"You'd pass me—just like that?"

"Sophie, you have the greatest telepathic abilities I've ever seen. I'm not sure I'm qualified to test you. Even if you can't do this, I'll find some other excuse to pass you. It'd be wrong not to."

Her heart lightened at his words. One exam down. Seven more to go. "I'll work on it tonight and let you know on Thursday."

"I look forward to hearing your results."

Sophie decided to practice with a different animal, so she chose their resident T. rex. Verdi's thoughts were more defined than Iggy's but less intense than Gildie's, and when she sent Verdi an image of her right paw over and over, Verdi finally got the hint and raised it. Then Verdi's thoughts told her she wanted a tummy rub as a reward. Sophie giggled and rubbed the soft, downy feathers. She could transmit thoughts to animals—how awesome was that?

"What are you doing out here?"

Sophie spun around, backing up a step when she saw the fury in Edaline's eyes. "I'm reading Verdi's mind for homework. I think she wants to eat the verminion, so you might want to keep her away from him."

She waited for Edaline to laugh—or at least smile. Instead

her eyes narrowed. "I thought I made it clear that you're not supposed to be outside."

Sophie kept waiting for things to go back to normal after the allergy incident, but it'd been four days and Edaline was getting worse. "I have to be allowed outside sometime."

"If I tell you to do something, I expect you to do it," Edaline snapped.

"But I'm fine. You have to stop acting like everything could kill me!"

Edaline paled. She looked anywhere but Sophie. "You're right. I'm worrying too much."

"I promise I'll be careful," Sophie said, desperate for something that might erase the pain in Edaline's features. "You don't have to worry."

Edaline was quiet for a long time before she shook her head. "Yes. I do." Then she turned and went inside without another word.

Edaline didn't join them for dinner. Sophie tried to ask Grady about it—tried to apologize—but he just told her not to worry and stared out the window.

Loud pounding on the front door broke the silence between them.

Sophie answered the door and an out-of-breath Alden raced in. The smell of smoke and fire trailed around him like an aura.

Grady leaped to his feet. "What happened?"

"There's been a development." Alden glanced at Sophie before turning to Grady. "I need your help."

Their eyes held for at least a minute before Grady stepped back, recoiling like he'd been struck. It took Sophie a second to realize Alden had transmitted a message.

Grady leaned on the table, panting breaths shaking his chest as he ran his hands through his hair. "I . . . can't," he whispered.

"You know I wouldn't ask if it weren't imperative."

Grady shook his head. "I'm sorry. Ask the others."

"You're the only one I trust."

Sophie held her breath, watching Grady. Alden's face looked desperate, and if he was worried, it *had* to be vital.

Grady sank into a chair looking thirty years older. He hid his face in his hands. "I'm sorry. I can't."

Alden closed his eyes. Listening to Grady's thoughts? Transmitting another plea? Not since the cheating incident had Sophie been so tempted to violate the ethics of telepathy and find out what was going on. But if Alden somehow caught her, Bronte could use it to have her exiled.

Would he catch her?

She could probably sneak in without him knowing, but what would she do with the information? If she said or did anything about it, he'd *know* how she found out.

It wasn't worth the risk.

Alden let out a full body sigh. "I'll have to find another way then. Excuse me." He nodded to Sophie as he turned to leave.

"Wait." It took her a second to realize the voice was hers. She cleared her throat as Alden faced her. "What's going on?"

Alden opened his mouth, but Grady cut him off.

"Go to bed, Sophie!"

"But—"

"Go to bed now!"

She'd never heard Grady so angry. Even Alden took a step back. She blinked—her eyes burning with hurt and humiliation—and fled to her room.

Grady and Edaline weren't home when Sophie came down for breakfast. They left a note on the table for her: "Gone out."

No "good morning." No "love, Grady and Edaline." She tried not to let it bother her . . . but it did.

They were still gone when she got home from school.

As much as she wanted to practice telepathy with Verdi or Gildie, she stayed inside and studied. She was determined to do what she could to cooperate.

At sunset the gnomes shared some of their dinner and she ate alone in her room, wondering if she should worry. When the stars came out, she decided it was time to call Alden. Before she could, the front door slammed.

She raced down the hall, freezing when she heard hushed conversation. She peered over the railing, catching a partial view of Grady and Edaline.

"It was the right decision," Grady told Edaline, sweeping the hair off her face as he pulled her closer. Muffled sobs drifted up the stairs. "It's best for everyone. Alden will find someone else."

Edaline cried harder and Grady cleared his throat. "Come on, I'll take you upstairs."

Sophie barely had enough time to sneak back to her room. She crouched by Iggy's cage and rubbed his cheeks through the bars as Grady peeked his head through the door. "Oh, you're awake."

"I wanted to make sure you got home safe before I went to bed."

Guilt twisted his handsome features. "Sorry. Didn't mean to worry you."

"It's okay. Where were you?"

"On an errand."

She stared at her hands. "Did it have something to do with Alden's visit last night?"

"That's none of your business. You should go to bed. It's getting late."

She didn't want to upset him, but she needed to know. "Something bad is happening, isn't it?"

Grady's sigh echoed through the silence. "It's nothing you need to worry about. Okay?"

"Okay," she agreed.

But when she crawled into bed, all she did was worry.

THIRTY-SEVEN

"CAN I TALK TO YOU?" SOPHIE WHISpered to Fitz on their way into the cafeteria the next day. "Somewhere private?"

His brows shot up at the request, but he shrugged and motioned for her to come with him. She could feel Dex's eyes burning into the back of her head as she followed Fitz down the hall.

"What's up?" he asked when they were alone.

"Do you know what your dad's investigating right now?"

"Why?"

She focused on his nose to think a little more clearly. His eyes had a way of turning her brain to mush. "He came over a couple nights ago, begging Grady for help with something. It seemed like it was important."

"I'm sure there's no reason to worry."

She rolled her eyes. He sounded just like his dad. "He looked *really* stressed, Fitz. I've never seen him like that. Do you know what he's working on?"

He hesitated. "It's some sort of fire—and I only know that because he comes home smelling like smoke. He doesn't tell me about official matters."

"But he sent you to find me, so he must tell you *some* stuff."

Fitz glanced over his shoulder, making sure they were still alone. "That was an exception. He needed someone close to your age to follow the leads he found—someone who would blend in. Otherwise he wouldn't have involved me."

She chewed her lip, processing his words. "And you have *no* idea what he's working on—at all?"

Something changed in his face. He knew more than he was telling her—she was positive.

You can trust me, she transmitted into his mind.

He sucked in a breath. "Whoa—I keep forgetting you can do that."

Please, she pressed. She may have sworn off investigating things after the Quintessence debacle, but this was big—and it was tearing Grady and Edaline apart. *I need to know.*

His eyes searched hers, then closed. "I shouldn't do this."

Please.

He leaned his head against the wall. "Concentrate."

She knew what he meant. He couldn't transmit into her mind—even Tiergan couldn't—so he wanted her to read his thoughts. She opened her mind and *listened*.

I heard him talking to Alvar, he thought. *It's not one fire—it's hundreds. All in the Forbidden Cities. All starting the same day. And the flames are this weird fluorescent yellow color. The Council ruled it a human arsonist and refused to investigate, but my dad thinks the Black Swan is involved. Alvar thinks he's crazy.*

Her heart stopped. Hundreds of human fires? *Do you know which cities?*

He didn't say. But I know they're all over the planet.

Are they near my family?

I'm sure they're fine. My dad was assigned to keep an eye on them—in case their memories come back.

Alden never told her that. But it was nice to know someone was watching them. *Do you know what the Black Swan is up to?*

No idea—I swear. And you can't tell anyone I told you this. I'm not supposed to know.

I won't. I promise.

"Okay? Can we go eat lunch now?" he asked.

"You can. I need to think."

"Don't worry about it, Sophie. I'm sure it's not a big deal."

She forced a smile. "I just want to think."

She wandered the halls, letting her mind spin with the new information.

Why would the Black Swan set fires around humans—and why were they yellow this time? Why did Alden need Grady to help? And why did Grady refuse?

She made her way to the atrium so she could switch her books before everyone else got there. She wasn't in the mood to talk.

A book was waiting on the center shelf of her locker: *An Insider's Guide to Pyrokinesis.* It came with a note: "Hope this helps you find what you're looking for."

She smiled. She'd forgotten the librarian's promise to send her anything she found on Pyrokinetics. There couldn't be better timing.

Alchemy was an even bigger disaster than usual. Sophie was way too distracted to concentrate, and after she accidentally turned a part of her own shoe to copper, Lady Galvin released her early, before anything could happen to her cape. Sophie used the time to head to the Level Six library, to thank the librarian for finding the book.

"Still looking for books on pyrokinesis?" she asked when she saw Sophie.

"No, the one you gave me is more than enough."

"What do you mean?"

"An Insider's Guide to Pyrokinesis." She froze when she caught the look of absolute confusion on the librarian's face. "Didn't you send me the book?"

"I've never even heard of it—and I thought I knew them all."

"Oh. Must've been one of the other librarians I talked to. I guess I'll have to thank them." She forced a tiny laugh.

"Let me know who it was. I'd love to read it when you're done."

Sophie nodded, keeping the smile plastered across her lips as she wobbled down the hall.

The other librarians never promised to send a book to her locker. It was possible one of them did, but she had a sinking feeling it had nothing to do with them.

She confirmed the suspicion an hour later when she was alone in her bedroom. A thick dog-ear marked a chapter toward the end. She flipped there, to a drawing of an elf surrounded by bright yellow fire.

EVERBLAZE: THE UNSTOPPABLE FLAME

The book slipped from her hands as foreign memories flashed through her mind. Half blind from the rush of information, she stumbled to her satchel and pulled out her Imparter.

"Show me Alden."

THIRTY-EIGHT

SOPHIE TOOK A DEEP BREATH TO FIGHT the drowning sensation she always felt when surrounded by the aquarium in Alden's office. She strangled her satchel against her chest.

Alden cleared his throat from the other side of his paper-strewn desk. "What was it you wanted to talk about, Sophie?"

She opened her mouth. No words came out.

"Is this about Grady and Edaline's decision?" he asked quietly.

She shook her head and swallowed, forcing her voice to work. "No—though I am worried about them. They've been acting weird since you came over that night."

Alden looked away. "They haven't told you?"

"About the fires? No. But they don't have to—I know there are hundreds of them. I know they're around humans. And I know you think the Black Swan's involved. So don't tell me there's no reason to worry because I know something's going on."

"The situation will be under control soon enough. The humans will put the fires out and everything will go back to normal." The words were confident, but she could tell from his eyes he didn't believe them.

She tugged out an eyelash, knowing the next words she spoke would change everything. "Not if it's Everblaze."

Alden was on his feet before she could react. He held her shoulders, forcing her to look at him. "How do you know that word?"

Her voice vanished. She fumbled in her satchel, pulling out the pyrokinesis book.

His mouth fell open. "Where did you get that?"

"Someone put it in my locker today. The chapter on Everblaze was marked." She pulled out her memory log and flipped to the pages she'd filled after she called Alden. "And when I read the word 'Everblaze,' I remembered this."

His rubbed his temples as he examined the complicated formula she'd projected. "Do you know what this is?"

"Not really. I know it's called Frissyn." She pointed to a symbol that looked like a Q with an X running through it.

"And that stands for Quintessence, but I have no idea what it does." The list of ingredients and instructions was so detailed only a master alchemist would be able to decipher it.

"Frissyn is the only way to extinguish Everblaze. The formula is *highly* classified—I've never seen the entire directions before." He ran a hand through his hair. "Do you know what this means?"

"Someone planted secret information in my brain." Her voice shook. The words were so much more terrifying out loud. She handed him the photo of her on the beach with the sand castle. "I found this a few weeks ago."

"Why didn't you tell me?" His voice wasn't angry, but guilt made her face hot anyway.

"I'm sorry. I was afraid I would get in trouble. But I also haven't remembered anything else until today. That's why I called you." She forced herself to meet his eyes. "The fires are Everblaze, aren't they?"

"I'm afraid they might be—but I've been overruled on that opinion."

"Overruled?"

He rose to pace. "The Council doesn't believe it's possible. They think it's much more likely the humans have an arsonist who's playing with chemicals on their hands, and since they excluded themselves from our help when they broke the treaty, it's not our concern. I can't blame the Council for feeling that way. Things like this are supposed to be unheard of. But our world is changing." He stared into the aquarium. "Your existence is proof of that."

"What do you mean?"

Indecision warred across his features before he moved to the desk, closed her memory log, and pointed to the silver bird etched into the cover. "Did you know that this is a moonlark?"

A chill ran through her as she shook her head. She'd barely paid attention to the cover.

"*Suldreen,*" Alden said quietly. "Moonlarks lay their eggs in the ocean and let the tide carry them away. The babies hatch alone, and must learn to survive without family. That's what the Black Swan called you. Project Moonlark."

She gripped the sides of her chair, needing something to hold on to.

"Twelve years ago we captured a member of the Black Swan and probed his mind."

"Prentice," she interrupted.

He nodded. "Prentice was a Keeper for the Black Swan, so the Council ordered Quinlin to probe his memories. His mind broke in the process, and Quinlin was only able to extract two pieces of information. A strand of your unregistered DNA, and your code name: Moonlark. You were the egg they cast out into the sea of humans, hoping you'd survive."

The words stung, like swallowing ice. They matched what Tiergan already told her but felt so much worse. *She* was Project Moonlark?

"So my parents belong to the Black Swan?" she asked.

"In a way . . ." His fingers twisted the fabric of his cape. "The thing is, Sophie, I'm not convinced you have parents—not in a conventional sense. I think the Black Swan created you, for some purpose I have yet to determine. I've done some research since I found you. Your human parents had trouble getting pregnant, so they saw a fertility doctor. I believe that doctor was a member of the Black Swan—posing as a human—and that he implanted your mother with your embryo to keep us from knowing about your existence."

The room spun as she tried to make sense of what he was telling her. "Why?"

"You're very special, Sophie. Your DNA has been manipulated. That's why your eyes are brown. Why your telepathic abilities are so outstanding. They even gave you a photographic memory, so you can easily learn and retain information—like cipher runes, and Council secrets—and an impenetrable mind to keep anyone from discovering them. I assume that's also why you have an allergy. Limbium affects the mind, and your mind is different from the rest of ours—not just on a talent level. On a genetic level."

She shook her head, wanting to shake the information away. "So I'm a mutant."

"Not a mutant. An anomaly."

"Same thing."

"It's not as bad as it sounds."

"How? You're saying a group of crazy renegades made me and hid me away, like I'm their secret weapon or something."

"I never said you were a weapon. I don't know why they made you, or why they wanted me to find you." He smiled sadly when her eyes widened. "It's safe to assume they're the ones who sent me that article about you. I'm sure they wrote the article—I doubt it's a coincidence the title uses the word 'prodigy.' They even burned their sign around the city where you lived to get our attention."

She rubbed her temples. The news was getting worse and worse. "What does that mean?"

"It means you need to be *very* careful." He pointed to the pyrokinesis book. "Clearly, they're trying to manipulate you. For what—I don't know. But they already made you illegally collect Quintessence, and the Council may not be so forgiving if you break the law again. So I need you to promise me that no matter what messages you get, no matter what you hear, or what you remember, you will come straight to me—just like you did today—and do nothing else. Will you promise me that?"

The fear was so suffocating she could barely choke out the word: "Yes." It was scary enough having secrets in her brain. The idea that she'd been designed and controlled, like someone's puppet, made her whole body shake.

Not to mention she now had no hope of ever having a normal life. Who would be friends with her when they found out she was an *anomaly*?

Alden wrapped his arms around her. "It's going to be okay. We'll figure it out."

She buried her face in his cloak and swallowed the sob fighting its way out of her chest. She was stronger than this—and she couldn't afford to lose her head. She shoved her fears away and focused on the bigger issue. "What if the fires really are Everblaze? They're yellow, right—just like in the book?"

"Many things could cause fire to be that color. I'm looking into it. Please trust that I can handle this."

She soaked up the hug for a few more seconds before she pulled away. "Okay."

He handed her the memory log, and she couldn't help staring at the silver bird, now that she understood the meaning. "Keep track of everything—and you can't let anyone see what's in there. That formula is *top* secret, but I want you to have it in case it triggers something else. Do you understand?"

"Don't worry. I haven't shown anyone—not even Grady and Edaline."

He frowned at the names.

"Are you still mad at Grady for refusing to help?"

"I'm just . . . disappointed. But what's done is done." He squeezed her hands. "Everything will be fine. Remember that—no matter what happens."

"I'll try." She glanced out the window, at the purple twilight sky. "I should get home. I don't want to worry them."

Alden nodded.

He kept the pyrokinesis book to see if it held any clues to where it came from, and he made sure the memory log was well hidden in the bottom of her satchel before he let her leave. "Do you need the Leapmaster?"

"Nope. I have my home crystal." She held the pendant up proudly.

Alden bit his lip. "Good. And, Sophie? Anytime you need to talk—no matter what time it is—call me, okay?"

"I will," she promised.

Then she stepped into the light, willing the warmth to soothe the chills rushing down her spine. As the scenery glittered away, she saw Alden's calm facade crumble, and then she was on her way home, hoping she'd imagined it.

Another note from Grady and Edaline waited for her on the table: "On errands. Be back later." Five words this time—more than double the last note. Maybe that was a good sign.

She missed Grady's throaty laugh. She missed Edaline's gentle smile. She wasn't sure what the problem was, but she needed to find a way to fix it—before it drove a wedge between them. She couldn't lose another family.

Edaline had left dinner for her in the kitchen. Sophie didn't want to be alone, so she brought Iggy and some homework with her. She was starting the last chapter of the firecatching book when the front chimes rang.

She raced to the door, afraid it was Alden with another

emergency—but it was a messenger, delivering a scroll from the Council.

She didn't hold it up to the light to see if she could read through the paper. She didn't test the seal, to see if she could break it and then reseal it. The curiosity was a fierce beast rampaging inside her, but she fought the urge and left it on the table. She did stay downstairs though, so she could see Grady's reaction when he opened it. Her willpower had its limits.

She curled up on the chaise in the main room to finish the last chapter. She mostly skimmed—firecatching was so boring—but the word "blaze" caught her attention. Sir Conley had taught her to place a copper bead in the bottles to seal in the heat of the flame, but the book said copper only worked with luminous flames. Nonluminous flames needed silver. And something called a "generated blaze" required gold.

A memory tickled the back of her mind.

Lumenite.

She wasn't sure what it meant, but she dug out her memory log to record it.

She projected the image in her mind: a squat, round bottle with a glowing, golden seal. Did that mean Everblaze needed gold *and* lumenite to be bottled? What was lumenite? And why was the bottle short and round? Sir Conley drilled it into her head that fire was caught with long, narrow bottles. The shape was essential to hold the heat without cracking the glass.

She closed her eyes, focusing on the memory to make sure she was seeing it right. The image was fuzzy—like something was missing that would clarify things. But she was sure the bottle was round.

A loud *rip!* shattered her concentration.

"No, Iggy!" she screamed, racing across the room. She yanked Grady's scroll from his grubby little paws.

RIIIIIIIIIIIIIIIIIIIIIP.

A huge chunk of paper stayed in Iggy's possession as he skittered away, clutching his treasure.

"Get back here right now or I'm feeding you to the vermin-ion!"

Five minutes of racing around the room and she was still no closer to retrieving the rest of the scroll.

"Stop!" she screamed. "Stop right now. Stop!"

STOP!

Her mental plea was so desperate it transmitted.

Iggy froze and turned to look at her—eyes wide with shock.

Let go of the paper!

The paper fluttered to the floor, and she grabbed the tattered page to assess the damage.

"Look at this," she groaned, laying the pieces on the rug to figure out how to glue them together. "What am I going to tell Grady? Do you have any idea how much trouble . . ."

Her voice trailed off when she noticed her name.

A tiny voice in the back of her mind begged her to stop reading. But her eyes had already spotted another word.

"Adoption."

She skimmed the rest of the page, struggling to figure out what the tattered document was saying. And then she found it.

"In accordance with your request, adoption proceedings for Sophie Foster have been canceled."

THIRTY-NINE

THE WORD RANG IN HER EARS, POUND-ing with every heartbeat. *Canceled. Canceled. Canceled.* As in started. Then stopped.

She closed her eyes to stop the room from spinning. It wasn't until her lungs burned that she realized she'd stopped breathing. She hugged her chest as her body shuddered. Iggy crawled up her shoulder and snuggled into her neck, like he knew she needed a friend. It didn't help.

She couldn't think. She couldn't move. She wasn't sure she would ever be able to function again. Then the front door opened and somehow she made it to her feet, scrubbing tears away with the back of her hand as Grady and Edaline entered the room.

"What's wrong?" Grady asked.

Her chest heaved from a choked-back sob. "A messenger brought this scroll from Eternalia, but Iggy ripped it."

Grady gasped and rushed for the scroll as Sophie turned and fled upstairs. He called her name, but she kept running.

She slammed her door, dragging a chair in front of it for added security.

Grady pounded outside, begging her to let him in, but she ignored him. She collapsed on the bed and buried her face against Ella to muffle the sobs.

Eventually the knocking stopped.

She lowered the shades and sank into darkness, wrapping it around her like a blanket of misery. Then she curled into a ball and cried herself to sleep.

The nightmares were unbearable. This time the whole world burned, leaving her alone. She woke up screaming and couldn't stop shaking.

Her eyes were red and puffy and her hair was a disaster, but she didn't have the energy to care. Getting out of bed felt like a tremendous accomplishment. The only effort she gave her appearance was to tear the Ruewen crest off her uniform. If anyone asked, she'd blame Iggy.

She went straight to the Leapmaster, but Grady and Edaline were waiting under the glittering crystals.

"Foxfire," she yelled, refusing to acknowledge them.

"I locked it down," Grady explained when the crystals didn't move. Edaline stared at the gaping hole in Sophie's cape, biting her lip. "We really need to talk about this."

"There's nothing to talk about. You don't owe me anything. I'm not your daughter."

Their faces crumbled at her words, but she was too angry to care.

"Sophie . . . ," Grady tried.

"No, it's fine. I thought we were a family but I was wrong. I can't replace Jolie and I guess you don't want me."

The words left a sour taste on her tongue, but she ignored it. Even when they both fell back a step, like the name Jolie was a physical blow. She wanted them to hurt—they deserved it. "There. We talked. Can I go now?"

"I want you to come straight home after school," Grady ordered, but his voice was hollow. "We need to talk, regardless of what you think."

She ignored him.

"Sophie, we're still your guardians. You have to do what we say."

Her eyes flashed as they met his. "Fine. If you want to keep up the charade, I'll play along. Would you like a hug while we're at it? Should I tell you 'I love you' again?"

Edaline covered her mouth to block a sob.

Grady paled. "No. Just . . . have a good day at school." He

snapped his fingers and the crystals spun to life, obeying her earlier command.

She looked away, but Edaline's muffled sobs made her stomach churn. Even the rushing warmth couldn't erase the cold emptiness as the light swept her away.

"You look like you lost a fight with a yeti," Jensi said, pointing to the hole in her cape. His smile faded when she didn't return it. "Everything okay?"

"Fine." She threw her books into her locker. One ricocheted and landed on her foot, and she kicked and muttered a few words she wasn't supposed to say.

"Ooooookaaaaaaay then," he said, slinking away. "Watch out," he whispered to Dex and Marella.

Sophie slammed her locker and stomped off without acknowledging them.

She tried hiding in the library during lunch, but Dex tracked her down.

"How long are you going to give everyone the silent treatment?" he asked, not even attempting to use a library-appropriate voice. The librarian glared at him.

"I don't want to talk about it," she mumbled.

"But I might be able to help."

"No one can help. But thanks for trying."

"You really want me to leave you alone?"

She nodded.

He sighed. "Okay. If you change your mind . . ."

"Thanks."

She watched him go, torn between relief that he was gone and loneliness so deep her chest felt ripped apart.

Dex must have warned everyone to leave her alone, because no one sat with her in study hall. Biana dropped a note in her lap when she passed by, though.

"Let me know if there's anything I can do."

Sophie blinked back tears as she read the note a second and third time.

She still had her friends—until they found out what a freak she was, at least—and they would help her through this. Once she was ready to tell them.

Bile rose in her throat when the bells rang. She didn't want to go home. It wasn't *home* anymore. If they didn't want her, what was the point of staying?

Maybe Grady and Edaline felt the same way.

Maybe they wanted to talk to her about leaving.

Totally sick, she moved slothlike to her locker to triple-check she had all her homework supplies. Then she took the long way to the Leapmaster, her footsteps echoing through the empty halls. All too soon she was there. She stared at the crystals, unable to give the command.

"What are you still doing here, Foster?" Keefe asked, coming up behind her. "Don't tell me you had to go to the Healing Center again."

"Nope. Just lost track of time."

He fanned the air. "Phew, those are some pretty strong emotions. Can't tell what they are . . . but they don't feel good."

She looked away, avoiding his close scrutiny.

"I'm assuming you don't want to talk about it."

She stared at the ground.

"And I doubt I'll be able to guess, so I'm not sure where that leaves us."

"Havenfield," she commanded, glad her voice held steady.

She could see him shrug out of the corner of her eye. "Candleshade," he called.

Their eyes met as the crystals spun overhead.

"Well . . . I hope you have a good night," he said as he stepped toward his beam of light.

"Don't worry. I won't."

Grady worked in the pasture, clipping Gildie's claws. Sophie waited for him to yell at her for being late, but when he met her eyes all she saw was sorrow.

"Do you want to talk now?" She kept her tone cold.

"Let me finish up here first."

She stalked inside, collapsing on her bed. She dug out her iPod, shoved in her earbuds, and switched to her "angry" playlist. The screaming was jarring at first—it'd been so long since she'd heard that kind of music—but after a minute the familiar numbness sank in.

She closed her eyes. This was what she needed. Not to feel. Not to care. She would never care about anyone ever again.

Someone grabbed her hand and she bolted upright.

Grady's mouth moved, but she couldn't hear him over the screaming and bass. She toyed with the idea of letting him keep talking—he didn't seem to realize she couldn't hear him—but decided to be mature.

She pulled out her earbuds. "What did you say?" The loud song continued to blast from the tiny speakers.

Grady frowned. "Is that . . . music?"

"Really? You want to talk about my taste in bands?"

He sighed. "No."

He sat on the edge of her bed and she scooted to the far corner—the more space between them the better. "Where's Edaline?"

"She couldn't . . ." He shook his head. "This isn't easy for us, you know."

She bit back the sarcastic comment on the tip of her tongue. She wanted this conversation over. "Look, it's your choice and you made it. No point explaining."

"But you understand why we can't?"

"I don't have to. You have your reasons. They're none of my business."

Grady bit his lip. "Well . . . we're sorry."

"Me too."

He stood to leave but turned back. "It's not your fault—you know that, right?"

She snorted. "Just let me know when I should start packing."

Grady said something else, but she'd already popped her earbuds back in.

Sophie leaned back and let the angry music tune out the world. When the playlist ended, it was dark outside. A tray of food waited for her on the table by her bed. She took a couple of bites but her stomach swirled in protest, so she took the tray back to the kitchen, hoping she wouldn't run into Grady and Edaline on the way.

She was almost back to the safety of her room when she saw light seeping through the cracks around Jolie's door. Curiosity triumphed over anger, and she tiptoed down the hall, pressing her ear against the smooth wood.

"This is only making it worse," Grady murmured. "Let's go to bed. You need some rest."

"I want to sleep in here," Edaline insisted.

"No. We agreed you wouldn't do that anymore."

A sigh cut through the silence.

"Do you think we made the wrong decision?" Edaline whispered.

"I . . . don't know."

"Me either." Fabric rustled. "She looks so hurt. Do you think we should—"

"Do you think she'd actually want to stay with us now?"

Yes, Sophie wanted to tell them. *Yes, if you really want me to.*

"Besides, I thought you said it was too hard having her around," he added quietly.

"She does remind me of her." A tiny sob cut through the silence. "How does she know about Jolie?"

"Alden must have told her. Or maybe Dex." Fabric rustled again. "Edaline, come on, you can't sleep here."

"Just for tonight," she begged. "I need to be in here."

Grady sighed. "Just tonight. And I'm staying with you."

The bed creaked and the light turned off.

Sophie stood there listening to the muffled sobs for a long time before padding back to her room and crawling into bed. She tried to imagine what it felt like for Grady and Edaline. How much they must miss Jolie. How hard it must be to spend every day without her. How lonely it must be to live in a world where no one else really understood what they'd lost. It was almost enough to make her forgive them. Almost . . .

For now, it was easier to try to forget them.

FORTY

THE NEXT MORNING EDALINE MUST'VE conjured her breakfast, because the tray appeared on her desk—and Sophie was okay with that. The only way to survive her remaining time there was to avoid Grady and Edaline as much as possible.

Dex stood waiting by her locker when she got to Foxfire. He stared at the hole in her cape. "How are you doing?"

"I'm fine." She brushed past him to open her locker.

Dex cleared his throat. "Are you mad at me?"

"Of course not."

"Then why won't you tell me what's going on?"

"Because I don't want to talk about it yet."

"But I'm your best friend."

"I know, Dex. I'm just not ready. I'm sorry."

His shoulders sagged. "Maybe I could cheer you up then. We could practice alchemy after school—start getting ready for finals. You could come to my house if you want, and I won't even get mad if you burn down my room."

The idea of a smile twitched around her lips, but it wasn't strong enough to fully form. "Maybe another time."

He sighed. "If you change your mind . . ."

"Thanks."

She leaned against her locker after he left, trying to shove his stricken expression out of her mind. She hated hurting Dex's feelings, but she wasn't ready to be "poor, unwanted Sophie Foster." She yanked her last book from her locker with unnecessary force, knocking an envelope to the ground.

Inside she found a scrap of newspaper with the headline: FIRESTORM CLAIMS FIRST VICTIMS.

There was also a note written in a hasty black scrawl— "You have to stop this"—and a Prattles' pin. A silver moon-lark.

She stared at the glowing metal bird, and somehow she knew it was made of lumenite.

Her hands shook as she folded up the note.

"You okay?" Marella asked. "You look really pale."

Sophie clutched her chest, taking deep breaths to calm her pounding heart. "Fine."

Marella laughed. "You might be the worst liar ever. Whoa—

is that a moonlark? Do you have any idea how rare that pin is? There are less than a hundred of them!"

"Oh, really?" She shoved it back in the envelope and hid it in her bag. "Well . . . cool."

"*Cool*? You have the *Prattles' moonlark*! You should be dancing through the halls!"

Marella's loud announcement turned several heads. Sophie slammed her locker shut. "Sorry, I have to get to session. I'll talk to you later."

Marella mumbled something about "waste" as Sophie fled the atrium, trying to think clearly over the words pounding through her brain.

You have to stop this.

She stumbled through the halls, searching for somewhere isolated to call Alden. She finally found a deserted corridor with stark-white walls and dug out her Imparter.

Alden's face appeared before she could finish saying his name. "Sophie? What happened?"

She glanced over her shoulder to make sure she was alone. "I found another note in my locker."

His jaw set. "We'd better not talk about it now, but I want you to come to Everglen as soon as school is over."

She nodded.

His image flashed away and she sank against the wall.

"Don't even *think* about claiming you're not mysterious anymore," Keefe said, and half a scream slipped out before she could stop it. He grinned as he stepped out of the shadows. "Surprised to see me?"

She sucked in huge gulps of air to calm her panic. "What are you doing here?"

"This is my ditching spot—remember?"

The white walls did look vaguely familiar.

"So, you want to tell me why you're sneaking off to talk to Alden about mysterious notes?"

"It's no big deal, Keefe."

He cocked an eyebrow. "Nope, sorry, I'm feeling way too much panic to believe that."

Empaths made lying annoyingly difficult. "I can't tell you Keefe, so don't ask."

"If you don't tell me, I'm going to tell everyone Valin is slipping you love notes."

"You—do what you have to do."

He laughed. "Wow. This must be important." When she didn't say anything, he shrugged. "Fine, have it your way. But at the end of finals I want a *really* awesome gift as thanks for my silence."

"Deal." They shook hands and Keefe listed off a few suggestions—but she wasn't listening. Thinking about finals gifts reminded her.

"How did you get into my locker after midterms?"

"I told you, I have my methods."

"I'm serious. How did you do it? It's supposed to need my DNA."

"Please. I never reveal my secrets."

"This is important, Keefe. If you don't tell me, I'll tell Alden and let you deal with him."

He seemed to weigh her resolve before he sighed. "It was already open, okay?"

"No way. I never leave my locker open."

"You must have. All I did was open it the rest of the way and drop my gift off."

The faint blush on his cheeks implied he was telling the truth—but it didn't make sense. "Nothing was missing. And you were the only one who put anything in."

"Yeah, which you never thanked me for, by the way. The nerve of some people."

He was right. She never figured out a way to thank him for his unusual gift. "Sorry. Thanks for the candy and the necklace."

"Necklace?"

"Yeah. You really didn't have to do that."

"Good, 'cause I didn't."

"What?"

"I gave you an extra large box of mood candy—that's it. Sounds like someone has a secret admirer. Seriously—how many boys do you have chasing you now?"

"A lot, I guess," she said, hoping he'd accept his own theory. But she had a sinking feeling a boy had *nothing* to do with the necklace.

* * *

Fitz and Biana didn't seem surprised when she caught up with them on their way to the Leapmaster to let them know she was coming home with them.

"I figured you'd have a lot to talk to my dad about," Fitz said. He glanced at Biana.

"Yeah, how are you doing?" Biana asked.

"I'm fine." Her heart skipped a beat—and for once it had nothing to do with meeting Fitz's eyes. Alden wouldn't have told them about the Black Swan, would he?

Fitz pulled her to a quiet corner. "Sophie. My dad told us about Grady and Edaline. I'm really sorry."

"Me too." Biana reached out and took her hand. "Is there anything we can do?"

Sophie looked away, blinking to stop the flood of tears she could feel coming. "Thanks. I'm fine."

One stubborn tear slipped down her cheek, and Biana wrapped her in a hug. Fitz draped one arm across her shoulders.

"It's going to be okay. Really," Biana whispered.

"Sorry." Her voice was thick enough to cut. She pulled away from the hug and wiped her eyes. "I don't want to talk about it."

"I know. That's why I didn't say anything yesterday," Biana said.

"You knew yesterday?"

Biana nodded. "My dad told us a couple days ago, because he and Mom are applying as replacement guardians."

Sophie's head whipped up. "What? Really?"

"Yep. I mean, the Council still has to approve it, but my dad made it sound like it would kinda be a done deal."

Warm tingling rushed through Sophie, and it took her a second to realize it was hope. It didn't totally heal the wound from Grady and Edaline's rejection, but it eased some of the fear and uncertainty. "I . . . don't know what to say," she whispered. "You guys wouldn't mind?"

"Are you kidding? Then I wouldn't be the only girl anymore. You have no idea what it's like having two brothers."

Sophie's eyes darted to Fitz, wondering how he felt about the idea. He grinned. "Of course I don't mind. You're already like my little sister—this would just make it official."

"Oh. Great." She knew he meant it as a compliment, but the word "sister" still stung.

Biana hooked an arm through hers and led her toward the Leapmaster. "See? Everything will be okay."

Sophie wanted to believe her, but she couldn't shake the feeling that things were going to get a lot worse before they got better.

Alden sat quiet after Sophie told him her recent discoveries. Too quiet. She'd tugged out so many eyelashes she was afraid there might be a bald spot. She dropped her hands to her lap.

Finally, Alden cleared his throat. "Can I see the necklace they gave you?"

Her shoulders slumped. "I didn't bring it."

"Why not?"

"I was afraid it might be a bug."

"An insect?"

"Oh. Sorry. That's what humans call tiny recording devices. I didn't want to bring it into your house in case it was a way to spy on us."

Alden smiled. "Human *technology*."

Her face burned. "But why would they give me a necklace, then? It's just a crystal pendant—nothing special."

"It has a crystal?"

"A blue one."

He dug out his black pathfinder from his pocket and pointed to the cobalt crystal at the end. "Was it this color?"

Her eyes widened. "I think it was. Do you think it's a leaping crystal?"

"Actually, I think it's an illegal crystal for leaping to the Forbidden Cities." He rose to pace, shaking his head. "They gave this to you at midterm?"

She nodded. "I still don't understand how they could get in my locker."

"A skilled Vanisher could sneak into Foxfire undetected, and we already know they have your DNA." He crossed the room back and forth four times before he spoke again. "I'll have to get that pendant from you—as soon as possible."

"I'll pick it up on Monday."

"Make sure you don't let anyone see it."

"I won't."

He let out a breath. "Good. You can keep the pin for now—maybe it will trigger more memories. I've never heard of lumenite being used for firecatching, but I suppose it's possible. Maybe you should read through your textbook again, see if it triggers anything else now that you know what lumenite is."

She nodded, though she dreaded the idea of reading the boring book again. "What about the note and the article?"

"You can't do anything about that. Remember your promise."

"I know. But are you looking into it?"

"I'm doing what I can. The Council banned anyone from going near the fires—even those of us with licensed pathfinders. So until they lift that restriction, my hands are tied."

"Why would they do that?"

"They're trying to stop the conspiracy theories from spreading any more than they already have."

"What if it's not a theory? What if it *is* Everblaze? It could destroy the world."

"It would never get that far. As soon as it threatens us or one of the Lost Cities, they'll investigate."

"But people are dying." She pointed to the scrap of newspaper on Alden's desk.

He sighed. "Humans die every day, Sophie. It's not our job to keep them all safe."

"It is if an elf started the Everblaze."

He studied her face for a second before he answered. "You throw the word 'Everblaze' around without realizing what a serious accusation that is. Have you heard the name Fintan?"

She closed her eyes as a word pricked her consciousness. "Balefire."

"Did I just trigger a memory?"

"I think so. But I don't know what it means."

He started pacing again. "Balefire was Fintan's trademark. It's a blue flame that requires no fuel. You've seen it in Atlantis—he sealed it inside the crystal spires to light the city. That was back when he was one of the Councillors. He retired when pyrokinesis was banned—which he fully supported after what happened."

"Marella said people died."

Alden nodded. "Because of Everblaze. I've never really understood the concept, but apparently there's a way to sense cosmic energy in the atmosphere, and if you pull enough of the force together, it will spark Everblaze. Fintan called it the 'fire of the sun on the Earth.' He was the only Pyrokinetic who managed to ignite it and live. The others who tried were consumed by their own flame."

Sophie shuddered.

"After that, the Council forbade anyone to learn pyrokinesis, and Fintan retired from the Council because he couldn't serve without a special ability. But he's stayed close friends with most of the Councillors, and he's the only elf alive who can start Everblaze, so can you see why the Councillors might have a hard time believing he's capable of this?"

"Do you think he's capable?"

Several seconds passed before he answered. "He doesn't seem like the type. Plus, someone's been setting suspicious fires all year—the white fires I've been investigating—and while they showed some signs that they might be someone *trying* to spark Everblaze, I never found any conclusive evidence. The Council is convinced this is yet another example."

"Still, shouldn't they at least investigate the fires, to be sure? Especially since these ones are yellow, like Everblaze?"

"They still see no need. When the first suspicious fires started in San Diego, I asked them to put all the Pyrokinetics under secret surveillance—including Fintan. There's been no suspicious behavior, so they're confident an elf can't be behind them."

"Why is the Black Swan so convinced that it's Everblaze then?"

"I'm not sure they are. Think about it, Sophie. The Black Swan are obviously the ones behind whatever's going on, so why would they go to so much effort to tell us what they're doing? They'd be ruining their own plans."

The words crashed into her brain like a stone. "But . . . what are they trying to do, then?"

Alden stared into the depths of the aquarium. "I'm afraid they might be trying to get you exiled—and trust me when I say you don't want to go there. It's a very dark place."

"Why would they want that to happen?" she whispered, hugging her chest, like the pressure might calm her racing heart.

"I can't even begin to guess, but everything they've done has put you at risk. They gave you an illegal leaping crystal as a necklace. They made you collect Quintessence. Now they're trying to get you to make a very serious charge against a former Councillor—without evidence."

It wasn't until Alden squeezed her shoulder that she realized she was shaking.

"There's no need to be afraid, Sophie. I'll do everything in my power to protect you, but do you understand why I don't want you to act on this? These fires may very well be a hoax to trap you—and you can't let that happen."

She took a deep breath to steady her nerves. "I won't."

"Good girl. I'm so sorry you have to be wrapped up in this, especially considering everything else you're dealing with." He took her hands. "I'm sorry about Grady and Edaline. I thought it might help them to have a daughter to raise again. Obviously, I was wrong."

Her voice failed her, but she managed to nod.

"Della and I would love to have you live with us. I'm still getting everything approved by the Council, but Kenric is confident he can overrule Bronte's objection."

"Why does Bronte object?"

Half a smile crept from the corner of his mouth. "He doesn't trust me. And he's never trusted you, given your past. So the idea of us living together . . ."

"Why doesn't he trust you?"

"Probably because my father's always off chasing phantom rebels," Alvar said from the doorway. Sophie and Alden both jumped. "Sorry. Sometimes I forget how easy it is to sneak up on people." He blinked in and out of vision as he crossed the room and leaned against the wall. "What are you guys talking about?"

Alden cleared his throat. "Sophie might be coming to live with us."

"Really? Cool, I guess." His eyes landed on the teal book on Alden's desk. "Is that a memory log?"

Alden snatched it and held the moonlark side against his chest. "I'm sorry, Alvar, you're interrupting an official meeting between an Emissary and a citizen. Anything you've seen or heard is confidential."

Alvar grinned. "Duly noted." He gave an elaborate bow and strode toward the door. "Forgive me for interrupting."

When he was gone, Alden turned to Sophie. "You should probably get home."

She cringed, but stood up, digging out her home crystal as he handed her the memory log.

"Keep searching your memories, Sophie. Maybe your next revelation will finally lead us to the truth."

FORTY-ONE

SOPHIE WASN'T SURE IF SHE WAS relieved or disappointed when she didn't find a note in her locker on Monday. She'd spent the entire weekend attempting to trigger hidden memories but hadn't found anything, and she was trying not to feel frustrated.

She studied in the caves, partly to avoid Grady and Edaline, but mostly because the walls at Havenfield pressed in—like there wasn't enough room for her anymore. Grady and Edaline left her alone as long as she came back by dark.

Nights were the hardest. She imprisoned herself in her room, sorting out the things she would take whenever it came time to move. Other than Iggy, she was determined to leave everything Grady and Edaline had given her. She didn't want any reminders of the people who'd kicked her out of their family.

But she'd decided to tell her friends about it. The thought of everyone's pity made her feel as if an angry imp were tearing around inside her body—but it was time.

Dex barely looked at her as he opened his locker, and his whole body radiated tension.

She cleared her throat. "Hey, Dex."

He didn't turn, keeping one very cold shoulder pointed in her direction.

"I'm sorry. I don't blame you for being mad. I know I've been a little distant lately."

He reeled around, his face twisted with so much anger she barely recognized him. "You weren't distant with Fitz and Biana on Friday! I saw you hugging them in the hall."

"Dex, I . . ." She hadn't realized anyone was around.

"Why would you tell them before me? I thought we were best friends."

"We are."

"Then why did you go home with them after you turned me down?"

"I was going there anyway. And I didn't tell them—they already knew." She took a deep breath, preparing for the next words. "Grady and Edaline canceled my adoption."

"Oh." He stared at his feet. "Are you okay?"

She choked back a small sob. The words hurt even more to

say out loud. "Not really," she admitted. "But that's why Fitz and Biana knew before you. Alden told them when he asked how they would feel about me living with them."

"What?" His voice was so loud half the prodigies in the atrium turned to stare. "You're going to live with them?"

She leaned closer so he would keep his voice down. "The Council still has to approve it, but I hope so."

"You *hope* so?" He slammed his locker closed. "Well, that's just great. You'll be a Vacker." He said their last name like it was a bad word.

"So?"

"So, Vackers aren't friends with Dizznees."

"I would be—and Fitz and Biana would be too if you made some effort with them."

"Right." He kicked the ground. "I don't get why you'd want to live there anyway."

"For one thing, there aren't exactly people lined up to adopt me." She cleared the bitterness from her voice before saying anything else. "Besides, they're my friends, Dex. I keep waiting for you to get over this—prejudice—against them, but it's like you *want* to hate them."

"I don't trust them."

"Well, I do."

"Yeah, because you have a megacrush on Fitz."

"*I do not!*" Blood rushed to her face. He'd said it so loud everyone giggled.

Dex snorted. "Whatever."

"It's the truth. And why are you being such a jerk? I tell you my guardians are kicking me out, and you pick a fight with me and humiliate me in front of everyone?"

"Maybe if you'd talked to me first—instead of running to Wonderboy—I could've helped. But I guess I should get used to that. Once you're living there, you'll ditch me anyway."

"Right now I kind of want to."

"Good!"

"Good!"

Dex kicked the wall and stomped away.

Sophie leaned against her locker, trying to figure out what to feel. Hurt, regret, and anger warred with each other, but anger won. She was in the middle of the biggest crisis of her life, and all Dex could think about was his silly competition with Fitz. It made her want to throw something. Hard. At his head.

Instead, she grabbed the illegal necklace from the back of her locker, shoved it in her bag, and stomped to elementalism.

Dex avoided her like the plague for the rest of the day—which was fine. She wasn't talking to him until she got a *very* sincere apology. Maybe with a little begging. And a present.

She'd planned to stop by Everglen to drop off the necklace, but Biana told her Alden and Della were in Eternalia all day meeting with the Council. So she went back to the cave at

Havenfield and tried to trigger memories until sunset. Once again, she found nothing.

She was up in her room transmitting commands to Iggy— her new, very successful method of training him—when Grady knocked on her door.

"Sophie," he called. "Can you hear me?"

"Yes." It was the first word she'd spoken to him since their talk.

He cracked the door enough to slip his head through, looking more uncomfortable than she felt. "Sorry to interrupt. A package arrived for you."

He held out a small parcel wrapped in brown paper. When she didn't move, he set it on the floor. "I guess I'll leave it here. Um . . . good night."

It was easy to hate Grady for what he was doing, but it was also hard. She really did love Grady and Edaline, and she'd thought they loved her. Her eyes blurred with tears as she tore off the brown paper, unwrapping a silver orb and a note.

"You must help them." Followed by three names: "Connor, Kate, and Natalie Freeman."

Her hands shook as the silver orb came alive at her touch, the word SPYBALL glowing across the center. She'd never seen one before, but she'd heard kids talk about them. They could show you anyone, anytime, anywhere in the world. You had to apply for a special permit to have one. And she had no doubt who'd sent her this one.

Still, she couldn't resist whispering, "Show me Connor, Kate, and Natalie Freeman."

Light flashed and the Spyball displayed three people huddled together.

The rest of the world disappeared.

Her mom's hair was longer, her dad looked a little thinner, and Amy looked older, but it was definitely her human family. Three echoes of a life where she thought she didn't belong. But they had loved her—which was more than she had here.

She wanted to reach through the orb and touch them, but she had to settle for watching as they huddled on the floor of a crowded room.

Why were they on the floor?

Her eyes found the words EVACUEE CENTER and she nearly dropped the ball.

They'd been evacuated. Which meant the fires were near them.

You must help them.

The note's words rang in her ears and she tried to shake them away—tried to remind herself she was being manipulated. But she couldn't take her eyes off the three people she'd once loved more than anything—the three people she *still* loved—looking tired and afraid as a deadly, unquenchable fire threatened them.

You must help them.

Something inside her clicked into place.

Her family never would've abandoned her. She couldn't abandon them. She didn't know how, and she didn't know when, but she *would* help them.

For now she would stay with them as a silent supporter, watching from afar.

FORTY-TWO

SOPHIE DIDN'T SLEEP.

She barely blinked.

The Spyball felt like a magic window that could close anytime, and she didn't want to miss a second of seeing her family.

Even though she'd tried to forget them. Even though they didn't know she existed anymore. Nothing could erase the love she felt for them. So when the sun painted the sky pink and gold, she stashed the Spyball in the bottom one of her desk drawers, dug out her Imparter, and called Alden.

"What happened?" he asked, rubbing the sleep out of his eyes.

"The fires are near my family, aren't they?"

He hesitated before he answered. "Yes, but everything is under control. Why are you asking? Did you get another note?"

She nodded. "It said, 'You must help them.' I know it meant my family." She left out the names and the Spyball. She wasn't ready to give up her only connection to her family—not after almost eight months without them.

"I don't doubt that's what they meant, but you must remember that they're trying to manipulate you. What better way to do that than to use people you love?"

"They're in danger, Alden. There must be something we can do."

"There isn't. Without evidence, we can't make an accusation, and until that accusation is made—or the fires threaten our cities—the Council won't order an investigation. These things take time."

"We don't have time."

"Yes, we do. Listen, I know you're upset, but promise me you won't do anything."

Her jaw set.

"Promise me, Sophie, so I don't feel like I need to send someone to watch you. Come to Everglen this afternoon, and we'll see if we can't find a solution you're more comfortable with."

She didn't want to agree, but she didn't want a chaperone following her around. "Fine."

"You promise?"

"I promise."

"Good girl. I'll see you after school."

She stared at the Imparter long after Alden's image disappeared.

She knew he was right. She was definitely being manipulated. But in all of human history there had never been a firestorm like this. Global. Deadly. Clearly organized. With bright yellow flames.

An elf *had* to be behind it.

Which meant an *elf* had to stop it.

She wasn't going to run to the Council like the Black Swan wanted her to, but she couldn't sit back anymore. Someone had to do something.

Alden said they needed evidence to make the accusation. She would get it. She didn't know how, but she would find a way.

She threw on her uniform and raced downstairs to get Iggy's breakfast so she could leap to Foxfire early. Her plan was to search the libraries for books on evidence laws.

She never made it past the front door.

Another package. Another note. Another pin.

This time the message was slipped inside a bottle. Her hands shook as she dumped the contents into her palm. The little golden flareadon pin glinted against her skin, and she examined the details, trying to understand its significance. The note only made her more confused.

"Left three, down ten, right two. You have everything you need."

Everything she needed for what?

She examined the bottle—searching for another clue she was missing. It was short and round, with a fluted neck and a wide opening. She nearly dropped it when she realized she'd projected the exact shape into her memory log.

Firecatching.

Lumenite and gold—the way to bottle a *generated blaze*. The way to bottle Everblaze.

The moonlark and flareadon pins supplied the metals, and she had no doubt the left, down, right directions told her how to use the necklace to leap where the fires were. Paired with the bottle, the gifts gave her everything she'd need to collect a sample of the fire. What better evidence could she provide?

But how was she supposed to get close enough to bottle the flame without killing herself—especially without fire-resistant clothing?

Fire resistant.

Gildie was fire resistant—probably why they gave her the flareadon pin instead of a piece of jewelry. They'd probably brought Gildie to Havenfield—she wouldn't put anything past them at this point. Was she supposed to guide Gildie with her mind to fly through the fire and collect the sample? Was that possible?

You have everything you need.

The Black Swan seemed to think so.

But then, she'd be doing everything they wanted her to—breaking several major laws in the process—and she couldn't claim ignorance like in the Quintessence debacle. This would be willful. They *would* punish her. Maybe even with exile.

A huge part of her wanted to leap to Everglen and tell Alden everything so she couldn't be tempted. The other part wouldn't forget her family huddled on the floor, clinging to each other. Or the article the Black Swan gave her: FIRESTORM CLAIMS FIRST VICTIMS.

Whatever consequences she might pay, it was wrong to let people suffer without trying to help. Tiergan said she would make the right decision if the time ever came—and this was the right decision. She *knew* it.

Before she could change her mind, she grabbed her satchel and ran for Gildie's enclosure. The golden pterodactyl flapped her wings as Sophie entered her cage.

Screech!

It's okay, Sophie transmitted, sending images of glowing flames, hoping to calm Gildie's nerves. Gildie settled on Sophie's wrist as Sophie dug the leaping necklace out of her satchel. Her arm almost collapsed under the weight, but she held strong.

Here goes nothing, she told Gildie as she counted the facets the way the note instructed. When the crystal locked in place, she took a deep breath, clung to Gildie's feet, and let the cobalt blue light pull her away.

The sudden blast of heat made her stagger. She could barely see through the thick smoke, but she could tell she was on a grassy plain, and the fires were in the hills all around her. Gildie screeched and flapped her wings.

Steady, Sophie told her, transmitting calming images until Gildie settled down. *Stay.*

She set Gildie on the ground and took off her cape, tying it across her mouth and nose to filter the smoke—finally, a use for the thing. She pried the digital displays off the back of the pins, dropped them in the bottle, and created an air seal the way she'd practiced. It took three tries to get it right, and it wasn't as thick as the seals Sir Conley made, but it was the best she could do.

Hold, she told Gildie, sending her an image of how she wanted Gildie to carry the bottle between her talons. Gildie didn't want to obey, but Sophie repeated the command over and over until Gildie flapped her wings, lifted off the ground, and snatched the bottle, holding it upside down, the way Sophie instructed.

She wasn't sure if she would be able to keep the mental connection once Gildie flew away, so she repeated the instructions until she felt Gildie understood. Then she gave her a warning. *Danger. Not normal fire. Be fast.* She transmitted images that might explain the threat and hoped Gildie's survival instincts would guide her through.

A sharp blast of wind blew smoke in her eyes, and she pointed to the fire. *Go, Gildie. Remember what I told you—and hurry!*

Sophie held her breath as Gildie flew toward the fire line. She tried to watch as her glinting body disappeared into the flames, but the fire was too bright, burning spots of color into Sophie's dry corneas. She closed her eyes, transmitting instructions to Gildie over and over.

Swoop through the thickest part of the flame three times and come back.

Thick, raspy coughs heaved through her chest and made it impossible to concentrate enough to locate Gildie. She didn't know how long she'd been waiting, but the heat of the fire was singeing her skin.

"Come back, Gildie!" she called.

The wind carried her words away.

How long was too long?

Gildie, please come back!

The shift in the wind put her in the line of the fire, which meant that if the grass kept burning at its current speed, she'd be overcome by the flames in a matter of minutes.

"Gildie," she screamed. A coughing fit brought her to her knees, making her voice useless. If Gildie didn't return in the next minute or two, she'd have to abandon her and escape.

The horrifying realization gave her a burst of adrenaline,

and she was suddenly aware of the buzzing energy at the back of her mind. Could she channel it as she transmitted?

She closed her eyes and shoved the energy into her mental call. *Gildie, come back now!*

She scanned the sky. Nothing.

Then a faint glint of gold sparkled through the smoke.

"Gildie!" she screamed, waving her arms. "Gildie, over here."

The gold flash changed course and disappeared into the smoke and flame. Seconds later the shimmering pterodactyl emerged from the inferno, circled once, and landed at Sophie's feet.

Screech!

Sophie threw her arms around her. "Ouch, you're hot!" she yelped, jumping back and thrashing her arms to cool the burn.

Gildie's coarse fur looked singed on the edges, and her enormous eyes were clouded and watery, but she seemed okay. Her foot still clutched the bottle, which was filled with tiny yellow beads of sparks and capped with a glowing golden seal.

"You did it!" Sophie transmitted images of the treats she would give Gildie as she wrapped the bottle in her cape and tucked it under her arm. Then she pulled out her home crystal—glad she hadn't given it back to Grady and Edaline—and leaped her and Gildie to safety.

* * *

"What were you thinking?" Grady demanded as he paced the living room. Edaline stayed outside, treating Gildie's scorched fur. She couldn't bear to look at Sophie's burns, and Sophie couldn't blame her after Jolie. She was surprised Grady could stand it.

Alden and Elwin were on their way.

This was the one thing she hadn't thought through. She knew she would have to confess what she did, but she'd expected to have some time to practice what she would say. Unfortunately, Grady had been in the pasture giving Verdi a bath when they arrived. Gildie screeched before she could even think about hiding.

"Do you have *any* idea how much trouble you're in?" Grady asked, tearing his hands through his already disheveled hair.

Before she could answer, the front door burst open and Alden and Elwin rushed inside.

"You promised," Alden said, his voice angrier than she'd ever heard. "Just this morning, you *promised*."

"I can explain."

"Oh, you'd better—though I'm not sure it will help at this point." The anger faded from his voice, leaving it flat and empty. Hopeless. "Bronte's calling for a tribunal."

She knew it was coming, but her stomach still contorted in ways that made her very glad she'd skipped breakfast.

Elwin cleared his throat. "Let's treat those burns, shall we?"

He squatted next to where she sat, flashing blue light around her arms. "These aren't so bad. I won't even have to use the yeti pee balm."

"Yeti pee?" She gagged as she remembered the stinky gold slime he'd spread on the burn from the stellarscope.

"Takes the sting out of the most severe burn. You're welcome." He spread thick purple balm on all the places where Gildie's scalding fur had touched her skin. "Any other burns you need me to treat?"

She shook her head.

He plunked two red medicine bottles and a bottle of Youth in front of her. "Drink up. This'll fix any damage the smoke did to your lungs."

She swallowed the sticky-sweet serums as Elwin wiped the balm off her arms, revealing fresh, healthy skin. "Thanks, Elwin."

He gave her a sad smile. "Yeah, well, I would say stay out of trouble, but I think it might be too late for that."

Her eyes darted to Alden, and her heart sank when she saw his grim expression.

"That should take care of her, but if you need anything else, you know where to find me." Elwin gave Sophie a look that seemed to say, *Hang in there.* Then he glittered away.

Sophie stared at her lap, not sure what to say.

"What were you thinking?" Alden demanded.

"You said we needed evidence to make an accusation. So I got us evidence." She pointed to her balled-up cape. "Take a look. It's unlike any of the flames I've bottled in elemental-ism."

It looked like part of him wanted to keep yelling, but he unwrapped the bottle. "Incredible," he breathed when he saw the tiny beads of yellow flame.

Grady ran his hands through his hair again and turned away.

"When the Council sees that, they'll have to admit it's Everblaze," she said.

"It isn't that easy, Sophie," Alden told her.

"Why? Because Fintan's their friend?"

"No, because *you broke the law.*"

"People are dying. Losing their homes. My family is camped out in an evacuee center right now afraid for their lives."

"They're humans, Sophie. Elves don't get involved in human affairs."

She pointed to the bottle. "Obviously, one did. I don't care that he's friends with the Councillors. I did the right thing."

"I hope so. Because there's no way I can protect you from the Council."

"I can," Grady interrupted, a wild look in his eyes.

"Grady—" Alden warned.

"No—it's not her fault. It's mine," Grady shouted. "I mes-merized her into doing it."

The words rang through the room as everyone stared at him.

"No, you didn't," Sophie argued. "I didn't even see you this morning."

"You did. You just don't remember because I told you to forget it." Desperation filled his tone, begging her not to protest.

"Grady, the consequences of that would be even more severe than what Sophie is facing," Alden warned.

"It's the truth. I mesmerized her."

Edaline gasped from the doorway, and all heads spun to look at her. "What are you doing, Grady?"

Grady looked away. "I'm telling Alden what I did so Sophie won't have to face a tribunal. I'm the reason Sophie broke the law. I used my ability to make her do it."

"No, you didn't!" Sophie screamed, launching to her feet. "Stop trying to cover for me—I don't need your help."

"Please let me do this, Sophie. It's the least I can do, after everything."

A hint of warmth and love was back in his eyes, but she looked away.

"I—I think you should listen to him, Sophie," Edaline stammered. Each word seemed to steal her strength as she spoke it. "Grady's right."

"No. I'm not going to let you lie to the Council and risk exile because you feel guilty about dumping me."

"It's not about guilt," Grady whispered.

The tenderness in his voice made her throat catch, but she cleared it away. "Oralie will know you're lying."

"I can be a very convincing liar."

"Yeah. I've noticed."

He sank into a chair. "I'm trying to make things right, Sophie."

"This is not the way, Grady," Alden interrupted. He stared at the bottle of yellow sparks. "Maybe when they see this, they'll decide her actions were justified."

"You know Bronte will never let that happen," Grady argued.

"We'll worry about that once we see how the Council reacts to this new evidence. In the meantime, Sophie has been ordered to act as though nothing happened. The official story is that you stayed home sick today and they expect you back at school tomorrow."

Alden sighed and turned to Sophie. "I'm not sure how the Black Swan convinced you to do this, Sophie, but can you promise me you won't do *anything* else they ask you to do?"

"I promise."

"I'm going to try to believe that."

"I'm really sorry, Alden. I won't break another promise."

"I hope not."

She stared at the floor. "I understand if you want to take back your adoption offer."

Edaline made a strangled sound.

"Sophie, we'd be honored to have you live with us." He looked at Grady and Edaline. "Sorry, I've been trying to figure out how to tell you."

Grady glanced at Edaline, then at the floor. "No—that's . . . great. I'm glad to hear it."

Edaline choked out something unintelligible. It might have

been her agreeing, but it was hard to tell. She turned and fled before anyone could ask her.

Alden sighed and held up the bottle. "I should bring this to the Council, get this process going. We'll worry about adoption concerns if . . ."

He didn't finish, but Sophie knew what he meant.

If she wasn't exiled.

FORTY-THREE

ACTING NORMAL AT SCHOOL THE next day was easier than Sophie thought it would be. Dex still wasn't speaking to her, Marella and Jensi were relatively oblivious, and Fitz and Biana already knew. She got a little choked up when Biana hugged her and told her things would be okay—and Keefe made a few jokes about what he kept calling her "mystery illness"—but other than that, it was like any other day.

Until study hall.

Sophie was sitting alone with Biana—ignoring the way Dex kept glaring at her from the next table over—when Stina plunked her beanpole body in one of their empty chairs.

"I never knew you were such a good actress," she sneered.

Sophie froze. "W-what do you mean?"

"Not you, Foster—you're not good at anything. I meant Biana. I know your secret."

Biana glared at her. "Oooh, I'm really scared."

"You should be."

Something about Stina's confidence seemed to get to Biana, because she shifted in her chair and her eyes darted to Sophie.

"She doesn't know anything. She's just trying to trick you into admitting something." Sophie grabbed her things and stood. "Come on. Let's sit somewhere else."

Stina slammed her bony arm across Biana's books. "Oh, but I do know something. See, since you've been ignoring Maruca lately, she and I have become quite close—and she's had some great stories to tell. This morning she told me the most interesting thing about the reason you and Sophie became friends."

All the color drained from Biana's face.

"What is she talking about?" Sophie asked quietly.

Stina flashed a wicked smile at Biana. "Should I tell her, or do you want to do it?"

"Tell me what?"

Biana sat pale and lifeless, like a statue.

Stina giggled. "It's really quite funny. She was *forced* to be friends with you. Her dad wanted to keep a closer watch on the freaky human girl who practically killed his son in a splotching match, so he ordered Biana to be your friend so you'd come around their house."

Sophie saw the panic in Biana's eyes and felt a little sick. "Is that true?"

"Of course it's true," Stina interrupted. "She hated you before that, remember? Did you really think she suddenly wanted to be best friends for no reason?" She studied Sophie closely. "Hmm. I guess you did. You're even dumber than I thought."

Biana sprang to life and reached for Sophie's arm.

Sophie jerked away. "Don't!"

Her mind was spinning, making connections she should have made a long time ago. She'd wondered if someone put Biana up to it. She'd just never considered it might be Alden.

"Sophie," Biana pleaded.

Sophie shook her head as traitorous tears pricked her eyes. The last thing she saw was the look of *I told you so* on Dex's face as she turned and fled.

She raced around a corner and plowed straight into someone.

"Sophie? Are you okay?" Fitz asked.

Of course she would run into *him*. And he was with Keefe— perfect. "I'm fine," she muttered, resisting his help as she struggled to regain her balance.

"Hey." He grabbed her arms. "What happened? What's wrong?"

She shrugged out of his grasp and tried to push by, but he blocked her path. "Let me go."

"Tell me what's going on first."

"Uh, Fitz." Keefe tapped him on the shoulder. "I'm feeling

some pretty serious rage right now. It's probably not a good idea to annoy her."

She glared at Keefe and he took a step away from her, holding out his hands in peace.

"Tell me what happened," Fitz pleaded.

The concern in his voice pushed her over the edge. "Ugh," she screamed, shoving away from him. "Just stop already."

"Stop what?"

"Stop pretending like you care. I know your dad put you up to it, okay?"

"That's crazy." Keefe looked at Fitz to back him up.

Fitz looked away, his whole body rigid. "What did Biana tell you?"

"Nothing," she hissed. "Neither of you had the decency to be honest with me. I had to hear about it from Stina."

Fitz muttered something under his breath. "Sophie, it's—"

"I don't want to hear it." Her voice cracked.

"Better leave her alone," Keefe said, pulling Fitz away. He glanced over his shoulder as he dragged Fitz down the hall—his eyes asking if she would be okay.

She shook her head, pulled out her home crystal, and leaped back to Havenfield.

"What happened?" Grady called when he spotted her, but she didn't acknowledge him. She threw her satchel on the ground and ran straight for the caves.

"Sophie, wait!" Edaline called.

Sophie kept going, but Edaline was faster than she looked, and in a minute she'd caught up with her. She offered a small furball. "In case you need a friend."

Iggy fluttered to her shoulder and Sophie wiped away a tear. "Thanks."

Edaline nodded. "Be careful down there. Looks like a storm's coming."

Sophie hadn't noticed the gray sky, but it seemed appropriate given her mood. She climbed down the cliff and wandered deep into the cave, reveling in the thick, gloomy darkness. She noticed a shard of rock on the ground and hurtled it at the wall. The clatter as it shattered into smaller bits was oddly soothing.

She threw another stone, and another, relishing the clang of each as they were pulverized to smithereens. When there were no rocks left, she kicked the edge of the nearest boulder until her foot throbbed. Dirty, panting, and in more than a little pain, she collapsed to the ground, feeling the tears she'd been holding back bubble over. She buried her face in her hands and gave into them, letting the violent sobs shake her body. She felt Iggy trembling next to her, frightened by her irrational behavior, but she didn't care.

Her life had officially fallen apart.

She had no friends. No family. Facing exile and expulsion.

She was totally and completely alone.

It was at that moment—when she thought things couldn't possibly get any worse—that they did.

A pair of arms pulled her to her feet and smothered her scream with a meaty hand. She tried to fight back, but a cloaked figure swooped out of the shadows and shoved a cloth over her mouth and nose. Something sickeningly sweet burned her throat and nostrils and her head instantly clouded.

A sedative.

She held her breath and kicked with all her might, but she couldn't escape the iron grasp, and she couldn't hold her breath much longer.

"Sophie?" Dex called, his voice echoing against the walls. "Are you in here? Fitz told me I should come find you."

The figure holding her cursed, and Sophie rallied her concentration.

Run, Dex! she transmitted.

She was too late.

She heard the scuffle, but her head was swirling too much from the drug to make sense of it. Then the arms holding her jerked away, and she crumpled to the ground as someone yelped. A ball of fur scuttled away.

Iggy!

He must've bit her captor.

Go get help! she transmitted, hoping he understood what she meant. He scurried out of the cave, so she took that as a good sign.

She tried to get up, but she was too weak. One of the figures grabbed her arm, squeezing so hard it cut off her circulation. "Let go," she rasped, surprised at how the drug affected her voice. Dex moaned behind her and she turned toward the sound.

A third figure had Dex with a viselike grip, and clearly no amount of struggling or fighting would help him escape. She held Dex's panicked stare as her captor pulled her to her feet and covered her mouth with his hand. "Drug them now!" he ordered in a deep voice.

"Both of them?" the figure holding Dex asked. "I thought we only wanted the girl?"

"We can't leave any evidence!" He turned to the second figure, who was already soaking the cloth with a small vial. "You said she only came here alone!"

"She does!"

They'd been watching her.

She watched in horror as the figure covered Dex's mouth and nose with the drugged cloth. His eyes held hers as he struggled against the sedative, but after a minute his head lolled and his body fell limp.

"Get his pendant," the one holding her ordered.

There was an ominous snap as Dex's registry necklace came free in his hand. Then he returned to Sophie, holding the cloth over her face. "Let's try this again."

Her nose burned and her head spun, and the last thing she felt was a tug on her neck as her pendant—her only hope of being tracked down and rescued—was ripped off her neck.

FORTY-FOUR

SOPHIE DRIFTED IN THE DARKNESS, unable to separate nightmare from reality. But the pain pulled her back to consciousness. Cold, thick cords sliced into her wrists and ankles. Bonds.

She was a hostage.

"They ordered a search and rescue," a strange voice whispered from far away. "They believed the tidal wave."

"Staging a suicide would have been better," someone else hissed.

"No one would've believed they both jumped."

"I know. The boy is an unfortunate complication."

Two men—or maybe three. She couldn't tell. She wasn't even sure she was awake. The mental fog felt so thick she could barely think through it.

"What are you going to do with him?" he asked.

"We're not here to answer your questions," a new voice hissed. A ghostly whisper. "Just do your job and wash the girl's recent memories."

Please, Sophie thought, scrambling to make her muddled mind concentrate. She transmitted as far and wide as she could. *My name is Sophie Foster. If anyone can hear me, please send help.*

She listened for a reply, but there was only silence as the darkness swallowed her again.

Loud voices yanked her out of the haze. She wanted to cry, but she didn't have the energy. Her body felt like one giant bruise. At least the pain meant she was still alive.

"Funerals are being arranged."

"They didn't care that there were no bodies?"

"They found the pendants at the bottom of the ocean. Everyone believed."

No! Her brain screamed. *We're not dead. Please, someone hear me. We need help!*

"Have they decided what to do with the boy?"

"They have to get rid of him."

Please! she transmitted. *Please help us.* She pushed the message as far as it could go.

"The girl's awake. I can hear her transmitting for help."

A strong hand squeezed her arm like a vise. "Stop it, Sophie! Do you hear me?"

"Relax. She can't reach anyone from here."

"I don't care. Knock her out."

Sharp sweetness tickled her nose, and she sank into the dark oblivion.

Time lost its meaning in the blackness. Each second felt like the next—until a burning in her nose jerked her back to reality. She wanted to sneeze and gag with every breath.

"Are you sure this is necessary?" The voice loomed over her.

"It's either this or give up."

A very loud sigh.

"I hope you know what you're doing."

Her chest constricted, heaving into a cough—but a cloth blocked her mouth, keeping the cough in. Her body thrashed in pain.

"The gag is choking her."

"She'll live," a gruff voice insisted. "I don't want her talking."

"This better work," someone else added.

The choking grew worse and she started hyperventilating.

"Wonderful. Well, go ahead—before she suffocates."

It felt like they pulled off her lips when they ripped the gag away. Her throat was dry and a sick, sour taste coated her tongue, but the cool air felt wonderful. She gulped as much as she could, coughing and hacking until her chest calmed down.

"Don't even think about screaming, Sophie. No one will

hear, and you will not like how we'll punish you. Nod if you understand."

Her head felt like lead, but she managed a couple weak nods.

"Good. Now let's get this over with."

Rough hands pressed against her temples, squeezing her already throbbing head.

"Why?" she croaked. She tried to open her eyes, but something covered them. "Why are you doing this?"

"You've served your purpose," a ghostly whisper hissed. "Now alter her memories so we can relocate her."

She held her breath, wondering if she would actually feel her memories being stolen—if it would hurt. But she felt nothing.

"Is it working?" the gruff voice demanded.

Silence, followed by an exhausted grunt.

"No."

The single syllable echoed through the room.

Something heavy hit the wall. Then a sweet cloth pressed over her mouth, and the drugs pulled her back to the darkness.

"Wake up, Sophie," someone called through the swirling mist of her mind. Her nose stung again. Then the coughing started.

She wasn't gagged this time, but her eyes were still covered and she was strapped to a chair, bound by her wrists and ankles. "Who are you?" she whispered, struggling to pull her mind from the haze of the drugs.

"That's not important," the ghostly whisper informed her. Shivers tickled down her spine. "What do you want?"

"Me? Oh . . . many things. Would you like me to list them all?" His voice was hollow, empty. She wished she could recognize it, but she'd never heard it before.

"What do you want from me?"

"Ah, see, that's much more specific." He laughed an eerie, breathy laugh—more like a wheeze. "I want to know why you're here."

"You tell me," she spat. "You're the one who captured me."

"Oh, I didn't mean *here*. I meant why you exist at all. Why anyone would go to so much trouble to create such a unique little girl? And what are they hiding in that impenetrable little brain of yours?" Venom seeped into the last words as hot hands brushed across her temples, leaving a trail of warmth everywhere they touched. "I don't suppose you'd be willing to tell me what you're hiding in there?"

"Get your hands off me."

Another breathy laugh. "You've got gumption—I'll give you that. But you leave me in quite a predicament."

Steady footfalls told her he was pacing.

"The easiest thing to do would be to kill you and your little friend and be rid of you both. But it's never easy, is it? Sure—it is with your friend. He'll be disposed of soon enough."

"Why? It's me you want. Why don't you let him go?"

"And cast suspicion on your disappearance? No, we can't

have that. Don't worry, he won't feel a thing. I'm not a monster, after all."

"You're worse than a monster!" she screamed. "You kill innocent children and don't even have the guts to show your face."

"Innocent? *Innocent?*" She could feel his hot breath on her face and pressure squeezing her arms. "If you're so innocent, how did you know the location of Elementine? How do you know about Everblaze?" He released her arms and the blood rushed back in a throb of pain. "No, Miss Foster. You may be ignorant, but you are certainly not innocent. The Black Swan made sure of that."

"Wait. Aren't you part of the Black Swan?"

He laughed—louder this time—almost a cackle. Apparently, that was all the answer she would get.

"So what do I do with you?" he asked, mostly to himself. "Do I keep you here so I can see what you can really do?"

"I can't do anything," she screamed. "I'm not special—I'm just *me*."

"Ah, but that's where you're wrong. You're their little puppet. So maybe I should just get rid of you and take their precious toy away."

Panic made her shake despite the bonds. Would he kill her now?

"You'll never get away with this," she whispered. "I already gave the Council the sample of the Everblaze. They'll come for you."

"How will they know it was me?"

"Because you're the only one who can ignite Everblaze."

"Am I? And I suppose you think you know who I am."

"You're Fintan."

He laughed. "I guess you've got it all figured out, then." He rushed her, gripping her arms again. "Tell me what your mind is hiding and maybe I'll let you live."

She screamed as the burning increased—like her skin was melting. "Please, you're hurting me."

His breath was hot on her face. "This is your last chance."

Please! She tried to concentrate so she could send out one last desperate call for help. She had no idea if she could reach anyone, but it was her only hope.

Her mind buzzed with a reserve of energy as she pictured Everglen until it was all she could see. *Fitz,* she transmitted, imagining him inside, eating dinner in the dining room. It seemed so real she could see his beautiful eyes widen in surprise. *Please, Fitz. I need your help. If you can follow my voice, please find me.*

But you're dead, he thought, his face twisting with pain.

I'm not dead—yet. Please, they're going to kill us.

"She's transmitting again," someone warned.

The pain in her arms became so unbearable she lost her connection—if it had even been a connection.

"Is that true?" the ghostly voice hissed as his hands squeezed tighter, twisting her raw skin.

"Stop," she screamed, contorting from the pain. "Stop, please."

"Knock her out again. And make the poison—I'm done with both of them."

"No, ple—" The sweet cloth blocked the rest of her plea, and she was jerked back to the dark.

Her mind swam through a pool of thick, inky black for an eternity. Sometimes she could find the clarity to picture Fitz's face and send another desperate plea for help, but most of the time she just drifted, feeling the rise and fall of her chest and wondering which breath would be her last.

At first she didn't realize she was moving. A rush of air across her face brought her to her senses.

"Don't struggle, Sophie," someone commanded as she tried to twist her body away. "I'm getting you out of here."

A rescue?

She couldn't feel the bonds anymore, and a strong pair of arms was moving her somewhere.

Her overwhelming happiness only lasted a second. "Dex," she grunted, her voice thick and raw.

"I'll come back for him."

"No." She twisted to break free. They were *both* getting rescued.

"I have to get you out of here, Sophie."

"No." She kicked her legs and almost managed to slip out of his grasp.

His sigh rocked through his body. "You kids are so difficult."

Something tugged at her memory, but she didn't have time to process it. "Dex," she insisted, thrashing harder.

He made a sound that may have been a growl as he spun her around, jostling her more than he probably needed to as he ran. When they stopped, he shifted his weight and pulled a body over his other shoulder. Her heart leaped when she felt Dex's warm breath against her cheek. He still seemed drugged, but he was alive—and they were being rescued.

Everything would be okay.

"Hang on to me," their rescuer ordered. "If I have to carry two of you, you have to pull some of your own weight."

Her brain still felt foggy from the drugs and her body was weak, but there was no way she was going to risk having him put Dex down. She wrapped her arms around his neck and held on with everything she had.

He moved quick and silent—occasionally stopping to catch his breath. Then they entered some sort of elevator, and her stomach lurched from the sudden jump in altitude.

"Who are you?" she whispered.

"It's not important." His voice sounded clipped, giving her nothing distinct she could recognize.

"Why are you helping me?"

"It's my job."

His *job*?

She'd been hoping it was someone who cared, but she wasn't in a position to complain.

"How long have we been gone?"

"It took us ten days to find you."

Ten days in that drugged delirium? Her whole body started to shake.

The doors opened and a burst of fresh air on her skin helped calm her panic. After a few minutes of running he lowered her to the hard ground, laying Dex beside her. Rough fingers parted her lips.

"Swallow," he ordered, pouring something bitter and salty down her throat. She gagged, but he clamped her mouth shut. "Swallow, Sophie."

She choked down the sludge. A minute later she heard Dex gag and knew he must be getting the same medicine.

"Okay," their rescuer grunted, placing something flimsy in her hands. "The medicine will take about an hour to work, and then you'll be back on your feet. That's the best I can do. You kids will have to take care of yourselves from here on out."

"What?" She couldn't even open her eyes—how was she supposed to take care of herself? "Don't go," she begged, fumbling to find him.

"I've been here too long as it is. If you don't make it back in a few days, I'll try to figure something else out, but I can't make any promises."

Tears pricked her eyes. "Please don't leave me," she begged, reaching out for him and finding only air.

He was gone.

Too weak and scared to move, she curled closer to Dex and cried harder than she'd ever cried before.

After a minute she felt a warm tingle in her mind—almost like a caress. Suddenly she was five years old again—before her telepathy manifested and her life changed forever. When she was just a happy, normal girl. She wrapped her mind around the feeling, clinging to the warmth and safety until her weary mind drifted off to sleep.

FORTY-FIVE

SOPHIE HAD NO IDEA HOW MUCH TIME passed before she forced her eyes open, ignoring the searing light. The warm feeling she'd fallen asleep to was gone, replaced with a heightened awareness of everything around her.

Maybe it was from being bound and gagged for so long, or the way the drugs had limited her abilities, but everything felt like sensory overload. It wasn't quite as bad as waking up in the hospital the first time her telepathy started, but it was close. She grabbed her head and moaned, wishing she had the strength to shield the barrage of sound.

They were in a city of some sort—a human one, based on the noise and the cigarette butts on the ground—in a deserted alley. The buildings looked like they belonged to a different century, and everything was stone, even the street. Dex stirred beside her and she squirmed closer, needing to feel his warmth. As long as he was alive everything would be okay.

"Dex," she whispered.

His eyes fluttered and he moaned as the light hit him. Then he bolted upright, his face wild. "Sophie?"

Their eyes locked and she held her breath, hoping he didn't hate her for getting him into this.

He threw his arms around her, hugging so tight it knocked the breath out of her. "I thought I'd never see you again."

She buried her face in his shoulder. "I'm so sorry, Dex. This is all my fault."

They clung to each other for a moment before Dex pulled away, wiping his eyes. "I'm just glad you're okay. And I'm so sorry for the way I've been acting—"

"Please. It doesn't matter. Let's focus on more important things, like staying alive."

He nodded, surveying their surroundings. "Where are we?"

"Somewhere human—but I don't know where."

"Why would we be in the Forbidden Cities?"

"Their hideout must be here. The guy who rescued us didn't leap, so it can't be far."

She checked her arms and wrists for wounds, but the skin was smooth and fresh. No sign of the burns she'd felt during the interrogation. Her nexus was gone too. She wasn't surprised the kidnappers took it, but why didn't the rescuer give her one? How were they supposed to get home? Unless that was what he slipped into her hand before he left. . . .

"What are you doing?" Dex asked as she scoured the ground, searching for anything that looked remotely elvin.

"He gave me something to help us, and I can't find it."

Dex helped her look, but all they found was a scroll of paper with the words "Alexandre, Lantern, Concentrate." Followed by the word "Hurry."

"Well, *that's* helpful!" She crumpled the page, ready to scream. Four vague, disconnected words? That's all they were giving her?

She felt her neck, desperately hoping her home crystal would still be there. But the kidnappers stole that too. Even her bottle of allergy medicine was gone. She had nothing left but the clothes on her back—and her stupid blue Foxfire uniform was only going to make it harder for them to hide among humans.

"I don't understand," Dex said, interrupting her venomous thoughts. "Why wouldn't he take us home? Why would he dump us here?"

"Because this was his *job*, and he didn't want anyone to know he was involved." She rose on shaky legs, the buildings spinning as the blood rushed to her head. "That's how the Black Swan operates."

"The Black Swan?"

"I'll explain as we walk. We should get moving—in case anyone's looking for us."

They wound through narrow, deserted streets, and Sophie finally confessed everything she'd hidden from him: her telepathy, Prentice, the notes, the Black Swan, Fintan, Everblaze, her upcoming tribunal. Dex seemed too stunned to process any of it—and she couldn't blame him.

The more she thought about it, the more she was sure the Black Swan had nothing to do with her kidnapping. *Their little puppet,* he'd called her. Who else could he be talking about besides the Black Swan? Plus, the kidnappers didn't seem to know what was hidden in her mind, and the Black Swan would know that. They put it there.

But if it wasn't the Black Swan, who was it?

And why?

Pounding noise interrupted her thoughts. Sophie stumbled back, clutching her temples.

"What's wrong?" Dex asked, steadying her.

"Human thoughts." She closed her eyes, taking deep breaths. "They're getting louder. Tiergan taught me how to shield, but I don't have the energy right now."

"I can't believe you're a Telepath," he mumbled.

"Does it matter?"

"No." He chewed his lip. "But . . . have you ever listened to my thoughts?"

"Of course not. I don't want to know anyone's secrets. Plus, it's against the rules. The one time I did it I got detention."

"That's what you got detention for?"

"I stole the midterm from Lady Galvin's mind."

Dex laughed and she couldn't help joining him. It felt wrong—given their current situation. But neither of them could seem to stop. They were still laughing as they rounded a corner, and Dex plowed into an old man sweeping the sidewalk in front of his store.

"Watch where you're going!" the man shouted as he struggled to regain his balance.

"We're so sorry," Sophie apologized.

He waved his broom at them. "You should be more careful. Someone could get hurt."

"We will." She pulled Dex away before the man drew more attention to them.

"What language were you speaking?" Dex asked when they were out of earshot. "It sounded like you were trying to clear your throat."

"What do you mean?"

"What do you mean, what do I mean?"

"I mean—wait—what?"

"Sophie, you do realize you were speaking a different language back there, don't you?"

"No, I wasn't."

"Yes. You were."

"Oh! I was speaking English. Humans don't speak the Enlightened Language."

"I know they don't speak the Enlightened Language. But I know English, and I couldn't understand a word you said."

She only half heard him, because her eyes had spotted part of a tower peeking over the roofs. "No way . . ."

She took off down a side street. Dex chased after her.

The street ended in a wide park, and Sophie froze. A hundred yards in front of her was a landmark so recognizable she had to blink her eyes a few times to make sure she was really seeing clearly.

"What is that thing?" Dex asked.

"The Eiffel Tower." She gaped at the graceful structure she'd seen in hundreds of pictures. "We're in Paris. Wait"—she turned to Dex—"we're in France."

"And that means?"

"You must have heard me speaking . . . French." She wrestled with the idea, but it wouldn't make sense. How could she speak a language she'd never learned?

"Okay," Dex said, interrupting her thoughts. "We know where we are. Now what?"

"I have no idea. I guess we keep moving."

They followed a crowd of Indian tourists, because their capes looked less out of place surrounded by saris. "We're going to need money," Sophie said as they passed a currency exchange.

"But unless you feel like robbing a bank, we'll have to figure out a way around it."

"Doesn't money come out of that machine?" Dex asked, pointing to the ATM. "That's how they show it in the movies my mom watches."

"Yeah, but you have to have an account and a code."

"Can we fake that?"

"No. They have all kinds of security measures."

He frowned. "Well, I'm going to check it out. Maybe I can make it work."

"How could you 'make it work'?"

"I'm good with gadgets."

She bit her lip. "Fine, but—be careful. They have cameras and stuff."

He waved her worries away as he got in line. Sophie fidgeted in the background, covering her eyes when he started pressing random buttons like it was a game. She kept waiting for police sirens and alarm bells, but a couple minutes later he was at her side.

"Is a thousand enough?" He held out a thick stack of rainbow-colored bills. "It's just paper, so I wasn't sure."

She gasped, glancing over her shoulder. "What did you do?"

"I told it we needed money and it gave me this."

"You *told* it? How?"

"I don't know. I just knew what buttons I needed to press. Why?"

"Because that's not normal, Dex. You just robbed an ATM."

"I did?"

"Yeah." She shoved the money under her cape so no one could see it. "How come you're so good with machines? Is that a special ability or something?"

He thought for a second before his shoulders fell. "It is. I bet I'm a Technopath."

"You say that like it's a bad thing."

"It's about as good as being a Froster. But I guess it's better than nothing. I'll have to look into it when we get home. *If* we get home." His voice trembled.

She squeezed his hand. "We'll find a way. I got us into this and I will get us out."

"How?" he whispered.

"I don't know." She glared at the spot where her nexus should be. "Why wouldn't he give us a nexus?"

"They can track a nexus through the field that holds you together."

Sophie tried not to worry about how easily they could be found. "Okay. Then the answer must be in this note. We need to do some research."

"Research?"

"Yeah." She scanned the street and pulled him toward an Internet café she spotted a few blocks down.

Since neither of them had eaten in days, she bought sandwiches—chicken for her, cheese for Dex, who was horrified at the idea of eating a once-living creature—and bought an hour of Internet time.

Dex giggled as he stared at the boxy black computers and at the way she navigated the web browser. "Technology," he mumbled, while Sophie Googled "Paris, Alexandre, lantern."

"That's it!" she gasped.

The number-one result was Pont Alexandre III, a famous bridge across the Seine. Ornate lanterns lined both sides. It had to be their way home.

The shopkeeper gave them directions, and after fifteen minutes of walking the famous golden statues at the top of the columns came into view. They sped up their pace, but their excitement faded when they saw how many lanterns there were.

"Maybe we should split up," Sophie suggested.

"What are we even looking for?"

"No idea. Just look for anything that looks elvin and we'll go from there."

"Easier said than done," Dex grumbled.

He was right. The lanterns were covered in elaborate carvings and decorations—some even with statues. They'd barely covered half the bridge when the sun sank below the horizon. They would need to find somewhere to sleep soon.

She was about to call it a day when she spotted a small, curved line at the base of a lantern toward the center of the bridge. An elvin rune—one she could actually read.

"Dex, get over here," she called. She pressed on it, searching for the edges of a secret compartment, but found nothing.

"Did you find it?"

"I found something." She pointed to the rune. "That means Eternalia. This has to be what the note wanted us to find."

"How does it help us get home?"

"I have no idea." Her eyes examined the lantern inch by inch, finally focusing on the tip of the highest lamp. "Look, Dex—there's a crystal. None of the other lanterns has that."

"You're sure?"

"Yeah. I know these lanterns by heart now, and this is the only one that has it." She squinted, smiling when she saw the crystal only had a single facet. "It's a leaping crystal—and I bet it leaps straight to Eternalia."

"You did it! We can go home." He threw his arms around her and spun her around. A second later he jumped back, blushing from head to toe. "Sorry. I'm just happy."

She shrugged, hoping her face wasn't as red as it felt. "No problem." Her smile faded. "But we still don't have nexuses. How are we supposed to get home?"

"People leap without them all the time."

"Yeah, people who don't need them anymore."

"We're close enough—and we'll concentrate extra hard when we do it. We might come back a little faded, but that only lasts a few days."

Easy for him to say. His meter had been three quarters full. She wasn't even to the half. If simple mathematics applied, that would mean she'd lose more than half of herself, which might make her fade away.

But it was their only option.

"Well, we can't do it until sunrise." She pointed to the angle of the crystal, which clearly needed dawn light to create a path. "Maybe we should find somewhere to sleep for the night."

Dex nodded. "I can't believe there's a crystal to Eternalia hidden in the Forbidden Cities. Do you have *any* idea how illegal that is?"

She frowned. "I wonder why it's here."

"So we can come and go as we please," a gruff voice said behind them. Sophie and Dex whipped around to find three figures cloaked in black pointing a silver weapon at their heads.

The kidnappers had found them.

FORTY-SIX

I WOULDN'T SCREAM IF I WERE YOU," THE
figure with the weapon warned them. "I'm not afraid to
use a melder, and you will not enjoy it." He pointed the
metal gadget at Sophie's forehead. "A few seconds will
only stun you. Any more will cause permanent damage. Do
you understand?"

"You wouldn't do that with humans around," Sophie said,
hating her voice for shaking. The bridge wasn't crowded, but
there were a few people out for evening strolls. One of them
would notice the three figures in black hooded cloaks threatening children and call the police.

All three figures laughed, and the one with the weapon—who
appeared to be the leader—moved a step closer. "They have no

idea we're here." He pulled a small black orb from his cloak. "This is an Obscurer. It bends light and sound around us like a force field. All anyone can see or hear right now is wind and a slight distortion in the air, like heat waves radiating off the ground."

Sophie reached for Dex's hand. They were on their own.

"I don't know how you escaped," the leader hissed as he handed a coil of silver rope to one of his goons. "But you can rest assured it won't happen again."

Sophie bit her lip so she wouldn't cry out as the goon jerked her hands behind her back and tied them tight. "How did you find us?"

"The Black Swan must've thought we wouldn't check our own pathways. Let that be a lesson to you. Never underestimate your opponent."

"If you're not the Black Swan, who are you?" Sophie demanded.

"Wouldn't you like to know," the goon sneered as he tied her ankles. The cold metal wire cut into her skin, but she barely felt it as she focused all her concentration on calling for help.

Please, Fitz, she transmitted, imagining him in the halls of Everglen. Her brain buzzed with energy, and she pushed her mind further than she ever had before. *We're in Paris—Pont Alexandre III. We need help. Tell your dad and please hurry!*

Maybe adrenaline enhanced her concentration—or maybe it was wishful thinking—but the message seemed stronger this time, like she could actually feel it swirl inside Fitz's mind as he struggled to ignore it.

Please listen to me. I'm not dead—but I might be if you don't come. Please send help.

Strong arms shook her shoulders so hard her brain rattled, severing her connection.

"She was transmitting again," the goon yelled. "Never heard a call that loud either. We should get out of here in case anyone heard her."

"Agreed—and don't try that again unless you want to find out what the melder would do to your powerful little brain. Understood?" The leader pointed the weapon between her eyes.

She swallowed the bile filling her mouth. "What are you going to do with us?"

"That's none of your business. Let's go."

Dex hadn't said a word since the kidnappers appeared. Sophie figured he was in shock, but he must've been channeling, because in one rapid burst he ripped apart his bonds and jumped free. "Duck, Sophie," he screamed.

She dropped to the ground as a beam of energy whizzed past her.

Another blast from the melder missed Dex as he slammed the leader to the ground and knocked the weapon from his hand.

The other goon grabbed the weapon and blasted Dex in the chest.

Dex flew backward and collapsed on the ground, his body jerking in a seizure.

"Maybe I didn't make myself clear," the leader growled as he dusted his cloak and snatched the melder from his goon. He pointed it at Dex's chest and delivered another blast.

Dex thrashed and flailed, strange gurgling sounds coming from his throat.

"Stop," Sophie begged. "We'll cooperate. Just stop."

"Of course you'll cooperate. You have no choice." He blasted Dex again, and this time Dex didn't move. His blank, lifeless eyes stared into nothing, and Sophie squeezed her eyes shut to block the image.

He'll be fine, she told herself. *He's just unconscious.*

"Get your hands off me," she screamed as a goon yanked her to her feet. A bony white hand squeezed her arm, and she memorized every detail of the pale scar between his thumb and forefinger so she could track him down and find him. The line was white and crescent shaped, with jagged points—almost like a bite.

The word triggered a flood of memories—vivid and clear—and this time they were *her* memories.

"You!" she gasped, jerking her head around to get a better look at him. The deep cowl of his cloak hid his face, but she knew who was hiding in the shadows. "I know you."

"You know nothing," he growled. But there was a dash of uncertainty to his voice. He shoved her forward, laughing when her bound ankles made her stumble.

"Stop playing around," the leader yelled at his goon. "Get rid of the boy while I take the girl back to the keep."

"You can't do that!" Sophie shrieked.

"How are you going to stop us?" the leader asked as he pointed the melder at her forehead. He snorted when she didn't say anything. "That's what I thought."

Something inside her snapped as she watched the scarred goon heft Dex's limp body over his shoulder to take him away and kill him.

She'd heard of *seeing red*, but this wasn't red. This was fierce, black *hate*. It clouded her mind until it consumed her.

All sound vanished and her whole body shook with a frenzy she didn't understand. She pushed the anger and darkness out of her mind, needing to be free of it. When the last ounce of hatred was gone, her vision cleared and all three figures were slumped on the ground, holding their heads and writhing in pain.

Her bonds snapped like they were made of paper, her muscles strengthened by the strange energy still pumping through her. She ran to Dex.

His body was limp as she pulled him free, but she could feel a weak pulse. If she could get him to Elwin, he would be okay. He had to be okay. He couldn't die because of her.

She fumbled through the heavyset figure's cloak and grabbed his pathfinder. She spun the crystal and locked it into place on the facet it stopped on, hoping it wouldn't take her to one of their secret hideouts. She didn't have any other options, so she just had to take the chance. It didn't matter where they went, just so long as there were elves there to help.

Then she flung Dex over her shoulder—barely noticing the extra weight—took a deep breath, and imagined her concentration wrapping around Dex's body like an aura. When she had a hold on him, she held the pathfinder up and stepped into the light, letting it pull them away.

The pain was almost unbearable, but she held on, refusing to let the leap beat her. The light was a force, battering her—pulling and pushing in so many different directions she couldn't tell if she was being ripped apart or crushed. When she was nearing her breaking point, the rushing slowed, the tug-of-war lessened, and the scenery glittered in around her.

She forced the last ounce of her concentration around Dex as the light whisked away, not allowing it to take any part of him with it.

The pain faded, and for one glorious second she thought they might actually be okay.

Then her legs collapsed.

They hit the ground hard, and Dex groaned from the impact. At least she knew he was still alive.

She tried to turn to see if he was awake, but she couldn't move her head. She couldn't feel her body. It was like her brain wasn't connected anymore, and she had an overwhelming urge to let go, drift with the gentle breeze tugging at her skin and follow after the parts of her that the light had dragged away.

She was fading. She must've lost too much of herself in the leap.

For a moment she surrendered, closing her eyes as the

warmth surrounded her. But she couldn't leave Dex. She had to hold on until he was safe.

She summoned every last bit of concentration and transmitted as far as she could.

It's Sophie, Fitz. Dex is hurt and I'm too weak to help him. Please come. I can't hold on much longer. . . .

She could see him with her mind's eye, in his room this time. It was a place she'd never seen—and she couldn't be sure if she was really seeing it now or if it was all in her imagination, but when she called his name, he turned and looked at her.

Please, Fitz. I need your help.

He turned away and his hands grabbed something. A tiny purple Albertosaurus, and the note she'd given him with it. If she could've felt her chest, her heart would've skipped a beat.

I went to your funeral, he thought.

I'm not dead—not yet. I need your help.

Her mind grew weak from the effort, but she fought against the weariness overtaking her and clung to the connection.

Please, Fitz. You have to come. Before it's too late.

Her hazy eyes scanned the scenery, searching for a landmark that might explain where she was. She was relieved they were out in the open, with no signs of the kidnappers. But that also meant they were on their own, and if Fitz didn't come . . .

There's a tree here, Fitz. Part of it has green leaves and part of it has flowers and part of it has snow. It's huge. If you know where that is, please hurry.

She projected the image to him.

I'm so tired. Please help us. We don't have much time.

She couldn't see Dex, but she could hear his labored breathing. She wondered how much longer he could hold on. Would it be long enough for someone to find him?

The gentle breeze tugged at her and she couldn't resist anymore.

I'm so sorry, Dex, she transmitted, not sure if he was conscious. *I'm sorry I'm not strong enough to save you.*

The warmth painted across her mind and she sank into it, to a world of blinding rainbow sparkle. No cares or worries. Just rushing air and freedom.

A faint sound yanked her back to reality.

Steady pounding, close by.

Footsteps!

Someone was coming.

Somehow she managed to pull her eyes open. The world was blurry, but she could see feet approaching her. Three pairs of feet, in dark clothes.

No!

She wouldn't let the kidnappers take her again.

She wouldn't go back to that dark, horrible place.

I'm sorry I couldn't wait for you to get here, Fitz. I tried. Then she released her last tiny hold on reality and let the blinding light sweep her away.

FORTY-SEVEN

SOPHIE DRIFTED WITH THE WARMTH. Time, space, life—they held no meaning in the brightness. But she was peaceful, more peaceful than she'd ever been. If this was death, it wasn't so bad.

A ghost of sound wove through the sparkle and color and heat. She tried to ignore it, but the noise persisted, and it sounded familiar. The same word over and over.

Sophie.

Awareness tugged her away from the light, and she fought against leaving the freedom. She didn't want to go back to the darkness.

But she couldn't tune out the voice.

Sophie. Sophie, can you hear me? Sophie.

The light turned teal and sparkled like a jewel all around her. The voice was soft, but still crisp, like it had an accent she couldn't place. . . .

Fitz!

The rainbow world lost its appeal. With a surge of newfound strength, she pooled every remaining ounce of her concentration and wrapped it around the sound of his voice, letting it pull her back to reality. She gasped as pain rocked her head so hard it felt like her mind cracked, and a thousand different aches splintered through her body.

She tried to move but only managed a slight shiver. Something strong and warm wrapped around her.

"Sophie," Fitz said again, clearer now, right next to her. "Sophie, can you hear me? Squeeze my hand if you can hear me."

She didn't have the strength to squeeze, but her mind was stronger than her body.

I'm here.

He laughed—a beautiful sound—and the warmth enveloped her again, tighter this time. "Everything is going to be okay," he whispered. "You're safe now. Just stay with me, okay?"

I'll try.

There was something she needed to remember. Something bad had happened. Someone was hurt. An image of a strawberry-blond-haired boy crumpled on the ground flashed into her mind.

Dex!

"Dex is fine," Fitz promised. "Keefe leaped him to Everglen, and Biana left to get Elwin. We weren't sure if it was safe to move you." His voice hitched at the end.

So many questions raced to her mind, but she was afraid to ask any of them. *Thank you for coming.*

"I'm sorry I didn't come sooner. I didn't want to believe you could still be . . . get my hopes up if . . ." He choked on the words. "I finally told Keefe and Biana about it, and they convinced me to come. If I'd come sooner, maybe . . ."

You're here now.

"I just hope I'm not too late," he whispered.

"Where is she?" Elwin barked, as running footsteps moved closer. He gasped. "Fitz, open her mouth."

Soft fingers parted her lips, and then a cool liquid slid across her tongue.

"Try to swallow, Sophie," Elwin ordered.

It took every bit of strength she had to push the sweet syrup down. The medicine rushed through her body, numbing as it went.

No!

She didn't want to be sedated again. She didn't want to go back to the darkness.

"It's okay, Sophie," Fitz whispered, his voice farther away.

"Don't fight the medicine," Elwin added. "Your body isn't ready to be awake. I promise it will be okay."

She was scared to sink into the blackness again. She wasn't sure she'd have the strength to come back.

Her panic eased as Fitz's voice filled her mind.

You're going to be okay, he promised. *Just sleep.*

She clung to his words as the darkness dragged her under.

Cool tingles across her forehead pulled her back to reality, and Sophie took deep breaths, luxuriating in the rise and fall of her chest. She'd forgotten how wonderful it was to breathe.

"That's my girl," someone whispered. She knew the voice, but her foggy mind couldn't place it.

Something touched her lips and she parted them, gulping the cool wetness that poured into her mouth. She wanted to drink forever, but the liquid stopped. Her face twisted in protest.

"I know," the voice said, "but you have to give your stomach a chance to adjust. It's been empty for a long time now."

She wanted to argue, but her stomach cramped as the cold liquid hit it. Her body contorted.

"Can't you give her anything for the pain?" another voice asked from somewhere nearby.

"I need her to feel right now, so I can check her progress. Then I can numb her again."

"No," she begged, horrified at her strangled voice. She'd had enough sedative to last a lifetime. "No medicine."

"Shhh," he whispered, rubbing balm into her dry lips. "I won't give you any medicine, I promise. Now please, lay still before you wear yourself out."

"Okay." She forced her eyes open, squinting in the light. A round face with dark messy hair hovered over her. The iridescent spectacles gave him away.

"Elwin," she whispered.

Tears pooled in his eyes. "I can't tell you how good it is to hear you say that. Bullhorn's been sleeping next to you for two weeks. We were starting to lose hope. But yesterday he moved, and now here you are."

Someone sniffled behind her.

"Alden?" she asked, recognizing the other voice she'd heard.

"I'm here," he whispered, stepping into her line of sight and taking her hand.

"You up for a few visitors?" Elwin asked.

"Sure," she whispered. Alden propped her up with a pillow, and she realized she was at Everglen, in the room she'd stayed in her first night as an elf. Outside she could hear some murmured debate over who should see her first, and then Fitz rushed to her side.

She swallowed back tears as she met his eyes. "Thanks for bringing me back."

Before he could reply, Biana raced into the room, threw her arms around her, and burst into tears. "I'm so sorry, Sophie. My dad wanted you around more so he could keep an eye on you, so he told me to reach out to you—but I really am your friend and then you were gone and . . ." Her voice trailed into sobs.

"It's okay," Sophie whispered, and she meant it. If Biana

cared enough to rescue her—cared enough to cry—that was enough. "Forget about it, okay? We're still friends."

Biana sniffled and pulled back to meet her eyes. "Really?"

"Really."

"All right, enough girly drama," Keefe said, shoving his way in. "I was part of the rescue too, remember? I'm the one who knew the tree you told Fitz about was the Four Seasons Tree, so if it weren't for me . . ." He faltered as he seemed to realize he was talking about her dying.

"Thank you, Keefe." She smiled to show him she didn't mind.

He shrugged. "Anytime. And by the way, *you're a Telepath?* I think that proves once and for all that you're definitely the Most. Mysterious. Girl. Ever." His face darkened. "My dad was very smug when he heard you'd been training with Tiergan. He always has to be right. And this time he was."

Sophie's eyes darted to Alden.

"It's okay. You won't have to hide it anymore. In fact, everyone seems to know every detail that's happened these past few months." He shot a meaningful glance at Keefe.

Great. Everyone knew what a freak she was.

Though it was kind of a relief. No more hiding. No more lying. Her friends would stand by her—and the others? She wasn't sure she cared.

"Things are changing," Alden added. "But we'll talk about that later. Right now you should rest."

"Not without this," Fitz said, handing her a bright blue elephant.

"Ella!" Sophie buried her face between the floppy ears, ignoring Keefe's snickers. She'd been through too much to care about being teased. She met Fitz's eyes, melting when he smiled at her. "Thank you guys for rescuing me."

"Just get better, okay?" Keefe ordered. "School wasn't the same without you. No explosions or emergencies. Boring."

"I'll try," she promised.

And if you need anything, you know how to reach me, Fitz transmitted.

Sophie gasped. "How?"

Fitz grinned. *I have no idea. I slipped in when you were fading, and now it's easy.*

Does that mean you can read my mind? she asked, preparing to die of embarrassment if he could.

He shook his head. *I can only transmit. Pretty cool though, huh?*

She nodded, trying not to worry about what might've happened to her brain to cause that kind of change.

"Hey—no secret telepathic conversations, you two—or I'll have to assume you guys are flirting!" Keefe laughed as they both flushed and looked anywhere but at each other.

"I think Dex is going to explode if I don't let him in," Elwin interrupted.

Dex burst through the door, and Sophie's breath caught in her throat. He looked perfect—not a scratch on him.

We'll see you later, Fitz promised as he pulled Keefe and Biana out with him.

Dex stomped past them. "Next time you try to rescue me, concentrate a little more on yourself, okay? You almost died because of me."

"Actually, you almost died because of me. Twice," she reminded him, her voice shaking as she tried not to think about his blank eyes after the melder blasts.

He bit his lip. "Call it even?"

"Deal."

He leaned forward like he wanted to hug her, then noticed Alden and Elwin and backed off. He squeezed her hand, color streaking his cheeks. "You're really okay?"

"Yeah. Just a little tired. How about you? Did the melder do any damage?" Her eyes searched for tiny injuries she might've missed from far away.

"Nothing Elwin couldn't fix. And nothing like what happens when you leap with all your concentration wrapped around someone else. Do you have any idea how dumb that was?"

"What was I supposed to do? My concentration's weak as it is, and you were injured."

"Actually, your concentration isn't weak at all," Alden corrected.

"Dex didn't lose a single cell in the leap," Elwin agreed. "If you'd kept a little more of that concentration for yourself, you wouldn't have faded, and I wouldn't have had to spend two weeks trying to bring the color and life back to a half-drained body."

"Sorry," she mumbled, cringing at the words "half-drained." "But . . . my nexus was barely at the half. Dex, you saw it. How could my concentration be strong?"

"We'll talk later," Alden said. "Right now you need to rest."

He pulled the blankets around her shoulders, and she snuggled Ella, wondering why Fitz had her. She'd left Ella at Havenfield. "Did Grady and Edaline come to see me?" she whispered, hating herself for hoping they had.

"They haven't left since Fitz found you. You have no idea what they've been going through these past three and a half weeks."

"Three and a half weeks?"

"You've been gone a long time, Sophie. They're waiting outside, but they understand if you don't want to see them."

Emotion caught in her throat and she cleared it away. As much as they'd hurt her, as angry as she'd been, she couldn't shut them out—not after everything she'd been through. "You can send them in," she whispered.

Alden squeezed her shoulder and led Dex toward the door. Dex waved as two gaunt figures crept into the room.

Sophie blinked. "Grady? Edaline?" She barely recognized them. They looked like they hadn't eaten or slept or changed clothes in weeks.

Edaline covered her trembling lips and raced to Sophie,

crawling into the bed to hold her so tight it was almost hard to breathe. Grady dropped to his knees on the floor beside them, squeezing Sophie's arm.

"I'll just . . . give you guys a minute," Elwin said, fleeing the scene as they all started crying.

Grady cleared his throat and wiped his eyes. "Sorry, we don't want to wear you out. It's just a little overwhelming to get you back. We went to your funeral. . . ."

Another sob shook Edaline's shoulders before she released Sophie and pulled herself up, squeezing Sophie's hands. "Losing you was one of the hardest things I've ever endured," she whispered, "but the worst part was knowing that you had no idea how much you mean to us."

Grady squeezed both of their hands.

"We never wanted to love anyone again after we lost Jolie," Edaline whispered. "But we love you, Sophie. You're just as much our daughter as she was. We need you to know that—not because we want you to forgive us, but because you deserve to know."

"Canceling your adoption was the worst mistake we've ever made," Grady added. "You'll always have a home with us at Havenfield, but we understand if you want to stay with Alden and Della. We just hope you'll come visit sometime. Let us be a tiny part of your life—even if we don't deserve it."

Sophie nodded, too overwhelmed to say anything other than, "Thanks." But when Edaline kissed her cheek and Grady stroked her hair, she added, "I love you guys too."

They both smiled, and even though they were still thin and tired, they looked more like themselves. Edaline kissed her cheek again.

"Oh, I almost forgot." Grady pulled a tiny furball out of his pocket.

"Iggy!"

Iggy flitted to her shoulder, nuzzling her cheek. Sophie gagged. "Ugh, I forgot about Iggy breath." She scratched his fuzzy head, and his crackly purr filled the room. "Thanks for your help in the cave, little man."

Edaline sniffled. "He did come and find us. Took us a while to figure out what he wanted, and by the time we got down to the caves there'd been a huge wave and . . ." Her voice vanished.

Sophie squeezed her hand. "I'm safe." She tried to believe the words were true.

Grady stood up as she yawned. "We'll let you sleep."

She didn't want to sleep after losing so much time, but her body demanded it, and by the time Grady pulled the blankets around her and switched off the lights, she was already asleep, with Iggy snoring like a chain saw beside her.

FORTY-EIGHT

SOPHIE'S DREAMS WERE A HORROR show of ghostly voices and black figures and fire. She woke up tangled in covers, only to find an enormous gray beast towering over her. She screamed as black fear swirled through her mind and her whole body trembled.

"Stop, Sophie," Alden warned, shaking her shoulders. "Stop, you're hurting him."

His voice washed the darkness away and her vision cleared. The gray beast twisted in pain on the floor.

"Sandor won't hurt you," Alden promised. "The Council assigned you a goblin bodyguard to keep you safe. It's not a good idea to inflict pain on him."

Her jaw dropped. *"Inflict?"*

Alden nodded. "It seems you're an Inflictor. A melder causes temporary paralysis, so Dex was semiconscious during your escape. He told me you made everyone collapse in pain. I wondered if that meant you could inflict. You just did it to Sandor, so it appears you can."

Her eyes widened and she turned to the barely conscious goblin on the floor. "I'm sorry—I didn't mean—"

"He'll be okay in a minute," Alden promised. "Goblins are tough."

And yet she'd incapacitated him—without even trying. "But . . . I'm a Telepath. How can I have two special abilities?"

"It is possible to have more than one. Rare. But considering how special you are, I wouldn't be surprised if you still have more abilities that you haven't discovered."

"What, I'll just wake up and suddenly be able to walk through walls?"

"Not quite. Most abilities stay dormant until they're activated—that's why we have ability detecting. It seems like the trauma of the kidnapping activated some of your latent talents. That's why you can inflict, why your concentration is stronger now—and Dex said you're a Polyglot."

"A what?"

"You speak languages instinctively, just by hearing them. It's a very rare skill. You'll be glad you have it as you advance in multispeciesial studies."

"I guess." She wasn't sure she would ever be excited about having *more* weird talents.

"We'll run some tests when you're stronger. See if we can find out what else you can do."

She shivered. She could still hear the ghostly voice of the kidnapper saying something similar while he interrogated her.

What if she didn't want to find out anything else?

Sandor heaved himself to his feet and moved back to his post in the shadows. "I'm so sorry," she whispered.

"It's all right." Sandor's soft voice would've made more sense coming from a bunny than a seven-foot-tall, buffed-out goblin. He turned to Sophie and bowed. "It's nice to know my charge can defend herself if I fail her."

She shivered. "I take it this means you haven't caught the kidnappers."

Alden squeezed her hands. "We won't let them get anywhere near you ever again. The nobility is working overtime following the leads we have." He handed her a memory log and flipped to a blank page. "Do you remember anything that might help?"

"I was blindfolded the whole time, and I was too drugged to probe their minds. Plus, I was saving my concentration for transmitting. But the leader was a Pyrokinetic, so it had to be Fintan."

"You're sure he was a Pyrokinetic?"

She rubbed where his hands had seared her skin. "Positive."

A deep pucker formed between his brows. "Then we have an unregistered Pyrokinetic. We're still monitoring every move of the other Pyrokinetics, and it couldn't be Fintan."

"Why not?"

"The sample you collected proved the fires were Everblaze. Fintan was arrested the day you and Dex disappeared, and he's been held in custody ever since, awaiting tribunal."

"That actually makes sense. He asked me if I knew who he was, and when I guessed Fintan, he laughed. Then he burned me again." She shuddered.

"I'm so sorry, Sophie," Alden whispered, choking up. "When I think about what—"

"Don't think about it," she interrupted, hating to see him upset. "It's over. I'm fine. And it's not your fault."

"In a way it is. I'm the one who declared your deaths and called off the search. If I hadn't done that, we might've found you sooner." He shook his head. "When they found your pendants in the ocean—and there had clearly been a tidal wave at the cave—I couldn't see how it could be anything other than a tragic accident. I never considered kidnapping. I never thought the Black Swan would sink so low."

"They didn't. I don't know who the kidnappers were, but they weren't the Black Swan. In fact, I think the Black Swan rescued us."

"That's what Dex said. Are you sure?"

She nodded, trying to organize her memories—they were

a muddled mess from the drugs. "I think the Black Swan are working against the kidnappers, and I think they sent me the notes and clues because they wanted me to stop the Everblaze." She paused, not sure if she wanted to know the answer to the next question. "Do you think the kidnappers are the ones who started the Everblaze?"

Alden fiddled with his cloak. "It's possible. Fintan claims innocence. But he also won't submit to a probe—so he's hiding something. And if we have an unregistered Pyrokinetic out there, I have no doubt Fintan knows something about it."

"Why doesn't the Council just order a memory break?"

"They want to give their friend a chance to see the error of his ways—and perhaps this new information will motivate him to confess. If not, they'll order one. They're just *trying* to avoid condemning him to a life of madness."

"That's his choice, if he won't confess."

"It is. But if you'd ever seen a memory break, you would understand their reluctance." His shoulders trembled. "It's haunting."

Her thoughts flashed to Prentice. She didn't know what he looked like—or even who he was—but he let his mind be broken to protect her, maybe from the same people who'd taken her and Dex. She wasn't sure she deserved that sacrifice. Especially since it had also destroyed the lives of his family.

"I'm sure the memory break will be ordered," Alden said,

breaking the silence that had settled over them. "The Council is simply giving their friend every chance to help himself. Plus, they don't want to believe he tried to single-handedly wipe out the human race. In the meantime, if there's anything else you can remember that might help us find the kidnappers, now's the time to tell me."

There *was* something else—something big. But the memory was out of reach, repressed by the trauma. She stared at Alden's hands as he fiddled with his cape. His pale, white hands.

She lunged for the memory log. "I've seen one of them."

"What? When?"

"The man who tried to grab me in the human world the day Fitz brought me here. He had a dog bite on his hand. The kidnapper had a crescent-shaped scar in the same place."

She projected the wound and the scar on a page and handed the memory log to Alden. One was fresh and bleeding and the other was a faded scar, but they were the same size and shape, and were even jagged in the same places. "See? He really was an elf—and he had been there to get me."

"Yet another way I've failed to protect you." Alden shook his head. "Do you remember what he looks like?"

She closed her eyes and concentrated on the memory, waiting until she'd recalled every detail before she sent it to the paper.

Her hands shook as she stared at the person who'd tied her up and drugged her—who'd been ready to kill Dex. He had short blond hair, piercing blue eyes, chiseled features—it seemed wrong for someone so handsome to be so evil.

Alden's eyes pored over the image. "I don't know him. It's amazing he let you go the first time, with only a human to threaten him."

"Well, Mr. Forkle could be . . ."

"Could be what?" Alden asked, when she didn't continue.

Her mind was racing in too many directions to answer. She rubbed her temples, trying to think through the chaos of memories. She needed to be *really* sure of what she was about to say.

"Should I call Elwin?" Alden asked, rushing to his feet.

She grabbed his cape. "It was *him*."

"What was?"

"Mr. Forkle." She shook her head as she met Alden's eyes. "Mr. Forkle rescued us." The sentence was so bizarre it made her want to laugh. But she knew it was true.

"Mr. Forkle," Alden repeated.

She nodded. "He started almost every sentence with 'you kids.' The man who rescued us said it too."

"That could be a coincidence."

"It was him." She scooted back, like she needed room to fit her huge epiphany. "Mr. Forkle is an elf."

Alden sank down beside her. "You're sure?"

She wanted to say yes, but . . .

She grabbed the memory log and projected Mr. Forkle the

way she remembered him. Wrinkled. Overweight. There had to be a mistake.

Alden gasped as he looked over her shoulder. "He *is* an elf."

"But he's old."

"That's exactly what someone looks like when they've eaten ruckleberries. See the way the skin looks stretched? The body swells *and* wrinkles as the berries digest."

"He did smell like feet," Sophie remembered. "That could've been from the berries."

Alden swept his hair back and stared into space. "That explains why the kidnapper backed down. He could tell your neighbor was more powerful than him. I'm sure the Black Swan had their most skilled operative guarding you." He shook his head. "I should've guessed they wouldn't leave you alone. They'd want someone nearby in case anything went wrong."

He was right. Mr. Forkle had always looked out for her. He'd called 911 when she hit her head. And he was always asking about her headaches. He must have known she was a Telepath. "But . . . why could I hear his thoughts? Shouldn't his mind have been silent?"

"Another part of his disguise. A highly skilled Telepath can broadcast thoughts the way humans do. He gave you what you needed to hear to not suspect him. I bet that's how they planted some of the memories in your brain. He certainly had enough access to you to broadcast subliminal messages when he needed to."

Mr. Forkle? A Telepath?

She sucked in a breath. "He was there when I fell and hit my head—the accident that started my telepathy when I was five. Do you think he did something to me?"

"It's possible. I'm not sure why they'd want to trigger an ability in you at that age. But he might have decided to take advantage of you being unconscious. Telepathy can be easier to activate that way—not that I've ever tried it. In fact, I wonder . . ."

"What?" she asked, when he didn't finish.

"I wonder if he's the reason you've developed more abilities. He might have triggered some after he rescued you. They were *exactly* the skills you needed to survive."

She didn't remember that much of what happened, but she did remember feeling five years old again. Was that because he'd done the same thing he'd done back then?

She shook her head. It was too much.

Her whole life she'd been controlled and manipulated—and they were still doing it.

"Why?" she asked, wishing she had something to throw. "Why put me with humans? Why all the secrets? What was the point?"

"I don't know," Alden whispered as he rose to pace. "I'd always assumed it was to hide you from us. But maybe there was more to it than that. Tell me this—why did you risk everything to bottle the Everblaze?"

She was surprised he had to ask. "People were dying."

"*Humans* were dying," he corrected. "And no one cared enough to stop it. Except you. I think you can hardly deny your upbringing played a big role in that decision. Maybe that's what the Black Swan wanted all along. If you're right—and they're working against these other rebels, who seem to want to destroy the human race—then perhaps they thought it would be wise to have someone who cared about humans on their side."

"I'm not on their side."

"That doesn't mean they don't want you to be." He paused to stare out the window. "The only ones who'll know for sure are the Black Swan. It's time we find them and ask them."

He made it sound so simple, like he could just look up their address in the phone book. "They've been hiding from you for years. What makes you think you can find them now?"

He held up the memory log. "We'll run these images through the registry database. Your neighbor might be hard to match, but we'll check every Telepath until we find him and force him to lead us to the Black Swan. In the meantime, we'll use the other picture to find the identity of the kidnapper. Once we catch him, we'll be able to probe his mind to find the others."

She curled her knees into her chest, shaking her head. "I told him I recognized him. I'm sure he's in hiding now."

"It's not that easy to hide from us."

"No offense, but it doesn't seem like it's that hard. The Black Swan hid me for twelve years—and you only found me when they led you to me. The kidnappers hid us somewhere in Paris and you had no idea. They have secret leaping crystals hidden among humans that no one knows about—except the other rebels. I think it's easier to hide here than in human cities. At least they have security cameras and detectives and police."

Alden sighed. "I see why you might feel that way, but you have to understand, Sophie. Humans have those measures in place because conspiracies and arson and kidnapping are common. Those are unheard of here. Or they used to be."

He shook his head. "For thousands of years the Council reigned supreme. They were the wisest, most talented members of our society, working together for the greater good. No one questioned their authority. But the past few decades have changed everything."

"Why?"

"Humans. They've developed weapons powerful enough to destroy the planet. So about sixty years ago a measure was brought before the Council to create a new Sanctuary specifically for humans, to relocate them for the good of the earth—and their own safety. It had a lot of support. Some very influential people have grown tired of hiding in the shadows while humans run amok throughout the globe. But the Council rejected it, refusing to imprison an intelligent species. For the record, I agree with their decision."

Sophie nodded. Humans would be devastated if their lives were uprooted that way.

"The supporters of the initiative were angry with the Council. Some called for members to resign—especially Bronte, since he was the most outspoken against the idea—and there were threats to go ahead with the plan anyway. The Council didn't take the threats seriously, but they forbade human contact of any kind and recruited Telepaths like myself to keep our minds open for suspicious activity. All talk of rebellion vanished, and the Council was satisfied. Crisis solved."

He sighed. "I'd always suspected the rebels moved underground—though I *never* would have guessed there was more than one group. I'm afraid I've been almost as blind as the Council." His shoulders sagged as he stared at the ground.

"Even when I found your DNA, none of the Councillors would believe you really existed, or that if you did, that it had anything to do with rebellion. That's why things have been handled so poorly. But they can't ignore it anymore.

"An elf tried to burn the Forbidden Cities to the ground with Everblaze. A team of alchemists had to spend days making Frissyn to put out fires all over the globe. Two children were kidnapped by an unregistered Pyrokinetic and held prisoner while we held funerals for them." His voice cracked, and he paused for a second, clearing his throat. "The Council has been forced to admit the rebellion exists, and you can rest assured that this threat *will* be resolved. We have tremendous power at our disposal. We just haven't been using it."

Sophie reached for Ella, hugging her to her chest to hide her shaking.

She wanted to believe him, but it was hard. The rebels were smart, and very well organized. If they wanted to get to her, she had no doubt that they could.

But she had a bodyguard now. He would keep her safe—though she wasn't in love with the idea of a giant gray goblin following her around all the time.

"I can tell you're still worrying, Sophie, and I don't blame you. But trust me on this. The rebellion will be stamped out very quickly now that the Council is willing to acknowledge it. Anyone involved will be brought to justice."

"I hope so," she whispered, trying not to think about the ghostly voiced elf who was out there somewhere, plotting revenge. "I'll see if I can trigger any memories that might help."

"No." Alden sat beside her. "I don't want you involved. You've been a big help, and you have incredible powers at your disposal, but you're twelve years old."

"Thirteen," she corrected, realizing her birthday had passed a few months ago. Elves didn't pay attention to birthdays—given their indefinite life spans—so she'd forgotten.

"Fine. Thirteen. That's still too young to be wrapped up in a conspiracy. I want you to make me a new promise." He waited until she met his eyes. "I want you to promise you will just be a normal, happy, thirteen-year-old girl. Go to school. Make friends. Get crushes on boys. Have fun. No more worrying about secret messages or plots or rebellions. Leave that to boring grown-ups like me."

"But I'm *not* a normal thirteen-year-old girl. I have abilities no one understands—and secrets stored in my brain that people are willing to kill me for."

"That may be true, but being special doesn't mean you can't have a normal life. You only get seven years to be a teenager. Enjoy them. Promise me you'll try."

A *normal life*. It sounded too good to be true.

It *was* too good to be true.

After everything she'd been through, she'd accepted that she would never fully belong. It was time to stop pretending that she could.

"I'll try," she agreed, "only if you'll promise me that if something big happens and you need me, you'll come to me—even if I'm only thirteen."

He held her gaze, like he was waiting for her to blink. She didn't.

"You drive a hard bargain," he relented. "But deal."

"Okay, then. I promise."

"The Council will be happy to hear that. It will help at your tribunal."

"Tribunal?"

His eyes dropped to the floor. "Bronte's still insisting a tribunal be held for the laws you broke to collect the Everblaze. Plus, the Council has to decide your future at Foxfire."

She tugged out an eyelash. She'd forgotten how uncertain her future still was. "When will it be?"

"Not right away. They've agreed to wait until you're strong enough."

"I'm strong enough."

"Three days ago you had a banshee sleeping at your side, and we were terrified we would have to hold a real funeral for you."

"Please don't make me wait. I can't stand not knowing."

Alden studied her face for a long time before responding. "If that's what you really want, I'll arrange everything for tomorrow."

She nodded. "It is."

FORTY-NINE

SOPHIE SAT NEXT TO ALDEN ON A PEDestal facing the twelve Councillors in Tribunal Hall—and this time it was a packed house. Friends, Mentors, strangers. Even enemies. Stina sneered at her as Bronte rose to read the charges.

Between the laws and the bylaws and the sub-bylaws, she'd committed five major transgressions and eleven minor transgressions—a new record. At least half of them carried the possibility of exile.

And yet, Sophie wasn't afraid.

She'd been drugged and interrogated, watched her best friend tortured for trying to escape, and had to fight her way back from fading away. No matter what the Council decided, it could never be worse than what she'd already survived.

So her legs didn't shake as she walked forward to speak her defense, and she didn't tremble under Bronte's glare. Her curtsy was as ungraceful as ever—she heard Stina snicker as she lost her balance at the end—but she held her head high as she faced the Council in all their regal glory.

"Miss Foster," Emery said, his voice warm. "On behalf of the entire Council I'd like to express our relief that you made it home safely. We'd also like to assure you that we will find whoever was responsible for your kidnapping and make them see justice for their actions."

"Thank you," she said, proud of the strength in her voice.

"That being said, you stand before us today accused of very serious charges. What have you to say in your defense?"

She'd spent all night drafting the perfect apology for her actions, but she'd thrown it away before leaving Everglen. She wasn't sorry for what she'd done, and she wouldn't pretend otherwise. Oralie would know she was lying, anyway.

Sophie cleared her throat and addressed the entire Council— even Bronte. "I never wanted to break the law, and I don't plan on doing it again. But people were losing their houses. People were dying. I know they were humans, but I couldn't sit back and let it happen. I'm sorry if that's a crime. I won't argue if you punish me for my choice, but I firmly believe it was the right decision. I'd rather be punished for making the right decision than live with the guilt of making the wrong one for the rest of my life."

Murmurs and whispers filled the room until Emery cleared his throat. Silence fell as he closed his eyes and placed his hands over his temples.

Most of the Councillors ignored her as they debated, but Terik glanced her way, shooting the tiniest wink when their eyes met. She hoped it was a good sign, but she couldn't be sure. Emery held out his hands to silence the arguments raging in his head. His eyes locked with Sophie's, his face unreadable.

"Thank you for your honesty, Miss Foster. While some of us"— he glanced at Bronte—"feel that your attitude is disrespectful and rebellious, none of us can deny that your actions uncovered a problem and conspiracy we ourselves had overlooked, and for that we owe you our gratitude. We can't, however, simply *ignore* the fact that laws were broken."

She sucked in a breath, preparing for the worst as the whispers and murmurs buzzed in her ears like static.

"There was much debate on what proper punishment would be," Emery continued, with another sidelong glance at Bronte, "but a decision has been reached— and it *is* unanimous." He cleared his throat. "Considering the fact that we, as your rulers, failed to protect you from recent unfortunate experiences, we feel that it would be inappropriate to assign any further punishment. Your transgressions will go on your permanent record, but your punishment will be marked as 'already served' and that will be the end of the matter. Is that understood?"

It took a second for the words to sink in—and another after that for her racing mind to realize he expected a response. "Yes," Sophie practically sang, as the murmurs turned into chatter around her.

Punishment already served. Could that really be it? Could it really be over?

"Which brings us to the matter of your Foxfire admission," Emery shouted over the din, his words like a giant pin bursting the bubble she'd been floating in.

The room fell silent. Sophie's heart thundered in her chest.

"Miss Foster, you were admitted to Foxfire on a provisional basis, and the matter was to be revisited once we'd seen your performance in your sessions. Due, however, to the aforementioned *unfortunate* experiences, you missed all of your final exams and are currently failing all of your sessions. And in order to preserve the integrity of our testing process, we cannot allow the exams to be made up at this time. So we're at a bit of a loss as far as how to proceed."

Bronte opened his mouth and Emery cut him off. "Your suggestion has been noted, Councillor Bronte. We are, however, hoping to hear a few other suggestions before we decide. I open this up to Miss Foster's Mentors. Can any of you see a solution to her grade issues?"

Whispers hissed through the auditorium as all of her Mentors rose from their front row seats and bowed their respect.

"If I may offer a suggestion," Tiergan said, smoothing his intricate blue cape as he stood and bowed. He'd dressed up for the occasion—it looked fancier than Lady Galvin's.

"Ah, Sir Tiergan," Emery said, his voice with a harder edge. "It's been a long time since you've stood before us."

"Yes. And I hope this time my appeal will be more successful," he murmured.

Emery waved his hand, signaling that the floor was his.

Tiergan shuffled his feet. "Sophie is the most talented Telepath I've ever worked with, and I cannot imagine failing her for any reason. If you need proof that her skills hold up under test, well, I can't think of any better proof than the fact that she managed to transmit halfway across the world to Fitz *and* send a mental image to guide him to her location—all while her body was fading away. For that alone I'd give her one hundred percent, if the Council would accept it."

Sophie resisted the urge to run across the room and hug him.

There was a moment of silence before Emery nodded. "We would. But if she were to continue her studies at Foxfire, she would require a Mentor, and our records indicate you aren't planning to return."

"I would be willing to extend my stay as Mentor, provided Sophie could remain as my prodigy," Tiergan agreed, looking only at Sophie.

She nodded, hoping he knew she appreciated his sacrifice. She knew how much he despised being part of the nobility.

"Excellent." Emery turned to the other Mentors. "Anyone else have anything to add?"

Lady Anwen stepped forward. "Sophie knows more about the human species than any prodigy I've had, so I'll gladly give her one hundred percent in multispeciesial studies. She was already passing with flying colors."

Several of the Councillors nodded their agreement. Bronte scowled.

"The fact that she was able to pull herself back from fading away settles the mind over matter debate quite nicely," Sir Faxon added. "And should definitely count for one hundred percent in metaphysics." He bowed, and stepped aside to let Lady Dara forward.

She dipped an elaborate curtsy. "Sophie didn't just learn history, she *made* history. Textbooks will be written about her someday, and I'll not have them saying she received anything less that one hundred percent in my session."

Hope flared in Sophie's heart, but she tried to squash it. She still had her toughest Mentors left. She held her breath as Lady Alexine stepped forward.

"I think the fact that Miss Foster was able to leap an injured friend without a nexus and both of them survived to tell the tale is more than enough to earn her one hundred percent on her physical education exam."

"And she found an unmapped star," Sir Astin added. "Not to mention *she has the stars memorized*. She definitely deserves one hundred percent in the Universe."

All the Councillors were smiling at this point—except Bronte. He turned his murderous glare on Sir Conley as he bowed and cleared his throat.

"Sophie successfully bottled a sample of Everblaze—something I doubt even I could've done. It would be absurd to give her anything less than one hundred percent in elementalism."

The room seemed to hold its breath as all eyes turned to Lady Galvin.

She stood behind the others, fingering the jewels on her dark purple cape.

"Anything you would like to add?" Emery asked when she didn't say anything.

Lady Galvin cleared her throat. "This will not be a popular decision, but Miss Foster barely passed her midterm and has struggled with my session all year. There's no way I can justifiably pass her."

Silence throbbed through the room as Emery frowned. "Nothing will change your mind?"

She turned to Sophie as she shook her head. "I'm sorry." She sounded like she meant it.

The crowd buzzed with murmurs of displeasure, but Sophie could hear Stina's cackle rise above it all. Right then she would've given *anything* to be a Vanisher and disappear.

"That is most unfortunate," Emery said through a sigh. He glanced at the other Councillors, who were shaking their heads—except Bronte, who was smirking like a spider with a trapped fly. "It appears our hands are tied. We cannot allow Miss Foster to advance if she does not qualify for eight subjects. Perhaps we can agree to let her retake the year?" He turned to the other Councillors.

The room swam around her and Sophie wobbled on her feet. Being held back was better than Exillium—for sure. But it would still mean being left behind by all her friends.

"If I may propose an alternative solution?" Alden interrupted, rising with an elegant bow.

Sophie held her breath as Emery gestured for him to proceed.

"The rules state that she must *qualify* for eight sessions to advance. Not that she must *pass* eight sessions. And recent events have revealed that Sophie has developed a second special ability." Alden paused for the murmurs in the crowd to quiet. "Obviously, that would *qualify* her for a session training her in her new ability. Therefore, it would seem not only practical, but prudent, to replace her alchemy session—which she obviously has no future career prospects in"—he flashed Sophie a smile—"with a session studying inflicting."

The rumble of the audience shifting in their seats mirrored Sophie's internal unease. She had mixed feelings about being able to inflict pain on others at will—and she wasn't sure she wanted to train in it. But if it got her into the next level at Foxfire, it would be worth it.

Emery stroked his chin. "That would be logical."

"Absolutely not," Bronte barked, a vein throbbing in his forehead. "I refuse."

"That's not your decision to make," Emery informed him with a smile. "An ability as volatile as inflicting qualifies for a majority vote decision and"—he closed his eyes—"we have it. Eleven to one in favor. That settles it. Miss Foster will continue her studies at Foxfire, and an inflicting session will replace her alchemy session."

Someone cheered—Dex or Keefe, Sophie wasn't sure—and the whole audience followed their lead, erupting into applause and chanting her name.

"So I passed?" Sophie asked Alden, shouting over the chaos. "I can stay?"

She wanted to smile when he nodded, but the glare Bronte was directing at her was so hateful it nearly knocked her over.

He cleared his throat, silencing the room. "You can force me to Mentor her in my ability, but her final grade will be up to me, and I can guarantee she will not pass."

Angry murmurs rose as Sophie turned to Alden. "Bronte's going to be my *Mentor*?"

She waited for him to tell her it was a mistake, but Alden nodded. "Bronte's the only registered Inflictor—besides you. It's a very rare ability."

Her mind reeled with horror. Bronte made Lady Galvin seem cuddly. "But . . . he's planning to fail me."

"We'll deal with that when the time comes. For now, just be glad you've earned another year at Foxfire."

She knew he was right, but it was hard to be excited about a year of one-on-one sessions with Bronte—learning how to inflict pain. She didn't even want to imagine how he'd teach something like that. Next year was going to be very interesting.

"There's one more matter we must address before we close," Emery announced, calling the room back to order. "It's a delicate matter, however, and one I think best left only to immediate friends and family. Everyone else, please see yourselves out." He waited until the crowd left, then turned to Sophie. "It appears we have two adoption requests for you, Miss Foster. One from Alden and Della Vacker, and the other from Grady and Edaline Ruewen. The Council feels it should be your choice, so we're leaving the decision up to you."

Sophie spun around, her eyes finding Grady and Edaline.

Grady gave her a small smile. "It's your call, Sophie. Whatever you decide, we'll still love you."

Edaline nodded her agreement. Her eyes looked misty.

Alden squeezed Sophie's hand and she jumped. She'd forgotten he was still next to her. "Della and I want you to be happy. Wherever you decide to live won't change anything."

Sophie nodded and swallowed the tangle of emotions, trying to sort them out.

She turned back to Grady and Edaline, taking in Edaline's tearstained cheeks and dark circles, and Grady's puffy eyes and rigid jaw.

She knew what she needed to do. What she *wanted* to do.

"Do you need some time to decide?" Emery asked her.

"No. I've made up my mind." She took a deep breath and cleared the emotion out of her voice as she turned to face the Council. "I want to stay with Grady and Edaline Ruewen."

She wasn't sure who cheered louder, Grady and Edaline—or Dex.

Then she dipped another curtsy as Emery concluded the tribunal, and the Councillors glittered away.

Alden wrapped Sophie up in a big bear hug. "I'm so proud of you," he whispered. "And I think you made the right decision."

"I think so too," she said, glad he understood.

Living with Alden and Della would've been awesome, but Grady and Edaline needed her. And she needed them too. She could never be Jolie, and they could never be the mom and dad she'd lost. But they could still be there for each other.

Alden led her outside, where all her friends had gathered under one of the Pures. Grady lifted her, twirling her twice before setting her down so Edaline could strangle her with a hug.

"You won't regret that decision," Edaline whispered, kissing her cheek. "I promise."

"I know I won't," Sophie whispered back. "I love you guys."

"We love you too." Grady crushed her with a hug, and when he pulled away his eyes were wet with tears.

Sophie scrubbed her own tears away with the back of her hand.

"For the record, I'm really glad they didn't exile you," Dex said as he gave her an awkward hug. "And I'm *really* glad you aren't going to be a Vacker," he whispered in her ear.

Sophie rolled her eyes, but her lips still twisted into a smile. Some things never change—and she wasn't sure that was a bad thing.

"So you don't want to live with us?" Fitz teased, nudging her arm. "I see how it is."

"I know," Keefe agreed. "You save a girl's life one day and the next day she trades you away like a Prattles' pin."

Biana shoved her way between them. "She probably couldn't stand the thought of having you guys around all the time—and I can't say I blame her."

Sophie giggled. "You guys don't mind?"

"Nah. One little sister is more than I can handle already," Fitz said as he sidestepped Biana's shove. "I guess I'll have to settle for being your friend."

"Friend sounds good," Sophie agreed. Her heart fluttered when their eyes connected, and she backed a step away before Keefe noticed the change in her mood. Friend was *way* better than little sister.

"You still staying with us tonight?" Biana asked.

"Actually, I think I want to sleep in my room—if that's okay." She glanced at Grady and Edaline. They smiled and nodded.

Della pulled Sophie in for a hug. "Just make sure you visit us sometimes."

"I will."

"You'd better. Oh, and we got you something." Della handed Sophie a small teal box. "To congratulate you for surviving another tribunal."

Keefe snorted. "Leave it to Foster to face multiple tribunals in nine months."

Sophie ignored him as she pulled a black nexus from the box. It was almost identical to the one the kidnappers stole from her, except it had tiny swirls of diamonds set into the sides instead of the runes. "Thank you," she said, fingering the glittering teal jewel in the center.

"I know you liked your other one, so I tried to find one close to that, but a little bit more feminine. I hope it's okay," Della said.

"It's perfect."

"Your concentration is strong enough to not need one, but Elwin doesn't want you leaping alone until you've given your body some time to recover," Alden explained as he locked the nexus on her wrist. "This one will only unlatch when Elwin decides you're ready, and uses a special key. And these just came from the registry." He handed her and Dex new registry pendants. They were fancier than their old pendants. Small copper beads framed each side of the crystal—which was now a triangle with three facets on each side—and extra cords had been woven into the chain, making it triply thick.

"Added security measures," Alden explained as Edaline swept Sophie's hair back and clasped the choker snug around her neck.

Sophie squeezed the pendant, feeling more like herself again. She would always be slightly different, but in her own way, she finally belonged. And with the extra protection she could almost let go of her worries about the kidnappers.

Almost.

She reached for Grady's and Edaline's hands, feeling safer with someone to hold on to. Not just someone. Her *family*.

"You ready to go?" Edaline asked, squeezing her hand tighter.

"Yeah. I think I am." She took another look at the smiling faces of all her friends. They were safe. She was safe. Everything was going to be okay.

Grady tightened his grip on her hand as he held the path-finder up to the light. "Well, come on then. Let's go home."

She nodded, letting his words sink into her heart.

They stepped into the path, and a comforting warmth that had nothing to do with the rushing light overwhelmed Sophie.

It had been a long and difficult journey, but she finally knew where she belonged.

Sophie Foster was going home.

ACKNOWLEDGMENTS

This might be the part of the book I've enjoyed writing the most, because I finally get a chance to thank the many, many people who've helped me bring this story into the world. I am not exaggerating when I say that I could not have done it without them.

To my incredible agent, Laura Rennert, thank you for taking a chance on the extremely nervous blond girl at the conference, and for bearing with me through all my rambling emails, incessant questions, and shenanigans. I could not have found a better source of wisdom, encouragement, or support to guide me through this journey.

I also must thank Lara Perkins for her brilliant insights into my story, and everyone at Andrea Brown Literary, who've proven to me that I'm with the best literary agency around. My deepest thanks also go to Taryn Fagerness for being a tremendous champion for this series, and for helping me share it with the world.

To my amazing editor, Liesa Abrams Mignogna, it is both an honor and a joy to work with you. I look forward to every email, every text, and every editorial note written on Batman notepaper. Thank you for giving me the chance to work with my Wonder Twin, and for helping me turn my draft into the book I always wanted it to be.

I also have to thank everyone at Simon & Schuster for believing in this project and giving it their time, love, and enthusiasm, including Alyson Heller, Lauren Forte, Bethany Buck, Mara Anastas, Anna McKean, Carolyn Swerdloff, Julie Christopher, and Lucille Rettino. Huge thanks also go to the entire sales team for their hard work and support, to Karin Paprocki for designing my gorgeous cover, and to Jason Chan who absolutely blew me away with his stunning artwork. Plus a special thank you to Venessa Carson for proving herself the best matchmaker ever.

To Faith Hochhalter, you didn't know me when I attended Project Book Babe, but I am so incredibly lucky to now call you my friend. Thank you for inspiring me, for your invaluable insights into my writing, and, of course, for the copious amounts of hugs and ponies.

I also must thank all of the authors who supported Project Book Babe. That event truly was a turning point for me, and I'm not sure any of this would have happened without it. Thank you for helping me realize what I wanted and giving me the motivation to get started.

To C.J. Redwine, thank you for telling me I was "the real deal" when I most needed to hear it. I could not have gotten this far without your constant pep talks, your #hitsend campaigns, and your hilarious and honest notes that pushed me to be a better writer. These . . . ellipses . . . are . . . for . . . you. . . .

To Sara McClung, thank you for reading this book as many times as I have, for wading through all the emails titled: "No—use THESE pages!" (especially since I tend to forget the attachment), and for enduring all of our countless (and infamous) brainstorming sessions. I would seriously be lost without you.

To Sarah Wylie, founding member of Team Keefe, thank you for always being there to dispense industry advice, spot-on critiques, and in-depth discussion of boy bands, *Friends,* or *American Idol*— whichever I needed most. You have definitely earned each and every, "I told you so" that you owe me.

To Elana Johnson, thank you for all the brilliant things you come up with—and for letting me be a part of them. And thank you for your fantastic notes, which helped me find my path back after I'd lost my way in the sea of revisions.

I also have to thank Emma Eisler and Laura Wiseman for a lifesaving brainstorming session that finally led us to the perfect title (after months of trying) You both are welcome to name my books any time!

To the entire WriteOnCon team, thank you for letting me be part of such a special project. My deepest thanks also go to all the agents, editors, authors, and attendees who share their time and make WriteOnCon what it is.

I will also never be able to properly express my gratitude to all of the authors who have tolerated my cyber-stalking and answered my questions and generally treated me like an equal. I'm sure I'm probably forgetting some of you (SORRY!), but I have to thank Jay Asher, Robin Brande, Michael Buckley, Kimberly Derting, Bree Despain, Carrie Harris, Karen Amanda Hooper, P.J. Hoover, Jon S. Lewis, Barry Lyga, Lisa Mantchev, Myra McEntire, Lisa McMann, Stephanie Perkins, Beth Revis, Lisa and Laura Roecker, Veronica Rossi, Lisa Schroeder, Andrew Smith, Natalie Whipple, and Kiersten White. And to the fabulous Bookanistas, thank you for being a source of knowledge, laughter, and the most incredible cheerleaders a girl could ask for.

The online writing community has also been a tremendous support group for me, especially Myrna Foster, Jamie Harrington, Casey McCormick, Shannon O'Donnell, Courtney Stallings Barr, Carolina Valdez Miller, and Heather Zundel. And to all of my awesome blog followers, thank you for clicking the follow button and leaving comments, and generally making me feel far more special and important than I am. I appreciate each and every one of you, and am constantly grateful that you share a small bit of your time with me.

To my parents, thank you for believing in every crazy dream I've pursued, and never doubting that I could do it. I could say more, but I think the dedication says it all.

Turn the page for a sneak peek at
Keeper of the Lost Cities Book Two:

EXILE

PREFACE

OPHIE'S HANDS SHOOK AS SHE LIFTED the tiny green bottle.

One swallow held life *and* death—and not just for her.

For Prentice.

For Alden.

Her eyes focused on the clear, sloshy liquid as she removed the crystal stopper and pressed the bottle to her lips. All she had to do was tip the poison down her throat.

But could she?

Could she give up everything to set things right?

Could she live with the guilt, otherwise?

The choice was hers this time.

No more notes.

No more clues.

She'd followed them to this point, and now it came down to her.

She wasn't the Black Swan's puppet anymore.

She was broken.

All she had left was trust.

ONE

I STILL CAN'T BELIEVE WE'RE TRACKING BIG-
foot," Sophie whispered as she stared at the giant footprint
in the muddy soil. Each massive toe was as wide as her
arm, and the print formed a deep, mucky puddle.

Dex laughed, flashing two perfect dimples as he stood on
his tiptoes to examine a scuff in the bark of a nearby tree. "Do
humans really think there's a giant hairy ape-man running
around trying to eat them?"

Sophie turned away, pulling her blond hair around her face to
hide her flushing cheeks. "Pretty crazy, right?"

Almost a year had passed since she'd found out she was an
elf and moved to the Lost Cities, but she still slipped sometimes
and sounded like a human. She *knew* sasquatch were really just

tall green shaggy creatures with beady eyes and beaklike noses—
she'd even worked with them in the pastures at Havenfield, the
enormous estate and animal preserve she now called home. But
a lifetime of human teaching was difficult to forget. Especially
with a photographic memory.

Thunder cracked overhead and Sophie jumped.

"I don't like this place," Dex mumbled, his periwinkle eyes
scanning the tree line as he moved closer to Sophie. The damp,
heavy air made his light blue tunic stick to his skinny arms, and
his gray pants were caked with mud. "Let's find this thing and
get out of here."

Sophie agreed. The murky forest was so dense and wild. It felt
like a place time had forgotten. The thick ferns in front of them
rustled and a brawny gray arm grabbed Sophie from behind.
Her feet dangled above the ground, and she got a face full of
musky goblin sweat as her bare-chested bodyguard shoved Dex
behind him, drew his curved sword from the scabbard at his
side, and pointed it at the tall blond elf in a dark green tunic who
stumbled out of the wall of leaves.

"Easy there, Sandor," Grady said, backing away from the
glinting point of the black blade. "It's just me."

"Sorry." Sandor's high-pitched voice always reminded Sophie
of a chipmunk. He dipped a slight bow as he lowered his
weapon. "I didn't recognize your scent."

"That's probably because I just spent twenty minutes crawling around a sasquatch den." Grady sniffed his sleeve and

coughed. "Whew—Edaline is not going to be happy with me when I get home."

Dex laughed, but Sophie was too busy trying to wriggle free from Sandor's viselike hold.

"You can put me down now!" As soon as her feet touched the ground she huffed away, glaring at Sandor and struggling to remove the giant wedgie he'd given her. "Any sign of the sasquatch?"

"The den's been empty for a while. And I'm guessing you guys haven't had much luck picking up the trail?"

Dex pointed to the scratch he'd been examining in the bark. "Looks like it climbed this tree and traveled in the branches from here on out. No way to tell which way it went."

Sandor sniffed the air with his wide, flat nose. "I should take Miss Foster home. She's been in the open for far too long."

"I'm fine! We're in the middle of a forest and no one besides the Council knows we're here. You didn't even have to come."

"I go where you go," Sandor said firmly, sheathing his sword and running his hands down the pockets lining his black military-style pants to check his other weapons. "I take my charge very seriously."

"Obviously," Sophie grumbled. She knew Sandor was only trying to protect her, but she hated having him around. He was a seven-foot-tall constant reminder that the kidnappers she and Dex had narrowly escaped were still out there somewhere, waiting for the right time to make their next move. . . .

Plus, it was humiliating being followed by an ultraparanoid goblin all the time. She'd been hoping she'd be done with the bodyguard thing by the time school started again. But with less than two weeks left on her vacation and the Council hitting dead ends on all their leads, it looked like her burly, slightly alien-looking shadow was coming with her to Foxfire.

She'd tried convincing Alden he could just keep track of her with the crystal registry pendant latched around her neck, but he'd reminded her that the kidnappers had no problem tearing it off the last time. And even though this one had extra cords woven into the choker and a few other added security measures, he refused to put her life in the hands of an inanimate accessory.

She repressed a sigh.

"We need Sophie here with us," Grady told Sandor as he pulled Sophie into a quick, reassuring hug. "Are you picking up anything?" he asked her.

"Not nearby. But I can try widening my range." She moved away from him and closed her eyes, placing her hands over her temples to focus her concentration. Sophie was the only Telepath who could track thoughts to their exact location—and the only one who could read the minds of animals. If she could feel the sasquatch's thoughts, she would be able to follow them straight to wherever it was hiding. All she had to do was *listen*.

Her concentration spread like an invisible veil across the scenery, and the chirping and creaking sounds of the forest faded to a low hum as the "voices" filled her mind. The melodic thoughts of the birds in the trees. The hushed thoughts of the rodents in the ground. Farther away in a small meadow were the calm thoughts of a doe and her fawn. And farther still, in the thicker parts of the underbrush, were the stealthy thoughts of a large cougar, stalking its prey.

But no trace of the heavy, thundering thoughts of a sasquatch.

She pushed her focus toward the snowcapped mountains. The stretch was longer than most Telepaths could handle, but she'd reached much farther when she was calling for rescue from her captors—and she'd been half-drugged at the time. So she was surprised when her body started to shake from the strain.

"It's okay, Sophie," Grady told her, squeezing her shoulder. "We'll find it another way."

No.

This was why Grady had brought her along for this rescue, despite Sandor's numerous concerns for her safety. He'd already tried three other times to capture the beast, and came home empty-handed. He was counting on her.

She tugged out a loose eyelash—her nervous habit—as she pushed her mind as far as she could go. Spots of light flashed across her vision, each one paired with a stab of pain that ripped her breath away. But the misery was worth it when she caught the vaguest whisper of a thought. A fuzzy image of river with mossy green rocks and white, trickling water. It felt softer than the sasquatch thoughts she'd touched when she practiced at Havenfield, but the thought was definitely too complex to belong to any of the normal forest animals.

"It's that way," Sophie said, pointing north before she took off through the trees. She was glad she'd worn lightweight boots instead of the flat, dressy shoes she was usually supposed to wear, even with her plain tan tunic and brown pants.

Dex sprinted to catch up with her, and his messy strawberry blond hair bounced as he matched her pace. "I still don't understand how you do that."

"You're not a Telepath. I have no idea how you do any of the things Technopaths do."

"Shhhhh, they'll hear you!"

Dex had made her promise not to tell anyone about his newly discovered talent. Dame Alina—Foxfire's principal—wouldn't allow him to take ability detecting if she knew he'd already manifested, and Dex kept hoping he'd trigger a "better" talent, even though it was incredibly rare to have more than one ability.

"You're being dumb," Sophie told him. "Technopathy is cool."

"Easy for you to say. It's not fair you get to be a Telepath *and* an Inflictor."

Sophie cringed at the last word. If it were up to her, she'd drop the dangerous ability in a heartbeat. But talents couldn't be switched off once they'd been triggered. She'd checked. A lot.

Sophie's muscles burned as the ground became steeper and the cold drizzly air stung her lungs—but it felt good to run. Ever since the kidnapping everyone kept her closed in, trying to keep her away from danger. All it really meant was that she was the one being held prisoner while the bad guys ran free.

The thought spurred her legs faster, like if she just pushed herself harder, she could get far enough from her problems to make them disappear. Or at least far enough from Sandor—though the goblin was surprisingly agile for his bulky size. She'd never been able to ditch him, and she'd tried *many* times over the last few weeks. The path grew narrower as they moved toward the mountains, and after several more minutes of climbing, it curved west and ended in a gurgling stream. White puffs of mist hovered above the rocks, giving the water a ghostly feel as it snaked up the rocky foothills. Sophie paused to catch her breath, and Dex bent to stretch his legs. Grady and Sandor caught up as she was checking on the sasquatch's location.

"You're supposed to stay by my side," Sandor complained.

Sophie ignored him, pointing toward the snowcapped mountains. "It's up there."

The thoughts felt sharper now, filling her mind with a shockingly vivid scene. Every tiny leaf on the lacy ferns was crystal clear, and she could almost feel the cool water splashing against her skin and the breeze tickling her cheeks. But the really strange part was the warm calm that wrapped around her consciousness. She'd never experienced a thought as such a pure emotion before—especially from a creature so far away.

"No more separating," Grady ordered as they started to follow the stream higher up the mountain. "I'm not familiar with this part of the forest."

Sophie wasn't surprised. The trees and ferns were so thick she was sure no one—human or elf—had set foot there in a very long time. Squishy green moss coated the ground, muffling their footsteps. It was also slick, and the third time Sophie slipped, Dex grabbed her arm and didn't let go. The warmth of his hand sank through the fabric of her sleeve and she felt like she should pull away. But he was steadying her balance, which made it easier for her to concentrate on what the sasquatch was thinking.

The beast must have been eating, because a satisfied feeling settled into the pit of Sophie's stomach, like she'd just had an extra helping of mallowmelt.

She hurried forward—afraid it would move on now that it was full—and accidentally stepped on a fallen branch.

Craaaaaaaaaaaaaaaack!

Goose bumps erupted all over her body, and even though she knew the emotion wasn't hers, Sophie couldn't ignore the shivering terror. She had no idea what that meant—but she didn't have time to think about it. From the images flashing through her head she could tell the sasquatch had started to flee.

She jerked her arm out of Dex's grip and took off after it.

The beast ran so fast its thoughts turned to a blur. Sophie concentrated on channeling energy from her core into her legs, but even with the extra strength she could still feel the sasquatch pulling farther ahead. It was going to get away—unless she found a way to boost her speed.

A brain push.

She hadn't been thrilled when she'd learned that she could perform the incredibly rare telepathy skill. But as she shoved the warm energy humming in the back of her mind into her legs and felt her muscles surge with a tremendous burst of power, she was suddenly grateful for the strange ways her brain worked—even if it did make her headache worse. Her feet barely touched the ground as she raced over the soggy soil, leaving Dex, Sandor, and Grady far behind.

The sasquatch's thoughts turned clearer again.

She was catching up.

The extra energy didn't last as long as she'd expected, though, and as her strength drained she found herself barely able to stumble forward.

It's okay, she transmitted, desperately shoving the words into the creature's mind. *I'm not going to hurt you.*

The sasquatch froze.

Its thoughts were a jumbled mix of emotions, and Sophie couldn't make sense out of any of them. But she took advantage of its momentary stillness, rallying the last of her energy to fumble toward a narrow opening in the thick wall of foliage. She could feel the sasquatch on the other side of the trees.

Waiting for the others would be the safer thing to do—but who knew how much longer the creature would wait around? And the creature felt calm at the moment. Curious. Three deep breaths spurred her courage. Then Sophie padded into the clearing.

SHANNON MESSENGER

graduated from the USC School of Cinematic Arts, where she learned—among other things—that she liked watching movies much better than making them. She's studied art, screenwriting, and film production, but she realized her real passion was writing stories for children. She's the *New York Times* and *USA Today* bestselling author of the award-winning middle grade series Keeper of the Lost Cities, as well as the Sky Fall series for young adults. Her books have been featured on multiple state reading lists, published in numerous countries, and translated into many different languages. She lives in Southern California with an embarrassing number of cats. Find her online at ShannonMessenger.com.